FORT GIRARD

Karine Hetherington

For Matthew and Leo

CHAPTER ONE

January 1940
The village of Voncq, Champagne-Ardenne

Daniel's hob-nailed boots cracked the thin ice puddles pitting the farmhouse track as he walked to the back of his military truck, clipboard close to his chest. Running his eye over the rows of jute sacks, he cried out, white vapour escaping from his lips,

"That's it, Marcel?"

"Yes boss," the farmer replied, rubbing his hands with satisfaction, "fifty bags of potatoes."

Marcel had done alright thanks to their battalion. Daniel gave him an indulgent smile, removing a thick woollen glove with his teeth so he could tick the last inventory box. *Farmers often fare better than others in war*, he thought. And who could begrudge them? Hadn't Marcel spent a lifetime eking out a precarious existence on this lonely plain? Just like Daniel's Uncle Charles. Daniel could still conjure the daily rumble of guns he'd hear while walking across his uncle's fields at dusk.

But that had been the last war. He slipped on his glove again and slid the bolts shut at the back of the truck. He walked over to Marcel who, having opened his gate, now stood gazing out over the snow-covered fields, which stretched forever. Daniel followed the farmer's stare to a patch of woodland darkening the horizon.

"How long will it last?" he asked, squinting into the sunshine breaking through the mist.

"The winter, you mean?"

Daniel gave a short laugh.

"Oh, the war." Marcel stuffed his hands into the pockets of his work jacket. "My son is stationed in Nancy, and he tells me the *boches* and our boys have got their fishing rods out – on both sides of the Rhine!"

The same old story doing the rounds. It was probably true, or had been true once, thought Daniel. Like the Maupassant story about two friends gone fishing along the Seine during the Franco-Prussian war. After one too many absinthes, they'd strayed into enemy territory and been captured and shot as spies. He felt himself shudder.

"Surely it's too cold to fish?"

The old man shrugged his thin shoulders. Marcel possessed the wiry build of a man half his age.

"Haven't had a big freeze like this in a while. Mind how you go up there. A customer of mine swerved into a ditch and broke his nose a few days ago."

Daniel nodded; had the truck rolled into one of those trenches his battalion had been digging up there?

He sighed. Those Bretons! As one of the few Parisians in their company, Daniel had initially struggled to understand their strange patois. And their living conditions beggared belief; their only consolation was the food Daniel found for them. He had done his usual round of farms today, collecting butter, eggs, milk, ending up with Marcel and his potatoes. All so that his fellow infantrymen didn't have to rely on their tins of sardines.

Daniel walked back to the truck and threw his clipboard in. It pained him to think of these things. It was useless to dwell on the state of the French Army, but that was how he had spent much of his time since coming to this God-forsaken place.

"*Bon*," he said, wearily preparing to leave.

The old peasant gave him a sympathetic look. "Got a minute?" He walked stiffly to his barn, returning with a metal canister.

Marcel was offering him his *eau de vie*. Nine o'clock in the morning. Daniel hadn't even had an acorn coffee. He'd been in a rush after arriving from Paris the night before. The train had been filled to bursting with soldiers, medical staff and their equipment. A young soldier, who'd given up his seat to a pretty nurse, had whipped out his penknife to scrape the blue blackout paint off the lamp above her head. All so that the young woman could read her romantic novel.

Daniel had looked on and smiled, too exhausted to read as a conversation started up between two soldiers.

"On the border, the *fritz* have started firing at our boys!"

"So, the war's started then!"

"*Eh bien non*," the speaker said, shaking his head and laughing. "The *fritz* raised a sheet with the words: 'French soldiers – *Entschuldigung!* Sorry! One of our soldiers fired by mistake. We weren't aiming at you!"

How they'd all laughed. A flask of warm rum had been passed around and Daniel had been relieved it had run out by the time it reached him. He hated the stuff.

But he couldn't refuse Marcel's offer of a drink now. It always served to keep in with farmers.

Marcel poured the clear liquid into a distorted metal cup and handed it to him.

Slowly, Daniel brought the spirit to his lips and sniffed.

"Juniper berries. My own brew," said Marcel, encouragingly.

Conscious of being watched, Daniel took a swig. His eyes watered as a band of warmth worked its way down his chest and settled uneasily in his empty stomach.

"*Encore un?*"

"*Merci bien,* but no," Daniel said, smiling, feeling light-headed. 'They'll smell it on my breath."

The old peasant laughed and tapped his bony nose. "You look better already," he said, patting Daniel on the shoulder. "A little pale earlier."

"Just come back from leave," Daniel said, self-consciously. The warm and loving world he had left just twelve hours ago came flooding back. Tatiana! He could still sense her warm, soft skin, feel the curve of her pale breast. He closed his eyes momentarily. Tatiana was his world and he was loath to share her with anyone.

He opened his eyes again and scrambled for a sentence, settling on a familiar grumble.

"Train took forever." He rubbed the blond bristle covering his cheek. "Could do with a shave."

"Plenty of time for that," said the old man, kindly. "Little else to do around here. War might be over before you see any action – haw, haw!"

The farmer's jests were unconvincing; Daniel knew he was

worried. These country people were tough, but they weren't going to forget the Germans trampling their soil last time around.

"Can't underestimate the *boche*s though," continued the old man. "I'm wondering whether I should join my daughter-in-law's family in Auvergne. My son is trying to persuade me to go south. They have a farmstead there. But I don't want to leave my land unless I really need to."

"It's good to have an emergency plan," Daniel said. Tatiana was in Paris, a day's drive south-west from where he was stood. The thought of her escaping with young Jeanne, baby Béatrice, and her parents filled him with dread. Etched in his boyhood memory was the look of wild panic on the faces of refugees fleeing Belgium during the Great War. Tatiana was fearless, but she was also impetuous. *She has the kind of dark looks those blond German officers love.* He clenched his teeth to stop himself from cursing and opened the driver's door.

"*Au revoir,* Marcel."

He mounted the truck steps, fell into his worn leather seat, and turned the ignition. With a judder, the truck sprang to life. He set off along the long, straight road iced with frost, past the misted fields and silent hills. Soon he was heading slowly up an incline leading to Voncq woods, alone again with his thoughts of Tatiana. She had often called him a Cassandra for his belief in the likelihood of war. Now that it was a reality, she had remained unwilling to listen to his concerns over France's unpreparedness for action during his Christmas leave. But, of course, there had been the children to indulge, especially four-year-old Jeanne, who had leapt onto his knee the minute he had sat down in the tiny apartment in rue de Grenelle, which they shared with Tatiana's parents.

"Papa, Papa, do the horsey."

His frozen lips broke into a smile as he thought of her black curls bouncing through the air. His first-born had travelled everywhere with him and Tatiana, all around the Auvergne and Brittany, moving on to Belgium and Holland when the French workers had occupied the factories in '36.

Baby Béatrice, however, was another matter. A war baby. Bad timing. She had cried every time Tatiana had offered to let him hold her. Sensing his low mood, Tatiana had asked her parents to take the children out to the Bois de Boulogne. Her father had grumbled. Elisabeta, his wife, had admonished him in Russian. Finally the apartment had been emptied of parents and children. Laughing, they had gone straight to their bedroom and had slipped, shivering, into chilled sheets.

How he longed to be back on that fine, sprung mattress with Tatiana's body pressed up against his.

A hole in the road jolted him out of his reverie. Daniel wiped the condensation from the windscreen, tried to focus on the narrowing road. Winding the window down for the bracing air, he listened for signs of life beyond the shudder of the engine. Leaving the dazzling white expanse behind him, he drove into the woods.

The interior of the truck darkened instantly. Daniel switched his headlights on and saw a startled deer leap across his field of view, its white markings disappearing into the thickets.

Turning down a frozen track, he finally halted beside a catering van. A few men with mossy beards and unkempt hair stood hunched over their metal cups.

"*Salut*, Dan," said a familiar grey-haired giant of a man with a prominent nose and large, sloping shoulders.

"Salut, Hervé."

Hervé's earth-lined face creased with displeasure as he threw his coffee dregs onto the forest floor. "Ugh! We're better off drinking our own piss. Any luck with the wine?"

"*Désolé*, my friend," said Daniel, descending from the truck. Before he had gone on leave, the wine had nearly frozen and was pouring slowly out of their barrels in clumps.

Not choleric by nature, Hervé bunched his fists with frustration. "What I would give to be back home in my warm kitchen with Fleur and the girls! Instead, cook tells me he had to take an axe to the bread this morning!"

Daniel gave him a sympathetic smile and got on with unloading sacks onto a wheelbarrow and trundling off to the stores.

On his way, he passed the new dugouts and tunnels which had become the soldiers' living quarters – if you could call them that. Hervé had shown him his, complete with wood-burning stove, oil lamps, bunk, rustic table and chair. Just like the pictures of trench life that Daniel had seen in the papers as a boy. No different from the quarters his young uncle Sam had endured at Verdun, not far from where they were camped. Sam had perished there. And, whereas nothing could compare with the horror of 1917, the inertia and freezing conditions were getting to the men.

Daniel felt a pang of unease as he conjured up the farmhouse in Voncq he shared with several other NCOs. Hervé and his colleagues would bind their rough army blankets around their uniforms to insulate themselves. If Daniel got too close, he could always smell the sweat, urine, and smoke seeping out of their greatcoats.

As head of transport and equipment, he had escaped the spade and shovel. He'd had Lieutenant Vilmoray, another Parisian, to thank for that, along with his own experience in the Colonial Cavalry in Morocco.

He heaved the last sack into the store, stepped outside and padlocked the door. At least a new colonel was set to take over in the coming week. Perhaps this one might inject some new thinking into their company. Until then, they were to stay and wait in their trenches, performing meaningless drills. It was a defensive game, they had been told. They had the Maginot Line and the Ardennes Forest to protect them.

He pressed his palms against his temples, feeling the beginnings of a headache. *Keep on moving,* he told himself. *Keep busy.*

He leapt back into his truck and waved to Hervé, who, having clamped the stub of a cigarette between his lips, was trying to light it.

"*A demain, mon vieux,*" Daniel whispered to himself. "*Bon courage*! You will need it."

CHAPTER TWO

May 1940

> *Au près de ma blonde*
> *Qu'il fait bon, fait bon, fait bon.*
> *Au près de ma blonde*
> *Qui fait bon dormir*

Daniel wound down his truck window to let in the evening air.

"Come on, sing!" Hervé elbowed him with his glistening, hairy arm.

Daniel raised his hand wearily in protest. It had been a long day. But how good the sun on one's back felt after the long, bitter winter. He yawned and watched the sun's weakening rays ripple and fleck the barley fields and woods with gold. He had been up since dawn, ferrying Hervé and his men around the region. All because the Mayor and the Colonel had decided to enlist their help on the land, for there had been a dearth of agricultural workers since mobilisation. Daniel had supervised the forking and carting of manure, the scrubbing out of stables. They had all piled happily into the back of his truck and continued on to Vouziers, where they had donned gloves to unload a truck full of rosebushes.

In the town square, with its grandiose *Hôtel de Ville,* they had uprooted the stony municipal beds and transformed the mournful, dead space that had greeted them. The sound of clinking spades, crunching soil and laughter, as young women offered cool pitchers of cider to the merry Bretons, had put the villagers in a festive mood. Even the square's two forlorn statues, of a long-forgotten poet and a historian, seemed to take on new life as the crimson rosebushes were lowered into position around them.

Daniel let an exasperated sigh out of the truck window as he remembered the conversation he'd had with Lieutenant Vilmoray, when, just a week ago, his superior announced the new round of morale-boosting duties.

"Roses!"

Vilmoray, seeing his incredulous expression, had looked pained. "At least it'll get the men away from their wood, Corporal," he'd replied, clearly a little frustrated himself. The same was happening all over the Champagne-Ardenne region.

Daniel had to concede that Hervé and his men had been relieved to be brought out of their repetitive, seemingly useless drills; the trenches and dugouts were now complete. There were only so many times one could dismantle and clean one's rifle. And hadn't relations improved today between the Army and the civilians, after a winter of disagreements and bar brawls?

The square had pulsed with music and gaiety. Young commissioned officers in immaculate khaki uniform had set aside their maps and papers and sat on the restaurant terrace, blowing smoke rings and eyeing the pretty waitresses. Even Hervé, a good family man, had noticed the girl with soft, fair shoulders and heavy straw-blonde hair piled high on her head. Monique – or had it been Marie – who had smiled so sweetly as she filled their cups.

Auprès de ma blonde…

Daniel thought of her soft, white neck – but only to compare it to Tatiana's. And the girl's eyes, so limpid and blue, reflecting the azure heavens, so different from Tatiana's dark eyes, which drew you into their fathomless depths.

The singing ended abruptly. Daniel steered the truck up the hill into the Voncq woods. Ahead, there suddenly appeared a family of wild boar, trotting hurriedly across the road. Realising that he might hit one of the trailing runts, Daniel swerved.

"Woohay, Daniel!" came a chorus from the back, as Daniel checked his side mirror. He was relieved to see the piglets scramble to safety.

A large elbow dug into his shoulder again.

"You risk our lives for that ugly little thing!" cried out Hervé, smiling. "We could have had him for dinner!"

Daniel frowned in protest as he turned down the dirt track back to camp. He loved all creatures and made no apology for it. Tatiana had always teased him about it:

"Talking to animals as if they could really understand you!"

He gripped the steering wheel. How different she was from him. No matter, he might just persuade her to live in the countryside, where he could paint and write and where their children could play freely. Tatiana still clung to the excitement of Paris, the musical concerts, the exhibitions, the fashions, even though they had little money and no real time to enjoy the city's delights. And now Paris was preparing for war. It made him nervous to think of her there.

He slowed the vehicle and pulled into the forest clearing that had been home to Hervé and his men for the past seven months. He applied the handbrake.

"A drink before you go back, Daniel?" Herve asked.

"Why not?"

As Hervé strode off to the newly-erected shower block, Daniel stepped down from the truck and savoured the aroma of browning sausages from the battalion canteen. He would eat back at the mess with Vilmoray. He ducked under a line of drying underclothes and set off through the woods to find the solitude he craved.

The men's laughter fading, he came upon a cool glade. A flutter of feathers above his head made him halt by a pine tree. Holding his breath, he stared up through its branches and waited. Chirp, chirp, trill – the song of the nightingale, the first that year. Leaning back against the trunk, he closed his eyes, felt the last darts of evening sun run over his cheeks. He imagined Tatiana leaning beside him, eyes half-closed. There had been a time in Montlhéry, at the little house in the woods, when she had enjoyed the seclusion and peace nature afforded.

The birdsong ceased abruptly. There was a flurry of feathers as Hervé's heavy tread became audible. He appeared suddenly before him, stripped down to his vest, his hair dripping.

"*Alors*, Daniel. Daydreaming again?"

Daniel shook his head, smiling. "Isn't a man allowed a little peace?"

"You mean you don't appreciate our company?" Hervé laughed.

Daniel had never seen him so happy. It took so little.

"So, the *Pinot...*" Herve continued, "isn't it about time we opened one?"

"Suppose you deserve it, *mon vieux*!"

"You're damn right we do!" Hervé replied, indignantly.

"Local cider good today?" Daniel teased.

"Yes, sharper than the one back home. And stronger."

"Those young women with their pitchers were a welcome sight too," Daniel continued. Hervé's face darkened.

"Yes, but I wouldn't have my daughter gallivanting around in a place full of soldiers."

Daniel smiled, uneasily. "Of course."

They joined the men around the campfire. Some were digging bent metal spoons into their beans, having already devoured their sausage ration.

Hervé reached over to an open bottle. "Here," he said, recovering his good humour.

"*Merci.*"

Daniel peered into his wine. *The colour of blood.* Tatiana had talked of Vladimir languishing in that TB clinic in the Alps. At least Albert Klug had been able to help out. They owed him.

Daniel gulped down his wine, then stared forlornly into his empty cup.

"More?" asked Hervé, looking at him with concern.

Daniel nodded and held out his cup.

A man broke wind.

"Is that a bomb going off, Alain?" said one of the others.

"Plenty more ammo where that came from," Alain answered, without looking up from his canteen.

"Forget the Maginot Line, we've got Alain!" cried out his neighbour, waving the smell away and grimacing. "Boys, gas masks!"

Hervé smiled in Daniel's direction.

Daniel shook his head. It wasn't the humour, or lack of it, that bothered him. The war was escalating beyond France. Poland had capitulated to Germany before the French forces could reach her, and now Norway. He hoped the French and British Expeditionary armies would fare better. And they had been provided with roses today! He looked around at his fellow reservists. Honest men. Some had fought in the Great War. But the months of waiting had created torpor. The trenches and tunnels were long finished, lying redundant.

Hervé, stretched out on the ground next to him, was displaying a heavy stomach under his vest.

"*Santé!* To absent friends and family."

Daniel raised his cup half-heartedly and drank in silence.

Hervé bounced his cup hard on the dry earth. "You're not yourself today. What's with you?"

"Nothing," Daniel murmured as he stood and brushed himself off. "Thank you. Some letters to write. *A demain.*"

He slipped away and drove back to Voncq.

That evening, as Daniel entered the NCO mess, a converted dairy with a low ceiling, he sensed all was not well.

"Bastard *boches!*" said one NCO, looking up from the newspaper he and his colleagues were sharing. "That's the problem with neutral countries. Belgians. Sitting ducks!" Without waiting to hear the details, Daniel walked over to Vilmoray, a lone figure at the end of a very long table. He was hunched over *Le Figaro*. A cigarette burned in his ashtray.

Daniel peered over his shoulder. "What's happened?"

"Look!" he said, handing Daniel the front pages. "It's yesterday's!"

'*L'Agression Allemande Contre la Hollande, La Belgique et le Luxembourg*'. Military bases, bridges, and railways had been bombed in a night operation. *All the months of waiting, waiting, and now it's really happening. Holland, Belgium, Luxembourg. All of them a day or two's drive from here.*

"Take it! I've read it." Vilmoray crushed out the burning cigarette and lit up a fresh one.

"*Salauds!*" Daniel shook the paper, sickened as he read the survivors' accounts of the slaughter. Women crying over blood-stained bundles. *Tatiana, oh Tatiana!* His heart started to pound and a sinking, falling feeling took hold of his stomach. There was no mention of the capital on the front page. He nearly ripped it as he turned it. And there he saw it: '*The sirens have sounded but very few Parisians have left their warm beds to seek the protection of underground shelters*'. *Tatiana*! She wasn't able to get out of bed early at the best of times. He could just see it, Paris in May, the blossom on the Champs Elysées, the beautiful birdsong.

Nothing had happened – at least for now! No bombs. The gas masks provided by the authorities last August had lain untouched at the back of Tatiana's wardrobe, behind the rows of shoeboxes. It must have been the same for all their neighbours in the fifteenth arrondissement, many of them White Russians, like Tatiana's parents. They had lived through revolution and they thought themselves invincible.

Cursing silently, he focused on the plight of his wife. During his last leave he had discussed what to do. After much heated discussion, he had persuaded Tatiana to go to his grandmother's house should they need to flee Paris. It was in a little village, Linas, 30 kilometres south of Paris. His grandmother had died there peacefully just before the outbreak of war. Tatiana had acquiesced, though it meant leaving her own parents.

'I've survived capture by the Bolsheviks!' Alexandre, her father, had proclaimed, flushing red from the vodka he'd brought out. 'My daughter, do you really think that I'm going to be frightened by the Hun? And what about the pillaging!?'

Vilmoray got up and stubbed out his half-smoked cigarette. "It's going to get a lot busier around here. I'll be back. I need to report to the Colonel." He marched out of the mess.

Daniel read the paper feverishly. French troops had shot down forty-four German planes over Northern France. The Stukas had been aiming at French and British Expeditionary troops heading for Belgium. A rage pulsed through him as he thought of the columns of refugees from the Low Countries.

He had seen it all as a boy at his uncle's farm in Champagne. The roads choked with women in headscarves, their dry, lined faces, men whipping exhausted beasts pulling overfilled carts. He had rushed into the cowshed where his uncle Charles was milking and had wordlessly drawn up a stool. Pressing his ear to the beast's velvet flank, Daniel recalled the comfort its loud digestive system had brought him. So many times their Uncle Charles had prepared their car for flight but the Allied front had always held – just. In the particularly bad winter of 1917-18, he recalled their sombre mayor, knocking on doors daily to announce a 'missing in action.' One terrible morning he had appeared on their own doorstep, for Charles's younger brother, Sam.

Vilmoray returned, making his way towards Daniel's table.

Daniel waited for him to speak.

"The new Colonel has arrived."

"With the Senegalese reinforcements. Good!"

Vilmoray bent his head, his expression grave. "There's a problem."

"A problem!" Daniel said, in a high whisper.

Vilmoray edged nearer. Daniel could almost feel his moustache brush his ear. "He's without his battalion."

"What! You're telling me we have two colonels, sir, one old and useless, the other without his men?"

Frowning, Vilmoray pulled himself to his full height and declared, in a loud voice, "The Colonel has asked me to assemble all the troops in the yard tomorrow morning. Get to it, Corporal!"

CHAPTER THREE

Daniel awoke with a start, unwrapping the sheet about his middle, his heart still pounding from a dream. Pursued by a lengthening shadow, he had been running over fields towards a tiny patch of yellow light.

He sat up on his lumpy mattress, his forehead and chest clammy, and stared at the bare, white-washed walls of his farmhouse bedroom. He heard the familiar grind of shutters, the yawns and muffled voices. The order had been to mass in the yard at 7am.

He swung his feet off the bed, onto the cool flagstone floor. Just a dream. He had never attributed much importance to them. Just a clearing of the system or a sign of fever.

A slight tremor shook his bed, then a juddering. He had woken to a similar sensation in his hotel room, in Bourg-Léopold in Belgium where he'd been on business in 1938, the time of the first mobilisation. It had been a false alarm. Everything had gone back to normal. 'Peace in our time' they had been assured after Munich. With relief, he had resumed his appointments, selling machine tools to the dairy industry. From Belgium he, together with Tatiana's brother, Vladimir, and Philippe Klug, had gone into Holland. Business had thrived.

His window rattled hard. Daniel rushed over; beneath him a long column of khaki armoured vehicles trundled by. An excited voice rose above the creak of tank wheels: "*C'est les Anglais!*"

Grabbing his trousers, he dressed hurriedly and raced down the stone stairs in his boots with the other NCOs. He was still buttoning his shirt as he came out onto the road. He crouched to tie his laces then stared up between the armoured vehicles, where Vilmoray, tight-jawed and unshaven, was waiting to cross. He stepped across at the end of the column, frowning.

"Sir, what are the orders?"

"I've just been with the Colonel. The French and British tanks are heading towards Belgium."

"I can see that. But the roads will be mayhem." Daniel pictured a clamour of troops and vehicles trying to force their way up to Belgium only to be held back by a torrent of terrified refugees fleeing south.

"It's beyond our control," Vilmoray said, irritably. "We've lost contact with the *Préfecture*, which is supposed to be managing the buses in the region for its own occupants." He clamped a cigarette between his slim lips. "And there's further bad news. The Stukas bombarded the airfield at Sault-les-Rethel early this morning. It's grounded our fighters."

"Damn!" Daniel watched Vilmoray light his cigarette. He had hated Paul Fort's snuff habit when he had been his secretary. Secretary to a poet. How far removed that early period of his life seemed. He watched Vilmoray puff elegantly and felt momentarily reassured by his self-possession. Sault-les-Rethel was, however, only half an hour's drive or more from Voncq. Half-way to Reims. "That's bad," he found himself saying. "Why isn't our artillery stopping the Stukas from getting through?"

Vilmoray knitted his pale brows. "I don't know. Our communications are a mess. No radio communication from HQ as they think the *boches* are intercepting them. Lines are being cut. By the time the written orders arrive they're worthless!" He screwed his eyes up in concentration. "Not wishing to spread panic, the Colonel, in his infinite wisdom, has ordered us to continue as normal since the matter is in hand, he says, and the troops will soon be taking up their positions in Belgium."

"What…?" Daniel stifled an expletive. "What does that mean exactly?" He wanted to make sure he'd heard properly.

"You are to maintain your present responsibilities."

Daniel stared at Vilmoray open-mouthed. "And Paris?"

"Nothing to report." Vilmoray smiled uneasily. "Paris remains quiet."

Daniel pictured Tatiana frantically packing whilst her mother Elisabeta looked on. At least the plans were set. She'd go to his grandmother's house with his own mother. Meanwhile, he had a job to do until the reinforcements arrived.

"The Senegalese…?"

Vilmoray's furious look stopped him from probing further.

Daniel walked dejectedly out to the yard. Seven meat delivery trucks and an old ambulance car were parked in a field behind their billet. Requisitioned in Fontenay-le-Comte, in western France, they had travelled all the way north-east with their regiment to the Ardennes. Daniel had hired a Voncq garage mechanic to paint the trucks a muddy brown.

He jumped into the first one in line and, shaking his head, set off south towards Vouziers, taking the quieter country roads.

It was another balmy spring day, unusually hot for May. He wound down the window and inhaled the sweetened air blowing off the fields. He turned left to join the main high road into Vouziers and was suddenly thrust into a long traffic jam: carts, cars, buses, bicycles, as far as the eye could see. He drew up behind a horse-drawn cart loaded with furniture and two mattresses, on top of which perched an elderly man and woman. The driver of the cart, a middle-aged man wearing a rough cap and shirt-sleeves, was pulling on the reins, grumbling. A woman seated next to him, in a headscarf and pinafore dress, twisted round and held up a tin cup to the old couple.

"There, *bonne maman* – have some. You need to drink in this heat."

The old woman stared blankly at her. Her mouth, which had several teeth missing, gaped obediently.

"I've had enough of this!" said the driver of the cart. He pulled off his beret and wiped his face with it.

"Never mind him, *bonne maman*," said the woman, administering water. "Your son can look after himself." She tilted the glass and let the water run slowly over the old woman's parched lips. "That's it."

A girl and boy, about ten and eight, pulled up their bikes beside the cart. The girl, a heavy straw-blonde plait running down her back, looked up.

"Maman. Can we just sit in the field? Eric and I have been going up and down for ages and we haven't moved an inch!"

"Yes, Maman," said the bony-legged boy beside her. "Can we have our sandwich?"

"Just wait a little longer, children. We're still moving. If you eat it now, you'll be hungry later."

"But Maman!" whined the boy.

A car started its engine in front of them.

"*Tu vois*, Eric!" said his mother, brightening. "Now back on your bikes." She turned to the old man and emptied her canister of water into the glass. "You see how *bonne maman* has drunk."

The old man's weather-beaten face nodded gravely.

Thinking of his own family, Daniel angrily started up the motor behind them and edged forward a metre, only to stop again.

"*Merde!*" He slammed his foot on the brake, then looked out at the wheat fields, and up at the cloudless sky. Cobalt blue. A sudden yearning entered him, to take off into the field with his paintbrushes.

There was a faint cry ahead. His gaze turned towards the road, where a soldier was pointing up at something. Two black dots had punctuated the blue. The orderly started to run up alongside the cars, speaking quickly, pointing skywards. One vehicle emptied. Then another. Bicycles were thrown to the ground. The dots dropped out of the heavens. Transfixed, Daniel's heart started to race as he watched them grow bigger. Two Stukas.

Merde! Wrenching the key from the ignition, he leapt out onto the road.

"Patrick, Sylvie, *sauvez-vous*," shouted the father over the airplane engines. Dropping the reins, he leapt down with his wife. "*Allez-y, vite.*"

The girl jumped off her bike and, torn between waiting for her mother and fleeing, hovered there.

"Maman!" the girl wailed, pulling at her creased woollen dress as she watched her parents coax the elderly couple down from their mattresses.

"Come, Sylvie!" shrieked the young boy to his sister from the verge.

Daniel saw the dull fuselage, the black cross level out and turn towards them.

"Come on," said Daniel, grabbing the girl and pulling her towards the coarse field grasses, to a ditch alongside her brother. He raced back towards the cart, where the man was unpicking the old woman's bony fingers from the mattress. "Monsieur, get under the cart!"

"Max!" cried out the man's wife, who was cowering by the wheel. "There's no time!"

It was true. The aircraft was now diving towards the column of traffic. Daniel raced to the side of the road, throwing himself beside the girl, who was trying to wriggle out of the ditch. Her brother grabbed her legs to stop her.

"*Reste ici!*"

They huddled close. Machine gun fire spat out in all directions. The family's horse reared with fright and then slumped onto its front knees.

Daniel squeezed the children's limbs. *Like chicken bones.* A second plane swooped and released its charge into the field behind them. A low blast shook the ground. The air grew hot and filled with dust, like the sandstorms Daniel had known in Morocco. Shards of wood and stones rained down.

Daniel felt the boy's shoulder blades tense against the palm of his hand, then push up. Daniel pressed him down again.

"*Non, mon petit gars.* They may be back for more." They waited for the engines to fade.

Daniel heard a moan and the sound of shifting wood. He got up and made the boy hold on to his sister.

"Look after her."

The boy turned to her. "*Sylvie, tu entends?* You stay with me."

Daniel walked over to the cart. Bullets had splintered its wooden sides and torn into the mattresses. The old man rocked onto his side and tried to mumble something. He cried out in pain and rolled back. Blood soaked his rough farmer's smock. Daniel looked across at the old woman lying very still beside him. Her eyes were still open and fixing the sky. Her stiffened hand clawed an exposed mattress spring.

The parents scrambled from under the cart. The woman locked eyes with Daniel. "She's gone, isn't she?"

Daniel nodded.

The girl ran over and buried her head in her mother's dress. The boy stood, pale-faced and stiff, watching his father gently unpick the old woman's fingers from their hold.

"Do you have a sheet, Madame?" Daniel said, stepping forward. He dropped his voice. "The old man. Your father-in-law?"

She nodded and gently pushed the children away whilst she climbed onto the cart. She threw him a blanket.

"It's all I have."

"That will do. Help me, will you?"

They bound the old man's middle, but he rolled over and the blanket unravelled, causing more blood to flow. As Daniel was attempting a tourniquet, the father approached them.

"Papa," he said, addressing the old man. "Try to keep still. Maman has left us," he said, gently. "It was her heart." He held his son against his chest, turning to Daniel. "Monsieur, can you take them to a hospital?"

He snatched a look back. Several cars burned fiercely, their occupants clutching each other in the fields. A cart had overturned in a ditch. A horse had been caught in the explosion. All that was left was a truncated flank.

Soldiers descended from an army truck ahead to receive the wounded.

Daniel breathed more freely. "We have to be quick. I'm sorry about your mother. But your father... we must hurry."

"Thank you, Monsieur. God bless you. Children, get in front, now!"

Having laid the old couple out in the back and bundled the parents in with a suitcase, Daniel pulled away. Taking a U-turn, he quickly left the main highway and took the forest roads. The smell of fresh blood emanating from the back made him open his window wide. He fished in his pocket for some *Vichy* mints and offered them to the children.

When they arrived in Vouziers, the market town was burning. Black smoke and orange flames billowed up into the once-perfect sky. *God forbid the hospital has been hit.* He looked behind him, at the children staring, frozen, through his windscreen.

"Will they come back?" said the boy, white-faced and gripping the seat.

"Here." Daniel handed over some more chalky sweets. The children's faces softened as Daniel drove through the central high street, past shops whose windows had been blown out. Shards of glass littered the pavements. A man emerged from one of the establishments with something under his jacket.

Daniel turned off the high street and was relieved to see the hospital intact. Three ambulances blocked the emergency entrance. He'd tell them to prepare for many more casualties.

"*Dieu merci!*" he whispered, and almost in the same breath, even though he wasn't a church-going man, he prayed inwardly for his own family.

CHAPTER FOUR

Daniel walked despondently away from the yard, head bowed in thought, towards the NCO mess.

"Ah, there you are, Corporal!"

Daniel stopped outside the former dairy and saluted Vilmoray, whose keen blue eyes picked out the blood streaking Daniel's shirt.

"What happened?" Vilmoray said, irritably.

Daniel felt a pain in his chest, a memory of a captain adopting that very same tone. It had been in Morocco. He had been transporting *Les Chasseur's d'Afrique* mail on horseback, through a mountain pass in the Atlas. Two Berber tribesmen had opened fire from a distance. Galloping off into woodland, he had been thrown from his horse and tore his jacket at the shoulder. That night, back at the fort, his Captain, far from being grateful for the safe delivery of parcels, had stared witheringly at the tear. It had brought him a demotion. It had taken months to regain that stripe. The injustice of it still gnawed at him. *A bullet wound would have earned me a military medal!*

Daniel broke in to explain, "A Stuka attack on civilians, *mon Lieutenant*. Along the road to Vouziers. I had to take a family to hospital."

Vilmoray's eyes widened momentarily then narrowed. "Cowards! And damn those telephone lines! They're still down!"

"Down?" Daniel repeated, mournfully. He recalled the emergency ward in Vouziers, the cries of distress, the chaos, the panic in the nurses' faces.

"But it would make sense," Vilmoray continued, pulling his lips back over his teeth as if he had trodden on something sharp. "Look," he said, dropping his voice, for a new batch of men had disembarked from a nearby truck and were now nervously awaiting orders. "There's been an important development."

Daniel was almost cheered by the gravity in Vilmoray's voice – something was happening.

"There are rumours, unsubstantiated, that the Germans have broken through the Ardennes and that Sedan has fallen."

Daniel's stomach sank with dread.

"Stukas, dozens of them, are firing on our boys, whilst the *boches* cross the Meuse River in inflatable boats."

"Inflatable boats!" It all seemed ludicrous. "But the British and our men who came through…"

"Were bound for Belgium. North."

"But…" Daniel stared at Vilmoray incredulously. "But if the best of our fighting forces are up there…"

Another truck arrived. There were shouts in the yard behind them as Hervé's men jumped down, clutching their rifles.

"They are not to know," Vilmoray said, quietly.

"Of course."

"Hurry and change. The Colonel's coming to address us."

"Which one?" Daniel found it hard to disguise his sarcasm.

"Our Colonel! The other hasn't returned yet."

"Hasn't returned! And the reinforcements? Some of our men have gone on leave…"

Vilmoray frowned. He was already elsewhere. Daniel watched him walk away.

Daniel ran back to his billet, scaled the stairs two at a time. It was only when he reached his room that the full horror hit him. Sedan was an hour away from Voncq. *Sédan again!* He threw his bloodied shirt onto a chair. Back in 1870 it had been the same. And then during the Great War. What was High Command playing at? The French front had to hold, for without reinforcements or effective armament, their hopelessly ill-equipped reservist unit didn't stand a chance. He thought back to the Stuka attack that morning.

Just one of our Amiots or an RAF Bleinheim would have been sufficient to stop that bastard from mowing down those people. How did that Stuka get through?

He removed a clean shirt from his knapsack and threw it on.

Their white-haired colonel had just climbed an equestrian mounting block when Daniel slipped in beside Vilmoray in the parade yard. They'd only seen him twice in the last eight months: on their long march from Sedan to Briquenay, when he'd been unable to control his horse, then again when their company had transferred from Briquenay to Voncq.

Daniel watched him puff his pigeon chest. In that high, feeble voice of his, he spoke of France's resolve to resist its old enemy and of the continuing importance of strong defences. Daniel looked up distractedly at the cloudless sky, at the swallows wheeling high above their heads as if it were any other summer.

Their colonel stepped down stiffly from his wooden box. "Vilmoray. I would like a trench to be dug here."

He can't be serious!

"Yes, *mon Colonel*," Vilmoray said, standing to attention and saluting. They watched the Colonel walk away on his arthritic legs.

Vilmoray turned to face their unit. "*Caporal Frey*. Will you supervise the digging?" He leaned in quickly and whispered, "Going to see about the Senegalese."

Daniel stared at the space that Vilmoray had vacated, then marched over to the wall and grabbed an entrenching tool. He went over to Hervé standing at the end of the row of men and plunged it into the earth. Slowly easing it out, he drew a serrated line down the row. Marching back to his starting point, he saw Hervé eye him with consternation. "Don't just stand there! There are Stukas in the area!"

"Yes *Caporal*," Hervé said, saluting him with a frown. He recovered himself and shouted at his men to take up their spades and shovels.

The ground was dry and unyielding at first. The sound of grinding metal on stone filled the yard. Someone cursed as a wall of dust flew up into their faces. They leaned hard into their spades, chipped away at the compacted earth with their pickaxes.

Daniel pressed himself against a wall, keeping watch over the quadrangle of blue sky above their heads. An hour passed. He rubbed the taut muscles at the back of his neck. *Bloody madness. In broad daylight!*

The first diggers rested. Another team shovelled earth into large hessian sacks, then piled them along the parapet of the trench; barely a parapet, Daniel thought.

They worked into the afternoon. Hervé rolled up his sleeves and mopped his brow, shooting a look of frustration back at Daniel. No one had uttered a word of rebellion. They didn't need to. The absence of crude banter and laughter said it all.

Daniel sighed and checked his watch. Four o'clock. They had been at it for hours. With a sense of foreboding, he approached, to assess the work. He stepped into the trench, aware of his men's belligerent stares. He propped up a measuring stick against the side of the trench.

"Seventy-five centimetres!" he said, shaking his head and feeling the ridge of the trench against the lower part of his thigh. "Only half-way!" He crouched down. In this position, they were still conspicuous from the air. Scrambling out, he screamed at them to continue.

Just as he returned to his position by the wall, he heard the rumble of engines.

"Stop!" he cried. His heart thumping with trepidation, he waited as all eyes focused skywards. Roaring propellers powered into the sky above their heads; two Stukas circled, turning to dive.

"Get down!" he screamed, and dashed towards the startled soldiers cowering in the trench. The men jumped in after him, almost in tandem, taking their shovels and tools with them. The air swelled with maddening sirens that screamed louder as the planes hurtled towards them.

His eardrums close to bursting, Daniel knelt in the damp earth and clamped his arms over his helmet. He felt the hairs on the back of his neck lift.

"Here," a voice said beside him. It was Hervé, offering him a spare shovel.

"Thanks," he screamed over the din, laying it over the top of his spine.

A mighty explosion erupted on one side of the yard, throwing he and Hervé backwards. Another explosion a second later hurled them forward. Daniel let go of the spade and felt the ground judder and shift madly beneath him. Columns of scorching clay and stones pelted down on his outstretched arms and helmet, for what seemed an eternity.

His ears still ringing, Daniel finally pushed back his helmet and peered down the line of men. One by one they rose from the trench, brushing the dust off their uniforms. He watched them stand in awe and shock before the smoking craters either side of the yard. Some of them fumbled for their cigarettes. Hervé let out an incredulous laugh.

"Bloody miracle!"

CHAPTER FIVE

'German Amoured Units Cross the Meuse', read the headline.
Daniel was hunched over a dog-eared copy of *Le Figaro*, which
the mechanic had brought over from his workshop. He brushed
aside strands of hair falling over his eyes and let the news sink in.
*Bah! The very Meuse whose banks they said were impossible to
scale! It's all been about confidence and daring for the Luftwaffe
and Wehrmacht. Poland was just the start of it!*

Daniel felt his neck tense as he read on. The Allied units in the
front line had suffered an 'avalanche of enemy attacks' yet, *Le
Figaro* assured its readers, they were 'resisting admirably'.

Daniel looked up from his paper. His gaze moved over to the
shattered window facing out onto the yard, now boarded up.
When would his company's luck run out? The newspaper was
talking about a battlefront stretching one hundred and fifty
kilometres, from south-east Sedan all the way north to Namur
in Belgium.

He set aside his coffee, which had grown cold. He needed some
air.

In the orchard behind the mess, he walked over to the long
line of trucks and vans which had been serviced that day. An
old ambulance brought up the rear. Running his hand over the
bonnet, he thought of the mechanic who'd left.

Limping into his depot, the man had handed him a newspaper.

"It's bad. Look, I said I'd be available next week... But I've
received a letter from my brother's wife. She needs help on her
farm."

"I understand."

"All your trucks are ready."

Daniel had pressed the money into his oily hands. He'd been a good worker and would be virtually impossible to replace. Stuffing the notes into his overalls, the mechanic had asked about Daniel's family.

Visions of Tatiana, Jeanne, Béa and his mother fleeing crowded his anxious mind at night now. As a boy, his Alsatian grandmother had left him with terrible tales of German atrocities: the burning of farms, attacks on defenceless women, worse.

For the next four days, Daniel waited for more information. Nothing from Tatiana, no newspapers. With no radio either, he numbly went about his duties, counting his infantry's pitiful equipment.

One afternoon, alone in his store, he hurled a pick-axe at the wall.

Heated discussions broke out in the Voncq mess.

"Why the Stuka attack on the yard and nothing since?" said one of the NCOs, voicing what they all felt.

Daniel brought a rolled map to the table. "You're right to be concerned. I think the *boches* are closing in. Look!" he said, emphatically, opening the map and stabbing the village of Voncq with his index finger. "Thirty kilometres west is Rethel, where there are reports of fierce fighting. And Sedan." He extended his third finger. "Forty kilometres north-east. If I join up the three locations like so, we have an obtuse triangle, with Voncq in the middle. We could end up hemmed in on both sides!"

They shook their heads. Vilmoray walked in.

"General Gamelin has been replaced by a man called Weygang. Don't expect to see any changes. It's all about defence with him too! Look at what's happening in Belgium. All those 'strategic retreats'."

The following day, on his way to the stores, Daniel pushed his wheelbarrow past Hervé morosely polishing his rifle.

"Any news on the reinforcements?" Hervé's tone towards him had sharpened lately.

"No," Daniel said, resenting being put in the camp of those in the know. "Sorry, your guess is as good as mine." He peered up into the sky, still that clear blue, and tried to ignore Hervé's scowl.

The end of May came. Vilmoray marched into the mess, ashen-faced. Throwing himself into a chair, he announced:

"Boulogne and Calais have fallen. All we have left is Dunkirk."

Daniel stared at him, aghast. "But how?"

"The German war machine just keeps on going. We just don't seem to be able to stop them!"

With a growing sense of foreboding, Daniel continued to visit the farms as ordered, but the farmers, alarmed by the news, were starting to join the remaining evacuees fleeing south. He was now relying more and more on his canned food. And for good reason, for there were rumours that German units had launched an attack on Attigny, eight kilometres west of Voncq.

The hot weather did nothing to lift Daniel's black mood. On the contrary, nature's inability to sympathize only heightened his frustration and confusion.

One late afternoon, as he headed to his quarters, he noticed a familiar-looking farm truck chug down Voncq high street. It slowed and pulled in abruptly at the kerb. The driver rolled down the passenger window, which was caked in dust.

"Daniel!"

Marcel's lined face squinted at him over his hen cages, the birds pecking furiously at the wire. Marcel pushed one of the cages aside angrily.

"The *boches* are coming down the *nationale* from Charleville in armoured vehicles and tanks! They'll be making their way in this direction. I'm clearing out of here! *Bonne chance!*" He drove off in a cloud of squawking hens and rattling furniture.

For a while, Daniel stood there, unable to move. Hot air blew off the fields, making a window shutter creak on its ancient pins. With no good weapons, their tiny reservist unit was doomed. Where were Vilmoray and the rest of the men? Running a circuit in the fields around Voncq woods. He looked down the street and saw an old woman in an apron carry a platter out of the inn, the staff officers' mess. They had holed themselves up there for months. *Surrender is inevitable. Now is the time to go and have it out with them.*

He stepped out into the empty street, running through a familiar, terrible scenario. Night after night, he had imagined the sound of boots in the yard and the harsh, triumphant, guttural voices of the enemy.

He halted by the inn door, lifted the brass knocker in the shape of a horse's head and found the door open. Stepping into a darkened hall, he heard laughter erupt from behind a door at the far end.

"*Santé!*" There was a scraping of chairs and the clinking of glasses. Rich cooking aromas came through the door. Rosemary-infused *gigot*. He couldn't remember the last time he had eaten such a meal.

Turning the brass doorknob with force, he entered a cloud of pungent cigar smoke. Through a half-open shutter, the afternoon sunshine streamed, illuminating the starched white tablecloth. It was strewn with gravy-encrusted sauceboats, silver platters with the remains of the officer's lamb, bottles of *Nuit Saint-Georges* and white Loire wines.

A grey-haired, stout-looking officer with ruddy cheeks broke away from the men finishing their toast. Registering Daniel's single stripe, he puffed out his chest.

"*Caporal,* what the hell do you think you're doing here?" He swayed, correcting his balance as he put his glass down.

"Pardon, Messieurs!" It was the maid. She brushed past, placed a generous selection of fruit on a side table and left.

Daniel's stomach tightened as she retreated into the shadows.

"You know this place is out of bounds to you, *Caporal*," said the officer, eyeing him with unconcealed contempt. "This had better be good!" He leaned into him. His breath reeked of crushed garlic.

"Sir," Daniel said, stepping back slightly and remembering to salute. "An armoured division of German soldiers has been seen proceeding south down the highway from Charleville, on the road to Chalons. We could be separated from our supply lines in Vouziers by morning."

"What? On whose information?"

"A farmer I trust."

"A farmer!" The officer sneered. "The area has been awash with rumour for weeks now. All unfounded. We would have heard…"

"Sir," a young man with large, brown eyes and a finely-tended moustache interjected, politely. "Don't you think we'd better check?"

The stout officer reeled towards the young man and then turned angrily back to Daniel. "This is ridiculous!" He pushed past and stormed into a room just off the dining area. Daniel saw him seize the telephone. A large-scale map of the Ardennes rose up over his bent figure. A series of bold, zigzagged lines ran along the Belgium and Luxembourg border: the Maginot fortifications. They had taken years to build and had nearly bankrupted his country.

The sharp essence of burnt grape wafted up and prickled the hairs of his nose.

"Eh! Pass over that Armagnac!" someone cried rudely across the table. They had all sat down. A surly officer with tufty hair had removed his jacket and was peering gloomily into his balloon glass. Others continued to drink and smoke in silence, glancing towards the office.

They act as if I'm not here!

"*Allô?*" shouted the officer from next door. "*Allô! Allô!*" The officer stormed back into the room.

The dining room door swung wide open behind Daniel.

There was a loud scraping of chairs on the flagstone floor as the officers stood to attention.

Daniel turned and stepped backed hurriedly as he saw their diminutive Colonel standing there with Vilmoray. Daniel and Vilmoray stared at one another in astonishment.

Recovering himself, Daniel saluted the Colonel.

"One of your men, Vilmoray?" the Colonel asked.

"I have come here of my own accord, *mon Colonel*. Our company is in great danger. The Germans are on their way…"

The Colonel nodded impatiently. "Yes. Yes, *Caporal*." The blood rushed to his face. "Now step aside!"

The stout officer hid a smile as he walked over from the map room and slotted into place at the table. "*Mon Colonel*. No doubt you are aware that our lines are down," he said, by way of apology for not foreseeing the current threat.

The Colonel nodded gravely and invited him to stand at his side. "Now, men," he said, his short arms behind his back. "I have received a communiqué from High Command. It contains the painful news that they have been obliged to withdraw from our HQ at Vitry-Le-François."

"Withdraw!" cried the young officer with the fine moustache. "If that is so – our orders are to go to Lannemezan in the Pyrenees…"

"But that's impossible," said the curmudgeonly tufty-haired officer. "It's just too far!"

The rest of the officers eyed the Colonel with stupefied expressions.

Daniel looked at them all in turn. *They don't have a clue. They haven't prepared for such an eventuality. Our new Colonel and reinforcements have disappeared and all we have is this cretin here!*

He stepped forward hesitantly. "*Mon Colonel*, I have a plan to get us out of here, tonight."

The Colonel seemed flabbergasted by his intervention.

Seizing his advantage, Daniel continued, "I know the roads better than my own family. It's our only chance to escape."

There was a ringing silence. Everyone's eyes were fixed on the Colonel.

Through the haze of cigar smoke, Daniel heard him announce their official retreat, giving him, Corporal Frey, the honour of leading their Third Company out through enemy lines.

Daniel sighed behind the wheel and shifted in his seat as he stared out anxiously into the summer night. With their headlights off, only the moon lit up the narrow, uneven road their convoy was crawling along.

What he had told the Colonel hadn't been bravado. Orienteering had always been a skill of his and map-reading a passion. As a boy he had pored over maps. Indo-China, the Congo, North Africa, even Russia, so vast, dreaming of escape from all the doom and gloom reigning over his home and going out into the world. His time in Morocco with a colonial cavalry unit had, for a time, satisfied his *wanderlust*. But life in the cavalry was strict. He would never forgive that dressing down his Captain had given him for ruining his uniform. And as for the Colonel...

The injustices of army life. At least he was a survivor, he told himself. His experiences had taught him to trust his wits. *But here I am, leading one hundred men!* It was best not to think that way. Best to think of his company as one man. One against the enemy. He wouldn't tolerate dissension tonight. If those officers played up… Well, he would leave them to their fate. In this very field.

He checked his side mirror as the moon went behind a cloud. It was almost impossible to make out the ambulance slowly bringing up the rear. He worried about it, for the road across the fields rose and dipped in the middle, challenging for a vehicle with a low chassis. It would serve those officers right if they encountered difficulties, but their fate impacted on the whole company. He recalled the chaos of the past hour. The panic in the officers' faces as they packed their regimental silver, wines, cigars, books. It had delayed their departure. And then a dispute had broken out about the ambulance. It was against war regulations to ride in one. With relief, Daniel had watched them pile into the back of it, with their precious cargo.

Hervé shuffled nervously in the leather passenger seat and brought his cumbersome rifle in from the open window.

"How far to the *nationale*, boss?" he said, impatiently.

A nervous cough came from the back of the truck. Hard to imagine that it was filled with breathing men. Daniel had overhead snoring. The culprit had been elbowed awake immediately.

He turned to Hervé and said, in a low voice, "At the crossroads back there we passed the village of Chuffily-Roche. Once we get to the hamlet of Colommes-et-Marqueny, we will have nearly reached the *nationale,* but I have decided to head south again for a while, to go through more fields and join it later. The *fritz* are unlikely to employ these roads."

Hervé nodded. Daniel could tell that the names meant nothing to him. He wasn't a local. He was a Breton and had barely left Voncq woods for the past eight months. Even the officers and the Colonel, all used to poring over military maps of the region, were practically ignorant of the minor roads and villages outside their particular sphere of interest.

They trundled past dilapidated farm buildings. Some, Daniel had heard from Marcel, had lain in disrepair since the last war. The region was poor and sparsely populated. Farmers had preferred to move south to richer lands.

Daniel looked away. He'd soon arrive at the point where he'd decided to stop and make it to the main road on foot.

A little cry through his truck window made him glance in his side mirror and curse. Several commercial trucks had stopped just behind them. The back of the convoy was in darkness. Craning his head out of the truck window, Daniel counted backwards.

Nine delivery trucks, a car. *Damn the ambulance*! *It's rolled into a field!* He raised his hand as a signal to stop. Where on earth had the officers got to? He looked over to Hervé, staring ahead and patting the side mirror with his large hairy hand.

The distant sound of an engine revving came through the window. Daniel released the hand-brake, sighing, and peered outside. The moon had reappeared. Its shimmering blanket swept down the column of bumpers, lighting up even the ambulance's radiator rising from a ditch.

Shaking his head, he set off, a little faster this time. He turned to Hervé. "The *nationale* is five minutes' walk from here. Once we're on it, we drive three kilometres north until the crossing on our left. We mustn't miss it. I'm hoping the *boches* will be guarding the more major junction, further north at Attigny."

Hervé nodded and went back to scanning the field. "It's so quiet here. You wouldn't think…"

Daniel nodded, stopped the truck, left the key in the ignition.

Hervé turned to him. "I should come with you. One of the other lads…"

"No. I'll go on ahead," Daniel assured him. "No use engaging the whole convoy before we're sure."

Without waiting for Hervé's reply, he opened his truck door. Hervé joined him on the driver's side.

"Alright, if I'm not back in ten minutes," Daniel said, frowning, "try your luck going in the opposite direction down the *nationale*. But unfortunately, that way, you'd be committing yourself to the major roads."

"Sounds like this is our only option, boss," Hervé said, looking Daniel straight in the eye.

Daniel nodded. "Now get in. We mustn't waste time."

Clutching his torch, Daniel ran the first 50 metres.

At the junction, the fickle moon disappeared behind the trees. Daniel held his breath and stared out at the starless night. He could hear the faint grinding of machinery. Curling his toes inside his boots, he stood there, unable to move. Had he imagined it? On a still night like this, the silence seemed charged with something intangible and difficult to define. And there was the thudding of his own heart to consider.

He stared into the blackness and reached for his flashlight. Steadying his hand, he waved the beam from one side of the road to the other. Trees, hedges, a flurry of large wings. An owl? He stepped forward, distinguishing a low, black mass on the right-hand side of the road. He extinguished his torch. An abandoned Citroen truck? Fuel was scarce, after all. He felt for the pistol Vilmoray had given him and eased it from its holster. As he released the safety catch, he heard someone run up behind him. He swerved and took aim.

It was the Medical Officer, looking startled. "*Caporal*," he whispered. "The Colonel wants to know why you've stopped. He orders you to continue!"

"I have to check that it's safe."

The man gripped Daniel's shoulder and shook it. "The area is teeming with the *boches!*"

Daniel dug his teeth into his bottom lip. He tried to recall whether he had driven past the car before. He did remember seeing several abandoned vehicles further up the highway a few weeks back. But surely it had been further northwards, up near Attigny. Perhaps if they waited for the moon to reappear.

"*Caporal!*"

Torn by indecision, Daniel ran back to the convoy with the Medical Officer. Hervé had already driven up to the junction. Daniel watched him regain the passenger seat and jumped up behind the wheel.

He reached for the ignition and slowly set off, allowing the medic to return to the ambulance. He turned onto the main road, changed into second gear, and edged forward. The moon was starting to break through the trees. The road at least was smooth here, no bumping or crashing of the underside, and his convoy was keeping up this time. *But there is no turning back. Damn that Colonel!* He clenched his wheel, murderous impulses clouding his thoughts. The road had narrowed. The ominous dark shape he had observed was now looming.

Hervé peered through the windscreen. "What's that, boss?"

Daniel started in his seat as the shape reared up in front of them. It was an armoured car mounted on huge wheels, with a 20mm cannon.

"Close your window, Hervé," he hissed. Keeping the same steady pressure on the pedal, he tugged on his own window pull. *Gently does it.* He felt Hervé clutch his rifle. "Put it down!" he said, firmly. The truck's engine thrummed loudly in the silence.

Daniel gritted his teeth. They had fallen upon a Panzer unit.

Daniel tensed in his seat as his truck passed the line of immobile armoured vehicles. Every one of them able to ram them down if they were to come to life now. And their guns, quick-firing, armour-piercing; explosive German shells could obliterate the whole convoy in seconds.

Please God! He was reaching the end of the silent column of turrets. Just as he had started to breathe more freely, he remembered the convoy following him. He looked in his side mirror; every commercial truck, which Denis had camouflaged a non-descript brown, had kept up, and there was that wretched ambulance.

Taking a deep breath, he turned his attention back to the middle of the road ahead, where a yellow glow, a lantern, lay upturned on a grassy bank. A metre or so away from it a dark helmeted figure in a coat was standing against a tree. A jeep was parked by a red halt sign in the middle of the road. The soldier rocked back on his heels, pulled up his fly, then lurched back to the sign as he heard Daniel's convoy approach.

Hands trembling, Daniel switched his headlamps on to full beam. He scanned for evidence of other soldiers, security dogs – nothing except the guard and their convoy. He continued on slowly towards him, his limbs tensing as the guard raised his submachine gun and pointed it at his windscreen. Daniel slowed, turned back to his sidelights and rolled his window down.

"*Enschuldigung!*" he announced, raising his hand in apology. On the left, out of the corner of his eye, he had spotted the slip road.

"*Halt!*" said the guard, dazed.

Originally from Alsace, Daniel had picked up a little German. "*Guten Abend!*"

The guard stared at him, confused.

"*Danke,*" Daniel said, grinning inanely and pulling down his indicator baton to signal left. He gave the guard another friendly wave. *Gently does it. Act casual. You could be one of them. The blond hair. Regular features.*

The guard hesitated, rubbed his red-rimmed eyes. Daniel flashed him his most dazzling smile. The guard, despite his stupefied expression, waved him through.

For the next minute or so, Daniel frantically checked his mirror as he drove. As the convoy joined him, he mentally ticked off the men. *And there goes the ambulance – the little runt at the back!*

Several kilometres down the road, when he felt them far enough from enemy lines, he pulled over. He jumped down and, pinching himself, made his way along the convoy to the back of the ambulance. No sound came from within. Furious, he pounded on the door. A sleepy officer opened it and eventually their red-faced Colonel.

"*Mon Colonel*, we have passed through enemy lines," he said, not without some pride.

"*Eh bien, Caporal Frey*, what are you waiting for?" the Colonel replied, trying to loosen a crick in his neck. "We'd better get the hell out of here!"

CHAPTER SIX

Daniel's eyes were dry and strained from hours of driving through the night. The circuitous route he had been forced to take through the Champagne countryside had greatly lengthened their journey south. He checked the arrow on his fuel gauge, willing it to stay in position.

By the end of tomorrow, our jerry cans will be empty. He was tempted to join the *nationale. But no – what am I thinking, after that encounter with that Panzer division!* How many other armoured units crouched in the darkness waiting for dawn to break? He relived the slow procession his convoy had made past the sleek killing machines and thought bitterly of the rifle and horse training he'd received in Morocco. All of it was now redundant in this new war dominated by planes and tanks. He pressed his foot down hard on the accelerator.

Alongside him, Hervé's muscular bulk rose and fell with slow regularity. Daniel fumbled in the darkness for his water canister, found it and tipped it over his parched lips. Only a few drops dribbled down his chin. As he tossed it aside, a maddening thirst took hold. He wound down the window and unbuttoned his woollen shirt. A tepid air blew in and passed over his clammy chest. The softness of it brought forth Tatiana.

He imagined her being swept further and further away from him, with Jeanne, Béa, his mother, all of them engulfed in a swirling mass of petrified women, children, and aged relatives. *But she is strong*, he kept repeating to himself. *She has lived through revolution.* And yet, what he had experienced with the refugee children outside Vouziers had triggered a terrible anxiety. He feared not only for his daughters but all children. No brother or sister should have to watch their grandfather howl like an animal. And with what terror they had watched the skies.

He hoped Tatiana would be able to shield Jeanne and Béa from the worst. Jeanne was a restless, sensitive child. Had the war aggravated her fears? During his last leave, how fast her little heart had beat up against his breast after she had danced to Charles Trenet's *Boum* on a gramophone in rue de Grenelle.

"Just like your heart, Papa, when you see Mama, Béa, and I. Stay with us, Papa."

He was conscious of the sky paling around him. A signpost marked 'Châlons' reared up in his windscreen. *This is where the German tanks are heading.*

He glanced at his wristwatch. Four thirty in the morning. Going on what Marcel had told him, he would avoid the town and head straight for Vitry-le-François, thirty kilometres south-west.

On the outskirts of Vitry, a flimsy wooden barrier barred the route into town. Behind it, Daniel saw a group of exhausted-looking artillerymen scanning the dawn sky, one of them wheeling a 75mm field gun. A group of soldiers had built a fire in a pile of broken bricks. Behind them, a collapsed apartment building emerged through the black smoke. The air reeked of powdered plaster, bricks, and charred wood.

One of the gunners walked towards Daniel's truck, his face black with soot, his eyes bloodshot.

"*Suivez la deviation à votre gauche*," he said, irritably. He turned back to join his colleagues squatting by the fire. "*Alors ça vient ce café*!"

Daniel pulled away with a heavy heart. The gunner had woken Hervé, who leaned into the windscreen.

"With that old cannon they hope to stop the *boches*?!"

Daniel frowned. *What they must think of us. But we can do nothing.* He turned towards Hervé. "Any water?"

Hervé shook his head but reached for a bottle by his feet. "Pernod?" he asked, producing the bottle, which he'd barely touched.

Daniel shook his own head. "We'll stop somewhere in Vitry, but not linger. This looks bad. If the planes have been through town, it means the Panzers are not far behind."

"How far to Lannemezan?"

"Another full day's drive or more."

"We'll run out of juice before then."

Daniel sighed and took the diversion. It brought them back into the centre of town. The condition of the road worsened considerably as they drew up to a central roundabout, potholes and displaced cobbles everywhere. He rolled up his window, as smoke and burnt tar caught in his throat, stopping as he came upon a cracked fountain still issuing water.

Everyone got out and took it in turns to fill their canisters and tin cups. Bleary-eyed, they joined Daniel, staring silently down the central avenue of town, which had been razed to the ground by incendiary bombs. What had once been apartment buildings, hotels, churches and government buildings had been reduced to matchstick and rubble. All of it stretching out to infinity.

Only one monument rose up defiantly amidst the devastation – Vitry-le-François's Hôtel de Ville.

"Where are the people?" someone asked.

"Gone," Daniel said, flatly. "The Prefect must have ordered an evacuation."

Out of the corner of his eye, Daniel saw the Colonel, who had had water brought to him, spread out a map on the ambulance's bonnet.

"Want me to take over the driving, boss?" Hervé asked.

Daniel rubbed the back of his sweating neck and splashed it with a cupful of fresh water. What he would give to plunge into a river, wash away the dust, the grime; the guilt.

"Not now. Further south."

And then they heard the blast of cannon fire from the entrance to the city.

"Not again!" Hervé said, emptying his Pernod bottle and filling it with water.

The Colonel's aide came running over to him. "Next stop, the town of Bar s/Aube. Get a move on."

They scrambled to their trucks and drove off.

By late morning, they were outside Bar s/Aube.

A harsh light had prised open Daniel's weary eyelids. Had he blanked out for a second? Through his dusty windscreen he saw an old stone washhouse. A *lavoir*, he thought, happily.

Climbing stiffly down from his truck, his head still throbbing with the sounds of the engine, he walked over the yellowing grass, sat beneath the *ardoise* roof, and stripped to the waist. He peered back at the officers and the Colonel grouped around the ambulance's doors in the glaring sun. Probably coveting their own supplies! His head span with dehydration. *To hell with them!* Hervé and the men had gone off scavenging. The hamlet seemed to have been evacuated. The food could wait. He threw his shirt into the pool and leaned in towards the still, dark waters. A pinched face stared back at him. Opening his mouth, he plunged head-first into the water.

He went to dry off in the sun. As he let his long limbs sink uneasily into the dry, prickly grass, he heard footsteps; Vilmoray.

"The water good?"

He nodded and smiled faintly, without bothering to open his eyes. Vilmoray's shadow fell upon his face then disappeared.

His vision swirling with yellow and green, he let himself roll onto his side and lose consciousness.

He was jerked awake by shouts from the hamlet and aircraft engines. He rolled onto his back. The roar of propellers above made his blood curdle. Five yellow planes, circling above their heads. *Bastard Mussolini!* The Italians must have just entered the war. One of the cumbersome machines fell out of the sky.

Heavy-legged and still drugged with sleep, Daniel staggered back towards the washhouse for shelter.

A dark form was lying by the water's edge. "Vilmoray!" Daniel screamed. Clutching Vilmoray's shoulders, he heaved him into the water and pulled him down with him. As they hit the stone bottom, the water's surface erupted with stars, the stone shuddering beneath them. Vilmoray struggled, distanced himself from Daniel to avoid a piece of falling masonry.

His lungs started to strain for air, Daniel came up gasping. The propeller sounds were fading. Vilmoray kneeled in the water beside him, gripping the sides of the *lavoir* and panting.

"*Viens,*" Daniel said, helping his superior up. "Quick, back to the truck."

They ran back, their drenched clothes clinging to them. Cries came from the village. The houses behind the washhouse had taken the full force of the strike. Hervé came running from the village with a full kit bag of provisions. The ambulance was already starting up and moving off.

Daniel leapt into the driver's seat of his truck and turned the ignition. The men piled on, Hervé in last. As he threw his gains to the floor he pulled out a bottle and uncorked it with his teeth.

"Want some *pinot?*"

Daniel took a hasty swig. The coarse red was comforting. A bit of rural France. His country's soil. One less bottle for the *fritz*.

Outside the village, they caught up with the ambulance and were soon waved down. Lieutenant Vilmoray went to talk to the Colonel and came running back.

"*Caporal*," he said, through Daniel's window, "our fuel is low. We're heading to a military fuel depot in Moulins. Put your foot down! And… thank you," he added, in a low voice, before marching off officiously.

They reached Moulins early afternoon, by which time it was blisteringly hot. The main bridge on the River Allier was eerily empty. A wooden barrier had been erected across it and several French soldiers stood guard. They frowned as the convoy halted several metres away.

"The depot must be on the opposite side."

Vilmoray came over. "The Colonel wants to know what you're doing."

"I plan to cross the bridge with a small team of men."

Vilmoray looked unconvinced. "The depot is clearly being guarded."

"Let me talk to the guards. We can load the drums onto my truck."

Vilmoray pondered. "Alright. Be quick." He marched back to the Colonel.

A red-faced officer not belonging to their company drew up in a military car. "What do you think you're doing?"

Daniel pulled himself up to his full height. "My Colonel orders us to fuel up."

"So?"

"Look, sir. I can see the depot from here, over the other side of the bridge."

The officer stiffened. He checked Daniel's stripe. "*Caporal*, this bridge is mined. In the next twenty minutes, it's going up!"

"Leaves me just enough time then!"

In the distance behind them, however, they heard planes.

"Don't be an idiot! This bridge will blow before the *fritz* try to cross it. The land forces won't be far behind the circling Stukas." Taking a look back, the officer ordered the guards into the car and drove off.

"Hervé, bring five men and remove that barrier."

"But…"

"Do it. Now! And tell Vilmoray to inform the *Colonel* that we'll meet them at Varennes, at the next bridge."

Now at the steering wheel, Daniel stared across the bridge. He noticed the wires from the charges.

Hervé ran back to the truck with his team. Daniel's foot tensed as he waited for the men to board. Without looking at Hervé, he pressed hard on the accelerator. They thundered across the bridge, the canisters rolling and bumping in the back, Hervé gripping the sides of his seat.

On the opposite bank, the men jumped down as he turned the truck round to face the town. The canisters were unloaded and taken over to the pumps. Each man grabbed a hose and started pumping manically, whilst Daniel watched the German planes scream over Moulins. *The Germans won't hit the depot. They need the fuel too badly. And that officer wanting to blow the bridge – he'll wait*. But the following second, a voice inside his head had decided otherwise. *You think the fritz won't jump at the chance at blowing your truck to smithereens! And as for that officer, he doesn't care two hoots about you – he wants to stop the fritz from advancing south! Keep the engine running!*

He turned to Hervé and glowered at him, but Hervé was already disconnecting the hose and pumping fuel into another canister.

Loud explosions punctuated the air. Drums were hoisted onto the back. Others followed.

"Hurry!" he shouted, though the men could go no faster.

Hervé was dripping with sweat. Another explosion, this time nearer the river, made them all gasp.

"Right, that's it," Daniel bellowed. "We can't wait. Get in!"

He heard a last canister being heaved on board.

"Leave the last one."

"Nearly there, boss."

"Do you hear me? That's an order!"

"Yes, boss." Hervé hauled in the last one, half-filled, and jumped into the passenger seat.

Daniel pushed his foot down. A bomber flew above their heads, and in his panic, Daniel scraped the sides of the bridge. He could sense the bomber getting ready to release its charge. The truck flew off the bridge and landed on the dry track running along the Allier. They bumped along at speed without looking back.

Great tremors passed right through the truck.

"Christ, boss!" Hervé cried, looking back across the river. "It's all gone up!"

As Daniel finally joined the road to Varennes, he glanced back through Hervé's side window. The depot roof had taken a direct hit. He ran his eyes back along the bridge, on the Moulins side, just in time to see its third arch collapse into the Allier's calm waters.

CHAPTER SEVEN

At Varennes, Daniel and Hervé were able to join their convoy on the other side of the bridge.

Vilmoray broke through the fray, ordering the men to unload the fuel. The place suddenly became alive with activity and purpose as a team of men gathered behind the truck.

Daniel stepped down to meet Vilmoray.

"Good work, *Caporal*. The *Colonel* informs us that we are clear of the battle zone."

Daniel watched him walk away. Leaning back against the bonnet of his truck, he stared at the white *Charolais* cattle grazing peacefully in the field opposite.

"Boss, I'll take over from here." Hervé had a map in his hand.

Daniel rubbed his eyes and tried to focus on the diagonal route they had taken across France since leaving the Ardennes. They had reached central France, the Auvergne, and were now half-way to Lannemezan in the south-west.

"Alright," he said, mounting the steps and crumpling into the passenger seat.

When he regained consciousness, it was to fresher breezes. He looked through his side window and saw a chain of conical hills with lopped-off peaks hurtle by.

There was a dull thud. The truck raced down a hill. Hervé swore and crunched the gear lever. They bumped over a narrow stone bridge. The sound of gushing waters lifted his spirits momentarily. A road sign came and went: St Flour.

Daniel rolled onto his side and sank again into oblivion.

It was only when he awoke that he was conscious of having slept. The morning sun pierced the windscreen, blackened with dust or ash.

"Where are we?"

Hervé's red-rimmed eyes were having trouble focusing on the road. "Past Toulouse, boss."

"Toulouse?" The Midi-Pyrénées region. Lannemezan, he remembered, was further west. He wound down his window and gazed out onto pale green mountains. A car horn sounded behind him. In his side mirror, the medic in the ambulance waved at him and pointed ahead.

People had massed outside a village café set back from the road.

"Slow down, Hervé. Pull into this village." Daniel thrust his arm out of the window and waved the convoy in.

They parked a little away from the throng and made their way to the café. Hoards of grubby children chased one another around a square, while groups of ill-fed cats sniffed at overspilling bins.

"Shoo," shouted an older boy, stamping his foot and scattering them in all directions. The youth watched Daniel, Vilmoray, and the men pass.

The crowd Daniel joined was mainly of exhausted-looking women with unbrushed hair, straining their ears in the direction of the café table where a wireless had pride of place. Around it, older members of the village sat, victims of the last war, judging by the eye patches, crutches, and missing limbs. Daniel took his place in the crowd next to them with several of the men. One of the seniors tapped his good leg with a cane, then looked up and glowered at Daniel. 'Not a scratch on him,' his eyes seemed to say. But the friend with an ear trumpet next to him was already diverting his attention:

"*Il a commencé le Maréchal?*"

"*Chut*! It's starting."

A ponderous, grave voice cut in.

"*Le voilà le Maréchal*," someone said in the crowd. "Turn it up!"

"*It is with a heavy heart that I say to you today, fighting must cease.*"

Daniel leaned in.

49

"I spoke last night with the enemy and asked him…"

"Maman, Maman!" A little girl who had ducked under Daniel's arm was tugging at her mother's skirt. "Bruno won't let me play!"

"Stop it, Mathilde! Can't you see I'm listening!"

Several mothers standing next to her gave the woman censorious looks.

"… the means to an end to the hostilities. May all Frenchmen rally to the government over which I preside during this difficult ordeal. May I calm their anxiety. May they listen and place all their faith in their fatherland."

People looked at one another with a mixture of shock, resignation, relief, and consternation.

Was this it? The end to the fighting?

Vilmoray walked away. Daniel joined him, feeling unwelcome. He was quiet, like the rest of the men.

The Colonel gathered those around him near the other side of the square.

"We'll have a fifteen-minute break," he said, in a cracked voice.

Daniel turned away and went to sit on the low wall around the square. The boy who had terrorised the cats had picked up a stray *boule* and was throwing it up in the air, jumping clear of it just as it missed crushing his sandaled toes. A woman in a headscarf and her friend came to sit beside Daniel, placing their leather suitcases bound with string at their feet.

"It's my only pair of shoes, Muriel," said the woman in the headscarf, rubbing her swollen ankles. "I can't walk anymore. Where are we to go? The trains will probably be out for months." She turned her despairing face to the unruly youth with the boule. "And just look at Patrick!

"The *Maréchal*'s talking about us going back to work," she continued. "Resuming our lives. But we don't even know if we have a house to get back to, let alone husbands!"

Watching the boy, Daniel was reminded of his own youth. *Pauvre gars!* He had got up to far worse after the Great War. Not that he didn't respect authority. Often it was the individual exerting it that was at fault. School had been his prison, the fields and nature his teacher.

Vilmoray marched over to him. "Coming? Best to keep going, judging by the state of the drivers."

At Lannemezan, they arrived only to be told that plans had changed and they were to go back towards Rodez, west of there, to a town called Villefranche de Rouerges, a medieval, fortified town.

Numb to the beauty of the mountain forests and gorges they passed, Daniel was relieved to finally reach their destination at dusk. He got down from his truck, ignored the sun setting over the Aveyron's swirling waters, and went to join the others in unloading.

Marooned in Villefranche de Rouerges, the waiting began for all of them.

The destruction of the railways had halted the mail. Endless games of *belote* and chess were not enough to fill the monotony of their days. Daniel often wandered through the town alone or with Vilmoray, absentmindedly jingling the few francs he possessed in his pocket. It was impossible to plan without news of Tatiana.

It took several weeks for her letter to arrive. He almost wept when he saw her ragged, loopy writing.

Noyer, Cher
June 13th 1940

Chéri

Your mother and I have reached the Cher and are lodging in a hamlet called Noyer with a clog maker and his family. Don't ask me how we got here. Many days on our feet, feeling we could not carry on. Two officers took pity on us on the outskirts of Paris and gave us a lift for a while. But all that seems far behind us now.

Baby Béatrice is cutting her teeth and keeping me and Jeanne awake all night. I have little to pacify her other than the corner of the sheet. During the day she grizzles and drinks milk, which I have to beg from the cobbler's wife. The old woman is so parsimonious and wears a permanent scowl on her pinched face. Jeanne tried to amuse Béatrice the other evening by donning Monsieur's clogs and performing a jig on his stone floor. The noise! Even I threw up my hands in alarm! Madame was quite stony-faced as she dished out her broth at dinner.

Dan, I'm praying that you are alive. At night we huddle together in a single bed, the cobbler's son's, who, I've just heard, has had the misfortune to be captured and taken to a German prisoner of war camp. They are talking about millions having met the same fate. Is it true? I pray that it isn't for you! I now have more sympathy for the Madame and have told Jeanne to keep quiet.

Please write the minute you get this.

Tatiana

P.S. Vladimir has left the TB clinic and is living in Jurançon near the Spanish border, with his fiancée and her mother. Unbelievable that he has found love in these dark times!

Daniel replaced the letter in its envelope. They were all alive. The letter was six weeks old. It seemed a miracle it had got through at all.

Daniel leaned over Vilmoray on the bunk next to him. He was reading a newspaper; a map of France dominated the front page. To the north and west of their country now lay German-occupied France.

Vilmoray looked up. "The *boches* have wolfed up Paris, our heavy industry, our best farmland, our most prestigious vineyards. And yet I will be returning to Paris to join them. What is there left in the south – the so-called Free Zone? How can you feel free when you have no job prospects?"

Daniel frowned. "I would rather my family live as far from the *fritz* as possible!" He stared at Tatiana's envelope, which he'd inadvertently crushed in his hand.

Vilmoray gave him a quizzical look. "Everything alright?"

"Yes," he said, apologetically. "I know I should be grateful that Tatiana and the children are alive. But life is tough in the Cher. The minute I can get money to them..."

"Oh!" Vilmoray said, glancing back at the newspaper. "Doesn't the demarcation line go through there?"

Daniel ran his eye anxiously along it. The river Cher bisected the department of the same name. The village Tatiana was in was just north of the river, in occupied France!

"Don't worry, Daniel," Vilmoray said, reading his mind. "They're already talking about repatriation. Even if it takes a while." He patted Daniel's shoulder. "We must keep positive. Heaven knows how many thousands are in a worse state than us…"

In the weeks that followed, Daniel slept fitfully. The noise and smell of communal living didn't help. Squabbles over mislaid clothes, shavers, and shoes were inevitable. They all had so few possessions.

To bolster himself up he wrote to Vladimir and told him that he'd landed in the Free Zone. Explaining his situation, he asked whether he could use Vladimir's address. Without it, he couldn't demobilise and get his pay.

Postcards started to arrive, with the briefest of news. The German authorities, keen to limit information between the two zones, had created ready-made answers. His father had ticked the box 'in good health'. Having undergone drastic stomach surgery during the Great War, he clearly wasn't. Stoical to the last, but at least his father hadn't had to flee Paris, Daniel told himself. That would have killed him.

Daniel's thoughts turned to the millions of soldiers writing home from German camps. Vilmoray was right, his company had been spared prison. But his spirits didn't lift.

He started to sift through his pitiful belongings. No clothes other than the khaki shirt and trousers he was wearing. His most prized article of clothing, his leather driving jacket, would no doubt last like his army boots, but what if he needed to present himself for interview?

"Find yourself a tailor in Jurançon," Vilmoray suggested. "Where your brother-in-law is living. That officer's cape of yours can be made into a pair of ski trousers!"

To date, Vladimir hadn't replied to his letter. Surely he'd received it by now.

"Why the long face, Daniel?" Vilmoray said, reading the paper he'd snatched off one of the officers. "Look here, there's something to cheer us all up. The financial terms of the Armistice. Twenty million francs France is having to pay. Enough to finance Hitler's army here. The *fritz* are claiming eighty percent of France's total food production. We will all starve, including the farmers!" he said, raising his hands in horror.

"Far worse than Versailles," Daniel said, shaking his head gravely. "Best to grow your own food and stay in the Free Zone."

Daniel said goodbye to Hervé, whose wife and daughters had returned to Rennes.

"Not a moment too soon," the Breton cried in frustration, "now that the *fritz* have stopped correspondence between the two zones again! Blackmail. What more do they want from us?"

Vilmoray, meanwhile, was impatient to regain Paris, eager to take up the reins of his clothes store in the ninth district.

"It'll be a mess, but my deputy assures me that business was brisk last week. The store was full of German officers on leave, profiting from the strong deutschmark." He handed Daniel his calling card. "*A bientôt!*" he said, jovially. "Don't hesitate to come by. You'll be requiring a new suit!"

"*Merci.*" Daniel slipped his card into his wallet, doubtful he would need it. Vilmoray had a good job to go back to, unlike him. Paris full of Germans! He had every intention of staying in the Free Zone with Tatiana. He was sure the cessation of correspondence was merely temporary. A log jam in the postal services. No – he had to concentrate on his family's immediate needs. He had no savings and his army pay would barely last a month; he needed paid work, and then to get Tatiana away from the Cher.

A day later, before setting out to Jurançon with a few notes in his pocket, he received Vladimir's short reply. Although his brother-in-law had seemingly recovered from TB, Daniel found it hard to read Vladimir's spidery print.

September 20th 1940

Daniel

 Brother – Relieved that you are safe and well. Of course, you must come the minute you can! We're staying with Gisele's mother, but you are most welcome, brother.
 Much love, Vlad.

CHAPTER EIGHT

Daniel boarded a packed train westwards, to the ancient town of Pau. There he was relieved to catch a quieter tram, to Jurançon, a suburb south of the city. Alighting, he continued on foot along a country road, delighting in the birdsong and fresh breeze. The Atlantic Ocean was an hour away, and south lay the Pyrenees, across which so many of his countrymen, those who could afford it, had fled into Spain.

He turned his gaze to the green foothills – the high escarpments, dotted with small vineyards. The white Jurançon wines produced here were less well-known than the sweet Sauternes dessert wine they resembled. He had developed an interest in wine when he'd toured the Bourgogne region, selling his machine tools.

Closing his eyes, he sniffed the faint, sweet aromas wafting around him. *Yes – a fine spot*, he told himself. The low distant thrum of a tractor made him open his eyes again. *The vignerons have access to fuel I see. I'll need a car if I am to work.* But he remembered seeing few cars out on the road. Maybe he should first concentrate on the *vendanges*, for he would be ideally located for agricultural work. But that wasn't until October, a month from now, or possibly later, for he remembered that a sweeter dessert wine required a later harvesting.

He stopped, wiped his forehead with the back of his sleeve, removed his leather jacket. Cramming it into his knapsack, he thought of Paris, thousands of kilometres away, where he might this very moment have been walking through the Champ de Mars gardens with Tatiana and the girls. He imagined the balding yellow lawns, the dust, the ill-fed, flea-ridden donkeys Jeanne would want to ride on and the Eiffel Tower, now thick with German uniforms.

"Ah Paris. Good riddance to her!" he found himself saying out loud.

He filled out his chest and looked about him. *Fertile earth – the climate is temperate.* Yes, he could see how this place was right for Vladimir. And it would suit Tatiana and the children too. Here his girls could run freely, without fear. Why would Tatiana wish to return to her beloved Paris, now transformed into the German HQ? Her father would object, Alexandre still didn't believe in him. *Bah! Surely, he cannot expect us all to squeeze into that two-roomed apartment! And every day having to look for work and to receive Alexandre's reproachful looks!*

He had reached a lane with a row of modest stone houses. An old, black Citroen was parked outside one of them. Seeing no bell, he knocked at the door.

A small, handsome woman with a dignified, lined face appeared on the threshold. "You must be Daniel. Welcome!"

"And you, Madame Ferali, Gisèle's mother?"

She gave him a world-weary smile, wiped her hands on her apron and shook his hand.

"Just in time for lunch. Vladimir and Gisèle are through there." She lowered her voice. "As you can imagine, they've been told to eat, eat, eat by the doctor."

Mme Ferali studied him with her ferocious dark eyes. Daniel tugged at his matted blond beard self-consciously. He had wanted to shave it off the past week, but the queues for the washbasins had been at their worst at the demobilisation centre when they knew the railways were running again.

Mme Ferali's expression softened, however. "You must be relieved to be out of there," she said, inviting him in.

"Yes," he said, following her through a dark, narrow kitchen where she had prepared a vegetable soup in a large pot. The smell of sweet spices filled the little hallway they crossed, reminding Daniel of Morocco.

"Go through," the woman said, returning to her pans.

"Ah, Daniel." The weak cry had come from the couch, where Vladimir was sitting with a tray of chickpea soup balanced on his long, bony thighs.

Still in his Prince of Wales suit. It was how he remembered his brother-in-law. Always so elegant, though the suit was now threadbare. He put his soup aside and stood up.

Daniel gripped his shoulder and discovered bone. Shocked, he removed his hand.

"Good to see you, brother," Vladimir said, beaming. He turned to an elegant, dark-haired woman sitting in an old chintz armchair opposite. She was taller than Mme Ferali and Tatiana. With her yellow cotton dress and glossy, shoulder-length hair, Daniel was suddenly reminded of his wife. But she was painfully thin, like Vladimir.

"Good to meet you, Daniel," she said, stretching out a pale, graceful arm. "Can I call you that?" She smiled.

"Of course." He peered into her eyes, almond-shaped like Tatiana's and Vladimir's. Beautiful eyes but grave.

"I hope you like Maman's chorba soup," she said.

"Ah, Madame Ferali. You are most kind," Daniel said, as she walked in with two bowls. "I do – very much. Chorba was our mainstay in the Atlas where I was stationed. The spices kept us warm at the fort." Daniel perched on the arm of a chair.

"We are in fact from Algeria," Mme Ferali said, kindly. "But it is no doubt the same. When my husband died in Algiers, Gisèle and I came back here. But I am Corsican by birth."

"Dan!" Vladimir's eyes were twinkling with gentle mischief. "Dan, your beard. Better shave that off before Tatiana sees it!"

The two women laughed. Gisèle reached across and took Vladimir's hand. She turned to Daniel.

"I am looking forward to meeting Tatiana. Vladimir has told me so much about her."

"You are not dissimilar," Daniel said.

"Yes, stubborn," Vladimir added, smiling.

Incredible, thought Daniel. *What a piece of divine luck this terrible illness has brought him!* His brother-in-law's body, once so tall and broad-shouldered, was alarmingly thin, but the ardour and life force simmered in those dark eyes.

"Daniel – some bread and goat's cheese with that?" Mme Férali enquired.

"Merci, Madame Ferali. You are too kind. But I really don't want to inconvenience you…"

"On the contrary, you will be a help." She paused to see whether

Daniel had grasped her meaning.

"Of course, Madame Ferali."

She nodded. "Meanwhile you can make up a bed here in the sitting room."

"And from tomorrow, I shall be out looking for work."

Mme Ferali looked satisfied with his remark. Vladimir, on the other hand, looked a little uncomfortable.

"Eat, Daniel," he said.

"Yes, yes, brother. Look, I've nearly finished. But can I ask you about the Citroen parked in the lane?"

"I bought it from someone at the clinic," Vladimir said, seemingly relieved to change the subject. "It got us here, but it's out of petrol and, as you know, petrol cannot be got nowadays. Unless you work on the land, and even then..."

Daniel spooned the last portion of spicy chickpeas and tomatoes into his mouth. "Delicious," he said, putting down his spoon. "I have an idea, Vladimir." Turning to Mme Ferali, he let out a laugh. "You see, Madame Ferali, your soup has inspired me!"

She smiled wistfully. "That's what my Pierre used to say."

"Vladimir. Do you remember that engineer in Belgium in thirty-eight? We were talking about the likelihood of war and fuel shortages."

"Of course," said his brother-in-law, now sitting up. "Gas generators as an alternative to petrol to power engines. But isn't that difficult?"

"No, he sketched a diagram for me and Philippe Klug in that bar. Philippe told me to hang on to that piece of paper. As a business idea! It's in my head."

Mme Ferali's eyes lit up. "I've just remembered. There's an engineer in the neighbourhood. A heating engineer. I went to him when I was wondering what to do about the car. Asked if he knew a *garagiste*."

"Excellent!" Vladimir slapped his thigh. "And by the way," he continued in a more serious tone, "talking of Philippe Klug. I've not heard from him or his father... I sent a letter to their Paris address..."

Daniel exchanged an unhappy look. The Klugs had been good to them both. But surely, they'd stay well clear of Paris.

"I've been wondering about them, too. But let me get on," Daniel said, rising. "First things first."

CHAPTER NINE

In the following weeks, the home-produced gasification unit took up most of Daniel's time and thoughts. The engineer, a burly middle-aged man called Laurent with a flamboyant black moustache, took to the task with great enthusiasm once Daniel had discussed the possibility of developing a business together. But the prototype had to work first.

At least the main parts were to hand, Laurent assured Daniel. The yard was a treasure trove, filled with scrap metal and piping. Laurent even produced an old cylindrical water heater, perfect for the main body of the gasification unit. After that, all that remained to be found were the wood briquettes to power the system.

Every day, Daniel rose early to go to the woodland near their home. Early afternoon, having trundled many cartloads of logs home, he'd sit on the sunny doorstep with Vladimir, hacking the logs into briquettes, whilst Vladimir shovelled the pieces into sacks.

Two weeks later, Laurent arrived late one afternoon in a horse-drawn cart to pick up the sacks. Mme Feralie wanted the driveway cleared.

"It looks unprofessional, and you'll give the game away."

Daniel leapt up onto the cart and accompanied Laurent to the workshop to help him unload. Rubbing his hands, red raw with blisters, Daniel felt the exhilaration and trepidation of an inventor as they entered the yard. What if the unit didn't work? So much time and money would have been wasted. And what could he do otherwise? Tatiana was waiting for news many miles away. He needed to see the prototype in action.

"Well – can I see it?"

"Tomorrow!" Laurent said, laughing.

He found it hard to sleep that night, one minute buoyed by enormous optimism and the next racked with doubt.

He rushed over to the workshop the next morning. Laurent was double-checking his measurements and calculations. The length and angle of the piping was crucial, he told Daniel. It had to curve smoothly over the main body of Vladimir's car, so that the gas didn't encounter any friction as it passed out of the cylindrical bin. They had to visit the old Citroen several times. Each time, the engineer made a slight alteration. By the afternoon, they were soldering the pipes back at the workshop and piercing airholes one third of the way up the bin.

Finally, the unwieldy contraption was brought up the lane to Vladimir's Citroen. Vladimir had insisted on helping Daniel clean the car up, for by now, word had got around the neighbours, through Mme Ferali, that a gasification unit to rival the market's Imbert would soon be tested and, if successful, be available in the area at a fraction of the price.

Thus, one fine Saturday morning, a clutch of families gathered around the gleaming Citroen to witness the launch of the prototype.

Daniel and the engineer had attached the boiler to the back of the car and run the pipe along one side of it, so that when it dropped down to the windscreen, the driver had an unobstructed view. The pipe continued and snaked under the bonnet, through to the engine. All of this Daniel pointed out to his audience.

'The next part is easy." He shovelled the woodchip into the cylindrical bin.

"Can we put in any old wood?" asked a man in the crowd.

"No, I would strongly advise you to go through us." A vision of his former employer, Albert Klug, passed before his eyes. 'Always give them a reason to come back to you, Daniel.' Drawing strength from the image, he continued, "It needs to be dry and the pieces need to be of a regular size. Too small, they will burn too quickly, too big, the air won't circulate. Be careful how you pack it. Two kilos of wood should take you eight kilometres, enough for several deliveries in the area, a binload, eighty kilometres. If you want to go further, you make a stop for lunch and start the whole process again."

There was a general murmur and nodding of heads.

The bin was now full. Daniel asked Vladimir to come forward and handed him a match.

"Vladimir, please set us on our way." He leapt into the front seat.

"Why the hurry, Daniel?" Laurent said, winking at the crowd as he closed the bin Vladimir had just lit, before turning his attention to the fire heater.

All went quiet as everyone waited.

Daniel wound down his window, grinned at the crowd nervously.

The engineer stared at the heater, held a pair of bellows up against a nozzle, and gave a few short pumps of air before checking his watch.

In the next ten minutes, the audience's attention was severely tested. Daniel did his best to involve them in the process. He asked the men about their businesses – where they needed to transport their goods. A little boy at the front of the crowd turned away in boredom, but his mother tugged at his sweater.

"*Attends*, Gustave!"

The engineer withdrew a thermometer from the boiler nozzle, marched over to Daniel's window.

"*Vas-y!*"

Daniel smiled nervously and turned the key in the ignition. The engine whirred then coughed into life. A miracle, he thought, and yet Laurent the engineer had been quite sure of his calculations. With a royal wave, he drew slowly off down the lane. Looking in his rear-view mirror, he watched several boys in shorts run down after him, cheering. Daniel thought of stopping and giving them a lift, but he didn't want to tempt fate.

He shifted down a gear and pushed right down on the accelerator. He was coming to a hill ahead. The boys stopped and turned back. Daniel now focused on the gradient. Not too steep – gradual. In a vineyard running alongside the road, a wine-grower walked between the rows of vines, stopping now and again to inspect the golden Marsand grape. He picked one to taste it. The noise of the car engine made him look up and peer at Daniel's gasification unit with interest. Daniel waved at him. He took off his cap and waved back.

How he wished Tatiana and Jeanne were here in the car. *Once I've built up the business, I may even buy a vineyard!* He saw himself lunching at the head of a long table, with Tatiana at the other end, Jeanne, Béatrice, his parents, the Ivanovs, perhaps more of his own children seated around him. Several sons to help him with the business. And then he started to dream of the Sunday afternoons he'd spend painting outdoors, the land, the workers, subjects he would never tire of.

At the top of the hill he turned and made his way back to the house. The women had dispersed back inside their homes. The men hovered, talking to the engineer, who was taking down orders in a cashbook.

In business already, Daniel thought, smacking his lips. *We make the units and service them. We make the wood chip too. The clients will be forever coming to us. Daniel Frey, you are a genius! Vladimir can keep the accounts, the engineer and I will split the business fifty-fifty. I'll handle sales.*

He got out and handed Vladimir the keys with great pomp. "For you, *mon vieux*."

However, Vladimir seemed a little distracted. "Daniel. There's a letter in the hall for you."

The engineer turned to him excitedly and showed him the seven orders he'd already taken, plus two question marks by two other names.

"*Un moment*," Daniel said, marching into the house. He stared at the envelope, at the loopy, rushed script. Why had Vladimir looked at him like that? He tore open the letter.

Daniel, Chéri

I can't take this life as a refugee anymore. With the money father sent us and since the network is working again, I have bought a ticket back to Paris for the children and your mother. Please don't be angry with me! Wouldn't you prefer your children to be properly looked after, with a proper roof over their head? In Paris, there will be work, you'll see. You are resourceful.

I'm rushing around trying to sort out an ausweis with your mother to go back into the occupied territory. Please write to the rue de Grenelle to tell us when you'll be coming back.

P.S. Send my love to Vladimir.

Daniel slumped down at the kitchen chair. Life as a refugee. He had left her to fend for herself for months, winter was around the corner. No doubt it would be getting colder in the Cher, unlike here. He drew in a deep breath. He couldn't be angry with her, for hadn't she had her fill of wanting and scraping over the years? And there were the children to think of.

He threw the letter aside. He wasn't angry with her, he told himself, just life. And Alexandre. Always meddling.

That week, Daniel, having been urged by Vladimir, sold the car with the ready-installed gasification unit at a premium and split the proceeds two ways.

"It's the least I can do," said Vladimir, smiling in front of Gisèle, who had walked into the room. He seemed relieved – as if a great weight had been lifted.

Daniel paid the engineer for his work, and he in turn gave him a cut of the business he had just brought in.

"Don't worry, Dan. I'll be paying Vladimir to do my accounts. And once he's good and strong, he can help me with sales, though Madame Ferali has already shown promise in that department!"

Relieved that he wasn't leaving Vladimir and his fiancée in the lurch, Daniel purchased a one-way ticket to Paris. But first he too needed to go to the *Mairie* to get an *ausweis*. Vladimir and Gisèle, feeling a little stronger, had fixed a date to get married there. Sadly, it would be after he'd left, for now there was no time to lose.

The morning of his departure, he sat at the table with Mme Ferali, Vladimir, and Gisèle.

"Laurent is to be our other witness," said Vladimir, laughing.

Daniel remembered his own wedding, four years previously. Tatiana had had to make do with a witness his employer, Paul Fort, had provided – an old country woman who had simply stared at Tatiana's swollen stomach with consternation. It was only after Paul had flattered her, charmed her, that the woman had felt happy to confirm that Tatiana had been born in Vladicaucase in 1911. How mortified Tatiana had been, and how terrified of her father at the ceremony. But then what a ceremony, in a traditional Russian church, all lit up with candles, his beautiful Tatiana pregnant with Jeanne. He shouldn't have left his wife to fend for herself in the Cher. But the trains had been completely disrupted since the war, he reminded himself. *And besides, I've been able to help her beloved brother.* He now ached to see her; Occupied Zone or Free Zone, he needed to be with her.

He got up to go and pulled a few notes from his wallet. "Madame Ferali, a little towards my keep."

"Thank you, Daniel," she said, placing the notes in a tin in the kitchen. "And here is some *Jambon de Bayonne* to keep that little family going. I've heard the food queues are…" She stopped mid-sentence, perhaps because she had seen him frown.

CHAPTER TEN

The train banged and shunted along the rails as they neared the outskirts of Moulins, the town which Daniel now associated with both retreat and defeat. The German advance had stopped there in June – the day he and Hervé had frantically filled up with petrol on the River Allier. Once a prosperous provincial garrison town, it now marked the frontier into the German-controlled Occupied Zone.

The compartment suddenly went quiet as they experienced their last minutes of freedom. All returning French soldiers, they reached into the racks for their knapsacks and jackets, pulled out their identification cards and passes.

Daniel's neighbour, an ex-brigadier who had spoken about his exploits fighting the Germans in late June, causing a few of them to shuffle irritably in their seats, pummelled his rucksack nervously.

Daniel pulled his own papers from his knapsack and rifled through his wallet, which still contained some old visiting cards. He set aside the Belgian and Dutch addresses – he wouldn't be needing them – and left Vilmoray's card in the middle fold. 'Madelios' it read, 'Gentlemen's outfitters, Paris Ninth district.' Behind it, Paul Fort's Paris calling card for his apartment in the fourteenth arrondissement. Daniel imagined he would remain holed up at his country house in Montlhéry for the remainder of the occupation. *Nazis – not overly fond of poets and artists.*

A card had slipped down. He eased it out. 'Albert Klug Enterprises – rue des Rosiers, Marais.' Together with the Belgian and Dutch contacts, he ripped up the cards and scattered them out the window, over the River Allier.

The others looked up at him with interest.

"Anything else?" Daniel said, as nonchalantly as possible.

They all shook their heads.

"In which case, I'll shut the window."

The train slowed and finally ground to a halt. Outside, a strident voice sounded over the tannoy, announcing their arrival into Moulins. Daniel peered out and saw a guard with a gun slung over his shoulder stand in profile behind a glass sentry box. Daniel looked away and clutched his papers.

The door was thrown open, causing all of them to sit up in their seats. A tall German soldier in immaculate uniform and shiny boots stooped into the compartment.

"*Ausweiß bitte. Vos papiers,* Messieurs."

The German-accented French had been unnecessary for Daniel, who understood German perfectly. He probably would have been a very adequate speaker if his grandmother hadn't banned all things German from the house at the end of the Great War. Schubert's Lieder, sheet music, and records had all been thrust to the back of a cupboard and his father no longer recited Goethe's poetry. What a difficult time that had been. Goethe had re-emerged later – when Daniel had worked for Paul Fort – this time in translation. Yes, he could see what his father had meant about him – a master. And yet up until a few months ago, Daniel had barely appreciated the importance of his father's education. His few words of German, uttered to the guard in the Ardennes, had not only saved his skin, but the skins of ninety-nine others.

Withholding his usual smile of greeting, Daniel presented his papers. He had an address in Paris, a wife to go to, children. His papers were in order, he had nothing to fear, and yet his heart hadn't ceased pounding since he'd disposed of Albert's card. The soldier peered hard at the bulk in his rucksack. He had wrapped Mme Ferali's Bayonne ham in a blanket. He was now resigned to handing it over, but suddenly the border guard was looking over to his neighbour, who was still fumbling, this time through his pockets and then his rucksack again.

The border guard handed back Daniel's papers and narrowed his eyes.

Conscious of being watched, the Brigadier was muttering to himself, careful to hide the panic no doubt rising within him. He looked up at the guard and smiled nervously.

"*Un moment,* Monsieur."

The soldier's features darkened. "*Allez schnell, schnell!*" he said, holding onto his holster.

Daniel felt the Brigadier's muscly shoulder stiffen next to him. His face had gone a deathly colour. "I can't understand it..."

The German border guard frowned. "*Keine Papiere?*"

The Brigadier looked bewildered and didn't move.

"*Verlassen Sie den Zug!*"

Daniel understood that the man was being told to leave the train, but didn't dare intervene.

The guard grabbed the Brigadier's elbow. "*Venez,*" he said, indicating the door and pointing to a small queue of men on the platform, waiting to be interrogated. "*Darüber, là-bas.*"

The Brigadier took his limp rucksack and, grim-faced, got down from the train without looking back.

An agonising ten minutes ensued, as papers and bags were checked. No more arrests were made. The relief was palpable as the soldier left the compartment.

Daniel tried to justify his inability to intervene. Of course, it would have been pointless to get himself into trouble. He had a family to support. And there were his parents, Tatiana's parents. He needed to keep his head down, seek work, just concentrate on Tatiana and their wellbeing. The rest, well he could only wait and see.

CHAPTER ELEVEN

Daniel reached Paris at dusk and forged his way through the swirling crowd at the Gare d'Austerlitz. Plunging down the metro steps, he saw a woman struggling with her case.

"Madame. Let me."

"Bless you, Monsieur. Marguerite!" she shouted, turning to a girl in pigtails clutching the ramp behind her. The little boy holding her hand had started to cry.

"He's dropped his *nounours*, Mama."

And suddenly, the boy was gone.

"Gabriel!" the mother screamed over the heads of the crowd. "My son, his bear! He cannot live without it!"

Standing at the bottom of the stair with his case, Daniel watched two young German soldiers dash down and carve their way through a river of people. Mercifully, the boy was recovered and had not been crushed.

"*Merci* Messieurs," the mother said, blushing.

The soldiers inclined their heads and went back up into the station.

"*Ils sont aimables*!" Daniel overheard one woman say, as she descended the stair towards him.

"*Oui, si ça reste comme ça, cette occupation ne sera pas si mal!*" said an older woman, being supported by her daughter.

Decent boys, yes, but who wouldn't do as they had done? Daniel thought. He would tell Tatiana to avoid such situations.

At the Tour Maubourg, Daniel walked briskly along the platform and mounted the steps into Paris's fifteenth arrondissement.

Inhaling the damp, autumnal air, he entered an empty street dimly lit in blue, the new black-out lighting. He continued on, conscious of the noise his worn leather boots were making on the cobbles. He looked nervously over his shoulder, convinced he was being followed, but there was no one.

As he stopped in front of the *boucherie*, with its empty hooks in the window, he felt his knapsack. The ham was still there. Night was falling fast. He looked up at the low-rise apartment buildings, all with their shutters closed. *Curfews. If only Tatiana had held on…*

He paced quickly past the Protestant church, wondering when he would see his mother. It couldn't have been easy, leaving his father in Paris to look after Tatiana. His heart swelled with gratitude, and by the time he had reached the unprepossessing wooden door between the *épicerie* and a café, he could barely breathe with longing for his family.

The familiar smell of leek soup wafted through a narrow passageway. He ran up the rickety wooden stairs to the first floor Ivanov apartment and stood outside the door, straining his ear. Faint murmurs were just audible in the kitchen, low adult voices. He checked his watch. Eight o'clock. Tatiana was reading to Jeanne and Béa, who were no doubt over-excited after the journey. He rapped on the door.

"Who is it?" shouted a gruff voice, with a hint of trepidation. Alexandre Ivanov had spoken.

"*C'est moi*," Daniel replied, self-consciously.

Shuffling slippers came to the door. Locks were released. The door inched open.

"Come in, Daniel." His father-in-law's hair had greyed around the temples.

And he never wore those spectacles before, thought Daniel. *Too vain*. Alexandre's eyelids had reddened and his forehead seemed creased with worry. All that puffing of the chest, the posturing, was not in evidence here. Feeling pity for the man who had endured such a change in fortunes, Daniel decided to give him a warm handshake.

Alexandre wearily led him into the galley kitchen. "Tatiana's not here."

"Oh," said Daniel, feeling the energy drain out of him.

Alexandre touched his forehead and winced. "I went to the

station this afternoon. There's a problem with the Vierzon line. They talked about a delay of forty-eight hours."

Mrs Ivanov came rushing in, carrying teas on a tray. She put it down and took Daniel's hand. Her hands were strong and warm, unlike Tatiana's, which were always so cold.

"Daniel, come in and sit down. Alexandre, take his jacket and his luggage."

"No it's alright, Monsieur Ivanov, I'll do it," Daniel interjected, not wishing to aggravate his father-in-law.

"Something to drink perhaps?" Alexandre said, opening a drinks cupboard. "We have vodka, thanks to Sergei at the kitchens of the Shéhérazade."

Mr Ivanov was pouring out his beloved Stolichnaya into two small glasses. Perhaps his father-in-law was warming to him at last, or wanted an excuse to have a glass himself. Elisabeta put a glass of steaming tea before her husband.

"Remember what the doctor said!"

Alexandre frowned and let the glass of neat vodka land loudly on the kitchen table in front of him. Daniel gulped it without pleasure.

"May I also join you with some tea, Elisabeta?"

"Has our daughter finally converted you, Dan?"

She and Daniel burst into spontaneous laughter. He wasn't sure – he wasn't sure why he suddenly wanted a strong, sweet black Russian tea. He pictured Tatiana at the brass samovar in the little sitting room behind them, filling his glass, her red lips curling in merriment.

"Sugar, Dan?"

He nodded.

"Saccharine I'm afraid. But you must be used to that." She smiled, sadly. "If we had our catering business still, we might have been able to... but Vladimir must have told you that we had to wind it up recently?"

"Yes," Daniel said, shuffling in his uncomfortable kitchen chair. He'd been so wrapped up with the gasification unit he had quite forgotten.

He saw Alexandre pass his wife a steely look as if to say: *Why did you have to mention that?*

Alexandre Ivanov, former oil baron. Everything he'd touched had turned to gold, once, Tatiana would say. Then the spell had been broken in 1919. By the time he had reached Paris, his luck had run out, along with most of his money. And to make things worse, his beloved daughter had married Daniel, a Frenchman, a common *moujik* – he'd never said as much to Daniel, but Daniel felt it, even in the way Mr Ivanov was now eyeing his hiking trousers. No doubt this time he thought better than to criticize his son-in-law, a returning soldier.

"So, Daniel. You are alright?"

"Yes, under the circumstances…"

"When Tatiana returns," Mr Ivanov said, turning to his wife, "we're moving out to a little hotel in the street. The owner has a Russian wife. We've managed to negotiate a reasonable price."

Daniel wondered how much was left of their savings. He remembered Tatiana mentioning a pay-off her father had received, money owing from his defunct partner in the oil business.

"We are very grateful, Mister Ivanov. Just until I find work…"

Alexandre dismissed Daniel's anxiety. "It was very good of your mother to take care of our Tatiana in the Cher. I know it was a difficult time." He cleared his throat, perhaps a criticism of his own handling of their separation or his mother's inability to comfort Tatiana in the Cher. "Of course," his father-in-law said, puffing up his diminished chest, "we have savings. However, if… But it would be sensible to take our main meals here… that is if you…"

"Of course," Daniel said, now resigned to the fact that he would not have Tatiana to himself. "It makes sense to pool our rations." He sipped his strong, sweet tea, thoughtfully.

"Daniel, you look tired. I'll make a bed for you in the sitting room," said Mme Ivanov, getting up.

He nodded. All the weight of the last few months seemed to bear down on him.

"A little more vodka, Daniel?"

"*Merci non.*"

"No?" Alexandre said, a fierce look on his face.

Perhaps Alexandre was missing his son, or was he offended that his French son-in-law had declined the honour? A little bit of both, no doubt. Daniel didn't mind the drink, but a good Alsatian beer was what he dreamt of, strong and refreshing after the long journey. To make amends, he dug his hand into his rucksack.

"Before I forget." He produced the Bayonne ham. "From Gisèle's mother, Madame Ferali, who you will no doubt meet one day."

"Oh, how generous of her! And what of Gisèle? Do you like her?" said Mme Ivanov, excitedly.

"Almost as beautiful as Tatiana."

"Ah, but we are biased, Daniel. Tell me, is Vladimir as happy as he sounds?" Elisabeta chirped.

"More so," said Daniel, relieved to finally settle on good news.

Alexandre Ivanov hurrumphed. "So they're getting married, Vladimir tells me."

"Yes. Today in fact. At the *Mairie* in Jurançon."

Alexandre twisted his lips in displeasure and downed his vodka in one.

CHAPTER TWELVE

Daniel rose early to visit his parents in the Pré St Gervais, a remote neighbourhood in the north-eastern corner of Paris.

In the packed métro car, he closed his eyes, eager to blot out the misery on his fellow commuters' faces.

At Concorde, he was jolted awake by the appearance of a group of German officers inside the compartment. In elegant light raincoats, they clustered self-consciously by the door, hugging their purchases and speaking in low, guttural tones. Perhaps the first-class carriage set aside for them was full, or perhaps they had been unable to reach its door in time. Whatever the reason, Daniel felt a mountain of resentment as he ran his eyes over the boxed shirts, silk scarves and lingerie. All acquired so easily, without a second thought for the price, for one deutschmark was presently worth twenty francs. Twenty francs! Daniel closed his eyes again and was relieved when the grinding cars drowned out their conversation for the rest of the ride.

At l'Opéra, everyone spilled out onto the platform. The German officers forged ahead of the grim-faced Parisians. Outside the station, Daniel ran into a group of ordinary German soldiers on leave clutching their guide books. He imagined their itinerary: Fouquets, les Deux Magots and the Tomb of the Unknown Soldier at L'Arc de Triomphe. He had already decided to avoid them.

He started to walk along a busy boulevard where a line of taxis rumbled in, powered by gasification tanks. A blonde woman in a dark grey uniform stepped out of one of them, followed by a tall middle-aged civil servant with steel-rimmed glasses and attaché case. As they were paying the driver, a General with a bluish, fleshy scar running down his cheek got into their taxi.

"L'Hôtel Meurice, *s'il vous plait*," he uttered, in a sophisticated, soft-sounding French.

Other lower ranks boarded bicycle taxis, barked out destinations as if addressing their troops in a yard.

Daniel turned away and walked on, declining to peer into the department store windows. Soon he'd be out of the city centre, and good riddance to it. He thought of the Jurançon hills he had left, of the plump, sweet grape ready to be harvested. Of the gasification business he'd left behind. He didn't blame Tatiana, he told himself once more.

Soon, he was walking uphill, into the rougher parts of *Belleville*, only to leave the bustling quarter for the outer *faubourgs*, lined with plane trees. The thrum of traffic, the urgent ringing of bicycle bells was starting to fade. Slowing his pace, he listened to a blackbird sing. Its mellow call brought memories of the meadows behind the apartment building he was approaching. As a boy, he'd lain in its grasses, watching the silky clouds float by. Smiling wistfully, he recalled the goat herder passing with his golden-eyed creatures, playing a tune on his pipes. He would stop to sell his milk at his parents' apartment building. He wasn't the only tradesman, a whole host of vendors came: a woman who sold watercress from a little cart, arms glistening with water from the stream, an old man with leathery skin and glittering eyes who sold scissors, razors, saws, who came back to sharpen your knives and instinctively knew when his mother's needed sharpening.

"Daniel!" The window on the first floor of the apartment building opened. "Come up, *mon Chéri*," said a sweet voice carried by the breeze.

How long had she been there waiting for him? He went up the central staircase with a knot forming in his stomach. Why did he always feel like this before seeing her? There she stood now, at the threshold of the shadowy apartment, a dusty apron tied over her sober dress, strands of greying hair hanging loose from her chestnut bun, her long, thin face flushed and happy. She was taller than Tatiana, her facial features more angular, and she was big-boned like her Alsatian ancestors.

He leaned over and kissed her on both cheeks. She still smelt of lavender water and Vichy mints, her only sweet indulgence. She pushed him away gently.

"Let me take a good look at you. I thought of you every day in the Cher. You must have missed Tatiana terribly…" She turned to the study, where Daniel's father was getting up shakily from a desk cluttered with papers and book ledgers.

"Daniel," he said, breathlessly. "Just coming."

"André, take your time, *Chéri*."

Daniel watched his father approach him, a little hunched and even more pigeon-chested than he remembered. It still hurt Daniel to see him like this. Once a successful businessman and a fluent German-and-English-speaker, he was reduced to filing accounts and book-keeping.

"Son," he said, patting his arm. "Go through with your mother. Nearly finished."

As Daniel sat down with his mother, she sighed. "I've come back and our home is in turmoil. Your father insisted on staying in Paris and helping out the Friedmans, not that he could've fled in a hurry. Tatiana and I were down in Montlhery at your grandmother's house sorting out her papers when the war broke. Thank goodness she'd brought the children too. By sheer luck we were able to get a lift out of town with two French officers. *Dieu merci*, it was all over quickly, and our families are safe."

She dropped her voice and went over to the stove. "I don't think you've ever met the Friedmans. Your father and he were friends at school. Well, before I knew him, he went over to Manchester to work for their import-export company. The family have had to leave Paris. We're hoping they've reached the Free Zone by now. With the Sonnenthals." She peered at him anxiously. "What about the Klugs, Albert and his son Philippe? Had Vladimir heard from them?"

"No news." Daniel frowned. "They have our Grenelle address if they want to get in contact. But I suppose they too have left the occupied territory."

"Not everyone was able to, Dan. When we were in the Cher, the village was full of Jewish refugees." Her hazel eyes suddenly darkened. "Anyway, let's talk of you."

"Oh – there's not much to say. I was lucky."

She took his hand and squeezed it fervently. "And you've been reunited with your little family…"

He pulled his hand away. "Tatiana hasn't returned. Delayed

forty-eight hours."

"Oh!" she said, now visibly perturbed. "I should have waited with her!"

"No mother. Tatiana can take care of herself. Besides, Papa…"

"It wasn't easy, Daniel. Your father needed me. Tatiana didn't know whether to return to Paris or join you. It was her father in the end who advised her to move back…"

"He did?"

"Don't blame him, Dan."

Daniel frowned.

"The money. It wasn't enough to stay any longer… You can't imagine the squalor of the place. The scramble for food. It just wasn't possible anymore."

CHAPTER THIRTEEN

"Daniel!" Clean-shaven and smiling, in an immaculately pressed, double-breasted suit, Vilmoray's prosperous appearance seemed at odds with the empty window behind him, where two nude male mannequins were treading space. "Good to see you," he continued, rubbing his manicured hands. "Afraid there's no heating. Follow me up to the office – I have an oil heater there."

They mounted the green and gold-carpeted stairs, strewn with clothing labels.

"What's happened here?" Daniel asked, keeping up with Vilmoray's regimental pace. The department store felt bitterly cold, out of the sunlight and emptied of goods.

"The *boches* have cleaned me out. Dandying up for those victory parties. I'm finding it hard to replenish my stock, what with textiles being diverted to German uniforms. I'll soon be handing over silk shirts and scarves for parachutes." By now he was on the landing and disappearing behind a door.

As Daniel entered Vilmoray's office, his colleague was already leaning against his desk and lighting his cigarette with a beautiful gold lighter. He snapped it shut, held out a silver case engraved with his initials.

Daniel declined. It was an expensive habit he could do without. "So, what do you plan to do?" he asked, running his eyes over Vilmoray's desk.

A heavy onyx ashtray half-filled with cigarette butts, several leather ledgers put to one side. Vilmoray had left out a note from someone, hurriedly-written, judging by the faint, jagged script.

Daniel leaned over discreetly as Vilmoray opened a drawer in his desk. *'Pense à toi mon amour. Elsa'*.

"Ah, here it is." Vilmoray had fished out a key. He strode over to a curved walnut armoire the other side of the room. "I'm not sure what to do," he said, peering into the armoire's smooth interior. "I'd like to stay in Paris. This town is full of officers with deep wallets. Make hay while the sun shines, I tell myself. Then perhaps move out of the capital. I have a sister in Bourgogne." He let out a short laugh, clearly not enthused.

Daniel was poised to encourage the idea, for wasn't life easier in the provinces, more food, fewer *fritz*? But already, Vilmoray was getting down to the business of procuring him a suit. He ran his slim fingers along a row of neatly pressed trousers.

"How was Jurançon by the way?"

"Good," Daniel said, biting his tongue. The temptation to talk about his gasification system and the burgeoning business he'd left behind was too great.

"I've been told the Free Zone is not the Eldorado one would like it to be! Pau is full of refugees: Spanish, Jewish and the rest." Vilmoray's hand stopped on a hanger, as Daniel wondered whether the woman who'd written to him had anything to do with his information.

"Really?" he said. "Suppose some are trying to cross into Spain." In truth he hadn't seen anything of Pau other than the train station. "France is full of displaced people," he continued. "Tatiana is still marooned in the Cher."

"*Vraiment!* I'm sorry to hear it!" Vilmoray said, turning to him.

"They're back tomorrow, thankfully…"

"And you'll be looking for a job I imagine?"

"Yes, it's quite urgent now."

"Good." He shot his hand up. "I mean good that you'll be seeing her. All this separation is no good for a family."

Vilmoray's expression was sympathetic. He had made no attempt to hide the letter on his desk, and yet Daniel didn't want to pry. He felt Vilmoray's seniority, his superior rank, even in civilian life.

And now Vilmoray was sizing him up. "We're virtually the same height, one metre eighty-eight, I would guess."

"Correct." Daniel smiled. They were tall for Frenchmen, long-limbed, fair-haired, lean. At least two kilos lighter since the start of the war.

"Here we are!" Vilmoray rolled a pair of high-waisted wool trousers off their hanger. "These should do for most occasions. Your wife could always make some adjustments if need be."

Tatiana was handy with a needle and could work a sewing machine. She had made all the soft furnishings with her mother at the Rue de Grenelle. Their main bedroom, with its deep red and midnight blue velvet and silk covers had taken on the appearance of a harem. It had taken him a while to feel comfortable reclining on a mass of cushions like some tyrannical *pacha,* which had been highly amusing for Tatiana. The thought of her lying next to him on the bed, laughing, made his blood quicken.

"Daniel?" Vilmoray was now handing him a brown jacket with padded shoulders to go with the trousers he'd forgotten he was holding.

"Are you sure?"

"Of course I'm sure! A versatile jacket." He turned to the shelves running along the sides of the wardrobe, took a white shirt out of a pile. It was still folded and pinned.

"But it's new…"

"Take it."

He opened a drawer filled with rows of folded tartan socks and fished out two pairs, still sewn together.

"There," he said. "Oh, I almost forgot." He opened the armoire again and drew out a hanger, from which hung an assortment of silk ties. He handed him a beige one. "This will go with everything. One of our best-selling ties before the war. Shoes, I'm afraid they've all gone."

"Look, I can't thank you enough."

"As you see, it wasn't difficult. Lunch?"

Daniel jingled the remaining change in his pocket. Enough for a metro ticket. He hadn't factored in lunch.

"On me," Vilmoray said, reading his mind. "The *patron* owes me a favour. And the bistro's serving wine today."

He felt himself weep inwardly with relief as he inhaled the warm rosemary aroma escaping from the kitchen. That morning, the queue for the *boulanger* had stretched right down the rue de Grenelle, down to the Protestant church. He had had to forego breakfast.

They passed a diner hunched over his food, spiking his rabbit and tearing at the flesh. The meal would be devoured with a few stabs of the fork, and with no bread or butter to soak up the gravy the poor man would be left yearning for more. Grown men couldn't survive on such a diet. And what about Tatiana and their daughters, who had been left hungry in the Cher? He now knew from his mother how hard it had been to feed themselves in a village overrun with refugees. He needed a proper job – and fast.

The owner led them to a table in a little alcove next to the kitchen.

Vilmoray sat down and dug his hand into his pocket. Out came a little cufflink box.

The proprietor nodded and smiled.

"Do your best today, will you?"

Daniel blushed. His Protestant upbringing rebelled against this sort of thing.

Vilmoray lit a cigarette and smiled at him. The proprietor served them a full-bodied, Burgundy wine, greatly superior to the table wine on offer.

"*Santé*, Daniel!"

They raised their glasses. Daniel let the heavenly libation slip down his throat. The dimly-lit bistro was bathed in a warm glow. He relaxed in his chair and for a while said nothing.

"Good, isn't it?" Vilmoray said, refilling Daniel's glass. "So, this business of work…"

"Well my career to date has been interesting and illogical, as you know. One minute a secretary to a poet, a spell in publishing, then a travelling salesman. Well-trained, mind you. I can sell books and patented machine tools!" He swilled his wine.

Vilmoray laughed. "I know!" He flicked his ash pensively. "I saw what you were capable of in the Ardennes. We'd all be languishing in a prisoner of war camp if it hadn't been for you."

"Thank you, sir."

"Georges, please."

"Georges." But Vilmoray was engraved in his memory.

"Well," Vilmoray said, inhaling, "your visit has not been in vain. Not only have we been able to share lunch, but something happened today."

"Oh?"

"An old friend, Cochet, came to see me. I told him of our great escape and we had a good laugh about that German guard letting us all through. I talked about you and your mad plan. Anyway, he's been taken on by Vichy's new National Education Department, now amalgamated into the Ministry for Youth. They're setting up these new youth centres for adolescent boys from broken homes. Youths who, left to their own devices, might get into trouble on the streets. Some are from the juvenile courts. They're looking for men, ex-army, to run these centres. I have his calling card if you're interested. But let's eat first."

Several hours later, Daniel was waiting at the Gare d'Austerlitz, his head buzzing with excitement. So many things to tell Tatiana. Troubled youths? He had been one himself. He had just time to call Cochet. Tatiana's train was due in ten minutes.

He ran into a cafe. After going through several intermediaries, he was finally put through to the man.

"Monsieur Cochet? Daniel Frey here."

"Ah, *bonjour* Daniel! Vilmoray's just called. Yes, good to hear from you. Your timing is impeccable. Can you come and see me tomorrow?"

"Yes, sir!" Being a soldier, Daniel delighted in decisiveness, and this man's informality was music to his ears. He had always hated snobbery. Vilmoray must have really sung his praises.

"You'll be coming to the former air force building, Boulevard Victor, in the fifteenth district. Come at fourteen-hundred hours."

"Yes, sir. Thank you, sir. I'll be there." Daniel put the receiver down and dashed over to the platform where Tatiana's train had just pulled in.

The area was thick with dishevelled-looking travellers spilling from the train with their children, older relatives, cases, boxes, parcels. Cries of joy spread through the crowd, interspersed with, "Attention Monsieur – you're treading on my boy's foot!" Or, "Madame, will you please not stand there!"

German guards looked on impassively, for there was nothing to be done with such an unruly mob. Meanwhile, every pretty, dark-haired woman with her back to Daniel caused his heart to leap, until they turned to face him. A spirited child with brown curly hair jumped off the train, but it wasn't Jeanne. He listened out for Béa's cry, but different wails rose above the swarming mass of coats and hats careering towards the exit.

Having pushed half-way up the platform, Daniel stood to one side and mounted a luggage cart. Right at the end of the train he spied an anxious dark-haired woman atop the carriage steps holding a nine-month-old baby in one arm, restraining a curly-headed girl with bony knees with the other. Her pale face, fixed on the crowd, was so forlorn that Daniel was relieved to see a man offer to help her with her heavy case.

"Tatiana!" he cried. Daniel started to wave frantically and call her name – how good it felt to do so! *Look this way, chérie. Jeanne, look this way.* He had jumped down and started to weave his way through the thinning crowd, but still, her bewildered expression showed that she was oblivious to his cries, as already she and Jeanne started to search for a luggage cart. "Tatiana!" he shouted. "Jeanne!"

His daughter seemed puzzled as she stared in his direction. Then he saw her dark eyes light up. She was pointing. "Look, it's Papa!"

Jeanne broke away immediately and bolted in his direction. Her little body landed with a thud against his chest as he crouched to receive her.

"Mind, my little chicken," he said, scooping her up and kissing her burning cheek.

"Oh Papa! Papa!" She nestled in his neck. Her little heart was beating so fast. Her curly hair dripped with perspiration. How crammed the train compartment must have been.

"Dan!"

He slowly unclamped Jeanne's arms and said, softly, "Just let me say hello to Maman."

Jeanne nodded reluctantly and let her mother break into their tight circle. Daniel pulled her towards him and felt her warm lips brush his collar-bone. Baby Béa, meanwhile, chomped on her dummy and started to play with her mother's hair. Daniel closed his eyes and felt all their hearts beat in time with one another.

Tatiana pulled away, laughed and then started to cry. He wiped her warm, salty tears with his finger and felt himself choke in wordless emotion.

"Why are you crying, Mama, Papa?" Jeanne was peering up at them with consternation.

Tatiana laughed.

"It's alright, my little *poulette*," Daniel said, staring into her mournful eyes. "But you're not so little anymore, are you?"

"I'm four," she said, primly, "and Béa, she's nine months."

Daniel took Béa from Tatiana. She had grown longer and had wispy brown hair now. He leant over her pale cheeks, felt a pair of little hands come up under his chin. He leaned in further towards her but felt the little hands push him back. Shocked, he looked to Tatiana, smiling apologetically.

"She's not been used to having a male around." She cupped his cheek. "Don't worry, it won't last."

Daniel sighed and handed Béa back to her. He felt a tug at his trouser leg.

"Come on, Papa, let's go and see Baboushska and Dedouska."

Daniel picked up the case and saw Tatiana eyeing his bag of clothes with an approving eye.

"An army colleague. And I have an interview with the Ministry of Youth tomorrow, would you believe, through him."

"You see!" she said, teasingly. "I was right to bring us back to Paris. Only just arrived and you already have a job!"

Daniel laughed. "Not quite."

She was right, however, and besides, now that she was here, he didn't care where they were. Home was where Tatiana was.

He placed his hand in the curve of her spine. "I'm so happy, *chérie*. I can't quite believe you're here."

"Me too," she said, and in a low whisper, "I wasn't sure you'd be here."

Any residue of resentment now disappeared into the air of that central station.

CHAPTER FOURTEEN

Daniel slipped out of bed. Gently opening the shutters of his bedroom, he watched the sun pour onto the bed covers. From the street came the sound of shop grilles being opened and clinking spoons in the café.

He slipped back under the covers and turned to Tatiana, stirring beside him. Daniel smiled to himself. How soft, deep and warm the mattress felt under him and how good it felt to be in bed with his beautiful companion. He lifted the cover and moved closer behind her. She smelled of hair oil and soap, having lain in a hot tub the previous evening, her first bath in months. They had used the last of their coal to heat the water. She knew it was a luxury, but had wanted to 'wash away what she had lived through.' Daniel had asked her what she meant by that, but then Jeanne had rushed into the little kitchen, wishing to join her mother.

"No, you're too big now. You can wait your turn!" she had said, a little sharply.

Seeing that Jeanne was hurt, Daniel had taken her away to teach her draughts.

He placed his palm upon Tatiana's soft stomach. Her waist had always been tiny but her womanly hips had allowed her to bear him two children without complications. And now, they would have more. They had discussed having a boy, one as fine as François, Paul Fort's son.

He nuzzled her hair and closed his eyes. Slowly emerging from sleep, she arched her back and stretched her legs.

"Good morning, *chérie*," he whispered.

She turned over towards him and smiled sleepily.

His hand ran the length of her spine. She shivered and closed her eyes.

A baby's cry came from next door. Tensing, Tatiana broke away from him.

"Later," he said, calling after her. "Your parents promised to take the girls."

"It'll have to be after the *mairie*. We have the ration books to organize!"

"Mama, is Papa awake?" Before he knew it, there was the sound of running feet. Jeanne leapt up on the bed beside him. She snuggled under his armpit and patted his chest.

"Papa, what are we going to do today?" and, in the same breath, "I'm so hungry."

"Come along my little Jeanette," he said, planting a loud kiss on the top of her curls. "Let's get up and go see what Maman has for us."

She jumped off the bed into his arms. The lightness of her shocked him.

He would feed his children. He resolved to make a journey outside Paris once he had a job. The importance of the interview was growing, it would probably be his only chance of obtaining such a sound position.

As they walked through to the kitchen, Tatiana was shaking a bottle and squeezing its contents onto her hand. At least Béatrice still had her allocation of milk, and her need for solids was small.

"Can I feed her?" Jeanne said, having devoured a little bread onto which Tatiana had spread a teaspoon of jam.

Tatiana presented him with the bottle. "Papa will do it."

The milk felt warm in his grip. He walked to Béatrice's cot and peered in. Béatrice's light brown eyes looked up at him questioningly and then at the bottle. She searched either side of him, anxious. Determined not to falter, Daniel put the bottle down, reached in, and ever so carefully, picked her up and kissed the top of her soft head. She started to cry. Daniel quickly cradled her and lowered the teat into her open mouth. Her little hands reached for the neck of the bottle and she started to suck hungrily. Jeanne was soon at his side, asking him anxiously about the Eiffel Tower and the donkeys.

"Have they taken them away?"

His attention focused on Béa, Jeanne tugged at his arm, jolting the bottle.

"In a moment, my little Jeanette, we'll go look for the donkeys. But please let me finish with Béatrice."

Tatiana came through. "Shall I take over now?" She was smiling, as if to say, "There, you see."

At two o'clock, Daniel was facing Cochet across a desk at the newly-formed Vichy Department of Youth Education. They shook hands warmly and sat down.

"I'll be brief, Daniel," Cochet said, furrowing his thick eyebrows and tapping his thumbs on the desk. "Since the June debacle our young men have been running riot. Not surprising – two million Frenchmen in POW camps and one hundred thousand fallen. a large proportion of our boys are finding themselves without a parent."

Daniel nodded. On his way there he had walked past the German Kommandatur. A poster with a rugged-looking German soldier in full uniform had caught his eye. He was carrying a young boy happily munching a slice of country bread smothered in butter, while two young girls walked at his side. '*Populations abandonnées,*' the poster read, '*faites confiance au soldat allemand!*' ('Abandoned populations – trust your German soldier!'). It had probably been up there for some time.

"These boys are confused. We've got to do something and fast, before they get into further trouble with the Germans."

"Of course."

Cochet rested his large hands on the desk. 'Tell me, Daniel. How would you handle a group of unruly boys?"

Daniel sighed. "Well, it's no fun for a boy entering manhood at the best of times. In war, of course, where the boy sees the male world fall apart, there is confusion, as you say. Figures of authority become crucial."

"Yes, Daniel. Having worked in education, I have always been able to spot a troubled youth, their restlessness, their inability to make eye contact."

Daniel held Cochet's gaze; a former headmaster, Vilmoray had told him. Daniel had been thrown out of two establishments despite his love of literature, his knowledge of the sciences and natural history, most of which he'd gleaned away from the classroom, spending summers in a field with his encyclopaedia and sketchbooks. He felt the colour rise in his cheeks. It took all his willpower to master his feelings of inadequacy.

"There is everything to redo. Number one is to take the boys away from the city. Number two, physical education. Number three, diet – I imagine the stealing is the result of hunger."

"Absolutely – this is what we plan to do. But what makes you think that you could get through to one hundred disorientated youths, for these are the numbers you'll be dealing with if you were to run one of the Youth Training Centres we're setting up."

There was a silence whilst Daniel conjured one hundred surly, scrawny young men. They weren't going to be like Paul Fort's son, who had followed him around the poet's estate like a puppy. François's education had been eclectic to say the least. Daniel had taught him to mend fences, chop wood, shoot cans with a rifle, and the natural sciences, while Fort took care of his son's literary education, when he was sober.

No, these youths weren't poets' sons. He hesitated.

"Well, as I said earlier, taking them out of their environment is key. I remember myself, a rebellious youth, working on my Uncle Charles's farm during the Great War and, under his patient guidance, enjoying the new responsibilities of milking the cows, feeding the horses, bringing in the hay. I was eleven."

"These youths will be older. Between fourteen and eighteen years of age. Perhaps older."

"Oh," he said, a little deflated.

Cochet waved away his doubt. "No, you're right. All young men need responsibilities and to expend energy."

"And to build things and grow things, I imagine."

"Yes, they'll be learning new practical skills, carpentry, metalwork, learning about agriculture. Do you like country life?"

"Sir, I am happiest there."

"And besides, we're keen to get them away from the Germans." Cochet dropped his voice. "If you see what I mean."

Daniel was suddenly thrust back into the war. "And the Germans… what will they think of these centres?"

Cochet dropped his chin. "Officially these organisations are banned in the Occupied Zone. The Germans are naturally suspicious of them. Breeding grounds for underground resistance."

"I can see why they would think that," Daniel said, slowly.

"And so, with this in mind, our organization will be run under the aegis of a Scout Association. The Sully Committee will fund it."

"I see – apolitical and unthreatening."

"And to make things easier for ourselves, we have deliberately chosen remote locations. Deserted chateaux, away from anywhere. They will all need to be restored. The restoration work will be carried out by staff and the boys. It will be part of the cure – if you see what I mean."

There was a silence. A secretary knocked on the door.

"My next appointment, Daniel." He rose and offered his hand. "So, can I take it you'll be interested in signing up?"

Daniel shook Cochet's hand vigorously. "Yes sir, very."

"I can't promise anything. First of all, you'll have to go to Sillery sur Orge, to a *château* near Juvisy, for your training. However, I have no worries about your ability to communicate and inspire these young men. You're not an old fogey like myself. And aged thirty-one, you're young and fit enough to take on such a challenging project, which will have you working long hours. You'll need to use your initiative, too, as our resources are limited. However, if your performance in the Ardennes is anything to go by, I have every confidence in you." The Lieutenant patted him on the shoulder. "There," he continued, "if you're selected, you'll be nominated a certain grade: Centre Chief, Assistant Chief, Team Leader, and so on."

"I have a wife and children, Lieutenant."

"Yes, of course, they can join you once the centre is up and running. We like our leaders to have a stable family life. It sets a good example. This is an exciting project and I'd love to have you on board." He got up and shook Daniel's hand once more. "Bonne chance!" They saluted one another.

Daniel rushed home in a state of agitation; what would Tatiana think of moving to the country?

She was alone when he returned, in heels and a midnight blue silk dress with padded shoulders, which accentuated her slender form. A light had come into her sultry eyes.

"Well?"

"I have a job," he said, tentatively, and before he could rectify the statement she had leapt into his arms.

Her warm breasts pressed up against his chest. They were steps away from the bedroom. In an hour's time the parents would be back. There would be endless questions and days of logistical planning to make sure they could cope without him for a while.

She took his hand. "Come on," she whispered.

"Why are you whispering? There's no one…"

"I don't know," she said, letting out a short laugh. She seemed nervous but anxious to press on towards the room.

She closed the door behind them. The bed lay waiting for them, in shadow. Outside their shutters, the housewives were queuing and gossiping in the street. Tatiana shut the window and pulled back the silken coverlet.

CHAPTER FIFTEEN

Six weeks later, Daniel walked out of Sillery training school ranked Chief of Staff. Almost immediately, he boarded a train bound for Vendôme, two hundred kilometres south-west of Paris, in the sleepy Loir-et-Cher region.

On the train, feeling both exulted and apprehensive, Daniel peered out of the window and got lost in a landscape of forests, lakes, and medieval domains.

Lefèbvre, one of his deputies, sat opposite him, his face buried in a leather-bound volume of *Le Grand Meaulnes*. Having worked for a prestigious Paris school, Lefèbvre, a thirty-year-old teacher, embodied all the qualities Daniel admired: including intellectual rigour and an ability to play down his intelligence. Like so many of his countrymen, he had returned to Paris disillusioned after his country's humiliating defeat. Seeking a change from the classroom, which he viewed as unable to tackle the thorny youth problem, he had been persuaded by his brother, a Protestant pastor, to lend him a hand in the charity he ran for boys orphaned by the war. It was there that Cochet had spotted Lefèbvre, crouching in the street outside the church, speaking softly to a terrified boy hiding in the gutter. With his hands tightly cupped over his ears, he had been terrified by a demolition ball.

"It's only the works, *mon petit gars*," Lefèbvre had said, holding out his hand. The boy had finally got up and gone back into the church.

Lefèbvre looked up from the book.

"Do you think our lot would prefer *The Last of the Mohicans* or *Treasure Island?*"

"Probably. *Le Grand Meaulnes* may appeal to the older ones. The story is, after all, set near here…"

"True…"

"And I have to confess," Daniel said, "a personal interest in the book. Its author, Fournier, was my former employer's secretary. I took over his position."

Lefèbvre raised his dark eyebrows. "I didn't know you'd had a literary career."

Bitter-sweet emotions played with Daniel's heart. It all seemed so long ago. "For a while."

Lefèbvre clapped the book shut and eyed him carefully.

Daniel went back to the window. They were passing a ruined château. "It was before I was married. When I met Tatiana… Well, as you know, there's not a lot of money in poetry."

"It must have been fascinating though," Lefèbvre said, ignoring the rueful tone. "All that burning of the midnight oil and parties." He gave him his kind, almost apologetic smile, as if to say, *but what do I know?*

"Yes," Daniel replied, determined to say no more about it. What was the point in reminiscing?

"I envy you," Lefèbvre continued, carefully. "To have experienced all that – before the war."

Daniel understood without him having to explain. *It is all about survival now.*

Lefèbvre laid the book aside. "But looking on the bright side, what we're setting out to do here is good. No?"

"Of course," he said, feeling a tingle of renewed purpose; he had to admit that at first all he'd considered was a job that would put food on the table.

There was a cheer from the adjoining seats. "Full flush!"

"Aw! Bouillot, not again!" said a tall, slim, dark-haired young man, Cintract, one of the two youth group leaders Daniel had recruited, whose father had died in the final battle for Vitry-le-François. Daniel wondered whether he had met him that fateful morning, during his own retreat through the destroyed city.

Cintract had come to Sillery through the scouts, as had Labarre, who was smaller and stockier than his young friend. His father had survived the Battle for France but was languishing in a German Stalag.

"Calm down, Labarre." Bouillot waved a muscled, hairy arm in his direction. "Come over here and watch the master at work!"

Daniel got up and peered over the seat. Bouillot was shuffling the cards in his large hands, nails still blackened with car oil. Bouillot, his other 'number two.' *As rough as Lefèbvre is polished*, Daniel thought to himself. *But he'll probably be my most valuable member of staff as Chief Technician.* Hailing from Belleville, Bouillot had spent his time under cars and trucks, which he, like Daniel, liked to drive at break-neck speed.

"Aw, I can't believe it, Bouillot!" Cintract threw down his cards.

"Too bad, *mon gars*." His wide jaw cracked into a sympathetic grin. Labarre sat down beside Cintract and watched Bouillot scrape his matchstick winnings into a cigarette box.

The train began to slow.

Daniel reached for his things and went over to Bouillot. "Have you been over the map with Labarre and Cintract?"

"Yes boss, but that was yesterday. One more time eh, *les gars*! Labarre, make yourself useful and get the map!"

"Hurry, Labarre," echoed Daniel. "We're almost in Pezou. In fact, give it over to me."

Daniel spread the ordnance map over the table. "Once in Pezou, we'll be walking north-west, towards la Ville-aux-Clercs, our nearest village. We'll be turning right at this point, as we reach the forest edge. Our destination is an estate named Fort Girard. Any questions?"

"How many kilometres, sir?"

"Work it out, Cintract. See the scale of the grid."

Cintract leant over the map, his fine roman nose snagged near the bridge, like Daniel's, and a scar on his forehead from a piece of shrapnel. Cintract frowned in concentration as he quickly totted up the squares.

"About nine kilometres, sir."

"Good, so get your bags."

"Yes, sir," Cintract and Labarre said in unison, before grabbing their overstuffed rucksacks.

The train had started to slow. Daniel felt his stomach clench in readiness. Winter was setting in and, a month from now, one hundred boys (not all at once, he was relieved to hear from Cochet), would arrive from Paris.

The train juddered to a halt. Slinging their heavy rucksacks onto their backs, they alighted onto a deserted platform. Most remaining passengers were heading for Vendome, one stop further. He looked up at the cold November sky, then paced on with his team, out of the station.

With only the sound of boots pounding the country lane, they walked in silence until they reached a barren-looking field on the outskirts of the hamlet. Daniel pushed open the farm gate and walked out onto the rutted, frozen soil.

Daniel pointed out a wood on a hill towards which they were heading. As they left the hedgerows, a biting wind blew across the field. A party of crows took off from its centre, their raucous cries filling the chill air. Daniel turned back to Cintract and Labarre, surveying their new environment. Several rabbits lolloped up and down, surveying them in turn.

"My aunt has started breeding rabbits on her balcony," Labarre said.

"Stop it!" Cintract clutched his stomach. "All I can think of is my mother's *lapin à la moutarde!*"

Daniel increased the pace until they finally reached the edge of a dense wood. Daniel checked the map – officially, they had arrived in the domain of Fort Girard.

Labarre picked up a stick and swiped it through the brambles and overgrown grasses. "Look at that painted cross on the trunk!"

"Good work, *mons gars.*" The light was dimming, they would have to hurry. "The house is in the south-east corner of these woods. A few minutes or so to go," said Daniel, setting off to the right.

"Hope so," Cintract said, wincing. A blister no doubt. He was keeping quiet about it.

Good, Daniel thought. They were here to toughen up.

He led them down a woodland path through the silver birch trees, which now creaked each time the wind blew. *These woods feel centuries old.*

Ahead, their way was blocked by a wall of thorns. Bouillot took a pair of long secateurs from his rucksack and started to slice his way through. He stepped back and blocked Labarre from rushing to the front.

"Uh. Uh. Labarre, where's your manners, son? The boss goes first. Always in an 'urry you are."

"Sorry, sir," said Labarre, stepping back with an embarrassed smile to let Daniel by.

"*Merci!*" Daniel marched through breezily, quickening his pace.

Behind him, he heard Cintract curse. "Blinking nettles!" Nature in its raw state was disconcerting for them, an irrelevance when you lived your life in the streets of Clignancourt or Belleville.

But they will learn.

Daniel inhaled the pungent odour of wild mushrooms, earth, and decomposing detritus and was reminded of Paul Fort's house in Montlhéry. The months he had spent clearing the tangled woodland around Paul's estate to make space for the orchards Paul had prized. Between his fruit trees, kitchen garden plots, rabbits and chickens, Paul was set up to survive the occupation. Daniel intended to bring the same knowledge here.

He now wondered about the state of the house. The Paris office had been evasive. It was part of the challenge after all, for the boys and staff to rebuild not only a house but a community. 'Rebuild'; time and time again the verb had been mentioned in the Maréchal Pétain's speeches after the debacle and again at Sillery, where it had become a tenet to live by.

The woods were beginning to clear. Over the fringe of trees appeared a roof and tall brick chimneys.

"We're here," he said, excitedly marching up to the back of the house, which seemed to block out the sky.

They wound their way round to the front and, in the fading light, tried to make out the extensive lawn outlined with trees. One stood out, a giant sequoia in the middle of the expanse, a lonely sentinel keeping watch over the house.

Daniel turned to face the mansion. Ivy had spread over the colossal façade, set on three floors. A central balcony on the first floor had broken through it, but long trails cascaded down in great, ugly clumps.

Daniel smiled at his team. "It needs work, as you can see."

They climbed some steps and came out onto a large terrace. Daniel walked over to a shuttered door; it had been forced open. Behind it, a French window had been shattered. He walked through the frame and stepped into a hall. Bouillot directed his torch beam towards a light switch. Daniel flicked it; they remained in darkness.

"There must be a fuse box in the kitchen or the hall."

Bouillot walked on ahead, his beam casting light momentarily over a large wood-panelled hall and central staircase.

The rest of them followed Daniel through to a large reception room.

Lefèbvre ran his torch over a trail of glittering shards.

"We'll block the windows tomorrow, Lefèbvre," Daniel said, moving over to a grand fireplace.

Bouillot reappeared. "Not the fuses, boss. Could be the wiring, or cabling even."

"To be expected. Labarre, Cintract, go and get some logs and kindling. I've been told there's a log store at the side of the house." Daniel leant into the mouth of the chimney. "Large enough to roast an ox!" he intoned, wishing to maintain morale, but then realised he had planted an image of succulent roasting meat in all their heads. His stomach was crying out for food, as theirs would be. He turned to Lefèbvre. "Candles."

Lefèbvre melted several wax bases and stuck them to the marble mantelpiece. The flames flickered precariously in the cold air blowing in through the broken windows.

Daniel started to draw up a list of materials in his head. A glazier was urgently needed. He prayed the windows on the floors above were intact, for there were twenty or more on the front façade. With luck, it was only a case of a break-in at the front. However, the criminals had managed to take off with the carpet and furniture judging by the sparseness of the room. Cabling for the electrics a possibility.

The boys returned with logs and kindling and lit a fire. As the flames started to flicker and cast long shadows over them, they each got out a metal cup. Cintract went off in search of water. He was back in seconds with a defeated expression on his face.

"No water coming out of the taps!"

Daniel shook his head. That, he wasn't expecting.

Bouillot and Lefèbvre offered the young group leaders a little wine with their black bread and *saucisson*. They stretched out over the cold parquet floor, draped themselves in coats and blankets, and stared into the chimney.

As his team drifted off to sleep, Daniel cast his blanket aside and crept out onto the terrace. The moon was out as he leaned up against the stone balustrade and, buttoning his greatcoat, he watched the night sky slowly fill with stars.

CHAPTER SIXTEEN

The very next day, with the frost still on the ground, Daniel set off early to the Ville aux Clercs, leaving his team to tackle digging a well in the garden, once the sun had warmed the frozen earth.

A brisk fifteen-minute walk through the woods brought him to a road signposting the village. On the church square, he made for the café, with its fogged windows. Daniel stepped in. A group of men leant over a stove. In the middle of them an affable, balding fellow was holding court.

"One thousand German bombers Hitler sent to London last month."

"Just as long as the British don't start dropping their bombs over the *fritz* here," said a man throwing some change onto a table.

The café owner slipped the money into his apron pocket and came over to Daniel at the zinc counter.

"Monsieur, *bonjour*! What can I get you?" He gave Daniel's place a cursory wipe. "*Café*?"

Daniel nodded.

"You are new here, *n'est-ce pas*?"

"Yes. Moved into Fort Girard last night."

"That old mansion!" The man laughed and went off to get his coffee. When he returned, Daniel continued,

"We'll be housing a hundred lads up there." Seeing a flicker of wariness in the man's eyes, Daniel tempered the statement. "Their fathers are in German prison camps or have died fighting."

They both glanced down at a newspaper lying on the zinc

counter. The Maréchal Pétain's winter appeal for French prisoners dominated the front page.

"Of course, of course," said the owner. He crossed his arms and frowned. "My boy doesn't know how lucky he is. I don't know whether it's the war or his age!"

"Maybe a bit of both," Daniel said, sympathetically. "When we're up and running, bring him up to Fort Girard. He might want to take a look at the carpentry and metal workshops we'll be building."

"A fine offer, Monsieur."

"In the meantime... You wouldn't know anyone with any transport? I could do with a lift to Vendôme. I need to go to the *prefecture* with my begging bowl."

"I am having to go there myself for supplies." The man turned to address a thin woman in an apron. "Jeanette. You're ready to take over?" She nodded and adjusted a loose pin in her hair. He turned back to Daniel. "I'll get the horse harnessed."

"Thank you, Monsieur," Daniel said, finishing his coffee and relishing the thought of a cart ride. "You'll be helping a good cause."

Daniel made his way to a tiny water closet at the back of the café. Leaning over a grim-looking basin and finding no soap, he thrust his handkerchief under the tap and gave his skin a rudimentary rub. At least he'd shaved the day before. Just a little blond down, nothing too sinister. The Prefect – or was he the Sub-Prefect, he would have to check – would understand.

He stepped out into the courtyard where the café owner pulled up several moments later in a farm cart. Just five years before, Daniel had picked up Tatiana in a similar cart, only theirs had been painted brown with yellow roses. How the poor donkey had staggered up the hill to Paul Fort's woody domain. Tatiana had left her beloved Paris to be with him. He recalled Tatiana's paleness and how she had clung to him against the biting wind on that hill. It had been the start of their lives together.

Loud trotting and the horse's neigh brought him out of his reverie. They were on a straight, flat country road on the outskirts of Vendôme. A watery sun was beginning to break through the dull sky, turning blue in places. In the distance, Vendome's medieval walls loomed.

The cart rumbled over an old stone bridge and they entered the town through an ancient portal.

"Porte St Georges," said the café owner, indicating it with his whip. "See how charred it is. The June bombing. But it held. Unfortunately we can't say the same for the rue de la Poterie. Two hundred dwellings destroyed by German incendiary bombs."

"Terrible," Daniel said, quietly. "Safer to live outside the town. No?" No sooner had he said it than a pang went through his heart. It would take months to make Fort Girard habitable. Tatiana and his girls, meanwhile, would have to wait up in Paris. But he had to remain positive, he told himself. Look at all these *Vendômois*, now rendered homeless.

The cart had stopped outside a gold-tipped gate where a bronze plaque bore the words: '*Sous Préfecture de Vendôme. Bureaux ouverts.*'

"We're here," the café owner said, gathering the reins.

"Thank you, *mon vieux*."

"Pleasure. It's Eric, by the way."

"Dan," he replied, shaking his hand.

"I'll meet you in the market square. Look, it's turning out to be a fine day."

"Monsieur le Sous-Préfet Buissière is expecting you." The secretary ushered him across a cobbled courtyard, through to a light-airy building. "His office is on the first floor." She led him up an echoing staircase and rapped on the door.

"*Entrez!*"

She opened the door. "Daniel Frey."

"Yes. Yes. Bring him in." A genial-looking fellow, with dominant dark brows, got up from his magnificent desk. A large framed photograph of Maréchal Pétain in kepi hat and uniform hung over him.

"Settling in alright at Fort Girard?' he said, walking across the room to shake Daniel's hand. "Thank you, Carole. You may leave us." Once she had gone, he continued, "Not been over there myself, but Paris tells me there's quite a lot to be done. Sit."

"Thank you." Daniel settled in a chair. "Monsieur le Sous-Préfet," he said, hesitantly, "I am so very grateful for you making the time to see me."

"Pleasure. So what can I do for you?"

Daniel detected a tightness in the voice. "Well, at Fort Girard we are lacking the most basic things. Water, electricity. My team have started digging for a well and will need water pipes. We have many broken windows. And once the main house has its utilities working, we plan to build outside dormitories and workshops – for which we need bricks and roofing material. As you see, there is everything to be done."

The Sub-Prefect leaned forward in his chair and pressed his thumbs together. "I can tell you straight away that we don't have the funds available for restoring this wreck of a house. We have our hands full rehousing our own residents."

Daniel winced. Surely Cochet had primed him.

"However…" The Sub-Prefect reached into his drawer and took out a sheet of government-headed paper. He scribbled a short note, signed and stamped it. "There," he said, handing it over. "The Chateau de la Gaudinière, in the forest of Fréteval. The Duc de La Rochefoucauld owned it so I believe you have some rights over it. For many years, it was a centre for Armenian children after the Russian revolution. More recently we put up some Spanish refugees there. Unfortunately, there was a fire and they had to move out."

Daniel felt a pang of unease. Was he profiting from the misery of others? On the other hand, another opportunity like this was unlikely. He thanked the Sub-Prefect profusely.

"Quite alright," he said, rising. "Keep me informed. Here is my card."

"Thank you, sir. Oh, Monsieur le Sous-préfet, before I forget…"

"Yes?"

"In order to run the centre efficiently… It would be most useful to… well…"

"Yes? Go on."

"It would be most useful to have a telephone."

Bouillot had found a telephone line at Fort Girard that morning.

The Sub-Prefect laughed. "No running water, no electricity, and a telephone line with no telephone. I will ask my secretary to search the departmental buildings – but that may take some time."

Daniel marched out of the courtyard jubilant. Checking his watch, he strode over to the centre of town, but slowed his pace as he passed several streets lined with mounds of brick and rubble and splintered timber. He was relieved to see Eric waving cheerfully at him on the square.

On the return journey, they passed a car workshop outside the Ville aux Clercs.

"Do you mind stopping here for one moment, Eric?"

Around the back of the *garagiste's* yard was an old Citroen hidden under tarpaulin.

"It'll start, but won't go very far. No petrol around here. You could run it on alcohol I suppose. But you'd have to change the carburettor jets and–"

"I'll be back!" Daniel said, simply. "Don't offer it to anyone else."

"Unlikely to be any takers!" the mechanic said, lifting his beret. "The *boches,* if they ever come snooping, are the only ones…"

After being dropped off at the café, Daniel ran back to Fort Girard. The team were coming up the lawn with several bucket-loads of water.

Lefèbvre put a pail at Daniel's feet and wiped his pasty brow. "There's no telling whether it's drinkable."

"We'll get the water tested in Vendôme," Daniel said, exultant at his recent successes. He'd borrow the café owner's cart, but they'd need something more substantial to go up to the Chateau de la Gaudinière for the materials. He turned to Bouillot. "At the end of the week, you'll go up to Paris. A water pump is priority. I'll draw up a list. And, of course, we need a truck to get us to the château and back. Who said Rome wasn't built in a day?"

CHAPTER SEVENTEEN

November 5th 1940

> *Princess,*
> *I'm writing to you by candlelight, missing you and the girls.*

Daniel pulled a page from his sketchbook. He started to trace the house's grand façade, its windows, stone balconies and trailing ivy from memory. In the foreground, on the terrace, Tatiana leaned across the stone balustrade and watched bony-legged Jeanne chase her toddler sister over the lawn below. A few butterflies hovered above them. It wasn't the season, but he knew it would delight them all.

Laying the sketch aside, he continued:

> *We have graduated from bare floorboards to straw mattresses and pillows, ever since Bouillot came back from Paris with a truckload of essentials.*
> *Thanks to the water pump and engineer provided by the Paris office, we will have running water in the following weeks, which you can imagine we are very much looking forward to. At present we are using several old wine barrels from the cellar as water butts, which we have placed outside on the terrace. Some mornings we have had to break open the ice forming on top.*
> *Meanwhile, the new engineer, an ex-Air Force officer,*

is causing me problems. Whereas I cannot fault his work, he is of a surly disposition. I have done my best to welcome him to my experienced team, but he looks upon his placement at Fort Girard as a disappointing demotion. It is not the technical college for young pilots he had in mind. During our last discussion, I was tempted to ask him to leave but thought better of it, feeling that over time, once he meets the boys, once we have built the workshops, things may change. He's already said he would prefer to live in the village, which I've encouraged and organised without too much effort. He has been my only human obstacle so far – and a manageable one.

I have, on the other hand, been buoyed by the enthusiasm of my team, and the Sous-préfet, Bussière, who has allowed us access to a nearby château. We went there with the truck yesterday. In the ruins of this grand house, which, my Princess, you'll be pleased to hear served Armenian children and Spanish refugees, we were able to gather essential construction material.

I imagine you reading this and being far more interested in its former usage – so here is the story I've managed to glean from the Sub-Prefect. The property was bought by an Armenian businessman in New York in 1920, someone who'd managed to smuggle out his money successfully from the revolution, rather like your father's business associate –though what a sorry affair that was in your case! The château housed one hundred children, girls and boys, and Armenian and French teachers were brought in to teach them a useful trade. Rather like what I'm doing now, twenty or so years later – isn't that extraordinary? Wars and revolutions create a bad start in life for young people, but with a few mentors, n'est-ce pas, good things may be achieved. You and I know all about that, my darling.

The way things are looking, the boys will be down in December. As for you, chérie, I will not contemplate you moving down here before the house is habitable and the weather warmer. I am sure you will agree. But I'll be home for Christmas, ma chérie.

Please find enclosed a sketch.

Bouillot will be bringing you up a food parcel this week.

All my love to you, Jeanne and Béa

Dan

CHAPTER EIGHTEEN

Daniel drove Bouillot to Pezou train station in the newly-acquired Citroen. The exultation he'd felt at getting the car working had come to an abrupt end that morning when he had opened Tatiana's hastily scrawled note.

> *I am pleased to hear that things are going well for you at Fort Girard. My news is less heartening. Paris has completely run out of powdered milk. It was hard for me to see Béa scream with hunger. Luckily, Sacha was able to obtain some on the black market...*

He'd stopped reading after that. The withdrawal of the "*Chéri*" had hurt him more than anything else. And as for the mention of Sacha...

"Dan. Are you alright?" Bouillot said, breaking the silence.

"Tired, that's all."

"Must be those mattresses. Tough little blighters."

"Yes," Daniel said, rubbing his forehead. He was relieved that Bouillot wasn't the prying sort.

One hundred disinfected mattresses stuffed with fresh straw were now laid out in rows in the upstairs dormitories, which had been scrubbed and swept clean by Labarre and Cintract.

"Still, there's Christmas and, before long, your Mrs will be down here," said Bouillot, as if reading his mind.

Poor Bouillot. He'd lost his wife in June. At Sillery, over a glass of beer, he had spoken of his wife's asthma attack, of the suffocating heat during the exodus that had brought it on. Bouillot had demobilised in time to bury her in Paris. His two daughters had been there to comfort him and were now living in his apartment with their children, waiting for their prisoner husbands to return.

I have much to be grateful for, Daniel thought, tossing the matter aside with fury. Béa had her milk and Sacha could conjure all the caviar, champagne, powdered milk he wished. Tatiana was his.

"Here we are. Just in time." Bouillot checked his wristwatch.

Daniel looked up at his grinning colleague, who, despite his recent loss, had found joy in his daughters and grandchildren.

"Have a good evening. And thanks for taking those eggs and milk. Tatiana will really appreciate it."

On his return, Lefèbvre was in the sitting room, reading the local paper.

"Morning, Lefèbvre."

Sighing, Lefèbvre passed over the article he had been reading. "Look at this." It was tucked away on the back page. The body of a Catholic priest had been found in a lake in the region. The police were trying to hunt down the group of youths he had chaperoned from Paris.

"Oh," Daniel said, in a low voice.

"I know."

"It's hard to imagine a group of boys could really do that!"

"I don't understand," Lefèbvre said, shaking his head. "When I was working at my brother's church, our charges were always so passive – it was a problem! I put it down to malnourishment, to trauma." Lefèbvre was leaning over the stove by the fire and pouring some ersatz coffee. "Want one?"

"Not all priests will have a way with boys," Daniel said, taking his cup from Lefèbvre. "But for them to commit murder..." He sat down and stared into the fire.

"It's just a freak of nature. Or a trouble-maker in the pack. Could be an older boy with a grudge who led them to stone him."

Daniel took his coffee over to the little library he was building up, of books Bouillot had picked up in Paris. He chose *The Life Cycle of a Dragonfly* and started to flick through the vividly-coloured illustrations. He was back at his uncle's farm in Champagne, aged eleven, watching a beautiful Blue Emperor land elegantly on a bulrush to the accompaniment of guns.

CHAPTER NINETEEN

"Everyone stand in a line and pipe down!" From the terrace, Daniel peered down at the youths engulfing the lawn below. Nervously swarming at first, they broke away and started to form an uneven line.

One red-haired young man, however, was refusing to follow suit and had walked over to the stairs leading up towards the terrace. With his hands in his trouser pockets, he whispered something to one of the older boys jutting out from the first row. Both of them looked up, sneered at their surroundings, at the house, and then focused on him.

Bouillot, who had been guiding the rows since his arrival with the boys, stared at the jittery boy, perhaps now in a better position to do so, for nothing was worse than walking through a forest with a trouble-maker behind you.

The older lad, perhaps conscious of Daniel's stare, shrugged his shoulders.

The trouble-maker threw his canvas bag to the ground and, adopting a swagger, made his way up the stone steps, to where Daniel was waiting for him.

"Well?" Daniel said, calmly, trying to wipe away the insolent expression on the youth's face.

The youth bunched his fist. "If you think we're going to take all of this!" He didn't look like a back-street fighter and yet his whole rangy body seemed to be trembling with incandescent rage.

Out of the corner of his eye, Daniel saw Bouillot and Lefèbvre mount the stairs; he raised his arm to slow them. Bouillot finally halted alongside Daniel, whilst Lefèbvre stood guard on top of the steps. Cintract and Labarre positioned themselves at the end of two of the three rows.

Unperturbed, the agitator continued, "Form a row here, do this, do that…" He shook a fist. "*Eh bien!* You've got another thing coming." His strident voice, not quite fully broken, sounded hurt. "*Moi et les gars*, we're not 'appy about it!" He turned to his captive audience down on the lawn.

A lonely cheer rose up into the wintry air. Daniel saw the older guy and a handful of others incline their heads with uncertainty. Others were perhaps too timid, too exhausted, it was hard to tell. He passed his eyes over his fifty charges. Some seemed older than their years, others, perhaps stunted by malnutrition, appeared to have been taken from the school playground.

"Bunch of twerps."

Daniel scanned the second row. A small, shaven-haired youth was kicking his bag. Boys sniggered either side of him.

Daniel's neck and shoulders, clammy with sweat, started to prickle. He had left the team at the station and hurtled back to Fort Girard to talk to the new cook, just arrived from the ocean liner *France*. Daniel had tasted tonight's nutritious offering, a pork and bean casserole, prepared in four great vats.

Daniel smiled inwardly.

"Go and join the others," Daniel said, still managing to control his voice.

"This is just like the boot camp we've just left."

"No, it's not, *mon gars*."

A withering look broke out on the youth's face: *Don't think you can get around me like that.*

Daniel glanced at Lefèbvre; his smooth, serene features had contracted. Bouillot, his arms behind his back, was observing the scene with ironic interest.

Daniel pulled himself to his full height. "Look, you've had a long trip down. Stop wasting everybody's time, including yours. Do as you're told and there's a good supper waiting."

The lad seemed to take this in for a moment. He suddenly noticed the rows of jute sacks propped up along the balustrade, however, and his expression changed.

"What are those for?"

"For the workshops you'll be building."

"I knew it," he said, shaking his head.

Bouillot leaned forward in his boots, ready to rush in. Once more Daniel put his arm out to stop him, then turned back to the young man.

"That is enough," he said, sharply, grabbing the boy's shoulders to lead him away from the sack he seemed about to kick. "Don't be a fool!"

The youth pulled away abruptly and reversed into Daniel's chest. His hair smelt of smoke and sweat. His stringy back seemed remarkably resistant and strong.

"Get off!" said the youth, spinning round suddenly and pushing him away.

The priest, floating amongst the weeds in a pond, flashed into Daniel's mind.

"I'm not staying 'ere." The boy marched towards the stairs.

"*Viens ici*!" Daniel clamped his arms around the youth's chest. *He has pluck but is foolhardy.* He loosened his hold.

The boy broke free and landed a punch on Daniel's chin. A stinging pain came and went. The lad rubbed his knuckles quickly up against his shrunken sweater, eyes glistening with provocation.

He barely reaches my shoulder. But he could start a riot. Fifty boys against five members of staff. The engineer has a day off. And chef is in the kitchen lovingly preparing a welcome dinner.

Bouillot rolled up his sleeves.

As a scrawny fist flew up in Daniel's face again, he blocked it elegantly. Daniel unclenched his own fist and swung his large, outstretched palm through the air. It landed with a resounding smack on the youth's left cheek.

The boy was propelled to the stony ground and hit his side. He lay there, dazed, panting and cupping his red cheek.

"Get up," Daniel said, dully.

The boy exercised his jaw.

"Nothing broken. But first of all, I'd like you to apologise."

There was a moment's hesitation as the young man looked up at him, undecided. He was shaking his head, almost smiling.

"Well?"

"Sorry," he mumbled, looking at the ground.

"That's better." Without waiting, Daniel gripped the boy's chilled hand and pulled him up. "Now go and join your *camerades*."

Seeing the youth standing there, still so confused, Daniel bent his head.

"What you did just now was not only unacceptable but incredibly ill-judged. I am a soldier. I could have done you real harm. Know your enemy."

He saw a flicker of light in the boy's grey eyes. Something akin to respect? He couldn't be sure.

"And, just so that we're clear, this is not a boot camp."

Lefèbvre led the boy down the terrace steps. Cintract escorted the youth to his place in the line. Daniel, who by now had had time to gather his senses, felt his heart gallop with intent.

There was some murmuring in the group the youth had joined, but he avoided their gazes and looked up.

"Alright, alright," Daniel said, raising his hand momentarily. "It's been a long day for you all. But everyone now just listen to me." Daniel scanned the rows of boys, staring up at him expectantly. "We're soon going in to supper. To make one thing quite clear to all of you, I too am not here to take orders from anyone, least of all the Germans who are occupying our land. I have no intention of running this place as a boot camp. However, there are a few simple rules, rules for your benefit and mine. You will be expected to control yourselves, to treat others with respect. That includes your team leaders and your *camerades*. We are all embarked on an adventure here. I expect you to conduct yourselves like men, not sheep. I am looking to you to help rebuild this house you'll be living in, to help rebuild the workshops you'll be learning in, so that you can find work for yourselves. So that you can help your families."

Daniel allowed this to sink in. There was a silence. A few nodded and uncrossed their arms. He continued, now smiling as he spoke.

"Here I do expect you to call me 'sir', however, in the camp, I would like everyone to be open with one another, honest with one another. If you have any problems, we are here to help. Don't think I don't understand, because I do." He was relieved to see a few boys smile.

"Tonight, you will be eating a hearty meal prepared by our resident chef. I don't need to tell you how privileged we are, when the rest of France is finding it hard to feed itself."

The boys in the front row suddenly looked serious.

"We must work together. Build workshops. Grow our food.

Help the community. And I don't just expect *you* to work, but *your leaders* too. We will work alongside you, doing the same jobs. We will all eat the same food, at the same table. We will even use the same straw mattresses as you whilst we wait for proper mattresses to arrive."

Daniel smiled. "I want us to be proud of what we achieve here." He scanned the faces. Fifty pairs of eyes, fixed on him with interest. Was it the thought of food? Or what he had said? He would find out tomorrow.

"You may go now. Please follow Cintract and Labarre up to your rooms. Put your things at the foot of your bed. Then follow them down to the dining room. My deputies, Lefèbvre, Bouillot" – Daniel turned to them, they nodded – "will join you there. Alright. Dismissed."

There arose what seemed a more respectful murmuring as the boys made their way past Daniel and the others.

Bouillot rolled his eyes after the last of them had galloped up the stairs. "*Bien*, boss. Let *chef* take over for the moment, eh? Oh – and the red-haired boy's name is Roupp, by the way. Pierre Roupp."

"Food is what they need," said Lefèbvre, behind him.

Daniel marched to his little office, shut the door behind him and, tugging at his hair, lay back in a chair.

CHAPTER TWENTY

A chill wind blew across the garden, causing the leaves to scatter at Daniel's feet. He looked up and prepared himself to address the ten lines of youths filed around him in star formation. With their sleep-tousled hair and ill-fitting clothes they were a sorry sight –

But they are here, Daniel told himself. *No one has bolted these past few weeks.* The provision of regular meals and companionship had probably persuaded even the most recalcitrant amongst them. Pierre Roupp stood half-way round, to Daniel's right, in his shrunken sweater and ragged trousers that stopped half-way down his white freckled shins.

An uncomfortable heaviness rose in Daniel's chest. With a mere slap he had knocked Pierre to the stones. He had had the good sense to unclench his fist and not harm the boy. Perhaps Pierre had already forgotten about it. Doubtless, he was no stranger to fighting in the street. Perhaps, now that his stomach was satiated, his rage would subside. It was terrible to be hungry. Terrible to be passed from pillar to post by the authorities, however well-meaning.

And yet that morning Daniel had risen from a troubled sleep feeling both remorse and rage.

'Bless them that curse you,' his mother had told him long ago, after his brawl with the headmaster's son, mistakenly believing that Daniel had been taunted by him. And when he had corrected her, that sad, disappointed look had passed over her kind eyes. She was never able to admonish him. Neither of his parents ever could. All he had been left with was guilt.

Yes, young men needed guidance, some reining in at times. In the cavalry in Morocco he had learnt to channel his disparate energies and emotions. To tame himself. Calmness and strength were qualities that kept you alive, he had been taught. And decisiveness. If a horse sensed hesitancy, he would test you, at worst bolt and do harm not only to you but to himself. If it meant squeezing his flanks, tugging the reins now and then, so be it. Pierre had respected the back of his hand.

This morning, however, was not about reprimand, but discipline and inspiration.

He unrolled the flag that Lefèbvre had handed to him and clipped it onto the pole.

"What I'm doing now is strictly forbidden," he said, looking round at them row by row and pulling on the cord. The Tricolor set off on its journey upwards, and as it reached the summit, Daniel gave it a final yank and knotted the cord tightly. It caught the wind and rippled beautifully to order. "I trust that you will never breathe a word of this to anyone. Not even your families, do you understand?"

"That shouldn't be too hard!" said one of the older boys, guffawing.

Daniel caught Pierre smirking.

"What about my brothers?" said another lad, standing behind him.

Daniel shook his head. "No, not even your brother."

Out of the corner of his eye, Daniel saw Bouillot glance back towards the forest, but acres of woodland separated them from the outside world.

"It's our secret. Can I count on all of you?" He scanned each row, willing each boy to meet his gaze. He was in no hurry. He wanted them to know that each man counted. Even Pierre Roupp lifted his chin and mumbled a, "Yes, sir".

Daniel was sure that they'd never once given any thought to their nation's flag growing up. And why should they? He hadn't at their age. Not until he'd served in the peace-keeping force in Morocco.

Silence reigned as the boys stared at the flag. As a lone bird started to peep in the forest, Daniel quickly loosened the cord and let the Tricolor slide down in his hands.

"And now let's press on. This morning, it's forestry, as you know." There were a few groans. Daniel lifted his finger. "And," he continued, pointedly, "in exchange for our labour, the mayor has guaranteed us enough wood to fuel our ovens and our heating. All the necessary saws and axes are in their usual place. If you're not sure what you're supposed to be doing, check with your team leader. Team leaders are at the front of your row, in case you haven't quite woken up this morning." There were a few playful shoves. Daniel waited for stillness and then shouted, "Dismissed!"

He watched the boys set off around the back of the house with Cintract, Labarre and Lefèbvre, who was looking preoccupied. Exhausted no doubt. He'd been on night duty. The boys were one hundred-strong now.

Bouillot came to take the flagpole away.

"We're going to have to do something about their clothes, Bouillot."

"Proper ragamuffins, I agree," he laughed. "But they stood to attention alright."

Daniel smiled. "Not bad for their first parade. But they'll have a winter to survive down here. At the end of the week, I'd like you to take your begging bowl to the Paris office again."

"Uniforms would be good, boss. Saw some in the stores when I was stocking up on plates and kitchen items the first time. Narvik expeditionary force. Good as new."

And what a fiasco Norway was, Daniel thought to himself. Still, if the uniforms could clothe all of them…

"Can't see the *boches* sticking their noses in around here. Can you?"

"Better things to do, *mon vieux*. I think we'll be safe wearing them. Just tell them that's all we've got, anyway."

"How about Roupp, by the way. Any problems with him in the dorms?"

"He's keeping his head down. But there's one I've got my eye on. The 'twerps' guy. Little fella. Vilon is his name. Keeps himself to himself. Lefèbvre said he wet the bed last night. Barely speaks. Lefèbvre told him to change his sheets but, unfortunately, one of the other boys heard. Well, you can imagine…"

"Right. Vilon, you say. Keep an eye on him."

CHAPTER TWENTY-ONE

From his office Daniel listened to the clatter of boots filing past. *What a month it has been*! Letters had gone back and forth to the *Mairie*, the *Préfecture*, the Sully Committee up in Paris. Bed frames, mattresses, pillows, crockery, cutlery, armchairs, tables, corrugated iron, pipework, all to be ticked off, accounted for. Forty-seven mattresses had been disinfected. The smell still lingered in the dormitories and mingled with the overall fetid, sweaty odour of pubescent boys. *Once the barracks are built, we will at least have a shower block*. Weeks of incessant rain had unfortunately held up the works.

He drew the typewriter to him. He had another thank you letter to type to the Sub-Prefect Bussière in Vendôme. The bricks and pipes from the Château de la Gaudinière were under a tarpaulin in the yard. All they needed was several clear days. And that precious telephone had arrived today too. Buissière was a miracle-worker. With this instrument, Daniel knew he could transform the place.

He smiled at this small triumph and loosened his scratchy serge collar. To distract himself from the maddening itch, he stared out of his office window, at the giant sequoia rising into the grey sky. They'd be assembling there after breakfast for the raising of the colours. What a smart turn-out it would be, all of them in their navy button-down jackets, ski trousers, berets and lace-up boots.

He wished Tatiana were there to see them all looking so impeccable. He had started to feel her absence acutely. The night before he had lain awake watching the moon illuminate the four corners of his spartan room. He had thought of them in Paris, in the little apartment in the Rue de Grenelle. The German barracks at l'Ecole Militaire was just around the corner. He hated to think of their vulnerability.

But there had been progress, he told himself. A female of a different order had just arrived. Mlle Laviolle, the new nurse. A veteran of Verdun, she'd served in a field hospital during the Great War. Fiercely independent, refusing to have her luggage carried for her at the station, she would be a welcome addition when the seasonal coughs and colds started.

The sound of heavy footsteps made him look up. The door flew open. "Bleedin' creatures, boss."

"What's the matter, Bouillot?"

"Would you believe it! A couple of them boys were scratching at breakfast. And not just their 'eads! Mademoiselle Laviolle recommends a complete inspection."

Daniel sighed. "*Sacré uniformes!* Could only have come from them! I myself…"

Bouillot made a face and passed his hand around the back of his neck. "All of us, boss…"

"At least the boys still have their old clothes." Lefèbvre had just walked in, smiling. "Mademoiselle Laviolle is in the infirmary, getting things ready. She'll be over here in just – ah, here she is."

Mlle Laviolle quietly closed the door behind her.

"Mademoiselle Laviolle. I'm sorry to put you through this. You have barely settled in."

"Can't be helped," she said, looking at her worn, polished shoes.

"Will you receive the boys one by one? They will have to be shaved, everywhere. And I can't trust them to do it themselves."

"Of course," she said, crisply.

"We can't take any risks in the dormitories. Crammed in like that." Bouillot seemed more affected than Lefèbvre. "Them lice carry diseases."

"Yes, yes," Daniel said, remembering the typhus scares in the trenches of the Great War. "Tell Cintract, Labarre, and other group leaders to collect all the clothes and bed linen. I hope they've been marked. Chef won't be pleased that we'll be taking over his vats. We'll set up fires in the different rooms and hang everything over the spare cable we requisitioned from La Gaudiniere. This is the moment to encourage the boys to write home. We'll also light the fires in the rooms."

Daniel walked up the central stairs with Lefèbvre. They separated and he stepped into Roupp's dormitory, where he saw Roupp sat on the bed in his clothes. The others had already undressed and were swaddled in sheets, complaining and jumping up and down to keep warm.

"Roupp, get those clothes off. The sooner you do it, the better!"

"Yes sir," he murmured, without looking up.

"Roupp, I'd like you to look at me when I talk to you."

"What are you going to do to us?" he said, pinching his shirtsleeves.

"Nothing lad. But you're all going to have to see the nurse."

"Nurse!" he said, looking alarmed.

"Cor, 'ave we got a young nurse," said a dark-haired lad at the stove. He raised a dark, hairy leg and jiggled it.

"That's enough," Daniel said, smiling this time and eager to keep things pleasant. "Yes, Mademoiselle Laviolle just started with us today."

"A mademoiselle?" piped up the same prankster again, rolling his eyes and fluttering his eyelids.

"Yes, a mademoiselle and old enough to be your grandmother." There were a few moans. "I'd like you all to show her some respect."

"But what's she going to do to us?" said Roupp, his hand gripping his belt.

"She's going to be dealing with the problem quickly." And before any further questions could be asked, Daniel walked out of the room.

For the first time since its introduction, the raising of the colour was cancelled. The shaven-headed boys took it in turns to help Chef boil their sheets and went to wring them out quickly on the terrace. From the cables Labarre and Boillot had fixed along the wall hung their steaming jackets, ski pants, berets, underclothes, and sheets. All day the fires would be kept burning.

Lefèbvre had made the boys write their letters home at the refectory table.

"Remember – no mention of the raising of the flag!"

"Aw, sir!"

"What else are we supposed to say? Oh yea. I've shaved my

head."

Lefèbvre laughed. Daniel passed through with Bouillot. They stopped by Vilon, who was stabbing his paper with his pencil.

"If you don't want to write, *mon petit gars*, sketch something. You're just wasting paper."

The boy made an even bigger hole in his sheet.

Not wishing to make a scene, Daniel walked on with Bouillot.

"I've never seen that boy smile, boss."

Later that afternoon, Daniel left the door to his office ajar. One boy then another came to visit him, either to check the spelling of a word or to simply talk.

Daniel decided to prolong the exercise the following morning. It was Sunday, and slanting rain splattered the rattling panes. Daniel was running his eyes down the approved reading list he had received from the Paris Office.

"Sir?"

"Roupp."

Shaven, leaning in the doorway, the lad looked younger, more delicate, especially with that sprinkle of freckles over his nose. A purple tinge around his eyes suggested interrupted sleep, but his eyes had lost that hard, hurt look. "Sit down, son."

Pierre perched on the edge of the seat.

"Well?"

Pierre rolled his pencil in one hand and gripped a blank sheet of paper in the other.

"I can't, sir."

Pierre's file was one of the first Daniel had read. "Your mother will want to know how you're getting on, *mons gars*."

Pierre laughed, dismayed.

Daniel had watched Roupp around the campfire several times recently, mutely mouthing the words to the scout songs Cintract was teaching him. No one was forced to sing, of course.

"Can't see the point. She won't reply. What with my dad being in the Stalag and her taking up with someone else…"

"Someone else?" Sadly, it was a recurring story among the boys he had spoken to. "She's your mother. A mother never forgets her son."

"This one does."

There was a long silence as Pierre focused on Daniel's desk.

"What's that you're reading, sir?"

"A reading list. Do you like books?"

There was a pause. "Not sure. It depends. That book you've underlined, sir..."

"*Le Grand Meaulnes*, you mean?"

"Yeh."

"You left school early, didn't you? Nothing to be ashamed of." Daniel decided not to elaborate on his own experiences.

"All that worry about study. How's that going to help anyone? That's what my Dad said before going off to war."

He didn't want to be seen to contradict the boy's father so soon. "Where is he now?"

"Stalag X-one-A – wherever that is. Mum doesn't want anything to do with him. She always called him a layabout. At least my stepdad – except Mum's not married – is bringing home a proper wage, she says. My stepdad's in Germany too, only he wanted to go." Pierre frowned. "All he cares about is money, my Mum, and the baby that's on its way."

"I see," said Daniel. "Hmm. Have you heard from your father?"

"Once. He told me he hadn't meant it."

"Meant what, son?"

"That he'd been angry with my mum. He said that literature and knowledge were all that had counted in his world."

Daniel gaped. A whole world of poetry came flooding into the room. "Did you write back?"

He shook his head. "My Mum was begging me to see that priest. I hated that church, the smell of cabbage, being made to feel bad."

Daniel smiled encouragingly. "Not their fault, son. They're doing their best. Look, take this." He handed him his personal copy of *Le Grand Meaulnes*.

Pierre put his blank sheet of notepaper down and turned the book over and over. He opened it and read the first line aloud. "*Il arriva chez nous un dimanche de novembre 189....*" ('He arrived at our house one Sunday in November 189...') He looked up. "Funny way to start."

"Got to start somewhere."

Pierre clamped the book shut.

"Go on, take it."

Pierre turned it over again.

"A 'thank you' would be appropriate."

"Er, thank you! Sir."

"That's alright." Daniel held out Roupp's sheet and pencil.

Pierre took it and disappeared into the reception room.

Daniel leaned back in his chair again and took a deep breath. Then he laughed.

Not even Bouillot's long face around the door minutes later, complaining about the weather, the lice, and the threat of snow the next day could dampen his spirits.

CHAPTER TWENTY-TWO

The train pulled in at Pezou station and out of it leapt a young man in an unbuttoned raincoat with cropped dark hair, carrying a worn leather travel bag. He bounded up towards Daniel.

"Vic," Daniel said, simply.

"Yes, pleased to meet you." Daniel grasped a bulky gold ring as they shook hands; its reared unicorn emblem was no affectation. He thought of Vic's parental home in the Loire, with its stabled horses and aged servants, and looked down into the *vicomte's* close-set, trustworthy eyes. A head shorter than him, with strong, square shoulders, he now pulled them back as if to say, 'let's not stand on ceremony. I left that world long ago.' Aged twenty-three, he'd already distinguished himself in the French Campaign, earning a *Croix de Guerre*. This young man was coming to Fort Girard on his own merits.

"A pleasure to have you on board, Vic," Daniel said, addressing him with the informal 'tu'.

They left the little station and walked out into the yard, where Daniel had parked his Citroen.

Vic flung his leather case onto the back seat and bounced into the passenger seat next to him. The ring, with its crescent moon and rearing unicorn, winked at Daniel in the fading afternoon light.

At the end of the week, after Cintract had led them in song around the campfire, Daniel encouraged Vic to recount his war experiences to the boys, though not without discussing it with him first.

"These boys are impressionable, as you know. We don't want to stoke them up to fight the *fritz*."

"Of course."

"We don't want them getting ideas. Our main aim is to train them up for jobs, so they can feed themselves and their families."

Vic nodded.

"Which doesn't belittle what you have done, Vic."

Daniel rose before the boys sitting cross-legged around the fire. Metal plates and cutlery had been piled up in a corner. They had sung. This part of the evening was given over to talk.

"Vic. Would you tell us a bit of what happened to you in the Forest of Warndt, where you fought."

Vic took his place beside him. Complete silence reigned, aside from the occasional sound of animals moving through the thickets.

"It was September nineteen-thirty-nine," he said, calmly. "We had slipped five kilometres into enemy territory – the German Saarland. A small team. What you call a *corps*. Our mission was to get several injured colleagues out of a village where we'd been fighting the *fritz*. We knew the forest was mined and that some houses in the village had been booby-trapped. Earlier, we'd had to leave our injured colleagues behind a ruined dwelling. Our commander had ordered us to aid him in bringing them back."

All the boys listened intently. One boy lifted his hand.

"How many *fritz* did you kill, Vic?"

Vic looked over to Daniel. "It was not that sort of operation. Our orders were to slip out as quickly as possible. If we started firing, our commander warned us, the enemy would know our positions."

Daniel watched the boys' eyes gleam with the glamour of war. He couldn't stop them feeling excited about it. He felt the stir of battle in his breast too.

Roupp, who was sitting in the front row, seemed pensive. "Were you ever scared?"

Vic nodded. "My heart had never pumped so hard."

Roupp gaped in surprise. A soldier with a medal – fearful? He was clearly puzzled.

"But we knew exactly what we had to do," Vic continued. "This is key. We had the military intelligence and command to guide us. And also a lot of luck." He smiled sadly. "But not all of us got out alive."

Daniel understood the role fear played with the soldier. Too little was suicide, too much was paralysing.

"Did you learn anything from your experience?" Daniel interjected.

"Yes." Vic paused. "I learnt that a good commander is key."

The next morning, the boys came promptly into the refectory where Daniel had just finished having breakfast. Vic walked in after them, greeted him, and sat down at the head of the table. Those who had been slumping over their food sat up straight, looking sheepish.

My young deputy is working even better than I imagined. And what a good idea to organise a projection of Charlie Chaplin tonight too.

Vic's influence at Fort Girard went beyond the boys. His energy and pleasant demeanour permeated the staff. Lefèbvre became livelier, while Bouillot's booming voice softened. Even the taciturn engineer managed to crack a smile under his brush moustache every time Vic entered the workshop. Vic's military successes, despite him never alluding to them again, gave them all hope. And there was so much more to Vic, they said. You would never think that he was an aristocrat. He was one of them, a good sort.

Now all that was left to complete Daniel's team was an agricultural team leader.

In anticipation of his arrival, Daniel bought a sturdy workhorse called Ulysses from a local horse trader.

Daniel went with the new team leader, Patrice, to the farm, where, in exchange for labour, the farmer had loaned them a parcel of land. In a dark corner of his barn, under straw, they uncovered an ancient plough and dusty harnesses. As they attached Ulysses to the wheeled contraption, they eyed the earth nervously.

"*Allez!*" Daniel pulled on the horse's bridle and coaxed the horse out of the yard. Patrice, in galoshes behind them, gripped the handles of the plough.

"Let go," he shouted, as they entered the barren field. Slowly, man and horse set out, built up momentum until the blades were dropped. After several false starts, the plough's blades engaged with the soil, slicing and parting it.

Jubilant, Daniel raised his beret; of all the projects they had undertaken, this was the one which enthused him the most.

Meanwhile, in an attempt to raise morale, the Ministry for Youth in Paris had sent down some stars to be sewn into their uniforms: gold for the 'moral educators', silver for the technical staff. The award system had been used in the youth camps in the Free Zone, they were told.

Holding back four gold stars for himself, Daniel distributed three gold to Bouillot, Lefèbvre, and Vic, the equivalent in silver to the engineer and agricultural trainer, and finally two silver for Mlle Laviolle, who grumbled about the time it would take her to sew them into her uniforms when there were vaccinations to be done. Cintract, Labarre, and the team leaders were the only ones to show a little pride in their awards.

For Daniel, however, one far more important element of the uniform was missing, one which would unite and define them all.

One morning after the raising of the flag, instead of joining the others at the carpentry *atelier*, now drawing near to completion, Daniel walked to the bottom of the garden with a pencil and notepad. At the forest perimeter, rising through the hazy winter sunshine, stood a white stone portal, which had served the feudal castle that had once stood on the site of Fort Girard. He sketched it and, with growing excitement, strode back to his office. At his desk, he created an ink monogram of the portal with the words 'TENIR' at the bottom of it.

The shrill ring of his telephone made him start.

"Monsieur Frey, it's Jean Riou here."

The voice was warm, personable. He recognised the name, he'd received a letter from this man just the week before, notifying him of his new appointment as Regional Director of the youth camps in the Loir.

"*Bonjour*, Monsieur Riou."

"Jean, please!"

"In which case, will you please call me Daniel?"

"*Bien sûr!* Daniel, I'd like to come down and visit the camp in the new year."

"With pleasure," he said, feeling his chest tighten. A month of rain and high winds had held up the works.

"How are the boys settling in?"

"Oh fine, oh fine. A few teething problems…"

"To be expected…"

"Oh yes," he found himself saying. "But we're making headway…" Hadn't Pierre Roupp become quite civilized? He had finished *Le Grand Meaulnes* and was now embarked on Stendhal's *Le Rouge et le Noir*. But there was still that taciturn 'twerps' fellow…

"Daniel, are you still there?"

"Yes. Just getting my diary." He pushed his 1940 diary aside, already crowded with names and telephone numbers, and reached for a new 1941 calendar provided by the post office.

The calendar had an illustration of the *Maréchal*, out of uniform and resembling some kindly grandfather in a smart double-breasted winter coat, brown hat and cane. He was addressing a classroom of schoolchildren. But the *Maréchal* was no doddery grandparent; stories had come out of Vichy of the octogenarian's strength. His forearm was apparently so strong that he could lift a young child up on that cane of his.

"Around the sixth of January?"

"Yes, perfect." He put a ring around the date and wrote 'RIOU' in bold, black letters.

"The year has gone quickly, *non*?" Jean said, suddenly sounding less buoyant, wishing to remain on the line.

"It's easy to forget that we are at war out where we are. At least, well… you know what I mean."

"I do."

"But I have just designed Fort Girard's monogram to go on the boys' uniforms. 'Tenir' is our motto – we're holding fast."

"That is good, Daniel. Very good." Riou's voice had lifted. "I look forward to meeting you. And my best wishes to your staff and the boys. And to your family, of course."

"And the same to you. *Au-revoir. A très bientôt*." He put the phone down and found himself smiling. He got up to leave his office, but the telephone rang again. "Allo?"

"*Chéri*, at last! I'm calling from a café."

"*Chérie*, what a surprise!" It was unusual for Tatiana to call. She complained that his phone was always occupied, or how she didn't have any time, for her entire day was always taken up with procuring food.

"Stop pulling at my coat, Jeanne!"

125

"There's nothing wrong, darling, is there?" Daniel said, noticing Tatiana's rising tone.

"No – should there be?"

Daniel fell into his chair.

"Oh please," he heard, "please, please, can I speak to Papa."

Daniel felt the pull now of his daughter. "Pass her to me, *chérie*."

Tatiana sighed. "Maman hasn't much time, Jeanne."

"Papa!" Jeanne said in her high, breathless voice.

"*Bonjour, ma poulette*. Did you like the drawing of you and Béatrice in the garden, chasing butterflies?"

"Yes, Papa. But that was ages ago!" There was a pause. "Is it really a big garden, Papa?"

"Yes, very big. Like a park. You and Béa will love it."

"But will you play with me, Papa?"

"Of course, *ma poulette*."

"But when?"

Daniel heard whispering and the receiver move. "Soon, *ma poulette*."

"Yippee! Béatrice can stand now, Papa."

The telephone line started to click.

Tatiana came on the line. "Did you mean it?"

"*Chérie*," he paused. "Come the Spring. In April…"

"April, oh," she said, flatly.

"But I'll be up for Christmas, you know that…"

"Yes – I know that." Her voice had dropped.

"So, tell me what I've missed in Paris?"

She paused. "Jeanne. Go and sit there, will you." Tatiana seemed to lean into the receiver. "There was a demonstration at the Arc de Triomphe on Armistice day."

"Oh!" he said, fully aware that the German authorities had banned all public demonstrations.

"Schoolchildren, students and their professors laid a wreath in the shape of the Cross of Lorraine at the Tomb of the Unknown Soldier. Some shouted 'Long live De Gaulle'."

"Ah, De Gaulle." The Maréchal had put a price on the younger general's head, but Daniel couldn't help admiring the fellow. All alone in London, planning something. *I am sure he and Pétain are in secret talks. They are both patriots.*

"Dan. Are you listening?"

"Of course, *chérie*…"

"The demonstration included all sorts of people, thousands of them."

Daniel felt a fury take over. She was talking as if she'd been there. "Tatiana, you weren't present… You know the dangers…!"

"Of course not. Father saw some of it."

Daniel gripped the receiver hard.

A self-consciousness crept into Tatiana's voice. "He was there having a drink with Sacha."

"In Fouquets!"

"Yes," she said, defiantly. And eager to goad him, no doubt, she continued, "The Wehrmacht made arrests. Sacha tells us that some boys and their teachers have been beaten in prison. It's terrible!"

Daniel tempered his tone. "Yes, *pauvres gars*. But keep away from Sacha, Tatiana. Fouquets is full of German officers."

There was a pause.

"Jeanne wants to say goodbye to you. Goodbye," she said, crisply.

By the time he put the receiver down he regretted ever having taken the call.

CHAPTER TWENTY-THREE

Daniel leapt up the narrow winding staircase and banged on the door. From behind it rose a high, familiar laugh, and the door flew open.

"Dan!" Tatiana's red lips curved into a smile. She stepped back to display a new dark, belted dress that accentuated her slim waist and womanly curves, which had, nevertheless, hardened since rationing. Behind her, baby Béatrice had been strapped into a chair with a teacloth and was being fed by grandmother Elisabeta.

Daniel bent to kiss his wife, fighting the urge to pick her up in his arms and crush her against his chest.

"Papa!" Jeanne was tugging at his trousers. Drawing away from Tatiana, he picked up his wriggling daughter, whose legs had lengthened noticeably. Her hair had the smell of an excited puppy.

"Papa!" Jeanne's arms encircled his neck. "Papa! Papa!"

"Hungry, Daniel?" Elisabeta said, looking up from feeding Béatrice. On the stove she and Tatiana had prepared a borscht. He wondered how many ration tickets they had used up to prepare this feast. He frowned, as instinctively and logically the trail seemed to lead back to the one person capable of bestowing them with such a thing.

"It smells delicious, Elisabeta," he replied, careful not to show his displeasure.

Jeanne spread her hands across his brow and kissed the bridge of his nose.

"Dan, sit down," Tatiana said, shutting the door. "Jeanne, let Papa sit."

"Aww, Mama."

"It's alright, *chérie*." Daniel knew it would be impossible to loosen Jeanne's limpet-hold. She slid onto his lap at table and they watched Elisabeta feed Béatrice. Béatrice pushed the spoon of oatmeal away and fixed him with her dark brown eyes.

Daniel smiled. "*Allez ma petite.*"

"Yes, come on, Béatrice!" Elisabeta echoed, looking visibly distressed. His mother-in-law could never rest until every scrap of food had been eaten from the plate. Tatiana's childhood had been tainted by her mother hovering over her. Only when a chicken bone had been stripped clean, she'd told Daniel when they were first courting, would her mother return to her own paltry portion of food. Their guilt about their parents was one of the many things that bound them.

Béatrice continued to stare at him whilst her grandmother shovelled food into her increasingly reluctant mouth.

"Papa. Have you got some chocolate?" Jeanne said, looking up at him imploringly.

"Really, Jeanne!" Tatiana said, her smile leaving her.

"*Non, ma poulette*," said Daniel, giving her a squeeze. He stopped as he felt her bones. "But you'll see when you come down to Fort Girard, Chef will find you good things to eat. He has a big kitchen with big cooking pots like this." He stretched out his long arms across the width of the galley kitchen and watched his daughter's eyes widen and shine.

"There'll be lots and lots of food," she said, jumping out of Daniel's lap and skipping around the tiny kitchen.

Elisabeta smiled sadly. Tatiana let out a sigh.

There was a knock at the door.

"Ah, that must be Papa," Tatiana said, a little warily. She always put on that tone when Daniel and his father-in-law were around one another.

She went to the door and let Alexandre in. He had a high colour on him and the satisfied look of someone who had been royally entertained. *Well at least he's in good humour.*

"Daniel," he said, pulling a bottle of Stolichnya from under his coat.

Tatiana shut the door firmly and strode back to the kitchen, where borscht was boiling too rapidly. She moved it off the stove.

"Dedushka." Jeanne dipped her hand into her grandfather's

pocket.

Alexandre gave her a crafty smile. His eyes had that alcoholic glaze. Fouquet's again, the Shéhérazade (too early perhaps), but all pointed to Sacha's munificence. Alexandre fished out a tablet of fragrant dark chocolate and sniffed it ostentatiously.

Daniel frowned and scrutinised Tatiana, who refused to look up from her stirring.

"Dinner is ready. Papa. Jeanne, help *Babushka* lay the table. Put that chocolate aside for later!"

Jeanne inhaled the tablet in turn, then slammed it down on the table.

Béatrice jumped.

"You frightened your sister," Tatiana said, wiping her apron.

Béatrice started to cry. Before his wife could reach her, Daniel untied her and carried her over to the other side of the apartment, to the worn sofa in the sitting room, next to the newly lit wood-burning stove. Béatrice started to calm, giving out a snuffled whimper. Daniel removed his handkerchief and gently wiped away a salty tear that still glistened on her cheek. She arched her back nevertheless and started to call out for her mother.

Defeated, Daniel returned to the kitchen to find Elisabeta and Tatiana ladling out the borscht.

Alexandre was giving him a wry smile. "How are things at Fort Girard?" he asked, pouring out two glasses of vodka and handing him one.

"Good," Daniel said, eyeing the vodka and wishing once again that it was a cold beer. "It's taken a while to make the house habitable." Alexandre was giving him that inscrutable look of his, so he added quickly, "But now we have heating and hot water."

"Hmm – and all those young boys. No trouble with them?"

"We are a close-knit community. They're settling. And they'll be learning a trade. The workshops will be starting after Christmas."

Alexandre nodded gravely. "We see those German recruitment posters all around Paris luring them to Germany. Good wages I hear. Much better than..."

Daniel flinched. "Yes. But at Fort Girard, the boys are in France, where they want to be."

"Of course." Alexandre downed his vodka.

Tatiana laid a plate of steaming borsch before her father, then Daniel. Béatrice reached out her dimpled hand and tried to take

Daniel's spoon. Daniel spotted her own little spoon still on the table. He kissed the light brown curls sprouting on top of her head.

"Papa, can we go on the donkeys at the Champs de Mars tomorrow?"

"We will see, Jeanette."

"Will Dedushka and Baboushska be coming with us to Fort Girard?"

Tatiana came to the table with the remaining plates. "No, Jeanne. I've already told you. Dedushka and Baboushska are staying here to look after rue de Grenelle. We can write to them and we'll be back, don't worry."

"And in the meantime, my little Jeannska," said Alexandre, patting her hand, "Baboushska and I will be thinking of you in that garden. If you see any roses, I'd like you to draw me one. Will you do that for me?"

"Yes, Dedushka."

Tatiana had often spoken of Alexandre's magnificent rose garden in Vladicaucase, Georgia. He'd had them brought in from all over the world.

The mention of roses had Daniel thinking back to the Ardennes. That day in Vouziers when he, Hervé and his men had planted the rose bushes. Seven months ago. He preferred to forget those shameful things.

After dinner they sat around the radio to listen to the Maréchal's Christmas speech:

"*My dear friends, it's not midnight yet, but already some of you have started to celebrate. For the majority of us, Christmas will be a sad affair. In many households there are empty seats around the family table, where once loved ones would have sat. Many who were celebrating joyously last year during their leave will never return. May our first thoughts be with them: they saved France's honour.*

"*Others are waiting, far away from you, as prisoners on foreign soil. Perhaps they'll be lovingly unwrapping the parcel you have sent them. Never, in their exile, will they have felt closer to you.*

"*I think of those also, tonight, who are suffering. Those who have no logs or coal for the fire. Those who have heard that it's Christmas Eve but who don't know what they will eat tomorrow.*

Children who won't find any presents in their shoes. Refugees who will no longer hear their village bell ring."

Jeanne, who had been playing with a doll, got up and ran through to the kitchen, where a few squares of chocolate remained on a plate. Feeling blessed and surrounded by his family, Daniel forgot Sacha's intrusion into their family affairs. He watched Alexandre and Elisabeta on the sofa; Elisabeta's eyes welled with tears. So many relatives left behind in Tiblisi and Leningrad. Alexandre too, his mouth drooping, was no doubt regretting his beautiful garden, his stables with his thoroughbreds, the oil fields he had had to abandon in Baku. The Nazi-Soviet pact had been the final nail for their hopes of ever returning. His father-in-law's red-rimmed eyes closed.

"My dear children, Christmas, don't forget, is the night of hope, it's a celebration of the Nativity. A new France is born. This France is made up of your sufferings, your regrets, your sacrifices…

"My friends. Trust. Be courageous. Be sure to put all your energies into creating this renaissance, so that your children are able to experience once more the joy of Christmas. Gather around me tonight, and let this France, the new France, grow and become stronger."

Daniel felt a little hand land gently on his fist. He had forgotten about Béa in his lap. He unfurled her little hand and kissed the perfect little nails.

"Soon, you will see the star shine marking out your destiny. Bon Noel, mes enfants, et vive la France!"

Paris, like the rest of France, had embarked upon a harsh winter. Trying to save on their dwindling fuel supplies, Daniel and Tatiana took their daughters with them to bed at night, and by day trudged along the Champ de Mars, carpeted in white, bulked up with sweaters, stockings and heavy coats. They would stare enviously at the elegant women walking out of their heated apartments along the stretch, buried in their furs and woollen hats, walking their little dogs.

On New Year's Eve, Daniel declined mass at the Russian church at the rue Daru and went to order a longed-for beer at the café opposite. A customer was reading a newspaper at the next table: 'London and Liverpool targeted again by the German Luftwaffe.'

Nursing his drink, he recalled the British troops in Champagne during the Great War. They had been part of a communications unit that had pitched their tents in a village neighbouring his uncle's farm. In impeccable uniform, the men had sat on fold-out chairs, cheerfully chatting over endless cups of tea and biscuits, whilst their radio bleeped happily between them. The café had, by contrast, been filled with his sullen countrymen, getting drunk on bad wine and cheap spirits. Theirs had seemed a darker, less predictable world. He was only a boy then, but that image had stayed with him.

And yet his love affair with the British had been severely tested in July, when he had been waiting to demobilise. Twelve hundred French marines had been massacred at Mer El Kabir by the British! What a mess it all was! Still, now the British were having their fair share of suffering again – nothing justified bombing civilians.

He stared up at the frozen Paris sky and vowed to take his little family away before April.

CHAPTER TWENTY-FOUR

"Bonsoir, les gars." Jean Riou lifted his right arm to bid them all goodnight, his left sleeve flapping loosely at his side. The decorated Sub-Lieutenant from the Colonial Infantry had lost his arm fighting for their country the year before.

Since January of that year, Riou, delegate from the Sully Committee for the region of Orleans, had been a regular visitor. Daniel had warmed to him from their very first meeting, finding his gentle, understanding manner and natural authority of great comfort.

"Bonsoir," the boys replied in unison, stacking the tin cups and plates they had brought for the fireside dinner.

Daniel and Riou set off along the woodland path, Daniel leading the way with the lantern. Daniel looked up at the grand old house, with its closed shutters and roof rearing up into the night sky. It almost had a foreboding aspect tonight. A little yellow light, however, glowed in the hallway entrance, beckoning them. Tatiana had left it on for them.

Daniel inhaled the evening air greedily. They had entered a spring of mild evenings, where it felt good to be alive. And what a heartening couple of hours they had spent with the boys, in the bosom of the forest, around a fire, with only the ancient trees and star-studded heavens to watch over them. It made Daniel feel warm inside to think of these young people, and others like them, growing healthy and strong, in other centres like Fort Girard, working alongside each other, supporting each other, away from the negativity and cynicism reigning in the towns. For what had started as a tiny movement, Riou told him, was now succeeding elsewhere in the region. Life could be simple if man wanted it to be so.

Riou stopped next to him. "Ah," he said, in the darkness. "How good it was to hear the boys sing with all their hearts this evening."

Daniel nodded and smiled. Riou had often commented on the spirit of his centre.

Riou walked up the steps, slowing as he reached the terrace. His head was bowed. He seemed preoccupied. Turning suddenly, he made his way back to the balustrade. "Come here a moment, Daniel. I have a favour to ask of you."

Riou wasn't the sort to seek help; he usually dispensed it, from their very first meeting after Christmas, when he had assuaged Daniel's fears of having done wrong with Pierre Roupp.

"Something snapped inside of me. I had to hit him," he had said, shaking his head. "Lead by example they told us at Sillery. Not much of an example."

"Don't trouble yourself, Daniel," Riou had said, smiling. "It obviously worked. Roupp is spirited but respects you. As do the rest of the boys."

Riou rested his hand on Daniel's shoulder. His eyes burned with a fervour Daniel had not seen before. "I'd like you take three boys. Three brothers. The youngest is fourteen. I know, a little young..."

"Juvenile courts?"

"No," Riou replied, guardedly. "There's been a raid in the Jewish quarter, in the eleventh district in Paris."

"Oh, I see." Daniel sucked in the freshening air. He had been aware of the denaturalisation laws targeting foreign Jews the year before, of them being repatriated to other lands.

"If you take these boys, I'll take care of the rest, their papers. All you have to do is hold them for a while, until we find them safe passage."

Daniel ran his hand over his brow. Tatiana was inside, waiting for him.

"Look Daniel, I know you're worrying about your family and the centre. Don't think I haven't thought about that. But just think, Fort Girard is remote."

Daniel looked up at him. Everything he had built here, all could be lost if the Nazis found these boys.

"If your answer is no, I will understand. I too have a family, as you know. I haven't taken this decision lightly and nor did the man before me, who spoke to me of these boys."

Daniel nodded. "Of course," he said, hoarsely.

"I know I can trust you to say nothing of this to Tatiana."

Daniel continued to nod. How many times had he sworn to her that he wouldn't keep anything of importance from her?

"I'll turn in now. Sleep on it." He gave him an understanding smile. "If you can."

Daniel let him enter the house and heard Tatiana bidding Riou goodnight in that happy singsong voice she had had since coming to Fort Girard.

She had settled down almost immediately; she had colour in her cheeks now that she cycled in the sunshine every week, going to the neighbouring farms to prepare food parcels for both their families in Paris. She'd been horrified by a notice in the papers warning people not to eat cats as they fed on disease-ridden rats. She had found a woman in Ville-aux-Clercs to watch over Béa and Jeanne for a couple of hours, and at the end of this week, she'd hand over the brown parcels wrapped in string to him with a look of satisfied pride.

Her contentment was also a result of news that she was four months pregnant. They would tell no one until she was showing.

Voices were now coming from the forest. Daniel turned and watched the boys, swinging rucksacks and lanterns, come down the middle of the lawn.

Daniel waved to them and stepped into the house, where Tatiana was waiting for him, smiling, at the foot of the stairs.

CHAPTER TWENTY-FIVE

His nerves worn thin from a night of interrupted sleep, Daniel descended the central stair, hoping to take breakfast in peace, for he was in no mood for idle chatter with either the boys or staff. Knowing their routines so perfectly, he had timed it to the second – the boys were now filing out of the refectory on the Sunday timetable, two hours later than the weekday. Bouillot, taking up the rear, was nevertheless rubbing his eyes and looking paler than usual. He saw Daniel and waved the boys on.

"See you down here in five minutes," he shouted up at Cintract and Labarre, bounding up the stairs two by two. Were the balmier breezes blowing in through the open door putting a sudden spring in their step?

Whatever it was, Daniel was glad they were going out, as he longed for the house to empty, to ruminate on Riou's request. It had been a busy night on the dormitories due to Vilon's night wanderings. Bouillot's heavy tread past their bedroom hadn't helped matters. Tatiana, he hoped, would remain resting upstairs with his daughters, who had awoken and drifted into their bed.

"Sorry about that racket last night, *boss*. Vilon was up in the attic this time."

"I know. I heard." He hovered impatiently. He really hadn't wanted to discuss Vilon this morning.

"I'll let you get on," Bouillot said, rubbing and scratching his muscly arm, which he was inclined to do when agitated.

"This morning, Lefèbvre, Vic and I are taking the boys down to the lake for a swim and some fishing, seeing as the weather is clearing. And Vilon is coming with us this time. No more hanging around Mademoiselle Laviolle and getting dispensations. I know she means well, but that kid has to learn to take part."

"Very good, very good," Daniel said, now taking a step towards the refectory.

He had honestly tried. They all had. If only the boy weren't so tongue-tied and unreceptive. Vilon had flinched the other day when Daniel tried to give him an encouraging pat on the shoulder as he opened a letter from home. Hailing from Ivry, the only child of an alcoholic mother, life had not been kind to him. But he wasn't the only boy to have suffered at Fort Girard. Unlike the others, however, he was finding it difficult to make friends, preferring to hang around Mlle Laviolle's infirmary with his fictitious diseases.

Daniel filled his bowl with an ersatz coffee, cut himself a thick slice of home-baked black bread and took his platter over to his office. He closed the door behind him. Out of the window, he saw the first cohort of boys and staff work their way across the terrace, down the central steps, across the lawn. Cintract, lagging behind, was nudging Labarre. But why were all of them looking so overladen? Vic had a stepladder and Lefèbvre, who had just appeared, was carrying several side tables. Perhaps they had an errand to run along the way.

As the hubbub faded, he raised the bowl and drained the coffee in one. Then he buried his head in his hands. Tatiana, the girls. The last thing he wanted to do was upset their lives. They had had to cope with enough upheaval in the past year and were only just beginning to settle. And yet Tatiana would never want those young brothers to suffer, she and Vladimir knew what it was like to be on the run, to live in fear for your life. They had Jewish friends. The Klugs. They owed so much to Albert Klug. But weren't these young boys a separate issue?

He sighed heavily. *If caught harbouring Jews I'll go to prison. Bouillot, Lefèbvre, and Vic will lose their jobs, as the centre could be shut. One hundred boys turfed out into the street for the sake of three.*

No! He let out a cry and clasped his ears. He stared down at his cluttered desk, at his 1941 calendar with the Maréchal. To think that Pétain had come down on the side of Dreyfus as a young man. Had the Germans forced his hand on Jewish issues? How were Jews surviving now that they couldn't work? He couldn't remember whether Albert had been naturalised or not. But these young brothers were fending for themselves. Imagine how frightened they were. How desperate their parents were, to want to be separated from them.

The doorknob turned. Tatiana walked in, carrying Béa on her hip. Jeanne let go of her hand and ran over to Daniel.

"Papa, can I come with you to the lake?"

She must have heard the boys talking upstairs. Jeanne had become the boys' mascot. Cintract indulged her, laughed when she marched alongside them, waving a stick around as she imagined a commander would do. She insisted that they play with her on their days off, and if Cintract wasn't to hand, Labarre was there to keep an eye on her. He'd made her a little stool so she could sit and watch their games of football. They called her *Chefette* and joked that it was she, not Daniel, who kept them all in check.

He felt himself frown. He didn't like refusing her.

"*Non, ma poulette,*" he said, arranging the nearest papers on his desk. "Papa is busy, but…"

"We'll come back in an hour when you'll have finished?" Tatiana said, eyeing him carefully, before leading Jeanne out of the office.

An hour and a half later, Daniel was cycling down the forest path with Jeanne on the handlebars. He had finally given in to Tatiana and was glad of it as he gradually surrendered to the beauty of the day.

The sun's rays filtered down through the high conifers onto their faces, bathing them in a dappled light. With half-closed eyes he listened to the whirring sound of wheels and dead pine needles crackling beneath them. For a time, in the depths of the forest, he, Jeanne, the bicycle, trees and sun melded into one.

"Faster," Jeanne cried, gripping his hands.

Her legs had grown longer, slender and more athletic. A diet of fresh air and nourishing food had brought her back from the gauntness he had witnessed when she'd first arrived. Sacha's chocolate had not been enough – how relieved he was to have her with him again. He leant forward and felt her hair brush his forehead. It was lush and shiny, like Tatiana's.

They'd reached a clearing and rode along a country road, following the Gratte-Loup river, which flowed into the lake they were heading for, a popular resort for the region.

"There it is, Papa!"

Villagers from the Ville-aux-Clercs had come out to walk along its grassy shores, bordered with bulrushes. A lone, white-haired individual was swimming in its chilled waters with his dog. A group of mothers and children watched him as they picnicked under a weeping willow. Further on, some men had got out their fishing rods and were fishing from a jetty.

Jeanne's face fell. "Papa! They're not here."

"Of course they're here." How could one hundred boys disappear, along with his staff? There was a logical explanation, surely.

They circled the entire lake and dismounted again.

"I'm sorry, my *poulette*!"

"Aw!" She stamped her foot.

"Why don't we go home and see if Chef has baked something. Or maybe you can help him?"

Jeanne looked up at him and gave him a toothy smile. She had lost her two front milk teeth. He got back on the bike with her and sped back to Fort Girard.

Daniel watched the hands of the clock go round for the entire afternoon. At five o'clock he was greatly relieved to hear excited voices in the hall. Stood there with his hands behind his back, he waited for his senior leaders, Bouillot and Lefèbvre, to step in. He wasn't exactly angry, but he couldn't understand the subterfuge. Where had they been?

He'd feared the worst: imprisonment. Ridiculous! The *fritz* were confined to the towns – Vendôme was twenty minutes away by car. There were only so many troops at Hitler's disposal to spread over the Occupied Zone. They had better things to do.

Bouillot and Lefèbvre stepped in sheepishly.

"Where were you?" Daniel softened his brusqueness with a smile.

Jeanne emerged from the kitchen eating a biscuit and ran over to Cintract. "Papa and I looked for you everywhere."

Cintract picked her up and threw her in the air. "You can't go everywhere with us, madam! And I see you've been baking. I hope you've got some left for later."

She munched into her biscuit and offered him the final crumb.

Cintract laughed. "No, it's alright." He put her down.

Daniel brought her to his side, impatiently. He wasn't happy with his daughter's behaviour, but Vic, who had been taking up the rear of the party, made his way to the front. Bouillot waited until he came alongside him and Lefèbvre to speak.

"Well, *Chef*, our little *Chefette* has rumbled us."

"Oh?" Daniel said, relieved that he was going to get an explanation.

Bouillot, Lefèbvre, Vic and the boys exchanged amused looks.

Bouillot spoke. "Seeing as you have a growing family here, *Chef*." Word had obviously got around that Tatiana was expecting; Jeanne had probably let slip that they were waiting for a little brother. "We thought you would need a little more privacy. We've found this little house farther on, past the lake. With three bedrooms. Thought it would suit you."

"But," said Daniel, "there's no reason… and besides, it's not ours."

Bouillot shook his head. "Lefèbvre and I have already organised everything with the mayor. It's empty. The owner is abroad. The boys and I have cleaned it up, put a few sticks of furniture in. We were going to deliver the beds in the morning and take you over there."

"Stop. Stop!" Daniel lifted his arms.

"Dan, what are you saying?" Tatiana had just come down the stairs with Béa. Béa was holding onto a pale yellow and blue bunny rabbit, a soft toy that Mlle Laviolle had crocheted for her with spare wool.

"Bouillot," Tatiana said, smiling. "I couldn't help overhearing. How thoughtful of you all. We are most grateful for what you have done here. Aren't we, Dan?" She took his hand and beamed at them all.

"Of course we are," Daniel said, flushing with conflicting emotions. "How long has this been going on?"

"The past month. The forestry has suffered a bit," said Bouillot, giving them a lopsided grin.

"Thank you all," Daniel said, feeling his throat tighten. The best part was watching the boys faces, their happiness. The workshops and barracks with extra dorms had been built around the back of the house by their own hands too. *If they can do all of this, the war is not lost.*

He watched the boys file past, up the stairs, and suddenly resolved to call Riou Monday morning. *This is a busy establishment*, he told himself. *If Bouillot and one hundred boys can disappear so easily under my watch, three brothers will be able to. The land and forests are our cover. The Sully Committee set it up that way. It will be like searching for a needle in a haystack.*

CHAPTER TWENTY-SIX

Albert Klug was tapping his account book with his pencil.

"Daniel," he said, pushing the books aside. "I don't know how long we can go on like this."

Daniel awoke with a start. In deep sleep next to him, Tatiana barely stirred. From across the room came a tap-tapping at the window. Daniel got up and quietly went to open it. Just as he'd thought – the pear tree branches he kept meaning to chop back. He broke off a few with his fingers and threw them down onto the lawn below.

The sun was beginning to creep over his garden wall. A fresh breeze came through the window, brushing his cheeks. What could he do? Nothing until Klug got in touch. And in the meantime, Riou's associate would be dropping off his precious new charges that morning, when everyone else was at forestry – the time to acquaint himself quickly with the young men, he thought, direct them to hide away their personal possessions and their identities, and then on into lunch when the others were back. He would leave them with Lefèbvre and Vic thereafter.

He scooped his clothes up from the chair and dressed in the sitting room. Shaved and clean, he slipped out of the house and hopped onto his bike.

Riou had called him that week, not only to discuss the brothers.

"Daniel, now that the forge, the workshops and the barracks are near to completion at Fort Girard, the Ministry of Youth and Education has sent a memo asking us to form better relations with the villages in the region. You are now looking for would-be employers, as you know. Like gold dust in this present climate. We need them to see the boys at work."

"Yes of course. How do you propose we lure them in?"

"Mid-summer is approaching."

"I see what you're getting at. We have the perfect garden for holding a country fête."

"Exactly! Invite the boys' parents down from Paris, a few local dignitaries, employers, farmers and such-like. And the local press."

"But I thought we had to keep a low profile?"

"Yes and no." Riou paused. "We hide certain of our activities but show the ones that are likely to please the local population and not ruffle the *fritz's* feathers, in the unlikely event that they were to show up. We are a community-spirited establishment, our boys are well-disciplined, not would-be terrorists. Ever since that student demonstration last November in Paris, they've been jittery."

"Of course."

Riou hadn't even broached the subject of the Jewish boys. But perhaps he was right not to pay them any special attention.

Riou had rung to confirm the boys' arrival before lunch. By the time Daniel reached Fort Girard, he became nervous. Daniel passed by the infirmary and found Mlle Laviolle drawing up an inventory of medicines and dressings.

"*Bonjour*, Monsieur Frey." She was the only one not to address him by his Christian name.

"*Bonjour*, Mademoiselle Laviolle. It's quiet. I forgot to tell you yesterday, we have three brothers joining Fort Girard today. Name of…" Daniel hesitated. He knew their birth name: 'Bernstein'. "Let me get this right: Claude, Michel, and Joseph. Joseph is the youngest."

"Oh, good." Mlle Laviolle's keen blue eyes, however, looked at him quizzically. "But I didn't think we had any room left?"

"We have now that Tatiana, the girls and I have moved out. I've asked Bouillot to extend the dorm."

"Of course. How is Jeanne?"

"Moaning about not being able to play with the boys."

Mlle Laviolle laughed. "And Béa?"

"Inseparable from her bunny."

Mlle Laviolle flushed with happiness, leaving Daniel to proceed towards his office. He stepped in, was just about to swing the door shut when he heard Bouillot's heavy tread across the hall.

Daniel led him into his office and shut the door. Before Bouillot could open his mouth with his concerns, Daniel sat him down and proceeded with his own.

"I've decided to hold a big fête in our gardens for mid-summer. Invite the village, the boys' parents if they can make it, a few dignitaries, employers, etc."

"Alright, *boss.*"

"I'd like you and the boys to construct a small stage for the entertainment."

Bouillot frowned. "*Chef*, I thought we were keeping ourselves to ourselves."

"We were. Certain things will of course remain hush hush, like the raising of the colours. But now Paris is giving out the message that we've nothing to hide, that, on the contrary, we've got a contribution to make to the village and its people. I thought we'd organise a tombola for the prisoners. Send the boys to the village for contributions. A pot of jam here, *rillettes* there. All is welcome. The boys can pick up the donations the day before, so nothing goes off."

"Alright, boss." Bouillot was fidgeting.

"Is there something wrong, Bouillot?"

"No, sorry, I'm listening. But it's just that when we were out in the forest just now, I saw Vilon rushing off towards the house."

"Oh!" Couldn't they go one day without Vilon putting a spanner in the works?

Mlle Laviolle stepped into Daniel's office. "Vilon's hurtling up the stairs. I called out to him but he's not answering."

Daniel marched quickly out of his office, followed by his deputy. The noise of a door slamming several floors up made them break into a run.

"Vilon?" they shouted. His dorm was empty and still.

They rushed back to the little staircase up to the attic. Daniel mounted the steps two by two, fury pumping through his chest. At the top of them he peered into the attic's dim interior. Packing cases, spare furniture had been stacked in the middle of the room. Through the dimness, sunlight slanted through a little window at the end, where dust motes swirled.

Daniel rushed to the window. Narrowing his eyes, he leaned out and inspected the bare, sloping roof.

Merde! He couldn't have. Daniel glimpsed the tip of the dark sequoia and felt physically sick. A whimper made him turn to the right. There a crumpled, terrified boy clung onto the base of the chimney. He had slid down the *ardoise* tiles and caught it just in time. One foot dangled over the void, the other was wedged in the guttering.

"*Mon gars. Ne bouge-pas!*"

White-faced, his cheek pressed against the brick, Vilon twisted round. There were voices coming from down below. Daniel distinguished Vic's young, treble tones.

Daniel turned to Bouillot. "Get me some rope. Anything!"

Bouillot retreated into the room. Daniel focused on Vilon's desperate face, his wild, wide-eyed terror.

"We're coming to get you, son." The words sounded hollow, but to speak was to hold him there.

"No!" Vilon cried out hoarsely. "Never!" He wobbled, screwing his eyes shut.

Daniel half-turned to Boullot. "Quick! He doesn't know what he's doing."

"Boss. I've some harnesses. Around these trunks here."

"Hurry!" Daniel said, through clenched teeth. He hoisted himself through the window. Half out of it, he forced himself to smile. "It's alright, *mon gars.*"

Vilon buried his whole face in the chimney. Slowly, pushing with his arms, Daniel forced the rest of his body out of the tiny window. He heard Bouillot's steps.

"Now, *mon petit gars* – you stay right there. We'll get you up as soon as we can. Just don't move – do you understand?"

"Noooo. It's no use!" Vilon wailed.

"Boss, the harnesses won't work. They're rotten!"

Daniel took a deep breath to control his rising panic. What had they done in Morocco, when a soldier had fallen off his horse in the Atlas Mountains? He had fallen onto a ledge. They didn't have rope.

"Our belts," he said, turning. "Take yours off and attach it to mine. Quick!" Daniel dropped his gaze for one second as he unbuckled himself – there was a sudden scrabbling sound.

"Christ!" Bouillot exclaimed. "Let me go down, *boss.*"

"No!"

Bouillot could be relied upon for arm strength. He always won arm wrestles with Vic. Now he grasped Daniel's wrist and slowly eased him down. Daniel gripped the belt which Bouillot held in the other hand, which they used to let him swing over to the right, alongside Vilon.

Daniel's left boot engaged with the guttering. Bouillot was half-out of the window now. Daniel swung towards Vilon and lunged. Just as Vilon pulled away from the chimney, Daniel managed to grasp him. "Got you!"

For what seemed an eternity, Daniel shut his eyes and tried not to think of the lawn. Of Vilon's broken body splayed out on the terrace below. Of the scandal. Of the resentment he felt towards this boy.

"Here!!" It was Vic, leaning out from the window with a coil of rope.

Daniel felt Vilon struggle beneath him. He grasped the chimney with both hands.

"Vilon, I'm holding on to you. Now reach out for the rope, do you hear?"

The boy stretched out his feeble arm. Vic took aim and threw the rope accurately, but it fell short of Vilon's hand. Vilon broke out into convulsive sobs. Vic quickly retrieved the rope and aimed it at Daniel. Daniel let go of one side of the chimney and snatched it. He tied it around Vilon's middle before the young man could wriggle out of it.

"Now listen, *mon petit gars* – you're going up, do you hear? See, there's Vic."

Vic threw down a smile of encouragement. "Vilon, *mon gars*."

Daniel gave him a shove. "Come on, Vilon. You can do it. Ready now. *Un, deux, trois… Oh, hisse!*" He pushed him up as his colleagues pulled. The angle was awkward. The boy was in freefall for a second, but his shriek was cut short by the sounds of Bouillot and Vic hoisting him to safety. Daniel closed his eyes and held the chimney tight.

"Boss. Catch!"

Seconds later, Bouillot was grasping him by the back of his shirt and hoisting him through to safety.

Giddy with the effort, Daniel stood, unsteadily. Vic was already leading Vilon down the stairs.

"To my office," he called out after them, and Vic nodded and led the lad out of harm's way.

In the office, he and Bouillot parked their chairs in a triangle, Vilon in the middle. Daniel didn't want to be at his desk for this. Vilon flopped listlessly in his chair, his head bent.

There was a knock on the door. Vic came in with a few vitamin biscuits from the kitchen.

Vilon looked up slowly.

"Take one," Daniel said, gently.

Vilon peered down at the plate. His lips quivered, his nose ran. He shook his head, started to cry, wiped his eyes, his nose on his sleeve.

Daniel put the plate aside. "Alright. Thanks, Vic."

"By the way, boss," Vic said, cheerfully, ostensibly back to his usual engaging self, "a car has pulled up in the forecourt. Those three boys you said were coming – shall I take them to the kitchen?"

He had forgotten completely! Daniel stole a glance at Vilon, who hung his head and sniffed.

"Just a moment, son."

He came out to the forecourt with Vic. Three sallow-faced youths in crumpled coats, two dark, the youngest fair, emerged from the car warily. The eldest, a grave-looking young man, shook his hand. Daniel turned to all of them, wishing to proceed without delay.

"I'm Daniel Frey. I run the centre here. This is Vic."

The boys warily moved their gazes to Vic. Vic smiled and shook their hands.

"Vic will take you to the Chef. You can have a glass of milk with something to eat. Keep you going until lunch. Now, will you excuse me? I'll leave you in Vic's hands."

He smiled once again, watched Vic usher them away, and stepped back into his office.

Bouillot had got his handkerchief out for Vilon. The boy's chest was still heaving. His jacket sleeve had worn thin at the elbow.

"*Mon gars.*" Daniel leaned forward. "What is it?"

Vilon buried his face in his hands.

"How can we help you, son? No one likes to see you like this." Daniel felt a little disingenuous as he sat there. He'd found it hard to grow attached to the boy. "Do you miss your mother? We could arrange…"

Vilon looked alarmed. He gripped both sides of the chair.

Stupid question – his mother an alcoholic from Ivry outside Paris. But I need to get to the bottom of it. "What is it?"

"She gave Max away!"

Daniel continued gently. "Who is Max, Vilon?"

Vilon wiped his eyes on Boillot's handkerchief. "My dog."

"Oh! But your mother had a reason to," Daniel said, encouraged by this scenario. "Probably gave him to a good home…"

The boy fell forward into his lap and cried uncontrollably. Daniel patted his matted hair, ever so lightly.

"It's alright, Vilon. Alright." The boy looked up again, this time more trustingly. "Sit up, son, will you?"

Vilon raised his heavy head, tried to open his half-closed lids, swollen with crying.

"I want you to come with Bouillot and me."

Bouillot, without betraying his surprise, got up and went to open the door.

"Come on, son," Bouillot said, wearily, "let's follow the boss."

Vilon shook his head. "I don't want to. They'll all be looking at me."

"Not where we're going."

Vilon looked alarmed.

"Don't be frightened, we're off to the fields." Daniel took his arm and, with Bouillot, slipped out the back of the house.

Having crossed a woodland, they came out onto fields. In a corner, Ulysses was drinking from a trough. Daniel swung open the gate and called him. The old workhorse raised his head and plodded over, water dripping from his muzzle.

Vilon stepped back nervously.

"It's alright," Daniel said. "See, he likes you. He's a workhorse. He's used to humans."

As Ulysses planted himself before them, Vilon looked up at him hesitantly.

"And he's going to like you even more when you feed him." Daniel took the biscuit out of his pocket. He broke off little pieces and laid them in Vilon's clammy palm.

Ulysses let his heavy head drop. Vilon squirmed and started to close his hand.

"Help him a little bit. He won't bite so long as you make it easy for him. Tip your palm forward. Lay it flat. That's it!"

Vilon froze at first, but as Ulysses's soft lips made contact with Vilon's skin he laughed. "He tickles!"

"That's right. See how gentle Ulysses is. Big but gentle. Just like Bouillot!"

Bouillot smiled indulgently as they watched Vilon bury his tear-stained face into the horse's neck.

That evening, on Daniel's orders, Bouillot made up a bunk for Vilon in Ulysses's stable.

CHAPTER TWENTY-SEVEN

Daniel slowly swung the car into the forest track. '*Fête de la St Jean*' had been painted on a sign nailed to a tree. Through the crowd massing around the forest clearing, Daniel spied Cintract talking to a stout countrywoman in a pinafore dress. Two boys left her side and ran into the woods, chasing one another with sticks.

"Bernard, Laurent," she called to the boys. "*Venez ici, tout de suite!*"

"Go on lads, the fête has just started," Daniel said, leaning out of the window. Barely acknowledging his intervention, the boys whipped each other on the thighs with a stick.

"*Je t'ai!*"

"*Je t'ai aussi!*" and they continued headlong into the thickets.

Daniel sighed. He felt Tatiana's slim arm across his shoulder. "All will pass off well, you'll see. Have you got your speech?"

"All here," he said, patting his pocket. He wasn't one for formal speeches but today was an exception. He hoped the mayor, town councillors, and wealthier landowners would dig deep in their pockets for the Red Cross on behalf of the prisoners in Germany.

Labarre came over. "The songsters, the fakir and magician came this morning. Jean Riou has arrived from Orléans, the new Sub-Prefect from Vendôme and that regional delegate from the Ministry of Youth." Labarre searched for the name on his list.

"Pelletier," Daniel said. Good. He liked the man. Straight-talking and decent.

"Sir, Monsieur Pelletier came with someone else – from the

Ministry of Work. He wasn't on the list…"

"Oh?" *What is the Ministry of Work doing here?*

"I didn't catch his name," continued Labarre. "Funny sort. Not very friendly, like. Kept his head down."

Daniel felt his chest tighten. "Probably just a routine call."

Labarre shrugged. "Anyway, nearly out of programmes."

"Good work, *mon gars*. Just make sure everyone knows where to go."

Daniel started up the engine and drove on to the house, where a gleaming, black Citroen was parked in the driveway.

They got out. Béatrice gnawed at her little fist as Tatiana took her in her arms. Jeanne flew to Daniel's side and grasped his hand. As they were making their way round to the garden, they heard a snort and the soft pounding of hooves.

"Ah, Ulysses and Vilon," Daniel declared, revived by the sight of the two of them together. Daniel ran his fingers through the horse's silken mane.

Jeanne let go of Daniel's hand and tried to hug the horse. Unable to reach around it, she patted Ulysses's flank instead. "Lovely horsey."

"He is, isn't he, my little *poulette.*" Daniel ran his hand down Ulysses's smooth, grey-white mottled rump.

Vilon now slept outside the house, in a new facility housing the charcoal ovens. For now, Vilon wasn't just a stable lad but also responsible for monitoring the ovens. Fort Girard now supplied the whole village in charcoal. In exchange, the mayor had allowed Fort Girard to keep enough fuel to run the workshops and the house.

"Can I have a ride, Papa? You said I could."

Daniel turned to Vilon. "Here's your first customer," he said, giving him a few bits of loose change.

Vilon mumbled something close to a 'merci', stuffing the coins into his money belt. He helped Jeanne into the saddle and shortened the stirrups.

"Daniel, are you sure she's not too young?" said Tatiana, carrying Béatrice, who was still chewing her fingers.

Daniel shook his head. He hadn't told Tatiana about Vilon and was glad of it, for he now happily observed Vilon guiding Jeanne with the reins.

Her small hands grasped the reins tightly. She flipped them over, as shown by Vilon.

"*Allez*, Ulysses."

"Look at me, Béa!" Jeanne said, excitedly rocking in the roomy saddle.

However, Béatrice, whose cheeks flushed red, grizzled with teething troubles.

"I'll take her to the sitting room for a while, Dan," Tatiana said. "In the quiet."

"Yes, *chérie*." Daniel kissed her and his baby daughter and continued down the sloping lawn whilst Tatiana veered back up the stone stairs to the terrace, where he had planned to give his speech.

Stalls and sideshows lined the fine lawn, which the boys had spent the past few days mowing. Daniel saw a queue outside the gypsy tent where one of the boys had donned a turban and was telling fortunes. It was surprising, or perhaps not so surprising, to see this number of people putting their destiny in the hands of a young man. Daniel noticed Pelletier, his colleague from the Ministry of Youth, give his wife a few coins for the reading. Beside him a man in his thirties, in a light raincoat and steel-rimmed glasses, was hovering, looking around.

Pelletier looked up and saw Daniel. As if sensing Daniel's unease, he signalled that he and the man were coming over. Daniel was pleased to have taken precautions with the Bernstein brothers. He had sent them to the neighbouring farmer for the day; they'd be back for the bonfire later, under the cover of darkness.

"Afternoon!" Pelletier held his hand out and clapped Daniel on the shoulder. "This is Monsieur Dutourd. He's come down from Paris today to take a look at what we do." Pelletier gave him an apprehensive look.

Daniel shook the stranger's hand. An office clerk's hand.

"Monsieur Frey," the man said, eyeing him.

There was a burst of laughter from the stage nearby. They looked up and saw Pierre Roupp flounce around in a woman's wig and a country dress.

Grateful for the distraction, Daniel started to lead them towards the stage, but Bouillot, accompanied by a man carrying a notebook, stopped them midway. "This is the person you need to speak to."

"Afternoon, Monsieur Frey! We're from the Dêpeche du

Centre. We'd like to take a photograph." Relieved to break free, Daniel made his way through the crowd to the terrace, where the photographer was already taking shots of the grounds below. Seeing Daniel come over, he greeted him and ushered him into position leaning on the balustrade. "One profile, one three-quarter."

Daniel placed his hands on the roughened stone, warmed by the afternoon sun.

The photographer stepped back. "Ready!"

Down below, Daniel saw Pelletier lead the stranger to the tent where Riou was smiling with his wife, who had just emerged from consulting the gypsy. They exchanged greetings, but the stranger looked uncomfortable and spoke little. The ladies were laughing at the rosy, fabricated futures awaiting them. They looked up, pointed in his direction. Riou leant in to whisper to Pelletier, for the stranger was now being accosted by Vic and Lefèbvre selling tickets for the raffle; the first prize, one kilo of boar sausages. The stranger patted his coat pathetically. He hadn't brought any money.

"Monsieur Frey. Do you mind looking into the camera now? We're ready for you."

Daniel turned to the lens and bared his teeth.

CHAPTER TWENTY-EIGHT

Daniel woke with a start and rolled over towards the open window. A soft breeze had entered the room through it, lifting a lace curtain and sending long, quivering shadows across the parquet floor. He stared at them and remembered his dream.

Everyone had been holding hands around the bonfire, singing at the tops of their voices. A man with his hands stuffed in his raincoat pockets stood by a pile of glowing embers. He was speaking to a group of boys, but Daniel couldn't understand what he was saying. Vilon had suddenly burst into sight atop Ulysses, and with a flick of the reins, had disappeared into the forest.

Just a dream. What a day yesterday. Daniel rubbed his forehead. *And what a success the bonfire was, and the day itself. Except. Except…*

Daniel slid out of bed, dressed hurriedly and, foregoing his ersatz coffee, pedalled hard to Fort Girard.

Quarter of an hour later, he was belting up the stone steps, glancing back at the smoking fire in the middle of the grounds. It was the only evidence remaining of the midsummer celebration, for Bouillot, Vic and Lefèbvre had already cleared the area with the boys.

Daniel stepped through the open door. Everyone was at breakfast. A few guffaws came from the refectory.

Daniel slipped quietly into his office and went straight to the telephone.

The telephone rang and rang. A man's impatient voice picked up the receiver. "*Allô. Ici* André Pelletier."

"*Allô.*"

"Ah, Daniel. Thought it might be you." He sighed. "Look, let me assure you I had no idea that minion was coming down from the Works Ministry."

Daniel had thought as much. It was not in Pelletier's interest to lie, but his ignorance in the matter was an added worry.

"Really? Can the Works Ministry now intervene so easily in our affairs?"

"So it seems. It's probably just a fact-finding mission."

"What?"

"I have to concede that I, too, never thought they'd bother to come here. But there's talk of the Nazis wanting manpower, now that they've gone into Russia."

"Of course, the Russians coming over to the Allied cause is most welcome." Daniel paused. "But I thought our boys were out of bounds to them. If I knew that I was inadvertently training them up to go over…"

There was a prolonged silence.

"I'm sorry. I'm just surprised that…"

"That's alright. Maybe it's just routine."

"Routine?" Daniel asked. "Are our centres going to be regularly inspected from now on?"

"Maybe. Maybe not. That guy will probably send his little report to the Ministry of Work, assuring them that our young men are not hooligans and are doing what they're told. That they're presentable and not on the point of running off to cause trouble."

"Hmm…"

"The best we can do at this stage is to seem to cooperate."

"Cooperate!"

"What I mean is…" Pelletier paused. "Give them access to the youth camps. We have no choice anyway. Meanwhile, we get the local employers to pull their socks up and start assuring us of jobs when the first lot of older boys leave us next year."

"Yes, yes." Pelletier wasn't telling him anything new.

They both knew they faced a challenging task. What could local employers offer them other than prolonged apprenticeships? The boys were earning a small stipend at Fort Girard. But their time here was limited. They had already extended their eight-month stay because of the delay in building the workshops.

"Daniel?"

"Yes?"

"Look – I know we're up against it now. Employers are limited and want cheap labour. The Germans, meanwhile, if they decide to start looking for younger recruits, will be proposing hard cash, three times what they could earn here. They'll also be telling the boys their presence in Germany will help release their fathers, their uncles. Workers in exchange for POW's. Bah!"

Daniel felt his mood darken.

"But let's not despair, Daniel. I was impressed by your boys."

"Yes, they're good boys." He wasn't going to give up on them that easily. "One would hope that the work we do here, the values we encourage, the friendships they have forged, will dissuade them..." He wanted to say, 'from betraying their country' but that was unfair.

"Yes, of course. So now let's concentrate on those French employers and the boys. They have to feel supported."

"Agreed. Meanwhile, it would help if you could keep us posted of any developments. If you can."

"Yes, Daniel, but you do understand that we, the Ministry of Youth, are a separate ministry and therefore often the last to know about the Works Ministry's intentions in the capital. The best you can do now is keep those contacts you made yesterday happy. We have a small budget set aside for entertaining."

When Daniel eventually put the phone down, he felt anxious, but as was often the case with him these days, anxiety spurred him into action. He got up, threw open the door, and marched over to the kitchens to talk to Chef.

CHAPTER TWENTY-NINE

Smiling wryly, Lefèbvre walked in with the *Dépeche du Centre.*

"Here, look at this," he said, tapping the paper. "'The hundred boys of France at the Ville-aux-Clerc Youth Centre celebrate midsummer at Fort Girard'."

"What a jumble of typefaces," Daniel said, frowning. Having been employed at the publishing house, Flammarion, he had a keen eye for layout; this was frankly amateurish.

"Oh look, there you are," said Lefèbvre, laughing. Daniel was at the microphone in a smart gabardine jacket, tie perfectly aligned and with neat, pomaded hair. *Pity about the half-closed eyes! That guy from the Ministry! Damn him!*

Sighing, Daniel turned to a photograph at the bottom of the page. Happy mothers and grandparents sat on chairs in the garden in their Sunday best. At their feet, children were laughing at Pierre Roupp lifting his skirt and displaying his voluminous bloomers.

"Read it out." Lefèbvre said, sitting next to Daniel.

"'*In the Perche valley, north of the Forest of Fréteval, stands a grand manor house covered in Virginia creeper. An ancient wall once ran around it. A portion of it remains today with the words 'Hold Strong' inscribed upon the arch. It has become Fort Girard's motto.*'" Daniel looked up at Lefèbvre and smiled. "'*In this historic building, belonging to one of France's noblest of families, are one hundred French chevaliers in training.*'"

Lefèbvre and Daniel couldn't help exchanging bemused expressions. "'*No question of serfs, or épées, however, as they're the most modern of youths'."*

"Chevaliers, can you believe it?" Daniel exclaimed, laughing.

"You'll have to show it to the boys over supper."

He quickly scrolled down. "'*These joyful celebrations, however, took on a serious note as Daniel Frey, the centre's chief, standing on the terrace and addressing the crowds in the garden below, spoke of the French prisoners, a subject which unites us all.*'" A tremor went through him. The conversation he'd had with Pelletier still weighed heavily on his mind.

"Go on!"

"'*He spoke of the mountain that was left to climb to create a community based on the principles mapped out by the Maréchal.*'"

"Well there you have it," Daniel said, turning to Lefèbvre. "It's a start."

And with that, he slapped the newspaper down and walked out of the room.

CHAPTER THIRTY

At the other end of the refectory table, the Regional Inspector for Employment surreptitiously drew out a little black notebook and pencil. Letting his tortoiseshell glasses slip half-way down his thick nose, he peered over at Daniel and fixed him with a falsely benign expression.

Daniel wiped his mouth on a serviette, continued to converse with Pelletier over the provenance of the *Pinot Gris* and the *Pinot Noir* adorning the table and coveted by them all, for it had been a while since they'd had such wines.

"My friend René tells me that the producers are hiding their best from the *fritz*, but he owes me a few favours," Pelletier said. "I'd like you to meet him when you come up to Orléans. If ever you need anything done, he's your man," Pelletier said.

The Inspector peered down to check his watch. Riou, who was seated next to their unwanted guest, raised his eyebrows at Daniel. Was Riou thinking the same? The man scribbling heaven-knows-what into his black book resembled that conniving Laval with his white shirt, too tight about the neck, his small, rough-looking hands and thick moustache. Pétain had been right to throw him out of his cabinet at the beginning of his tenure. He hoped the rumours of a conciliation between the Maréchal and the former lawyer were unfounded, for Laval, while claiming he could strike a deal with the Germans regarding the prisoners, was cockiness incarnate and not to be trusted.

The Inspector shut his notebook.

Riou picked up the bottle of *Pinot Noir* with his good arm and went through the motions of offering him a drop, but the Inspector had already refused the *Pinot Gris*, so rich and aromatic, served earlier with the *carpe, tomates avec sauce verte* and the main course, *poulet avec pommes rissolées*. Too bad – more for them.

"*Une petite goutte avec le fromage?*" Riou suggested once more, handing the platter of Loiret cheeses over to him.

"*Merci,*" the Inspector said, helping himself to a moderate slice of *Pannes Cendré*.

The Inspector had asked them to forget about him on his arrival at Fort Girard. He had arrived late; Daniel well knew that his tardiness had been a way of setting the distance between them.

Who are you? Daniel had thought, grasping his stone-like digits. *Are you with us or the fritz?*

Daniel had made the mistake of trying to bribe the last Parisian Inspector with precious packs of butter. He had simply been replaced with another equally anonymous personage. Today, this one had simply been in a hurry to get to the lunch table, where everyone had already sat down. Oh, why had he come today of all days?

Now, barely dipping his lips into his glass of water, the Inspector rose, gave his mouth a final wipe, and made his way over to Daniel.

"Thank you for the fine lunch," he said, hardly concealing his displeasure at such culinary ostentation in wartime. "I am wanted in Orleans. I will be in touch."

"Of course," Daniel said, miserably.

Great sighs of relief and sufferance followed the man's departure.

"That's probably not the last we see of him," Pelletier whispered to Daniel as he returned to the table.

In his upset, Pelletier had managed to gulp down the precious fruity red Daniel had meant to savour with the cheese. Daniel sighed and lay back in his chair.

Daniel tried to push the Inspector to the back of his mind, but there was no denying the net closing around the centres. He resolved to spend every minute of every day on this question of employment and keeping his charges safe.

On the 11th November, Armistice Day, Daniel marched down to La Ville-aux-Clercs with the boys in uniform to commemorate those fallen in the Great War, and in May-June 1940.

The church had never been so full, he was told by the Mayor, as latecomers were made to stand at the back. After the mass, the Mayor joined him in laying a wreath on the monument to the dead. During the two-minute silence that followed, memories of his uncle surfaced, as they were inclined to do on this date every year.

'In a few hours' time, I will probably no longer be here. My body will be cold, inert, like so many I have seen here in the past few months. Bodies that were so full of life.'

In his final letter, his Uncle Sam had reconciled himself to joining his dear friends. He had written a line at the bottom of his letter: 'The warlike nations do not inherit the Earth; they represent the decaying human element.' He had run a line through it, however, perhaps wishing not to end on such a note.

A great follower of Norman Angell, the pacifist, it was all the more heart-breaking to think that Sam had suppressed his ideals in order to fight alongside his comrades.

Daniel half-turned to his boys, standing gravely in uniform behind him. Sam had been their age when his life had been snuffed out. At the same age, Daniel had left home to serve in a Colonial regiment in Morocco. Thirteen years later, France had been at war again. Still – today he and his boys had come to honour the departed and to support La Ville-aux-Clercs, whose inhabitants had braved the bitter winter wind to pay their respects. The fact that they were banned from taking part in such ceremonies by the occupying force had not fazed them one bit. The boys and the show of public resistance had lifted everyone's mood in the village.

Daniel spied Tatiana in the front row. His defiant mood softened a little as he saw her, drawn and pale, her bump pushing through her heavy winter coat. She was months away from giving birth. The new year, the doctor had said. Béatrice stood alongside her, dressed head to toe in Jeanne's woollen hand-me-downs and clutching Mlle Laviolle's blue crocheted rabbit.

Jeanne, meanwhile, weaved in and out of the crowd with the notary's daughter. They had resumed the game they had started before entering church.

Three weeks later, at precisely two in the morning, Tatiana went into early labour.

The temperature had dropped, and it had been snowing for days. Daniel slipped his boots on hurriedly and trampled through the deep snow to the café, where he woke Eric. Daniel had organised a special *ausweis* for him to ferry them to Vendôme the following morning.

Bleary-eyed and reluctant to leave his warm bed, Eric dragged himself to the car. As the engine spluttered into life, Daniel urged him to make haste. By the time they arrived, Tatiana was already frantic. The child-minder was making her a *verveine* infusion and offered to take charge of the children. Reassured by Daniel's presence, Tatiana, wrapped in her winter coat and carrying a pair of rolled blankets, stepped into the back of the car, closed her eyes, and willed the baby to hold tight. They drove off slowly, through the silent, moonlit, snowbound forests, and reached Vendôme at dawn.

The birth happened soon after. It was a girl, France, Francis if it had been a boy. It was not only an act of patriotism, Daniel had had a cousin with the same name, born in Alsace, during the last German occupation. As he beheld his rosy, fair-haired child, so different from dark-haired Jeanne and Béatrice, Tatiana and he exchanged half-resigned, half-relieved glances: 'She isn't a boy, but she is healthy'. And what a beautiful infant she was. He nestled her in the crook of his arm, whilst Tatiana turned to the window of falling snow. She talked about a sleigh ride she had regularly made with Vladimir and her parents to the church in Vladicaucase, Georgia. How happy she had been, sitting beside her brother, with their legs under piles of blankets and wolfskin.

France stretched her doll-like arms over her baby blanket and yawned. Tatiana turned back and, through half-closed eyes, her slender fingers searching his, remarked,

"She's our snow queen, look at her!"

And indeed, every little cell in Daniel's blood came alive as he hugged his rosy-faced snow queen from Alsace.

CHAPTER THIRTY-ONE

"Monsieur Frey, whilst conceding that your staff have given these boys a good moral education…" The Inspector frowned, inserting his papers into a file. "I am not satisfied that you are preparing them sufficiently for the sort of jobs that need to be filled."

Daniel smiled inwardly. He'd been expecting this and had braced himself for the inevitable barely-veiled threat. Sauckel, in charge of German labour deployment, had 'asked' rather 'demanded' that the French Ministry of Employment provide him with hundreds of thousands of 'volunteers' needed in the metallurgical industry, in construction and armaments factories.

The Inspector snapped his briefcase shut.

Everything we have worked for here – everything could spiral out of control. And to think that I could be coerced into sending our boys to a German munitions factory. It is supposed to be voluntary!

He watched the Inspector reach for his coat and made no effort to get up.

How can he sleep at night! France is at breaking point. Crippling war payments, endless requisitions. We're bankrupt. Four hundred thousand francs a day to the occupying forces. Four hundred thousand! Far from being a release, the Armistice has become a crippling yoke to bear. Our factories are closing in Northern France and the workers are up in arms. The Germans will run them into the ground and soon enough they'll be forced to take that train to the Ruhr. For what else can they do to feed their starving families? Where is Pétain in all of this? In the Free

Zone, letting Laval negotiate with the fritz, happy to leave him to do his dirty work for him. It is all such a mess!

"I'll let myself out, Monsieur Frey."

Daniel didn't even bother to look up.

"You'd be well-advised to take this seriously."

Daniel felt the cords of his neck tighten. To have a Frenchman reprimand him was shocking. He nodded grimly.

As the door clamped shut, Daniel plunged his head into his hands. *Think. Think.*

A shrill ring made him start. He wrenched the receiver off its cradle.

"Yes?"

"Daniel?" It was Riou. "Has he left?"

"Yes," he whispered.

"Look, there's a rumour that the Germans are going to close down some of the centres."

"What!?" Daniel pinched the scarred snag on his nose. He had not been expecting that. But he shouldn't have been surprised. What self-respecting centre leader would agree to send its youths to Germany?

Two thoughts buzzed around in his head. *I am not alone. They can't shut us down.*

Remembering that Riou was at the other end of the line, he continued, "If they think our boys are going to Germany for the money and spanking new accommodation, they'd better think again! As for Laval's so-called negotiations with the *fritz* – it's emotional blackmail. One French prisoner being released in exchange for three French workers, an outrage!"

"Yes," Riou added, quietly. "Be careful. No use taking them head on. They're too powerful. They'll bring you down and all your staff with you. Continue playing for time. At least make some pretence of starting additional technical training. For the time being, going to work over in Germany is only voluntary."

"Yes – but how long will that last?"

There was a silence at the other end of the line. "Look, Daniel," Riou said, clearly struggling himself, "all we can do is keep trying to place the boys on farms, local businesses, even if they moan about the pittance offered. They'll just have to get used to the idea of earning little until times get better. And then it could be another year."

"Oh, no! That Inspector's tone was threatening." He had never raised his voice with Riou. "And before we know it we'll all be pushed into that train."

Riou let out a loud sigh. No doubt he'd been getting an earful from other centre chiefs too. "Look, Daniel, I understand your concern, but remember it's simply a rumour. In the meantime" – Riou dropped his voice – "the Bernstein boys are still under your roof. You can't draw attention to yourself. I've been contacted by the same Jewish organisation that handed us the brothers in the first place. Their uncle has been living with false ID in the Free Zone and is ready to take them. He has the means to get them over the demarcation line. Things have got worse since they've enforced the wearing of the star. Tell them to pack."

Thrust into action, Daniel brightened fractionally. "Alright. Is that all?'

"Isn't that enough?"

There was a knock at the door. He replaced the receiver. "*Entrez*!"

Lefèbvre was standing there, frowning. "Has the Inspector gone?"

"He's gone."

"And?"

"Oh, the usual." Daniel groaned. "Not happy with the programme. We'll talk about it next week. Look, I need you to tell the brothers to pack."

"Oh!" Lefèbvre was surprised. "Just as they were beginning to settle."

"They're going to their uncle's, in the Free Zone."

Lefèbvre threw Daniel a questioning look. Both knew how difficult and expensive it was to smuggle anyone through now.

Lefèbvre started to make his way up the stairs.

Daniel called after him, "And make sure Chef gives them enough supplies for the road."

Daniel and Lefèbvre saw the brothers off.

The eldest, Claude, turned to Daniel and gripped his hand. "Thank you," he said, simply. His dark eyes gleamed with fear and excitement in equal measure.

A whinnying was heard from the stable. Vilon stepped out, a little pale and waving his grooming brush at Jacques, the youngest, who had spent some time helping him in the stable that day. In Vilon's company, Jacques had been relieved, or so it seemed, of needing to talk.

"*Vite, allez-y,*" Daniel said. Jacques got reluctantly into the car, followed by his two brothers.

That night, Daniel was plagued with conflicting emotions. Their departure had been timely given the turn of events. How long could he have hidden their true identities? He had to admit a feeling of relief that they had gone, tinged with a lingering guilt which had not left him since the beginning of the war.

Tatiana opened the door. "Daniel, you're late again," she said, concerned.

"Papa, you promised to read with me." Jeanne appeared in her nightdress behind her mother and, slipping under her mother's arm, pulled him in.

"Not tonight, *ma poulette,*" he said, gently guiding her to the kitchen table. He let himself fall into a chair and sighed.

"Papa! You're always too tired." She stomped off to her bedroom.

"Dan, come on!" Tatiana said, watching their daughter go. "You did say. Just for a while, whilst I brush Béatrice's hair. I've only just been able to get France settled."

Have I really broken my promise to her? And what about all the others I could be letting down? I need to think. But I can't think here. What I would give for a good stiff drink, not to think. But the war has taken all our pleasures, our comforts and our hopes.

Tatiana walked over to the cupboard, impatiently. She was wearing her wooden heels, which clanked hard on the stone floor. She leaned into a cupboard and brought out an inordinately large tablet of chocolate.

He flashed her an angry look. *Sacha.*

Tatiana looked away, sniffed, and broke off a piece.

"Again!" he said, exasperated. 'Oncle Sacha' the girls called him. In Vladimir's absence, he had usurped his brother-in-law. Tatiana had no business accepting gifts from him.

"Oh, don't give me that withering look, Dan."

Daniel shook his head and her dark eyes flashed.

"You don't know Sacha."

"What?" Daniel gave her a furious look. It's true – he had never

167

met him. And never would.

"He's no angel. But who is in this war?" She pressed down on the tablet and broke off two pieces.

Daniel shook his head. How many times had he heard that from people who used the war as an excuse to carry out unwholesome business with the *fritz*.

"And if you must know, he's keeping in with certain German officers for a reason." She had dropped her voice.

"That's what they all say!"

"No, Dan. It's not what you think. He has a friend, an actress, who sings at the Shéhérazade Club. She starred in his movie, remember?"

He remembered. How could he forget that Sacha had made a film. "Stay out of it, Tatiana – do you hear me!"

Jeanne crept in nervously and went over to her mother. The word 'chocolate' had also brought Béa, who had run in with wet hair. Barely acknowledging him, both girls seized the squares from their mother and dug their little teeth into them.

"*Doucement!*" Daniel said, snatching the chocolate out of Tatiana's hands and placing the tablet on the highest cupboard shelf.

Tatiana led the girls back to their bedroom. No sooner were they gone than a tingle of knowing ran through him. *Sacha is protecting a girlfriend. Probably Jewish. I have one hundred youths to protect. Maybe it's time I also made friends with the fritz.* He felt his gut tighten with resolve. *I have no other option left.*

CHAPTER THIRTY-TWO

"Shut the door and come in, quickly," Daniel said, motioning Cintract and Pierre Roupp to his desk.

Both youths looked puzzled, no doubt wondering why they'd suddenly been pulled out of forestry duties and called to the Chief's office.

Daniel waited for them to settle. *Cintract has become a man. Look at that strong jawline. His amenable expression has as good as left him. Probably just as well, for what I'm going to ask of him. And young Roupp – much more self-assured and a little calmer. Plucky, stronger. He's catching up with Cintract.*

"Now," he said, leaning forward and smiling conspiratorially. "I'd like you two to help me."

Cintract leaned forward and Roupp cocked his ear.

"Tomorrow we'll pay a visit to a very important man. our new Regional Military Prefect – a Doktor Küssling." Daniel watched their eyes widen in disbelief.

"A *boche?*" Cintract said, incredulous.

And a real hard nut – 'pacifier' of Czechoslovakia, I hear. But these boys don't need to know that. No need to scare or excite them further. "Yes – a *boche*, as you say, Cintract."

"But why, *Chef?*" Cintract turned to Roupp, who seemed just as surprised but had clearly decided to let Cintract, his group leader, lead the discussion.

Daniel continued calmly. "Let's just say that we need to go butter him up. Get this high-ranking German on our side."

Both youths scowled, as expected.

"I know this may seem illogical, but just for tomorrow, I'd like you to dazzle him, to show him what fine young men you are."

"But they're Nazis!"

"Yes," he continued, neutrally. "They are the enemy. But Fort Girard's independence and survival depends on this *fritz* leaving us alone. There are rumours they're suspicious of what we're doing here, and who can blame them." He broke off, allowing a moment of patriotic pride amongst them.

Both boys beamed, but then Cintract's face showed renewed concern. "Who's been spying on us? No one ever comes here apart from Riou, Pelletier. Oh – except the people from the village for that St Jean celebration last summer."

Daniel had had the same suspicions at one time but had put them to one side. The only black sheep had been the engineer. But now, whilst not on site at Fort Girard outside teaching hours, the engineer was quite happily living in the village. He had even met a local girl. He had nothing to gain from complaining about the centre to the *fritz* and jeopardising his employment. And the Bernstein brothers – he had never shown any particular interest in any one boy – so it was unlikely that he should take any particular interest in them.

"I doubt anyone has spied on us." He wanted to cut off Cintract's line of enquiry straight away. They'd be talking about the Employment Inspector next, and he didn't want to complicate matters by making them feel vulnerable. "The Germans are jittery," he continued. "They're suspicious of everyone these days. We're simply going to show this blockhead what fine *jünge Männer* you really are."

Both boys squirmed.

"You mean like Hitler's *Jugend*?" Cintract was looking uneasy.

"Yes," Daniel said, matter-of-factly. "Like the Hitler Youth – but you are obviously nothing to do with such an organisation. Rest assured that we will go dressed in our Narvik uniforms – no question of us being German."

Cintract looked up. "So, you're asking us to put on our uniforms and – what, *Chef*?"

"Appearance is everything. You'll need to shine up those boots of yours." Daniel could see Roupp was restless, rapping his hands on his thighs. He should come to the point. "And only then will you be ready for the parade."

"Parade?" both of them repeated, anxiously.

"Think of it as a show. I've seen what consummate actors you are."

Both of them cracked embarrassed smiles and glanced at one another.

"And this is your opportunity to play your finest roles to date. Don't worry, I'll do the talking. Now," he said, looking them firmly in the eye, "are you prepared to do this for me?"

They looked at one another, undecided.

"What exactly is involved?" Cintract asked.

"You already know the drills, but they need to be perfect. Let's start with a salute. Imagine I am Doktor Küssling. Stand up, both of you."

Both stood and saluted half-heartedly.

"Again! Put more energy into it. Pull yourselves up to your full height." Daniel got up from his chair, arched his back and threw back his shoulders. "Like this." He looked down at them. Both still looked undecided. "Now go towards the door and march towards me."

Cintract and Roupp turned and made their way to the door.

"Alright, march. When I say 'halt', click your heels together and salute."

They performed the drill.

Daniel hollered at them, knowing that only the nurse might overhear, "Look at your *führer* – not at your feet."

They had to perform the steps several times over before executing the drill with complete precision, snapping their heels together with earnest, serious expressions, eyes fixed on him.

Roupp looked troubled. "*Chef,* I'm not sure…"

Daniel patted him on the shoulder. "It won't be for long. Just a short visit. And then you'll be out."

Roupp shook his head.

"Remember, this is not you, Roupp. But you, of all people, have the gumption to do this."

"I know, *Chef.* I know how to act." His voice drifted off.

"*Écoute*, Roupp, you and Cintract are going to shine. Other peoples' lives are at stake too – not only your own. And remember, this is your second act of resistance. The first was to raise the Tricolor and to salute your nation's flag."

The following morning, the mist around the garden was only just beginning to lift when both boys clambered up into the front of the B14 truck, pale and silent, pulling on the trousers of their pressed uniforms. Before Daniel put the key into the ignition, he noticed Roupp rub a cloth over his boots and Cintract retrieve a comb from his top pocket and tug at his wet hair. The scent of polish filled the truck.

Daniel wound down the window and set off without a word. Only when the truck hit the high road in the direction of Orléans did he start to think through his strategy. They had all agreed that each youth would give truthful accounts of their family, their lives. It was risky but a better option than to lie, then forget a story or get confused if cross-examined. Both boys had practised relating their wartime experiences without letting any bitterness creep into their voices.

Daniel had kept his eye on Cintract in particular. At times, he still worried about Cintract's stoicism regarding his loss. And yet such traumatic experiences abounded at Fort Girard. He had always encouraged the boys to talk openly of their lives, however painful. The youths had, one by one, spilled out their sorrows around the campfire, under the cloak of darkness.

He drove in an easterly direction and, an hour later, pulled up before a château along the banks of the Loir. Two heavily-armed sentinels stood on duty at a newly-erected barrier before a gilded gate. Daniel halted the truck and wound down the window a little further to put the stars sewn into his left sleeve in full view. He announced that he was Chief of Staff of the youth centre stationed in the Ville-aux-Clercs and that he had come to see Doktor Küssling. As he enunciated the military Prefect's name for the first time, he made sure to pronounce the 'ew' of the umlaut correctly over the 'u'. It seemed to have the desired effect, for the soldier now asked them to descend from the truck in a fractionally less menacing tone.

"*Attendez-vous ici,*" he said, pointing his submachine gun at the stony ground. Daniel was sure that both Cintract and Roupp had never set eyes on such a weapon and that Vic's tales of war were now suddenly coming alive to them.

The sentinel walked away down a gravel drive and disappeared through the château entrance. His colleague searched them, then checked over the back of the truck and, unsatisfied with the fruitless search, proceeded to eye them suspiciously from under his helmet.

Ten minutes passed. Daniel checked his watch several times. The sentinel who had gone in search of Doktor Kusschling was returning.

"*En-trez* Meussieu," he shouted, in a strange, strangulated voice as he approached the grilled gate.

Daniel inwardly sighed with relief, gesturing for the boys to follow him.

"Nein. *Bleiben Sie hier!*" the sentry yelled at the youths.

Daniel realised that the three of them had misunderstood the guard. He had meant "Monsieur" not "Messieurs", which would have addressed all of them. Just a mispronunciation and what havoc he was causing.

His colleague jabbed his weapon towards the car. Cintract and Roupp edged back, confused.

Trying to play down the incident, Daniel turned to them. "*A tout à l'heure,*" he said, smiling awkwardly, then followed the guard through the gate and back along the gravel drive. He entered the chateau, found himself climbing a flight of red-carpeted steps to the first floor, and was ushered into a little *salon* by a young bespectacled male secretary.

Two exquisite Louis XV gilded armchairs covered in yellow satin were arranged in the middle of the room. Between them, on a little marquetry table, stood a half-empty bottle of schnapps, an empty glass, and a cafetière of what smelled like real coffee.

Daniel stared at the pale blue damask wallpaper ornamented with hunting prints of wild boar and deer. His attention moved to a little desk in the corner of the room, upon which two silver picture frames gleamed. Two officers were shaking hands in one of them – was one of them with the Führer? Daniel put a foot forward in that direction when a creak of parquet made him stand back. In the doorway stood a tall, blue-eyed, shaven-headed Prussian officer, in an immaculate white uniform. From his top left-hand pocket hung an iron military cross. Daniel saluted.

The Prussian scrutinised him. "Stand at ease. So, you are…"

"Daniel Frey, Herr Kommandant. I'm Chief of Staff of the youth centre at the Ville-aux-Clercs. Having heard that you have just been nominated as the Military Prefect, I've come to pay my respects."

The Prussian raised his grey eyebrows, amused and puzzled. "Your visit is most unexpected."

Daniel smiled and inclined his head. "Forgive me – I should have called beforehand, but..."

"Frey – I said to my secretary – he must be German. And certainly, you look like one of us."

Daniel shook his head. He hadn't anticipated this remark, nor the familiarity. Could it be the schnapps? He forced himself to smile.

"The name is probably of German origin, Kommandant Küssling, but I assure you that I am French, from Alsace."

The Prussian started to frown but Daniel fixed him with a dazzling smile as if to say 'Yes, Alsace is now a German territory. But we are military men, these things happen.'

The Prussian hurrumphed. "Just as I was saying. You are German," he said, with a wave of the hand. "Your appearance, your perfect presentation confirms this. You saluted me, not like a Frenchman, but like a German officer."

At this the Kommandant's face flushed red. Daniel wondered how many glasses of schnapps he had put away that winter's morning. Having left the battlefronts of the East, perhaps there wasn't much to do around here. Daniel saw the beginnings of a paunch strain the lower buttons of his military jacket. He was reminded of the caricature of the Prussian officer in the clandestine cartoons circulating Strasbourg in the 1914-18 occupation, which he'd seen as a ten-year-old boy. *An arrogant Prussian, who is now feeling magnanimous because he can be.*

"Of course, Kommandant Küssling. I'm flattered that you should think so." Daniel felt a pain in his heart, but continued, "The object of my visit, Herr Kommandant, is to inform you of the work we are doing in our centres – since we are now under your jurisdiction." He half bowed his head, causing the Prussian to smile. "I would welcome your comprehension with regard to the plight of our boys. I'm a great admirer of what you have done in your own country with the Hitler Jugend, and so I am sure you will understand what we're trying to do with our own youths, who have been sorely neglected and who are trying to find their way." He wanted to add 'in these troubled times,' and caught himself just in time.

The Prussian was frowning. But was he frowning in

concentration? He couldn't be sure.

"What I mean is that times have changed…"

"Yes, yes," the Prussian said, waving the matter away. He gestured for Daniel to sit.

"*Vielen Dank. Merci,*" Daniel said, sitting. "And so you will understand too that we are keen to build these *jünge Männer* up again."

The Prussian sat down heavily and nodded. "*Natürlich, natürlich.*"

"To make them strong. They have been so traumatized by war."

The Prussian nodded sagely. "I agree. It is most important for us to have leaders like you to direct the European youth of tomorrow."

Daniel felt a tightness in his throat and swallowed. "Thank you, Kommandant Küssling. Now, I'm sure you'd like me to introduce you to the two boys waiting outside."

"Of course, Herr Frey, have them come in. I want to meet them," he said, enthusiastically slapping his thigh.

Daniel left the room, descended the carpeted stair, just managing to hold onto his soldierly composure. It was only when he left the chateau that he was able to take a lungful of air as he marched up to the gate.

"Kommandant Küssling would like to see them."

In silence, they marched back to the château, to be met by the secretary. He waved them through, and Daniel marched up the stair with Cintract and Roupp in step. On the landing he stopped, pretending to admire a small statuette of a horse.

"Luck is on our side," he murmured. "Our man has had one too many."

Cintract and Roupp nodded and smiled at the sculpture, aware of the secretary's eyes focused on them from below.

They stepped into the sitting room.

"Here they are, Herr Kommandant," Daniel said, smiling and standing back.

Cintract and Roupp saluted. Their fresh countenances contrasted sharply with the room's opulence.

Daniel watched the lines of the *Doktor's* face soften.

"*Gut! Sehr gut!*" he said, walking around them with his hands behind his back. "But their hair is too long, Herr Frey," he said, wagging his index finger at them.

Cintract and Roupp stared ahead, whilst Daniel promised that it would be rectified immediately.

The Prussian was adopting a pally air. "Now, my man," he said, addressing Roupp, "what line of work is your father in?"

"My father," Roupp said, turning to the Prussian, "is a prisoner of war."

"*Ach*," he said, bowing his head and shaking it. "It is difficult without a father, *nicht wahr?* But you are strong, and it is the nature of war."

"*Danke, sir!*" Roupp polished off his reply with a salute.

The Prussian laughed. "Yes, you remind me of my nephew Franz, a handsome lad. On the Russian front now." He eyed Roupp carefully.

Daniel feared his mood had darkened. He saw Roupp getting ready to speak. *No, Roupp. Let me...*

"Giving those *Russkis* a real lickin' I hope, sir!"

The Prussian threw his head back and laughed heartily. "Just like Franz. The boy has spirit." He punched the air.

Daniel feared that the Prussian would launch into a tirade against the communists. He laid his hand on Cintract's shoulder.

"And may I introduce you to another fine young man, Cintract."

"*Ja.* Of course." The Prussian swivelled round in his boots. "You are older, *ja?*"

"Twenty-two, sir."

"Independent now. But you have a family, *ja?*"

Daniel drew in his breath.

There was a slight pause, as Cintract seemed to gulp. "Sir," he said, finally, "they were killed in the Vitry-le-François bombing."

"All of them?" There was a silence. Cintract nodded gravely. The Prussian was stunned. "But you are a fine *jünge Mann*," he said, recovering his senses and extending his arm as if he was going to pat his shoulder. He wobbled and let his arm drop. "Your family... one of the casualties of this war, yes."

He swung his portly body round to Daniel. "Herr Frey. Very pleased that you came today. We've been told that your youth camps are terrorist breeding grounds."

Daniel and the two boys looked suitably shocked and wide-eyed.

Daniel eventually spoke. "Terrorists? No. Not us!"

"In which case..." The Prussian eyed his drinks cabinet.

176

Daniel feared being invited for a drink. He now yearned to leave before implicating himself further.

"I'll make sure that your centre is left alone."

"I thank you," Daniel said, clicking his heels. He stood there, wondering whether he could make a plea on behalf of the other centres. He couldn't push his luck.

The Prussian swung his arm up. "*Heil Hitler!*"

"*Heil Hitler!*" Daniel intoned hoarsely, realising that nothing further could be achieved with the man.

The *Doktor* accompanied them to the landing. "My secretary down there will show you out. Franz!" he called, steadying himself on the stair ramp. "*Auf Wiedersehen*, Herr Frey!"

Daniel and the boys gave the *Doktor* a final salute and descended the stair.

Leaving the château, they walked to the truck in silence, passing the sentry guards with their heads held high. It was only when they were way out on the highway, twenty minutes later, that they were all taken with sudden convulsive laughter.

CHAPTER THIRTY-THREE

A month passed without hearing anything from Doktor Küssling. However, far worse, Daniel received a visit from the French *Commissaire au Travail des Jeunes* at the end of May.

He wondered whether the German Military Prefect had communicated with the Ministry of Youth up in Paris, but he doubted it. Daniel's improvised meeting with the Prussian might have staved off Fort Girard's closure, however high on the agenda in Vichy was Germany's renewed request for manpower. Laval had now undoubtedly become Germany's pawn, and one of the men brought in to do Laval's dirty work was standing before Daniel now, smiling and offering his clammy hand.

"Delighted to meet the man behind Fort Girard. May I?"

Daniel gestured for him to sit and waited for the unpleasant tidings.

"We are both busy people so I'll get on, shall I?"

Without nodding, Daniel watched him whip a newspaper article from a file with a flourish. Daniel stared at it dejectedly. He recognised it to be a recent interview he had given. And it had made its way right up to Paris. Barely hiding his disgust over this article being used for propaganda, Daniel scrutinised the photo of himself. It was a full body shot of him looking tough with his hands in his pockets. Alongside him, Lefèbvre and Bouillot and the team were looking out in all directions.

He had the urge to laugh in the official's face and bit his lip. 'Chef Frey, Builder of Fort Girard' was printed in bold letters. 'Youths of Fort Girard Build a Carpentry Workshop'.

"We'd like to compliment you yet again on your work with the boys, however..."

Daniel eyed the official warily. The *Commissaire* ignored him and went on to reiterate the need for manpower for Germany if they were to fight communism. Daniel had stopped listening. He pulled himself up in his chair.

"But surely these young men are not what you're looking for!"

The *Commissaire* pulled a fountain pen from his inside jacket pocket. "Some of these boys are nearing twenty, Monsieur Frey. The employment agency will be able to deal with any gaps in their training. You already know our position, you have been warned before and so now, I'm giving you the order to select your best workers and to direct them towards our office."

Daniel shook his head.

"If you fail to comply, I will have no other recourse but to relieve you of your duties."

Daniel gave a short laugh. "I cannot do what you wish me to do."

"I believe you are not thinking straight, Monsieur Frey. I'm giving you eight days to make up your mind. Otherwise you'll be packing your bags."

Daniel got up and opened the door, extending his arm towards the exit.

The *Commissaire* shook his head and gave him a supercilious look. "Really, Monsieur Frey." He calmly tucked the file back into his briefcase, slipped his pen into his inside jacket pocket, and let himself out.

As soon as he had left, Daniel phoned Pelletier at the Ministry of Youth's department in Orleans.

"Your call is timely, Daniel. My boss Chodekowitz has a position to fill. Interested?"

Daniel leaned forward in his seat. Such providence was unexpected. He smelled a rat. Orleans was an important administrative centre. They could have their pick of people.

"What exactly is the position?" Daniel said, warily.

Pelletier laughed nervously. "Head of Youth Propaganda?"

"You're joking?" Daniel squeezed his temples.

"No, not Nazi propaganda, if that's what you're thinking."

"Oh. Good," he said, hesitantly.

"You know – good propaganda. Raising the profile of the

youths in our centres and informing the bosses in the region what they're up to, what skills they have. I'll put him on, he's just come into the office."

Before Daniel could protest, there were muffled voices on the line. "*Bonjour*, Daniel. Pelletier has already mentioned your name. You come highly recommended. I hear the inspectors are giving you grief. Well, as you know, I have a position to fill here. Are you interested? Your experience running a centre would be invaluable. We need to help these young boys and girls all the more in light of the new developments. Why don't you come up and we can discuss all this. But the job is as good as yours."

He replaced the receiver, but felt the buoyancy quickly drain out of him as he thought of Lefèbvre, Vic, and everyone who had worked for him at Fort Girard. His team. There was a knock at the door.

"Come in."

It was Cintract. "Are you coming, *Chef*? Lefèbvre's set up the wireless."

They walked two floors up, stood in the darkened hallway outside Lefèbvre's room where whirring, bubbling sounds reached them from under the door. Daniel gave three distinctive knocks. Roupp, now a team leader, came to the door. They had all agreed to be cautious, for anyone found listening to Radio Londres faced imprisonment.

They walked in. Bouillot was perched on Lefèbvre's bed, Labarre and Vic on the floor. Lefèbvre, at his desk, was turning the volume up a fraction. Daniel seated himself next to Bouillot, whilst Cintract leant against a chest of drawers by the door with Roupp.

Out of the grill of the dome-shaped walnut radio came the words: "*Ici Radio Londres: les Français parlent aux Français. And now a correspondent signing herself N.S. writes from Nantes,*" said the broadcaster. "'*I went to my local cinema when a newsreel came on showing a meeting between Hitler and Mussolini. And you should have heard the din! Everyone whistling and shouting and stamping their feet, cursing these two old cronies with words I dare not repeat. We were told the following time we were to be silent. When the moment came, the whole of the auditorium succumbed to a sudden and noisy cold. Everyone was coughing and sneezing.*'

Roupp laughed, but Cintract grabbed his shoulder. "Shush."

"*And now a young woman signing herself 'The Stenographer',*
writes,

"'*While continuing to respect the Maréchal – because it is*
impossible to believe him capable of treachery – the French people
no longer believe in him. He has become a mere figurehead, a
façade.'"

Lefèbvre turned to look at Daniel, and what passed between
them was the knowledge of things changing.

"Right I'm off," Daniel said, getting up.

He had decided that he'd tell them all tomorrow – calmly.
He'd be up all night composing a speech, but for now he needed
Tatiana.

Tatiana was lying on the bed, feeding France with a bottle. Eyes
already closed, both mother and daughter lay almost motionless
across the coverlet. At odd intervals, France sucked lazily on the
teat, already having entered her infant dream world.

Daniel leant down and stroked Tatiana's cheek. Her eyes had
sunken a fraction. That morning, she had complained excitedly
of feeling nauseous. A boy was what they both wanted, but what
sort of world were they bringing their children into? And where
would they live after Fort Girard? Daniel let them sleep and
decided not to wake them.

CHAPTER THIRTY-FOUR

Daniel didn't put the moment off any longer; he gathered the core members of his staff the following morning.

"I have decided…" He was alarmed to feel his voice hoarsen. He cleared his throat briskly. "After much thought, I have decided to accept a new position in Orleans, working for the Ministry of Youth."

A fleeting look of shock mingled with disappointment passed over Vic's face. Daniel was, however, relieved to see his protégé recover his senses almost immediately as he adopted the ubiquitous soldier's stiff posture.

Bouillot, meanwhile, shifted from one foot to the other several times before speaking. "*Chef*, congratulations on the new position. I don't need to tell you how sorry we are to see you leave Fort Girard." They all nodded gravely. "And," he continued, decidedly uncomfortable, "I've some news of my own…" He turned to Lefèbvre and then back to Daniel.

Had they discussed the matter without him? Daniel felt a pinch of hurt. He had always strived for openness in his organisation. *But look at me – am I not also keeping things from them? I have been pushed, blackmailed even, by the fritz and Vichy, into accepting another job.* He winced inside as he foresaw the problems ahead. *The next Chief is bound to be a 'yes man', and where will that leave Lefèbvre and Vic?* Once settled in Orleans, he'd be better placed to help them, he figured, shaking himself out of this debilitating doubt. He trained his eyes on Bouillot, who was struggling to continue.

"Now is as good a time as any I suppose." Bouillot looked at his shoes. "As you all know, my daughter Agnes has been finding it hard in Paris, what with her husband being in the prison camp and food and fuel being… Well I don't need to tell you…" He looked up at them apologetically, for there was no doubt in his mind, it seemed, that he was letting them down.

They all nodded. Of course, Bouillot's negotiating and sourcing skills would be vital to his daughter's survival.

"In Paris, the women in our district are protesting in the streets. They're fed up with the hunger, the scrabbling around for hand-outs from the charities. And they want their sons, their husbands, their brothers back!"

"Of course. We understand, Bouillot," Daniel said, nodding. He needed to let him have his say. But he also needed to get on with the meeting. To not let it disintegrate into complete misery and despair.

"My daughter is scared."

"Of course she is. You must go. But you will stay until I leave in October."

"Of course, *Chef*."

Whilst giving him a smile, Daniel worried that Bouillot's announcement had made matters worse. He didn't want the others to feel they were being left to buoy up a sinking ship. Two years together. Their project had been a resounding success – in every way. He had to keep the spirit of Fort Girard alive.

"Anyone else planning on leaving?"

There was nervous laughter, though it was short-lived. Mlle Laviolle removed her glasses and gave them a wipe. She sighed and popped them on again. Lefèbvre was looking pensive but managed to maintain his calm demeanour and keep his eyes fixed on Daniel, as if awaiting further explanation.

"But *Chef*, who's going to replace you?" asked Vic.

"I'm sorry, but I can't confirm such details right away. I've been assured that he'll be a very competent fellow," Daniel said, feeling his conscience waver. "He will undoubtedly have his own style, but I'm sure he'll look to you all for guidance."

Vic's mouth twitched awkwardly.

Daniel soldiered on, "Lefèbvre will continue as Deputy Chief. And I'll be only a few hours away in Orleans, working for the regional department of the Ministry of Youth. My first task, having visited local centres, will be to set up a work information bureau for the boys and girls in this region. That means for our boys, too." As he spoke, he was gladdened to see their faces finally iron out and relax. They were not being left by the wayside – he was continuing Fort Girard's work on a higher level, where he could exert more influence.

He cut the meeting short. They filed out, people whose responsibility it was to keep things as they were. Lefèbvre lingered at the door.

"*Chef* – or rather, Daniel." Lefèbvre gave him his self-deprecating smile. "So, you're really leaving."

"Yes. I'm sorry. Between you and me, the authorities were making my life difficult." There it was. He had said it. He owed it to Lefèbvre, who would be discrete.

"Ah!" Lefèbvre frowned. "I feared as much. But thank you."

"Hopefully with me gone, things will get easier. And if they don't, you and Vic must get in touch. You are staying, aren't you?" Daniel said, suddenly realising that part of the reason he had the strength to go was because he knew that Lefèbvre, dear Lefèbvre, had the courage and motivation to take up the reins.

"Of course. Don't worry. There's still much to be done here, what with the war taking a turn and…"

Daniel gestured for him to sit and close the door. "And with the boys being asked to go to Germany."

"Yes, and with the Americans…" Lefèbvre threw him an enigmatic look. His eyes suddenly glittered with intent. "Germans are jittery, aren't they? Things not going so well for them in Russia…"

"Yes. We need to brace ourselves for a toughened regime."

Daniel and Lefèbvre had been encouraged, during their training at Sillery, to encourage patriotism and not speak of politics or the war to the boys, and by extension they had censored themselves, Daniel realised. True, there had been little time to reflect during the long work days. The emphasis had been on preparing a new generation of vigorous youth for work. Yet the BBC reports Lefèbvre had captured had opened up a new world of bewildering possibilities. Unable to hide behind ignorance, they had entered a world of complex decision-making on every level, from governments to the man and woman in the street.

Lefèbvre brought a pipe out of his pocket. "You don't mind me smoking?"

"No." There was a knock at the door. "That's Riou. Sorry, I would have liked to..."

"Don't worry. Vic and I will manage."

Lefèbvre shook Riou's hand warmly on his way out. Daniel watched his number two leave his office with a strange sense of loss. But Riou's cheerful, expectant face jolted Daniel into the present; a series of visits and discussions of a practical nature lay ahead. And afterwards, Daniel had an urgent matter to discuss.

Later that evening, after they had sung around the fire with the boys for perhaps the last time, Daniel and Riou finally found themselves alone, walking up to the house.

Their conversation turned to the Laval's *Relève* for workers in Germany, and the Maréchal. That Daniel had lost faith in the Maréchal was no surprise to his colleague. Hadn't they all? The Maréchal's vision of a new France rejuvenated and rebuilt with good, honest labour and morally strengthened by strong family values and patriotic feeling had all but disintegrated. They had only to look around them – Bouillot's son-in-law still in that camp, just one of the millions of absentee fathers. Broken families. Food shortages, factory closures. And the nail in the coffin for Vichy the month before had been Pierre Laval, now the returning premier, openly pledging France's support for Germany on radio and offering France's boys and factory workers up as sacrifices to the German war machine in his so-called *Relève*.

"But we mustn't give up on protecting the boys, *n'est-ce pas*, Daniel?" Riou said, staring hopefully up at the stars. Riou had trusted the Maréchal (the 'Hero of Verdun'), like Daniel, and now the shock of Vichy's betrayal was hard to fathom.

"How can he sleep at night? I can't understand it! The youth of this country were precious to him. It's all he talked about. Cared about. It's got to be that scheming Laval. His broadcast has shamed this country. What our Allies must think! To have said that he desired a German victory! He's never wanted war with them. It's too depressing. To be associated with Nazism and all the filth that comes with it. And amongst all this..." He bunched his hands into fists. "Part of me still believes that Pétain is in secret communication with De Gaulle."

"Daniel," Riou said, quietly, "these things sicken me too,

but we cannot dwell. Better to be angry and to do something. Whether Pétain is keeping his options open with the British and maintaining secret communications with De Gaulle is neither here nor there. The truth is – we don't know. It is good that you are angry. You must do something now."

Daniel felt a release. They were walking under the stars again, in the great garden where they'd always had their most important exchanges. The breeze had softened. It was high summer. Riou stopped and turned to him.

"Daniel," he said, checking behind him, "I think you're asking me what you should do. Well I'll tell you. It is now a sacred duty to resist and to follow De Gaulle, even though we don't know much about him and there is a death sentence around his neck. The Germans will lose the war – they're bogged down in Russia, the BBC tells us. Our Allies will land here, when the time is right. We must help them by joining the Resistance. I'm already engaged in the fight. If you wish to join us, I can charge you with several missions. You have already taken risks. You took those Jewish brothers in, you pulled the wool over that Doktor Küssling's eyes. But you can do more. You don't need to give me your decision tonight. And as always, never speak of our conversation."

By the time Daniel turned in that night, his mind was racing.

He was an ex-soldier – used to hierarchy, strict discipline, orders and sheer numbers. Resistance, on the other hand, required going out on a limb, taking the initiative, being independent. Students, young people without military training, had already engaged in it – at great cost. And there had been those who'd had little option but to go underground and fight: communists and Jews. Tonight, Riou, a military man, a family man, had revealed that he too had joined the fight with Pétain's supposed arch-nemesis, De Gaulle. The proud young general, waiting patiently across the Channel, gathering troops and allies to his cause, excited him, filled him with awe, a warmth he hadn't felt in years. He was being called to action.

But there was a great gulf between rebellious talk and action. Riou had already crossed the divide. And yes, Daniel could see why. He could see how, not taking that leap of faith, he would stay in the wilderness of fear. Prompted by Riou, he had already taken certain small steps, and now it was his sacred duty to join the fight. He was ready. Even if it meant keeping it from Tatiana. Did he want his daughters and, ultimately, their son, if she was expecting one, to grow up in Hitler's New Europe?

He rang Riou several days later.

"I'll do it," he said, simply.

"Good." Riou didn't seem surprised. "Your first mission is to procure an *ausweis* and drive me to Arnouville."

Thrust into a very new present, Daniel took a few seconds to respond. "Yes, Yes," he mumbled.

"That's all you need to know. And don't worry, Daniel. No suicide missions."

One Friday morning in late September, Daniel picked up Riou in Orleans. After hauling several back-breaking suitcases into the boot, they set off along the little forest roads of the Perche region.

Winding down his window and rolling up his sleeves to capture what seemed the sun's last rays for that year, he thought nervously of the precious cargo bumping and shunting around in the back.

They rolled past lakeside beauty spots. Riou's route avoided all the main arteries and junctions. No checkpoints. This wasn't Paris, thank goodness.

They plunged into the heart of the forest and marvelled at the mottled light running down the leaves. Had he been too rash, he thought suddenly. He could have opted to do nothing, to lead a quiet life. Plenty of people were doing it. He thought of Tatiana's complete ignorance.

'A change of air will do you good,' she had said, as she waved him off that morning. He'd been struck by her paleness. He'd had the sense to call the child-minder the evening before.

Several hours later, they drove up a straight gravel drive. Up ahead was the Château d'Arnouville, a very wide, low-rise edifice of pale grey stone.

"Arnouville Youth Centre," Riou said, with uncharacteristic jocularity. "Not bad, eh, for lunch?"

A first man emerged from the grand entrance, sporting thick, dark eyebrows. With his black pomaded hair and camel coat, he strode out like an Italian, throwing out his arms like an operatic tenor.

"*Bien venu à notre Centre!*" His bright eyes, meanwhile, narrowed as he looked Daniel up and down. He shook his hand warmly.

Riou had told him Duvillard seemed affable. "Don't be fooled. He's a political animal and excellent organiser."

Duvillard introduced Riou and Daniel to a placid-looking man in a beret and steel-rimmed glasses, who had walked out timidly behind him. *He could be a bookshop owner.* Was he in disguise? Daniel wasn't sure.

"Now," Duvillard continued, "you won't mind if we leave you, Daniel?"

"Of course."

"Good. Good! We have beautiful grounds to explore. Back later." He picked up one of the cases. "*Mon Dieu!*" he exclaimed, heaving the case up the central stair. The man in the beret followed with his case without complaint.

"*A tout à l'heure,*" Riou said, passing him and following them up the crimson-carpeted stair.

Daniel watched them disappear and, stuffing his hands into his pockets, strode out into the grounds, which so reminded him of Fort Girard. As he picked up his pace, he started to hum a scout marching song. *Un kilometre à pied, ça use, ça use. Un kilomètre à pied. Ça use les souliers. La peinture à l'huile, c'est bien difficile, mais c'est bien plus beau que la peinture à l'eau.*

Very soon he had walked the perimeter of the grounds, ending up at the central fountain. He peered at his wristwatch: 12.30. Three-quarters of an hour they'd been discussing their business. *Are they regretting bringing me? Perhaps they're arguing over me? No, impossible! Riou wouldn't have brought me if he wasn't sure.*

"Daniel!" shouted a voice. He saw Duvillard stride out towards him. "Follow me."

Without exchanging a word, they marched back to the house, mounted the stairs and entered a dimly-lit, wood-panelled room. Duvillard locked the door behind them.

Daniel's gaze was drawn to the long table at the end of it, over which the others were bending their heads. They parted and made room for him. Running his eyes down the heavy oak table, he found row upon row of submachine guns, pistols, packets of ammunition, rolls of Bickford rope.

For a while he was speechless before the haul he had transported.

The others just looked at him and smiled. The placid man who had worn the beret asked them all to sit and turned to Daniel.

"We apologize for the wait. It took a while to put this lot together."

Daniel smiled. "Of course," he said, his heart lifting.

"It is on Riou's high recommendation that I have decided to reveal to you what we do here. Be aware that this is a mortal secret we share." The man's voice was calm. Like a priest's, he thought. "You are not obliged to help us, of course." He peered at Daniel through his steel-rimmed glasses.

Daniel didn't know whether to respond. He sought Riou who gave him an empathetic smile. Presumably, he had gone through the same procedure.

"However, we need people with your military background. If you decide not to go ahead, we will forget having met you. Rest assured that we will understand, for this is your affair, not ours, but you should know this – we three, like you, are fathers with children, and therefore we have thought long and hard before making our decision. We are not working with the *maquis* but with the British intelligence Service. Our role is to gather intelligence, distribute arms and equipment, and to carry out reconnaissance work for parachute landings. In short, to prepare the way for the Allied landings which true Frenchmen desire. When you make your decision, you will tell Riou and you will only deal with him from then on. He will be responsible for your acts. That is all for today."

Daniel returned home in shock at what he had been party to. Possessing just one hunting gun could land you in prison. If they had been stopped today, they would have been interrogated, shot, at best taken to a German labour camp.

He made his way over to France's pram, parked under the old pear tree in the garden. Gripping its warm handle, he peered in and saw his daughter, dressed in Béatrice's white cotton dress, focus her large blue eyes on him. Her plump little legs kicked off the crocheted blanket excitedly.

"Papa!" Jeanne came rushing across the overgrown lawn, her hand covering the top of a glass jar. Béatrice followed, bare-foot and a little unsteady.

"Look Papa, a butterfly." Jeanne was nearly six-and-a-half and

Daniel had just taught her the life cycle of a butterfly.

Daniel peered into the jar, where a pair of turquoise and emerald wings opened. "He's a beauty. Where did you find him, *ma poulette*?"

"Maman found him on the windowsill. She said I could show you him when you got back."

"*Papi-llion*," shouted Béa, pointing her finger, glistening with saliva, at the jar.

"Well thank you, *mes chéries*, for showing him to me, but now we must set him free."

"Oh naw, Papa. Can't I just have him for a pet?"

"No Jeanne. You know it's cruel." He gently unclamped her hand and placed the creature on his large index finger. The butterfly fanned its wings. "See, children. He is quite happy on my finger, but he is free to fly off if he wants."

"Can I?" said Jeanne, wiggling her index finger.

"Yes. Here." Their two fingers joined. The butterfly, however, opened its wings and took flight. For a moment Daniel thought they had lost it, but then it landed on Béatrice's curly chestnut head. He and Jeanne laughed.

"Béatrice he's on you!" Jeanne cried.

Béatrice turned around to find the source of their amusement. "*Papi-llion*."

"On your head!" Jeanne said, excitedly.

The creature flapped its wings and nestled in Béa's soft sun-tinged curls. Béatrice frowned. She raised her little hand above her head and slapped it down.

"Naughty, *papi-llion*!"

"*Non chérie!*" Daniel grasped her hand, but there was an awful silence as he and Jeanne stared at the bent wings stirring for the last time on Béatrice's head.

Jeanne screamed and thumped her younger sister on the shoulder. Daniel got in between them as Béatrice started to cry. Tatiana leapt out of the back door into the garden.

"Jeanne, what have you done again to your sister?" She went over to Béatrice and crushed her against her apron. "Oh, Daniel, you're back. What happened?"

"Nothing, *chérie*. Just a mistake."

"Poor butterfly!" Jeanne was kneeling in the grass. She scooped up the motionless creature.

Béatrice retreated into babyhood, looked on and sucked her thumb.

A cry rose up from the pram and a pair of brown legs kicked. Daniel leapt to his feet and went over. He scooped his youngest up and stuffed his nose into her blonde locks. She smelt of fresh hay.

"Papa. Can we bury him?"

He turned to Jeanne, who was offering up the jar in which she had plopped the lifeless creature. "Yes, let's go over there by the rose bushes and give him a decent burial."

Béatrice looked on, now a little bored. Tatiana stood up.

"Come on Béatrice, *chérie*. Let's follow Papa and your sisters. It wasn't your fault."

"Papi-llion," Béatrice repeated, as she took her thumb out of her mouth and toddled over to the burial ground.

CHAPTER THIRTY-FIVE

The Tricolor snapped at the end of the pole as a chill autumnal wind blew down the garden. With a heavy heart, Daniel ran his eyes along the rows of boys, fanning out into a star formation for the last time.

A sprinkling of new recruits had come down from Paris that week. How small and scrawny they were in comparison to their rosier, sturdier, taller companions. Cintract, Roupp, and Labarre headed up their file. Strong-armed, muscular, Daniel was proud of the health and vitality they projected.

He mounted a small rostrum and started to speak. "And so today is a day of change, not only for myself but also for those of you leaving Fort Girard." Daniel swiftly acknowledged Bouillot, Cintract, and his companions. Daniel paused, making sure he was adopting a serious, matter-of-fact tone. "I'll be handing over the reins to our new *Chef* here."

His successor bunched his lips awkwardly. The former headmaster had arrived the afternoon before, expecting a school of sorts, and instead had found Fort Girard, where boys sang on their way to work and around a campfire, together with their group leaders. A place where everyone addressed one another with the familiar *tu*.

Daniel thought of the harvest of oats they had brought in that September. Of the carpentry and ironmongery workshops that were up and running. And there would be more initiatives after his departure – the music and drama workshops he and Lefèbvre had discussed would develop, he hoped. What school could provide all that? Traditional schools were too restrictive. He hoped the man would continue in the same vein.

Lefèbvre and Vic are staying, remember. But this man was the sort to take his meals inside his office – he had been uncomfortable eating at the communal table when the air around them had filled with high-spirited banter – he was the sort who preferred systems, timetables and reports. *The sort*, Daniel thought, wincing inwardly, *to follow policy*.

Daniel continued, "Change is sometimes necessary. We need to be able to adapt in these troubled times. However, some things never change. The love and respect for one's family and one's companions. Our love for France." He looked up at the Tricolor then back at them. "I'm asking you to hold strong. To remember Fort Girard's tenet: *Tenir*." He bent his arm and raised his fist. "And now, a song to set us on our way: *Ce N'est Qu'un Au Revoir* (Auld Lang Syne). Vic, please go and get Mademoiselle Laviolle."

Mlle Laviolle came to join them on the lawn and they started to sing. Her high voice rose amongst theirs.

Faut-il nous quitter sans espoir
Sans espoir de retour?
Faut-il nous quitter sans espoir
De nous revoir un jour?

Ce n'est qu'un au revoir
Mes frères
Ce n'est qu'un au revoir
Oui, nous nous reverrons
Mes frères
Ce n'est qu'un au revoir

The song was still ringing in Daniel's head that early evening when he, Tatiana, and the girls arrived in Orleans. They drove down several cobbled streets with burnt-out houses with 'No Trespass' signs, finally turning into an alley just wide enough for the car, to stop off in front of a low building with no windows and a rusty iron gate.

Pelletier had helped him secure their new home. It hadn't been easy in a town where entire districts had been wiped out by German incendiary bombs during the Battle of France in

June 1940. The Prefect had put into place a reconstruction plan, Pelletier had told him, but the Germans had blocked the funds needed to carry it out. Revenge? Undoubtedly. How sweet victory must have been after the humiliation of Versailles. And the people of Orleans, rendered homeless? Most had had no option but to leave the centre and settle in the surrounding villages.

Daniel had already warned Tatiana that the five of them would have to make do with two bedrooms, a washroom and a kitchen, all on one level. It would be a squeeze, but it would be near to his work. It would be so until the next baby arrived in May, seven months from now.

Tatiana had confirmed that she was pregnant that morning. Convinced by a dream she'd had that she was carrying a boy, Tatiana had accepted Daniel's news, brushing off their modest dwelling for now, already concentrating, it seemed, on the child growing inside her.

Cupping her barely protruding belly, she stepped out of the car with Jeanne and Béa staggering sleepily behind her.

Daniel scooped France up in his arms. Already in her nightdress, her eyelids fluttered. Daniel looked up and down the silent street, where every resident had retreated behind closed shutters for the coming evening. From the fourth floor of the apartment building overlooking their new home, however, faint music filtered down.

"*Mary-Lou, Mary Lou. Do you remember our first rendez-vous?*"

Daniel recognised the old romance from before the war: Tino Rossi's honeyed voice had been a backdrop to his first fateful meeting with Tatiana. They had been in the record shop she worked in, in the Latin Quarter. He had already fallen in love with her voice, her laughter on the telephone. He recalled her ruby nails running along the rows and rows of records when he first saw her – and those dark, almond-shaped eyes. Ah those eyes! How long ago it all seemed. Now Jeanne and Béatrice clung to her skirt and shivered. He needed to settle them quickly; it had been a long, emotional day.

He strode up to the rusty gate and opened it for his wife with a flourish. "*Et voilà!*" he said, extending his hand across their darkened courtyard.

CHAPTER THIRTY-SIX

As he stepped out into his yard the next morning, Daniel heard voices. Peering up through the lime tree dominating his back yard, he saw two women seated on their sills, conversing. The more mature woman was frowning up at the grey skies.

"You'll see. When we're queuing outside the butcher's, she'll be standing at the front and getting the best cuts. We'll be left with the gizzards again."

"We should be so lucky!" The younger woman leaned towards her neighbour and lowered her voice. "Standing all hoity-toity, made up to the nines."

"Shush! She'll hear you."

"She's sleeping. The shutters are closed. Heard her *boche* boyfriend coming round with his heavy boots."

They both laughed and went in.

Daniel shook his head and made for the gate. *That's all I need. A fritz peering down on us!*

It felt strange to be back in a town. Fort Girard's grand terrace, sweeping lawn and forests illuminated his mind. Tatiana and he had been happy there. He wondered whether he'd ever feel as fulfilled or motivated again.

He threw open the whining gate. He'd have to oil it. He didn't want anyone knowing their business. He wedged his trilby onto his head and headed out to town.

They were living in the north-west of Orléans, just within the old city wall. He headed south-east, down a long thoroughfare ending in one of the central squares. From there, his office was a minute's walk away.

It was quiet at this time in the morning, but that had been one of the few advantages of war – a drastic reduction in traffic. A lone Citroen chugged past with a gazogène engine. He thought once more of the business he had left behind in Jurançon. At that time it had been in the Free Zone. No longer. Hitler's troops had taken over the southern zone a month before, seemingly without opposition. The French had woken up to it. That was Hitler's way. Hitler's revenge for the US attack on North Africa. *And what had Laval done? Nothing! Still having cosy meetings with the Führer. He's finished. No self-respecting Frenchman worth his salt supports him anymore.*

Several cyclists bumped past him, over the cobbled street. Ahead, a rag-and-bone-man in a horse and cart was crying out, in a reedy voice,

"Rags, old bones, rags, old bones."

Daniel pulled up the collar on his raincoat. It turned his stomach to think that they were manufacturing soap out of bones. How he craved the scent of lavender and rosemary. He sniffed the damp air and felt heavier droplets land on his nose. Lowering his hat, he picked up the pace and headed to the Place Gambetta.

At the corner of the square, he checked one of the arteries, the rue du Faubourg Bannier. People were walking past a row of collapsed buildings without caring to look up. The rubble had been cleared and swept, the loose bricks neatly piled up away from the pavement.

His chest tightened as he crossed the square. Pelletier had warned him that the German military high command occupied the rue de la Bretonnerie and rue de la République, all a stone's throw from where he'd be working. But what difference did it make? It had shocked him to be ordered about by that insufferable French Inspector. On policy and laws, it was impossible to tell where Vichy France began and the Reich ended. As regional delegate in the Ministry of Youth, he'd be doing all he could to protect young people in the Loire region, though he would need to tread carefully.

Daniel entered Chodakewitz's pokey office. Files were stacked on his desk. He was on the telephone, listening intently and nodding.

"How many workers? You have to be joking!" His new boss

looked up and gave him a wave. "Must go. He's here."

A large framed poster of the Maréchal, in his *képi* hat and full uniform, bore down on them. *The 'Victor of Verdun'*, Daniel thought to himself, the words bringing on sadness and anger. *Still, he'll never be as bad as that wolf Laval.*

Chodakewitz came off the phone. "Ah, Daniel!" He leapt up and stretched out a warm hand. "Pelletier will arrive in a minute. Settled in alright?' He grinned. "Finding your way around the city?"

"Yes, quite simple." Daniel smiled. Chodakewitz had also been a scout. All of them were, almost without exception, ex-scouts and soldiers, to whom orienteering was second nature.

"Pelletier has been praising you to the skies. He says you're the man for injecting new life into these youth centres. We've quite a number – all over the region." Chodakewitz led him to a map hanging on one of the walls. "Your area of responsibility is the Loiret, L'Eure/Loir, Loire and Cher *départements*. You'll be visiting the territories, motivating young people to find work in the region." Chodakewitz leaned on his desk, as Daniel removed his raincoat. "Oh, apologies, just put that over the back of your chair. Now, as you know, the Germans are becoming more and more insistent. Top of their list are the older age groups – the nineteen-year-olds, who, if a labour law is enforced, will be the first to be called up."

"Conscripted, like military service?"

"Exactly, if Sauckel gets his way. We're just preparing ourselves. Our problem is getting the message across loud and clear and, of course, finding jobs for them here in France. It means bringing the youths up-to-date with what is available. We also – and this is very important – need to keep in close touch with the employers themselves. A regular fortnightly call, the odd dinner. Well, you did that at Fort Girard."

"Of course."

"I don't suppose you've had time to walk past the German recruitment office in rue Royale."

Daniel shook his head. "Not had the pleasure."

"There's a poster in the window: *Nos ouvriers sont bien nourris* (Our workers are well-fed). Photographs of restaurant chefs, two young ladies feasting, pictures of spanking new accommodation. You name it, they're putting it out for others to gawp at. And of course, they're being told that three workers will release one French PoW."

Daniel shook his head. "Any indication of the uptake?"

"We can only guess. Going on anecdotal evidence, not much at all. But the minute the *fritz* make it law, our job will be to lessen the blow. Operation TODT is an option – the building of defences along our Atlantic coast. Infinitely more appealing than an ammunition factory in Cologne." He raised his finger in the air. "We also face the thorny problem of our youths leaving our centres prematurely. We want to keep them off the streets, away from extremist influences and out of the *fritz's* clutches. This is where you come in again. Not only will it be your job to put the latter in touch with local employers, but also to keep those attending the centres happy and motivated."

"Yes, I see. At Fort Girard we had planned a drama department. I need access to gramophones, records, books, play scripts. Music appreciation, drama – that always goes down well with a young, mixed audience – for I take it I'll be responsible for the young women too?"

"Yes, of course. For that sort of equipment, you'll have to see that new Préfet that's been appointed – Bussière."

"Bussière!" Daniel's felt the room light up; he'd entered Daniel's life once more. He had been so helpful in Vendôme. "I know him. I couldn't have restored Fort Girard without him."

"*Formidable!*" Chodakewitz got up and patted Daniel on the shoulder. "There you are," he said, laughing.

"Sir."

"Call me Chocho," he said. "Everyone else does."

Daniel relaxed. It was like Fort Girard all over again. He now felt it was the right moment to broach the subject.

"I've been meaning to ask you... My job title? For I will need a visiting card."

Chocho cleared his throat. "Head of Propaganda." His eyes twinkled with mischief. "Don't worry, no Nazi propaganda here, as I've said before."

There was a knock at the door. Pelletier came in.

"Ah, Daniel." He shook Daniel's hand and sat down.

Chocho was now beaming. "Delighted to have Daniel on board, but I've called you both here on another matter. I have some funds for another office. There is a building in the St Paul district, an old

Scout association house which escaped the bombing. Now that scout organisations have been officially banned, we can use it."

"But that is fantastic," Daniel said. "It's the perfect opportunity to set up our rival recruitment centre."

"Recruitment centre?" said Chocho, looking puzzled.

"Well not exactly. Like an information, documentation centre, where jobseekers would leave their details, consult manuals and job adverts, and employers would leave calling cards, information about job vacancies."

"Yes, I see. That's good."

"And we have the 'propaganda' budget to fund this, no?" Daniel gave Chocho his broadest smile.

"I believe we have," Chocho replied, laughing and frowning a little.

"Enough for a permanent librarian, for I will often be out and about in the region?"

"I'm not sure our budget could stretch to that."

"Perhaps one that came in two afternoons a week?"

Chocho made a face.

"Does that mean yes?"

Within a week, Daniel had recruited Pelletier's friend, René Guichet, who had provided the wine for the lunch he had given at Fort Girard.

"Excellent wine, René, Pelletier must have told you. Completely wasted on our Inspector."

René laughed. "I heard." He pushed back his round spectacles on his button nose. He had a young, boyish face – it was hard to believe that he was married with four children.

He set to work immediately, rattled off countless letters to every employers' organisation he could think of. Maude, a quiet, retired schoolteacher, came to assist him.

Daniel had to wait several months to meet with the Prefect, Bussière – but those months were filled with travel around the region.

In the New Year, 1943, he was one of the first to be received by his old acquaintance. The authorization to buy radios, record players and records for the music appreciation classes was given at their first meeting.

However, Daniel's trip had to be put back, with the implementation by Laval, after many months of speculation in Daniel's circle, of the *relève*, a French law passed by Vichy, which now ordered all males 20-23 to make themselves available for work in Germany as a substitute to military service.

Daniel, although not surprised, was in shock. That cocky Laval had caved to Sauckel. Laval the German-lover, people were saying. He had offered the rest of France on a platter and now he was dangling those boys in front of the ogre, whose hunger would never be satisfied.

René, Pelletier and Daniel were doing their utmost to prevent the boys from ending up at the Siemens factory in Germany. For a lucky few, universities were proving a temporary haven. But inevitably, the older boys in the centres were beginning to flee and go underground. Pétain, meanwhile, had decided to protect the young women, believing them to be sacrosanct in their role as future mothers.

One day in April, several months later, Daniel was finally getting ready to make his trip to Paris. He and Pelletier had dealt with the most urgent cases around the region and Daniel was now focused on the younger members of the centres and the female population.

He was just preparing himself to walk over to the town hall to obtain his *ausweis* for Paris when Riou walked in, smiling, with an earnest-looking young man.

"This is Lerude. He works with us as a centre leader."

Lerude shook his hand warmly. He had blond hair, regular features like Daniel, but he was thin, pale, and his sunken eyes suggested a recent illness.

"Good to meet you."

René came in with a pile of letters, looking preoccupied. He marched up to Daniel with a pen, indicating that his signature would be needed, and then brightened when he saw Riou at the door.

"*Bonjour*, what brings you here?"

Riou smiled. "We need to talk with Daniel. Can those signatures wait?"

Daniel was surprised by Riou's abruptness. René nodded, sensing that it was important business.

"Just remember, Daniel, the Rector from the university is coming early afternoon."

"We won't keep him long. Here, Daniel, shall we go to the café on the square?"

"*Bien. Allons-y.*"

The men left the *Centre de Documentation et Information* and started crossing the square towards the café, before seeing a few *gendarmes* entering with a swagger. One of them had just taken out a notebook.

"Let's carry on," Riou said.

Lerude nodded. They set off down a side street and came out onto a little square with a church and a presbytery. From there they descended a narrow flight of old stone steps leading to the banks of the Loire.

For a time they walked in silence, away from the town centre. Riou came to a halt and turned towards the river.

"This won't take long. I know you're busy."

Daniel looked across the Loire's high, swirling, waters, flowing past at breakneck speed.

"Lerude and I were wondering, since you're already bound for Paris and will have the authorisation to travel, whether you would go and see a colleague of ours. His name is Durand."

Daniel felt himself flinch. Had he mentioned his Paris trip to Riou? Or had René been talking? He tried to recall the name. "Wasn't he…?"

"At Arnouville. Yes. At our lunch, remember? The one who led our meeting."

The dimly-lit table littered with weapons and bomb-making equipment came back to Daniel in vivid detail. He nodded.

"Well, would you be open to meeting up with Durand again, only in Paris this time?"

"I see," he replied, digging his hands into his pockets.

What was supposed to have been a simple business trip up to Paris months ago, a delightful jaunt, had not only been put back several times, but was now becoming something quite different.

Seemingly unperturbed, Riou continued, "We need someone to take two cases out of Paris and bring them here. And seeing as you have the *ausweis*… Will you do this?"

Daniel bent his head. So many conflicting thoughts nested in his mind. He looked back down the river. On the patchy island in the middle of the Loire, a heron was spreading its wings.

And then he heard voices. Two *gendarmes* were walking from the town centre towards them, probably the same individuals they had seen by the café counter.

The *gendarmes* must have noticed them, but one of them was busy surveying the waters. He stopped his colleague and pointed back towards the island.

"What do we do?" Daniel said, quietly, his heart starting to thump.

"You have nothing to fear," Riou said, keeping his eye on them. "We're taking a stroll for lunch. We're heading back towards the steps. Let's not change our route. Start walking."

Daniel stepped out of the river grasses and back onto the muddy path with the other two in tow. Riou was tailing him now. The *gendarmes* turned away, starting to march up-river, towards the nearest bridge. Something was bobbing in the water around the island.

"Ignore what they're looking at," Riou said, calmly. "Could be anything. We've seen all sorts float down, flotsam, dead horses," and almost within the same breath he continued, but now in a more urgent tone, "After picking up from Durand and boarding a train in Paris, you'll be getting off at a little station in the countryside, just outside Orléans. It's used by lots of Parisians who wish to stock up with country goods – you'll blend in with the rest of them with their empty cases."

Daniel nodded, already feeling the incredible weight of his own cases. What was he nodding for? He hadn't accepted.

They were back at the bottom of the large flight of steps, which led back to the church square. Daniel started to climb them, with Riou and Lerude on either side. He stared down at his shoes, which were splattered with mud, then at the top of the stairs. He started to climb them, breathing hard – though not because he was unfit.

"How will Durand recognise me?" he said, finally scaling the last step. The church square was still empty. "It was quite a while back. And to be honest, I don't remember–"

"No problem, Daniel. You will go with a torn note, you will ask for Durand, he will produce his half. Simple."

Daniel buried his nose in his collar. He turned to Riou and then to Lerude, who smiled encouragingly.

"Do you accept, Daniel? You are suited for this mission. You have the *ausweis* – it's the perfect cover – you have a trustworthy face and, as I say, you'll be able to remain relatively anonymous – you'll be boarding a packed train."

Daniel opened his mouth. They had started walking again and were passing by the little presbytery. He heard himself reply in the affirmative.

"In which case…" Riou handed him the torn bank note.

Daniel folded it and slipped it into his own wallet, behind Tatiana's photograph. It had been their first holiday ever together in the Auvergne – after Jeanne's birth. She had never looked so happy and free.

"But, but what about all the equipment I'm purchasing?" Daniel asked, now searching for problems.

"Do not concern yourself with these details. We will organise for the gramophones and wirelesses to follow you by train."

CHAPTER THIRTY-SEVEN

Clutching his cases, Daniel plunged into the afternoon crowds flowing down Paris's grand boulevards, which were teeming with German soldiers. *Right into the hornet's nest.* The thought of it was strangely thrilling.

The doors of a department store burst open. Out came a vigorous, portly man in a leather coat and trilby, accompanied by a young blonde woman in a green military uniform, laden with Dior perfume and toiletries. All that Tatiana dreamt of. The woman hailed a Mercedes that had been waiting for them.

"Avenue Foch," she said, getting in.

The man shut her door and was about to step into the street and walk around the vehicle when his beady, close-set eyes fell on Daniel.

He felt himself falter. *Just walk on. Keep your head high. You've a business meeting, you're buying music, having purchased your radios at the His Master's Voice factory. Simple.*

"*Komm Klaus, schnell!*"

"*Ja, ja,*" the man said, turning back to the car reluctantly. He walked around to the road-side door and got in. As the vehicle pulled away, he looked back at Daniel, as he stood on the edge of the pavement, clutching his cases, his heart hammering pathetically.

Idiot! He had nearly tumbled at the first hurdle – no hurdle at all. And what had his suitcases contained – nothing but air! What was wrong with him? He stared around him, realized that no one else had paid him the least amount of attention, and walked on.

Perhaps he had needed breaking in again. It had been a while since he'd been on that first mission with Riou. At least he hadn't buckled under the stare. But something had unnerved him more than usual. This *fritz* neither had the body nor the posture of the military man. He had seen men of the same ilk in Orléans, coming out of their HQ in boulevard Alexandre Martin. 'Avenue Foch'. Ah, Of course! The Gestapo Paris office.

He walked down a street into a sun-filled square. His pace slowed; still shaken, he was conscious of his shoes slapping on the cobbles. His eyes skimmed over the pavement, the spotless square, in the middle of which rose L'Opéra Comique, with its graceful white arches supported by colonnades and statues. Debussy's opera, *Pelléas et Mélissande*, was showing that evening to a full house, it seemed, for a diagonal strip with the words '*Complet*' had been stuck over the promotional posters. It would draw the cream of the German military and senior civil servants, no doubt eager to see the French equivalent of Wagner's *Tristan and Isolde*.

Daniel turned away. Ahead of him was a little street in shadow. He entered it with a pounding heart and stopped outside a music shop. Placing the cases at his feet, he checked his watch. Just a few minutes to go.

Wiping the sweat from his forehead with his handkerchief, he perused the window display. In amongst the black and white photographs of full-breasted divas and stocky, bearded tenors, an elegant violin rested on a velvet podium. He thought of his pigeon-chested father, playing the fiddle, as he liked to call it, with his mother accompanying him on the piano. He wouldn't have time to visit them today. They'd thanked him for the food parcels he and Tatiana sent regularly. Daniel suspected that his mother had made sacrifices to feed other mouths.

He unbuttoned the collar of his shirt. *Not one Jewish star have I spotted since I've been here. Not one.*

Inside the dimly-lit shop, a woman in a pale suit moved towards the counter. A young bespectacled man was ringing up the till and handing over her music. Daniel adjusted his trilby. It was time. On cue, as if conscious of Daniel's rendezvous, the customer made for the door. Daniel slowly picked up the cases and gripped the handles. The door opened, the shop bell rang out in the silent square. The bespectacled man was looking at him – was it Durand? He wasn't quite sure.

"*Un moment*," the man said, holding the door and peering over in the direction of his disappearing client. He checked the street and, with his free hand, gestured for Daniel to enter. It had to be Durand, but he was wearing different glasses or had had a haircut. Daniel needed to be sure. He removed the bank note from the leaves of his wallet and rolled it up in his palm.

The owner dived in after Daniel, stole a glance at the cases and smiled.

Daniel looked into his approving eyes. "*Je voudrais parler à un Monsieur Durand.*"

"And who do I say has called?"

On cue, Daniel produced the torn bank note.

The man produced the other half. Without speaking, he walked up to the shop entrance, turned the sign to '*Fermé*', and bolted the door.

"Follow me," he said, drawing aside a thick curtain and walking into a passage.

Stuffing the note back in his pocket, Daniel followed him through a draughty hallway, up some creaking stairs and into a little apartment above. They entered a tiny kitchen with condensation on the walls. The air smelled of boiled leeks.

"Something to eat?" Durand said, sitting him at a table laid with an oilcloth and where a basket had been put out with two slices of black bread.

Food was the last thing on his mind but Daniel, realising he may have a long day ahead, accepted the offer.

Durand laid two knives and spoons on the table whilst the soup heated through, then opened a drawer and brought out two checked napkins.

Durand smiled at him and went back to the hob. "It's my mother's soup. She's gone to the cinema with my father. There was a raid recently." Durand carefully ladled the soup into two bowls. "Twenty youths rounded up by the police."

"I heard," Daniel said, taking the bowl and laying it before him.

There was a silence between them. Durand sat down.

"Go on, eat. You're in for a long day," Durand said, shaking his serviette. He spoke gently and quietly, as if Daniel were recovering from a protracted illness.

Daniel lifted his spoon and accepted the bread that Durand offered.

Durand took several mouthfuls of soup then put his spoon down. "We haven't long."

Daniel sipped quietly, eager not to miss a word, for he knew Durand, like the others, would never commit any information to paper.

"You are to take the Métro Réaumur Sébastopol and get off at l'Odéon on the left bank. There, make your way to a café in the rue de Rennes, the one on the corner of the rue du Vieux Colombier."

"I know it," said Daniel. From his bookselling days, Daniel knew the Latin Quarter well.

"You are to go to the little room at the back and sit behind the counter."

Daniel looked up, puzzled. "Won't that look odd?"

"Don't worry, we know the owner and his wife. The wife will be expecting you. You are to say that Durand sent you. Wait behind the counter and put your two cases to your left."

"Alright." He broke off some black bread and mopped the soup bowl clean. "Anything else I need to know?"

"That's it for now."

"Well now it's your turn to eat," Daniel replied, half-laughing. He had noticed how thin the man was.

Durand took small, regular sips until his plate was empty, then wiped his mouth.

"Now, tell me what you did this morning."

"I was over at the His Master's Voice factory in the western suburb of Paris ordering radios, gramophones."

"Look, you'd better not linger." Durand went over to a little table piled high with sheet music. "I'm sure my father won't miss a couple of these. You might like to put a few sheets in both cases. You never know – if you're searched on your way to rue de Rennes. You can tell them you're down to your last Piaf and Charles Trenet – no?"

"Thank you," Daniel said, getting up and taking them. He opened both cases and put them inside.

"You'll be fine," Durand said, calmly. "You look like a *boche*."

Daniel left the shop, his whole body tense, and boarded a packed metro.

At Odéon, Daniel bolted out of the exit and, at street level, almost walked into a police van stopped outside one of the cinemas. A group of men milled around the vehicle.

"*Salauds*," he heard one man mutter under his breath.

Another man, in overalls, started to hum the *Marseillaise*, until he saw a *gendarme* appear on the cinema forecourt with a youth in handcuffs.

Daniel turned away in disgust and started down the boulevard of St Germain.

How can they live with themselves? Carting off their own like that. He plunged back into the streets and alleys of the Latin Quarter, eventually entering the square of St Sulpice. He passed The Fountain of the Four Cardinals and continued on, past the colossal Catholic Church with its giant colonnades.

By the time he'd reached the rue du Vieux Colombier he was half-running and in a sweat again.

He slowed as he entered the café on the corner. Only a few tables were occupied out front, where the sun's rays were beginning to penetrate the low-hanging cloud. Inside, the establishment was empty, and soon Daniel discovered why. No electricity, no heating. Daniel shivered as he walked to the back, to an area with a tiny, bare counter.

A pale woman with clipped back greying hair appeared from the kitchens.

"*Bonjour* Monsieur," she said, wiping her hands on her apron.

"*Bonjour* Madame. I have been sent by Durand."

She nodded. "Go, sit yourself down. Coffee, Monsieur?"

"*Merci*, you are most kind, Madame."

While the woman returned to the kitchens, Daniel sat and gently lowered his cases, making sure they were to his left. He buttoned up his shirt and raincoat, then blew hot breath over his fists and waited. Alone. Aside from a yellow metal Ricard advertisement and a wooden sign listing the prices of drinks by the glass, there was nothing to distract him. Daniel wondered whether the café had run out of alcohol, but then sniffed the faint aroma of cheap cognac lingering in the air.

At the café entrance, a man with a little dog peered in. Daniel gripped the counter. A woman had stopped before the man and was asking him for a light. He removed a lighter from his jacket pocket and lit her cigarette.

"*Café*, Monsieur."

Daniel jumped. "*Oh, merci*!" He sipped the lukewarm ersatz coffee and checked the café's exits. Two points of entry, perfect.

The pale waitress went to clear the cups and wipe down the tables outside. She stood, enjoying the warm spring sun. Daniel, slouched on his bar stool in the gloom, peered up at the clock over the bar to check that it matched with his wristwatch. Nearly one thirty.

Heavy footsteps came up behind him. A man in a belted raincoat and trilby, dressed exactly like him, held two identical cases. He was darker however, had grey, wiry hair and an angular face.

"*Un café s'il vous plait, Marion!*"

"*Oui.*" The woman scurried back to the kitchens.

The man fell onto his stool.

Daniel was alarmed to see the man with the beret being led into the cafe by his dog. He mock-saluted Daniel's neighbour.

"He's with us. Don't worry," Daniel's neighbour said. With care, the resistance agent laid his own cases to Daniel's right and in the same smooth manoeuvre grabbed Daniel's cases.

"Mine weigh a ton. But you're fit," the man said, looking Daniel up and down. The coffee came. "*Merci Marion,*" he said, distractedly. He added some saccharine and stirred it in. "You are to take a train leaving in exactly one hour. The two-thirty to Orléans. Once on board, leave the cases by the toilets – do not use the racks. Mind you get in there fast, that way your cases will be covered up by everyone else's luggage. You can be sure the racks will be insufficient for the crowds leaving Paris this Friday afternoon."

Daniel nodded.

"At Les Aubrais station, there will be Franco-German control checks. Go down three-quarters of the queue on the platform – get into the middle lane. That's it. *Bonne chance.*"

The man drank his coffee and left, followed by the man with the dog.

Over at the Gare d'Austerlitz, Daniel viewed the crowded platform with mounting concern. He stepped up onto a trolley, looking for spaces amongst the mass of passengers that had gathered there with their families. Everywhere Daniel looked, any spare spaces had been filled with luggage and picnic baskets.

And now, more worryingly, his gaze ran along rows and rows of green uniforms amassing on the edge of the platform. Germans soldiers off to join their regiment. Something was afoot – they made up at least 20 percent of the entire trainload. It would be impossible to avoid them, especially if they spread themselves through the train carriages.

Taking a deep breath and balancing his two heavy cases, which pulled so hard at his forearms that his elbows ached, Daniel threaded his way through the crowd.

"*Excusez-moi* Madame, Monsieur. *Désolé*, my wife is over there with our baby..." He stared straight ahead, focused on a young woman he had seen carrying a baby boy ten metres or so from where he stood.

"Ouch! *Attention* Monsieur!" a man snapped, holding his knee. "What have you got in there? Bars of gold?"

Daniel excused himself and laughed uneasily, thankful that the soldiers were too far away to hear. He moved more slowly now, taking infinite care with his burdensome cases. Now and again, he stopped, balancing them against his muscular thighs. He would look up and focus on the young mother ahead, who he seemed to be approaching at a snail's pace.

After ten minutes of stepping over baskets, children and cases he eventually reached his destination.

"*Bonjour,*" Daniel said, giving her his warmest smile.

The young woman looked up with surprise but seemed so hollow-eyed that she cared little. She wasn't wearing a wedding band. He parked the cases one atop the other.

"I thought you might want to sit down on these. Seeing as you've been carrying that baby of yours."

The woman hesitated and looked around, seemingly relieved that no one had noticed Daniel. Everyone was too focused on getting a seat on the train, which was now due.

As a precautionary measure, Daniel followed her gaze. No husband on the horizon; besides, the platform was so thick with people now that he would have trouble getting through even if he were determined.

Daniel leaned into the woman. "My own wife is expecting soon," he said, gently. "We'd be thrilled to have a handsome little boy like yours." He placed his finger under the baby's soft chin.

The mother's face relaxed into a faint smile. She sat down on the cases and, to Daniel's relief, the baby son gurgled at his touch.

Daniel didn't dare turn round, for to do so would spoil the ruse.

The train was delayed by 15 minutes, by which time Daniel had whispered to the woman that he would leap on the train early, secure her a seat with her child and then leave her in peace.

There was a roar of relief as the train pulled in. The passengers hurled themselves forward. Daniel let an angry-looking man go before him with his young wife and children and stepped immediately behind them, blocking the crowd to let 'his' young woman through with her baby. Checking that at least one of the soldiers mounting the steps to his carriage had seen them together, he stepped on.

Having seated his adopted family, he continued on down the carriage until he spied the toilets. There he placed the cases, impatiently waiting for others to load their picnic baskets atop them, which they did almost immediately. Ten soldiers had already boarded the carriage and were beginning to dump their bulging rucksacks around the picnic baskets.

"*Da drüben*," said one of them, sending Daniel further down the corridor. Daniel watched his precious cargo disappear under a mound of German equipment with a mixture of amusement and terror.

After a 20-minute unexplained break, the train lurched forward. Shunting along the ancient rails, it followed the Seine, passing the warehouses of Bercy, where thousands of bottles of wine were stored, some of them grand vintages, all destined for the tables of the German elite.

A Parisian leaning against the window next to Daniel was talking quietly to a colleague. Daniel heard fragments of their conversation, something about Allied bombings in Rouen.

Daniel shut his eyes and leaned against his carriage window. He wanted Allied victories of course – he accepted the disruption it brought to their daily lives– but he feared the American bombers, who bombed indiscriminately. He prayed for French pilots, for only they would take enough care with their own people.

Daniel peered through the window. Juvisy, one of the biggest railway junctions in France. They weren't that far south of Paris. Slowly, the train took a right fork and started passing a number of little villages, whose names ended in '*Orge*', the Seine's tributary. The train climbed to a plateau, barely picking up speed. 'Brétigny', a sign said. The daylight was dimming. Through the gathering dusk, Daniel distinguished a ring of familiar woodland. A medieval tower rose through it. The Montlhéry Tower. Daniel had seen it every morning when he'd worked on Paul's estate. With its Tricolor flapping proudly in the breeze, it had always lifted his spirits. Now the flag had been removed.

The train turned in a wide semi-circle and stopped. About a quarter of the carriage emptied. This was an important market gardening region. The closest to Paris. There would be rich pickings here. Daniel eyed his cases nervously as several women removed their baskets and sidled past them.

After a series of unexplained halts they reached Etampes. Staring out over Beauce country, where acres of young wheat fields stretched to infinity, Daniel frowned. At the September harvest, all of the cereals would be transported back in the opposite direction, to Germany.

He was feeling the gnaw of hunger. The aroma of *saucisson* and fine herbs filled the compartment. Several German soldiers were digging their teeth into their beloved pumpernickel. Meanwhile, everyone in the corridor had started to gather their belongings, dust their jackets. The two picnicking soldiers got up and walked over to the toilets. Seizing his opportunity, Daniel weaved through the carriage, prised his cases out from under the luggage, and, as nonchalantly as possible, staggered over to another part of the car.

The train stopped and the doors opened. The soldiers filed out. Daniel waited, then joined the queue's middle stream as he'd been instructed, making sure he was three-quarters of the way down the platform.

At the station's exit, several guards were checking luggage. The soldiers went through smoothly, leaving a widening gap in the queue. Before the last of them had filed out and just as Daniel feared being taken too quickly up to the front with his cases, he felt himself jostled on either side. A firm tug and suddenly, releasing his hold, Daniel felt the iron weight disappear. Relieved of his dangerous burden, he heard himself laugh manically. How the accomplices got out of the station was a mystery, for when he dared to look up, there was no trace of them.

CHAPTER THIRTY-EIGHT

In the reading-room of the episcopal palace of Orleans, now the municipal library, Daniel watched a sprinkle of dust motes spiral down from the ceiling. He looked out onto the tranquil gardens, picked up a pen, and wrote,

Debussy loved playing the piano but hated scales. One afternoon, when no one was listening, he let his hand drop up and down over the keys randomly. The chords he came up with possessed a strange, ethereal beauty. This is how he came to compose 'Clair de Lune', which I'm going to play to you now.

He had hoped Tatiana would help him compile the music programme today. On their marital bed, where she had lain with her feet up, he had produced a multitude of records of various genres. But she had soon tired and told him to take them away. She had it all in her head anyway. It was then that he had noticed her little icon of the Virgin Mary and Jesus, upturned on her bedside table.

"Have you thought of a name for the baby, *chérie?*"

"It's bad luck to talk about the birth, Dan."

Sighing, he picked up a script of *Portique pour une fille France* dedicated to Jeanne d'Arc. The dramatist, Charles Peguy, was Orléans-born. Daniel had decided to involve all the centres of the region in this celebration of her life and to stage it in cathedral cloisters. Her statue in the Place du Matroi had escaped the full impact of the terrible 1940 bombings. Jeanne was the perfect symbol of resistance, he told himself. The perfect foil.

Daniel returned, with reams of hand-written notes, to his own office.

René stood at his usual position, looking even more like an overgrown schoolboy with his short haircut, side parting, and round spectacles. He was on the telephone as usual.

"*Salut*, Dan!" he said, grinning, and then went back to his conversation. "Yes, it's him. Do you want to speak to...?"

"Who is it?" Daniel said, wishing to get behind his desk and catch up with his post and paperwork before embarking on his notes.

"Riou."

"Riou?" He reached for the receiver.

René stopped him. "Just a moment. Alright. I'll tell him. This afternoon."

"What's going on?"

"Riou will speak to you later."

"Oh."

René put the receiver back in its cradle. "So, the stranger returns."

"Yes," he replied, distractedly walking into his own office, René in tow. As he passed the fireplace in the back office, he spied several bricks piled on top of each other. "What are these, René?"

René looked excited. "I haven't time to tell you yet. That's what Riou and I were talking about."

"Oh," Daniel said, picking up a brick.

"It's to block off the chimney. Riou wants us to use it as a weapons cache."

"'Us'?"

René's face expressed a mixture of glee, pride and excitement. "I've joined your group," he blurted out. "Riou was going to tell you. Anyway, you'll see him this afternoon."

"Oh!" Daniel looked over René's big shoulders, out through his office door to the front office. Did he have to be so indiscrete? Anyone could have walked in.

"Don't worry – I'm listening out for the door," René said, pushing up his specs on his button nose. "Is this a problem for you, Dan?"

"No, no." At least he didn't think it was. René was resourceful and good with people, had first-hand knowledge of the region and its people. And Riou was a good judge of people. "Where is

214

our secretary?"

"Maude doesn't start today before three pm."

"Whose idea was it to hide the guns here?" he said, shaking his head.

"I joked about it and Riou took me up on it."

"What!" Did René have to be so honest!?

"They need to be moved somewhere, Dan. Lerude is coming with them this afternoon."

"It's too risky. If we're found out, not only will we be carted off to the Gestapo but our whole enterprise will suffer."

"Look, there's a modicum of risk, I grant you. But think…" He laughed nervously. "It's a pretty good solution. There's this perfect chimney at our disposal. Riou has checked it out. The space is large enough to…"

Daniel put his hand up to stop him. "I will wait and speak to Riou."

Riou came that afternoon, as planned.

"Let's go to the café opposite to talk."

Daniel nodded and, having sat down and ordered two ersatz coffees, waited for the explanation. He didn't want to openly criticize Riou's action – Riou who was always so reasonable.

"Daniel, it makes sense to have René. René knows everyone in the region. I've put him in charge of intelligence gathering and reconnaissance for the parachute drops in the Sologne region. We then relay the information to Durand. René will be careful. He too has a family to protect."

"Of course," Daniel said, pressing at his eyes with his thumbs. "Jean, I accept that René is now onboard."

"Accept? You work alongside him – do you think it's a bad choice?" Riou looked puzzled, even hurt.

Daniel shook his head. "No, no, I'm very fond of him. But he's a little indiscreet." There, he had said it.

"Indiscreet?" Riou looked alarmed.

"Well, not exactly, but we must impress upon him the procedures. Like locking the door, checking that no one is listening."

"I will have a word with him."

"I've already brought up the matter. But if he hears it from you… And this business of hiding arms here," Daniel continued, keen to press on and regretting his criticism of René, who trusted him completely. "I was hoping to keep our activities separate."

"You mean yours and René's?"

"No – the centre's and the resistance's."

"Oh, I see," said Jean. "I understand your concern, but it has always been this way. Remember the Bernstein brothers? And what about Duvillard at the Arnouville Centre, which continues to hide Jewish boys and receive parachute drops? We save time this way and, using the centres as fronts."

The wording is unfortunate. What about our boys and girls? Daniel let Riou continue, however, in his calm, methodical way.

"Besides, nothing is more dangerous and time-consuming than travelling around in cars, which we sometimes need *ausweise* for. Look, I can't force you, Dan…"

Daniel suddenly felt guilty. His reluctance sounded like cowardice.

"Sorry."

Riou sighed and waited for the coffees to be placed down. "Your job centre is the perfect shield,' he said, lowering his voice. "René is always here to receive the weapons and Lerude can bring them over with his cohort of youth from the centres."

Daniel rapped the table with his thumb. "Alright."

Jean nodded and patted him on the arm. "Don't worry. Everyone has too much to lose to slip up."

When Jean Riou had left, Daniel went through to the office around back. The chimney had been blocked with bricks. Maude, who had just appeared, was oblivious to its new appearance.

"Afternoon, Monsieur Frey. I have started typing the notes of your music programme you left on my desk. I'm already half-way through and I'm enjoying it immensely!"

Daniel reached the school steps just in time. He waved to his eldest daughter, standing first in an orderly queue of six-year-olds. Without waiting for her teacher's approval, she broke ranks, rushed down the steps in a creased summer dress, shouting,

"Papa, Papa!" her curly hair bouncing around her shoulders.

"Jeanne!" shouted her teacher, trotting down after her, after telling her charges to stay where they were.

"*Désolé*, Madame!" Daniel called, crouching down to receive Jeanne into his arms.

"Papa!"

He leant forward, intent on kissing the top of her head, but her teacher had arrived.

"You must be Monsieur Frey," she said, not unkindly, but with a trace of annoyance.

"Yes," Daniel said, standing, smiling, and shaking her cold, bony hand. "You must excuse my daughter, she's not used to me coming…"

"Of course," said the teacher, now turning to Jeanne. "She's one of the lucky ones though."

Jeanne gave her an uncertain smile.

Daniel bristled at the remark. The fate of French prisoners was still very much in the public eye and it was true, Jeanne and he were 'lucky'. But still. He waved the comment aside, now eager to get away.

"Say goodbye nicely, Jeanne."

"*Au-revoir*, Madame Flatôt.*"

"*Au-revoir* Madame," he said, turning Jeanne towards the street.

Along the pavement, Jeanne hastened to a march. *Am I walking that fast*? he wondered. But he had to get back to piece together the dismantled sten guns Lerude had heaved in as he was leaving. Ironically, the gun would feel comparably light once whole again. He looked forward to handling it, to tucking the automatic under his arm and aiming it at that bastard responsible for employment policy, Sauckel.

He felt a hand in his. Jeanne had started to sing *Maréchal Nous Voilà*.

> *Une flam-me sacrée A sacred flame*
> *Monte du sol natal Rises from our country of birth*
> *Et la France enivrée And a France in rapture*
> *Te salue Maréchal! Salutes you Marshall*
> *Tous tes enfants qui t'aiment All the children who love you*
> *Et venèrent tes ans Who venerate your years*
> *A ton appel suprême To your supreme call*
> *Ont répondu "Présent" All replied "I'm here"*

"Can't you sing something else!"

His daughter looked at him uncomprehendingly. *Maréchal*

Nous Voilà was a prerequisite in schools – the *Marseillaise* had been banned since the Armistice.

They carried on in silence and passed the German Soldaten Kaserne. Daniel narrowed his eyes. He'd noticed a marked increase in German troops around the town since returning from Paris. People had been complaining about their disorderly conduct in the evenings, their alcohol abuse.

Through the central gate, Daniel and Jeanne heard strident tones, pounding boots. The sentry, standing rod-straight on the pavement in front of his box, eyed them impassively from beneath his metal helmet.

Jeanne stared at him anxiously and squeezed Daniel's hand.

"*Viens, ma poulette.* Nearly home. We turn this corner and it's our street. And remember, Maman needs plenty of rest. Monique will be over to cook supper and put you to bed. You're a good girl," he said, kissing her black curls again. He was relieved to see her smile.

As they entered the courtyard, things were eerily still. Daniel slipped into the house, which was in shadow. The tree in the courtyard blocked most of their late afternoon light.

"Jeanne – Maman's left your glass of milk here. Sit here with your books." He heard a feeble voice from the bedroom.

"Dan, is that you?"

Tatiana was on their bed in a loose, linen summer dress, her feet raised. She set aside some stockings she had been darning.

"*Chérie, ma chérie!*" He lay down beside her and gazed into her sunken eyes, normally so dark and sparkling, but more recently dulled with fatigue. "What sort of day have you had?"

She touched her left knee, which was swollen.

"You are right to rest."

"I had some pain earlier. But I feel a little better now."

He took her left hand in his. It was glacial. He rubbed it.

"That's better." Tatiana smiled weakly. "Do the other and my feet."

"Ah, your circulation, Tatiana. What did the doctor say?"

"There's a midwife in our street. Just opposite as you go through our gate. Will you go and see her, Dan?"

"I will, *chérie.*"

Tatiana's proud, teasing voice had left her weeks ago. It worried him. He finished massaging her feet, where she had lost all sensation, it seemed.

In the street he knocked on the midwife's door. A woman in her fifties opened the door, already in her coat.

"Madame. I'm Monsieur Frey. My wife said–"

"Yes. Yes. You're over the road. Your wife and I have spoken. Not her first…"

"Fourth."

"No surprises at least. But each delivery can be different. Now, if you will excuse me." She reached for her keys hanging on a hook by the door. "The babies never stop coming." She picked up a bulging leather bag at her feet. "I'll come as soon as I've finished with this one."

Daniel thanked her but left anxious. He nevertheless had to return to the office whilst René held the fort out front.

When he returned that evening, Tatiana had had her first contractions. Monique had put the children to bed. Baby France's cot had been moved into Jeanne and Béa's bedroom, much to Jeanne's delight; she loved to play mother.

"Thank goodness you're here, Monsieur!"

"Monique. Can you stay here tonight? You can take Jeanne's bed."

"Yes, Monsieur. In any case, it's dark and, what with the curfew, it would take too long to cross town."

Daniel heard a groan from his bedroom. "Monique, go to her!" He rushed over the street to the midwife.

"I need to warn you, Monsieur. I have no medicines. I saw your wife earlier, she'd be better off in a clinic."

"Come over to our house at least."

The woman sighed. "You have plenty of clean towels, I hope. In which case give me quarter of an hour to prepare myself."

"Yes of course, Madame. Thank you."

By the time the midwife returned, Tatiana was pacing the room. The midwife reiterated the need for a clinic.

"*Chérie*. You're going to have to walk with us to the fire station. Can you do that? It will take us fifteen minutes, and from there we will get a lift to the clinic."

Tatiana nodded and scowled as a lash of pain passed over her face.

"Let's go," said the midwife. "It helps to move. No sense staying here."

Daniel put a coat around his wife, took her little bag with her toiletries, nappy pins, nappy cloth, baby clothes, and rolled a pillow and blanket under his arm, for emergencies.

Over at the station, the Fire Chief shook his head.

"*Désolé,* Monsieur. You should have stayed home, we have no authority to take you. The little fuel we possess is only to be used in fire emergencies."

Tatiana doubled up in pain. "My waters!"

"Monsieur," Daniel said, now wiping the smile from his face. "You can see – where can we put my wife?"

"Not here."

"But…"

Tatiana groaned and sat on the fender. She'd turned white.

"The only place is…" The Fire Chief looked at the fire ambulance, against which Tatiana was leaning.

The midwife led Tatiana up the steps into the back of the emergency vehicle. Daniel was made to boil water in the station's kitchen. He returned with a jug full of steaming water, into which the midwife plunged her instruments.

A strong smell of iodine filled the confined space. Tatiana was sitting at the end of a foldable bed, her skirt around her white thighs, gripping the midwife's arm and breathing through her teeth.

"It's happening quickly, the baby's head is already showing." The midwife removed her hand from between Tatiana's thighs. "Madame, don't push just yet, do you understand?"

Tatiana didn't seem to register, but pushed herself up from the bed and, crouching, snarled and started to expel short, sharp breaths.

"Monsieur." The midwife turned to Daniel quickly. "Get another jug, fast!"

Daniel rushed out, hoping the other pot of water he'd put on the stove had boiled.

It was simmering. Down through the station corridor, Tatiana's cries rose into the night. The curfew had silenced the town. He removed the vat when the water had boiled and filled two jugs.

A more urgent howling pierced his chest. He ran back to the ambulance, mounted the steps. The midwife was pulling the arms of their new-born through.

"Mon Dieu!" He rushed forward, filled another metal basin, and washed his hands in another.

The baby came, small, viscous and white in the midwife's towel. Daniel saw Tatiana's agonised face soften, but her eyes turned away.

"Madame. Do you want to hold her?"

The midwife presented what she thought was a prize for Tatiana's suffering. Tatiana lay back down on the metal bed, rolled back her head and closed her eyes.

"Madame, I will take her," Daniel said, receiving his daughter into his arms, her little face creased up in anger. The face, was so delicate, each feature so perfect and small as she bunched up her fists and cried.

"Oh, Tatiana, she's beautiful and strong."

The midwife, expressionlessly, snipped the umbilical cord.

"Come Tatiana," Daniel said, smiling at his daughter, "I'll bring her to you."

Tatiana rolled onto her side and faced the fire vehicle's metal wall.

"Madame, we still have the placenta to expel."

Tatiana rolled back, dull-eyed.

CHAPTER THIRTY-NINE

"Prop up your leg and rest, Madame."

"And how long will I stay like this, Doctor?" Tatiana said, looking at her bandaged leg dejectedly.

"About six weeks, Madame."

"Six weeks!" Tatiana raised her eyes to Daniel, flashing a moment's anger before they were engulfed once more in despair.

"I am sorry, Madame." The doctor didn't look sorry at all, only intent on relaying information and then escaping.

Daniel quickly took Tatiana's hand. "We will manage. The main thing is that you're alright, and the baby."

"Exactly," said the doctor to Tatiana, just as a father would to a child making unfair demands, he who was so busy with the war, after all – Daniel had to allow him that. "You are lucky, Madame, that the phlebitis was caught early and that it should be temporary."

Tatiana winced and held her calf.

"Hot flannel applications and rest, of course, should ease it."

"But I have four children, it is impossible to..."

"If I were you, I would concentrate on your baby daughter. Get her weight back up." The doctor and Daniel turned their eyes to the little baby, now grizzling in the hospital cot, on the other side of the bed.

"Yes, *chérie*," Daniel continued, in a more conciliatory tone, trying to ignore the resentment he saw in her eyes at his siding with the doctor. "Don't worry, Monique can extend her hours and I...."

But Tatiana was watching the doctor replace a clipboard with her notes at the end of the bed. The busy medic nodded to them and smiled, a smile probably denoting his own satisfaction rather than any consideration for his patient, then left the room.

"*Chérie.*" Daniel leaned over and kissed her clammy forehead. "Just consider it a temporary inconvenience."

"You're just like him," she said, gritting her teeth, angry tears welling up again.

Daniel had hardly ever seen Tatiana cry, always so stoical in the face of life's challenges, but this pregnancy had laid her low. And the doctor's tone had defeated her. The sooner they were out of this hospital, the better.

That afternoon, Lerude took them home. Daniel watched his wife turn the key in the lock, this way and that, her face creasing with frustration. She let out a cry of impatience as it slipped from her hands and bounced onto the courtyard stone.

"Let me, *chérie.*" Daniel knelt down with his daughter, picked up the stubborn key, which succumbed immediately to his turns, and let them in. It pained Daniel to see Tatiana so low. The slightest inconvenience was now bringing on silent, rolling tears. He pretended not to notice, and, focusing on his daughter, made his way to their bedroom. It was important to focus on the well-being of the child, he told himself, and all he could do was let Tatiana rest. He would stay with the two of them for a while, for Monique had taken the girls out on this sunny, spring day and he'd had little sleep. He watched Tatiana head straight for bed, pulling back the cotton blanket and getting in. She had at least aligned the cot on her side of the bed.

"Lie down, *chérie,* and I'll bring our daughter to you. We can place her here between us."

"Put her in the cot," Tatiana said, propping her leg up on several cushions. "And please draw the curtains. We must sleep as she sleeps."

"And what a deep sleeper she is," he said, smiling at his daughter, whose delicate, pale lids were closed. He pulled back the crocheted baby blanket, which had served for all their daughters, and laid her down gently.

Tatiana had thrown her head back onto a pillow, lines of worry furrowing her forehead. Her eyelids, puffed with exhaustion, were closing slowly.

"Sleep, *chérie*," he said. Sighing, he rolled onto the bed beside her, took her hand in his, and fell into a deep sleep.

Daniel woke with a jolt.

"Sorry to wake you, Madame, Monsieur," said Monique, entering the room with France, who was trying to wriggle out of her strong arms, Jeanne and Béa galloping behind her. Jeanne ran towards the cot first; Béa came up beside her, carrying a dark-haired waxen doll, whose head she crashed onto the side of the crib.

"Béa, mind how you are with your little sister," Daniel said, rubbing his eyelids violently and shaking himself awake. He checked that he was decent and realised he had fallen asleep fully dressed on top of the coverlet.

Tatiana turned onto her side and pulled her sheet tight over her angular shoulders, looking on without uttering a word. Monique lowered France so that she hovered over the cot, folding and unfolding her little hand to greet the newborn. France stuck her saliva-covered finger into her mouth.

Jeanne, who had been staring intently into the crib, now turned to her mother.

"*Elle est belle*, Maman. *Mais toute petite!*"

Daniel noticed Tatiana bite her lip. Their new daughter was on the small side.

Béa peered over the crib now and sat her doll on the edge. "*Bonjour, bébé*," she said, rocking the doll forward and bending it so low that the doll's long wiry hair brushed the baby's face. The baby awoke and look startled.

"You'll scare her, Béa," Jeanne said, pulling the doll up again into a sitting position.

"Jeanne!" Béa scowled.

The baby gave out a little sneeze, causing all of them to laugh, Béa the loudest.

"I'm hungry," she said, suddenly stomping off to the kitchen, taking the doll.

"Monique, would you mind preparing something for them?" said Daniel, keen to get some peace for his wife so that she could nurse their daughter. "And thank you for staying last night." The young woman had been a reassuring presence ever since they had arrived in Orléans.

"Of course, Monsieur." Monique went next door with France.

Tatiana sat up in bed and removed the sheet, exposing her bandages.

Daniel caught Jeanne peering anxiously at her mother.

"Maman – does it hurt?"

Tatiana observed her eldest through half-closed eyes. "No, Jeanne," she said, languidly.

"Have you got a name for the baby, Maman?" Jeanne continued, in the same breath.

She's growing up quickly, Daniel thought.

Tatiana shook her head. "No, Jeanne."

"But we will," Daniel interjected. "Now off you go, *ma poulette*." He turned to his wife, whose dark eyes indicated fever. *She needs air*, he thought. "*Chérie*, I'll just open the window."

"No, Daniel." She lifted her head, with effort.

"It's still warm outside." He opened the window – a tepid breeze blew into the room. Daniel leant out and marvelled at the china blue sky. High, urgent bird cries spiralled down from the lime tree. Daniel filled his chest, suddenly enthused with the day. "*Chérie* – what a beautiful day it is. The baby has brought us fine weather!"

Tatiana nodded, unimpressed, heavy-lidded, and turned to the bedside table. She tore open a sachet of aspirin and shook the powder into a glass of water.

France had crawled back into the bedroom, a mop of blonde hair at the foot of the bed. Tatiana watched her try to mount the mattress, then fixed her eyes on Daniel as if to say, 'take her'. Daniel fished her up and took her to the kitchen, where Monique had filled the girls' glasses with milk and had laid out some vitamin biscuits on a plate.

Monique removed France's bottle from the water she had boiled and retrieved France from Daniel.

"Don't throw the hot water out, Monique. After you've finished with France, would you take a warm flannel to Madame?"

"Yes, Monsieur."

But from the bedroom next door came a cry.

"Tatiana?" Daniel rushed back into the bedroom with Jeanne and Béa, followed by Monique with France.

Tatiana was sitting up in bed staring at a blue-winged bird

circling the ceiling. Round and round it went, its wings beating frantically as it finally stopped and hovered over the cot, bearing its white breast to the baby and bowing its beak, before flying out of the open window.

Tatiana wrung her hands. "Dan, give the baby to me," she said, rapturously, stretching out her arms towards the crib. Daniel noticed they were trembling.

Daniel reached down into the clean sheets Tatiana had so lovingly prepared for a baby son. His daughter was so warm and light in his arms as he brought her to his chest.

He sat down on the bed beside his wife. The baby opened her eyes and crinkled her nose as Daniel carefully placed her into Tatiana's thin arms. Tatiana peered down at her daughter, a heavy curtain of hair covering one side of her face. She swept back her hair to reveal her tear-stained cheek.

"She's so beautiful," she sniffed.

Daniel saw a trace of a pained smile form on her dry lips.

"The swallow," she said, finally. "He came to her and bowed to her. I would like to call her Alexandra."

Tatiana made a slow and steady recovery, helped in large part by Monique, who had witnessed Tatiana's fragility, perhaps with some consternation.

Daniel saw a change in Monique, who took more care in her appearance, her heavy flaxen hair now waved as she set off to school with the children in the mornings. As she wheeled France out in her pram, Béa and Jeanne behind, she looked a picture in her pretty grey summer dress with yellow and white flowers, her plump arms browning in the June sun. One morning, Daniel felt the urge to paint her, but suddenly saw Tatiana eyeing him with suspicion.

Tatiana went back to rolling her hair and applying make-up, and he was grateful, for it was the old Tatiana returning, only more beautiful this time, and he told her so one summer's evening, as they lay stretched out on the bed in front of an open window.

As usual, he then recounted his day, regaling her with his new project: the performance of a musical pageant based on the story of Jeanne of Arc. He told her, excitedly, how he'd asked permission for it to be staged in the gardens and cloisters of Chartres Cathedral.

A crash of iron in the courtyard made them jump and, limping slightly, Tatiana went to the window and stood there in the moonlight, a Grecian queen in what resembled a white tunic, her full breasts outlined to perfection. Alexandra had just been nursed and had fallen asleep in her crib. Tatiana peered out into the darkened courtyard.

"*Guck mal, Willi, eine schöne Frau*!"

"Down, Tatiana!" Daniel hissed.

"Ah, pull me up, *Dummkopf*, instead of gawping!"

Tatiana dropped down on the mattress beside him, trembling. "I can't believe it," she whispered, terrified. "I thought it was the cats. Two German soldiers."

Daniel slid off the bed silently and peered over the top of the windowsill. A dark figure under the tree was pulling his colleague up by the shoulder from an upturned refuse bin. The operation required several attempts. Daniel noiselessly pulled the windows shut and locked them, and drew the curtain quickly. He prayed for the soldiers to leave; why had the gate been left open? Probably Jeanne when she'd gone for the ball which had bounced over the gate. And then he had called her in for dinner.

The sound of boots approaching.

"*Frau komm hier!*"

"*Mehr schnapps*!" growled a voice in a graver tone.

As they started to pound on the door, Daniel slipped a pair of trousers over his pyjamas.

"Don't, Dan," Tatiana whispered, gripping his belt. "You know they're having people deported for no reason."

"I have to go," he said, releasing her fingers. "If we don't open the door, they're likely to use force. Get into the children's bedroom with Alexandra and make sure you are all quiet."

Tatiana's eyes widened with terror.

"Go, *chérie*. Now!" He made his way to the kitchen and heard a door shut quietly in the other bedroom. He stared at the door before him.

"*Aufmachen*!"

Only the wood of the door separated him from these thugs. He unhooked the chain, started to lift one of the latches – but then let it fall again. He had just caught sight of the leather slippers he was wearing.

The door began to rattle. "*Mach die Tür auf!*"

He pulled himself up to his full height and pulled the door back. Two dishevelled-looking soldiers were leaning against the doorframe.

"*Frau. Schnaps*!" said one, trying to focus his gleaming eyes on Daniel. Daniel inhaled a scent of fatty sausage and sweet spirits. He stepped back, relieved to see that the finer, younger, honed Teutonic specimens he feared were not in evidence here. These were middle-aged soldiers, of farming stock it seemed, with shorn haircuts.

"*Meine Herren. Meine Frau ist krank. Aber komm mit mir zu einem Café*," he said, clapping them both on the shoulder.

The men looked undecided, perhaps puzzled by his ability to communicate in their language, albeit a little ungrammatically. They looked at one another and then turned to him again, their eyes narrowing.

Daniel felt his stomach harden as he realised that the two, though the worse for drink, were tanked up for a fight. He gently but firmly turned them towards the gate.

"*Ja, schnaps!*" slurred one of them.

"*Gut.*" Daniel clapped him on the shoulder, then gave both of them a quick friendly shove into the courtyard, as if he were out with friends, pulling the front door and the gate behind him forcibly. Adopting their gait, he staggered into the street with them, leaning forward, but one of the soldiers seemed to be righting himself and pulling back. The soldier swerved suddenly to face Daniel and mumbled obscenities, the other, seemingly awoken from his drunken lethargy, dug his muscly fingers into Daniel's upper arm.

"*Allez!*" he screamed, now pushing Daniel to the end of the cobbled street.

Daniel dug his heels in, but his leather slippers gave way to the stone. The two soldiers hoisted him above the ground for a few seconds and brought him down hard. They were directing him towards a deserted alleyway.

I'm finished. Daniel screwed his eyes shut and felt all that was molten inside of him harden. Jerking back violently, he wrenched his arms from their vice-like grip. Squeezing the soldiers' thick necks to get a good hold, Daniel crashed their foreheads together; there was a dull crack and low groans as he threw them to the ground. One of them managed to stagger to his feet again, then pulled up his moaning colleague.

Horrified to see them revived, Daniel turned and took off, past the rue Chateaudun, away from his family. Behind him, he heard furious voices and the sound of heavy boots. He had to get them away from here, but his slippers slapping on the cobbles gave him away. He halted as he turned a corner and tossed them into a bin. Feeling lighter, he sprinted along the narrow streets of old Orléans, the cobbles cold underfoot, but felt no pain, only the terror of being caught and of his pursuers returning to his house in the rue Chateaudun.

Behind him, he heard the lumbering pair shout. As long as he heard them, Tatiana was safe. The thought of her cowering in the bedroom with his daughters filled him with unbearable pain. He wanted to scream but clamped his lips shut.

He headed south, in zig-zag fashion, towards the river, his head swimming with vile images – Tatiana being forced onto their bed, Jeanne jumping atop a soldier to stop him and the other raising his hand to her.

He swerved round just as one of the soldiers waved a revolver in the air.

Daniel sped off again as a bullet hit the wall over his head.

Minutes later, he'd reached the banks of the Loire. He was taking the route he'd taken that day with Riou and Lerude. It struck him as bitterly ironic to be pursued by two drunken soldiers who had by chance stepped into his backyard, when for a year his clandestine Resistance activities had gone undetected by the German military.

The narrow flight of steps heading back towards the presbytery flashed up before him. Increasing his speed, he scaled the stone steps two by two and pressed himself up against the church wall, listening out. The clock struck eleven. *Tatiana!* He propelled himself into the moonlit cobbled streets once more.

At the corner of the rue Chateaudun he slowed, tiptoed along the narrow pavement, hugging the shadows, and slipped in through his gate. He righted the bin, hid it behind the tree. Before entering, he heard shutters creak shut above his head, in the apartment building at the end of the yard.

No sooner had Daniel bolted the door behind him than the raised German voices returned, this time reaching him from an alleyway parallel to the one he had taken. He raised the kitchen table and swiftly jammed it against the front door. Then he ran to his bedroom and listened, his ear to the window.

"Daniel – is that you?" whispered a voice behind the children's bedroom door. He crawled over to it and whispered through the keyhole. "Shush, Tatiana. Don't move."

There was silence from outside. Not a shutter creaked. Not a door opened.

Had someone sent them somewhere else?

A key turned and Tatiana's petrified, white face appeared, with Alexandra in her arms. Behind her Jeanne tugged at her nightgown.

"Thank God! Dan!" Tatiana started to cry as Jeanne threw herself into his arms. "I didn't know what to do. I heard the neighbours through the bedroom window saying *'pauvre petite –* fancy that, with all those children'. But they didn't come to help! I would never have left a mother and her children alone, never. Never!"

"I know, *chérie*." Tatiana was no angel; she had a temper, but also a caring, passionate nature.

Jeanne buried her head into Daniel's chest.

"Don't worry, *mes chéries*," Daniel said, pulling Jeanne away a little so that Tatiana could join them. He encircled them in his arms. "This is the last night we'll be spending here." He kissed the two of them in turn.

CHAPTER FORTY

"I moved Tatiana and the girls out this morning," Daniel said over the phone, satisfied that Pelletier fathomed the length and breadth of his predicament. "They're staying on Monique's family farm outside of town."

"Good, good," Pelletier said, his voice dropping with concern. "Just a minute. I need to check something with Chocho. Don't go, he's just walked in – Chocho, Daniel had some problems with the *fritz* last night."

Daniel heard Chocho gasp. Chocho grabbed the receiver. "The property has two empty dependencies."

"Really?"

"But Pelletier will check. I'll hand him back to you."

Pelletier came back on the line.

"Thank you," Daniel said. "Tatiana will be relieved."

"Where is she exactly?"

"East of Orléans. In the countryside, in St Jean de Bray."

"Well, that'll be a few minutes' bike ride from where we are living!"

Daniel's heart leapt. "Call me!"

"Of course."

As he put the phone down, Daniel felt himself breathe more easily.

By early evening, Pelletier was driving Daniel along a track leading from the main house down through the parkland to his new home. Daniel rolled down his window and inhaled the warm, sweet aroma of freshly cut grass. They passed a small apple and pear orchard, a little meadow where the grass had been kept long, and pulled up before a stone cottage decorated with Virginia creeper.

As they got out of the car the sun's final rays were warming the old wall running around the house. They entered the enclosed garden, where bees droned sleepily around flowerbeds ornamented with dahlias and fragrant climbing roses. Daniel propped up an overturned watering can. They walked on through a vegetable patch with shrivelled tomato plants and sweet peas, into a kitchen with a wood-burning stove. They carried on into a sitting room with an overstuffed sofa and *bergère* chair, in front of a small fireplace. Two small bedrooms ran off the sitting room, one just large enough to accommodate Jeanne, Béa and France and, wonder of wonders, they discovered a bathroom.

"And there's a cellar full of coal I hear," said Pelletier, grinning.

Daniel felt his throat swell with gratitude. "Jeanne will go to school in the village. Away from the bombs and German barracks."

"Only Riou left in town now," Pelletier said, sighing.

"It's more convenient for his older children's school," Daniel replied, brushing a cobweb from a straw chair in the corner. "And he fears nothing, it seems." He pulled the chair alongside Pelletier in the *bergère* and sat down.

Pelletier nodded. "When you've lost an arm in battle and received the *Croix de Guerre,* I imagine you're not going to let yourself get scared, nor show your fear to others. It's almost a duty."

Daniel placed his hands on his knees and sighed. He felt low all of a sudden.

Pelletier's smile vanished. "Look, Daniel – what happened the other night was an accident. Bad luck. Your family will be as safe as mine here. We'll look out for one another."

Daniel looked out onto the garden. "Yes. It's good to be back in the country."

"No bombs, no *fritz*… that is… not like in town."

Daniel nodded, but felt the cold run through his veins.

Pelletier, perhaps sensing he had provoked this, continued, "And Tatiana will have company here, *n'est-ce pas*? The other wives? And it'll be good to have you too, Daniel. We three can cycle into Orléans in the morning."

It took a while for Daniel to rid himself of the sensation of being watched. At night, a tree branch tapping at the window was enough to propel him from his bed. He asked himself whether the soldiers had been tipped off that night in Orléans. Or the neighbour, the *fritz* lover? Night after night he ran through all the people he'd come into contact with daily and came up with nothing.

He was careful not to share his worries with Tatiana who, not wishing to dwell, had thrown herself into socialising with the wives; they exchanged information on food rations, sewed together, planned picnics, pooled records to play on the gramophone, watched over their children playing in the grounds. The men met and discussed the war and, the minute the women were out of sight, talked of resistance.

Riou was eager to tell Daniel that the two drunken soldiers had not returned, or made enquiries at his work, and that they wouldn't want to admit they'd been drinking to their superior. In any case, it was highly likely that they'd forgotten, caught up in their campaign to stamp out resistance in the Orléans region. And if they had found him to be a member of the Resistance, he would have been carted off straight away. All this Daniel knew, but these arguments were not enough to kill the fear lodged in his breast.

Riou, while advising them all to be vigilant and to cover their tracks, redoubled their underground activities. He had found someone at the *mairie* to produce false identity papers and forged stamps, and René, Durand, and Riou now occupied a good deal of their time intelligence-gathering, seeking out landing strips for British pilots in the adjoining Sologne region.

Daniel, finally encouraged by his colleagues' defiant spirit, threw himself into his work, interspersing it with several more trips to Paris, to Durand, all of which passed without incident. He was becoming a master at deception, he told himself, managing to keep it all from Tatiana, as the others did from their wives.

Instead he preferred to talk to her of his great theatrical project, *Portique pour une Fille de France,* now on the point of being performed in the cloisters of Chartres Cathedral. The historical extravaganza was an ambitious enterprise, requiring the participation of hundreds of youths, girls as well as boys, from the centres in the Loire region, bringing to life key stages of the heroine's life in ten different *tableaux.* The more articulate had speaking parts in the Greek chorus, whereas the grand majority were extras or singers in the two choirs they had formed.

The day came, and Daniel was nervous. There had been no time for a proper dress rehearsal for one thing; they'd all worked on a separate *tableau* in their respective centres. Daniel had visualised the massive project on paper, sketching his vision of the stage and the *tableaux* and costumes. He had consulted the plans for the original production performed in Marseilles, played to audiences of 25,000 plus in a giant stadium. But his production would be scaled-down, due to material shortages, and more intimate, perhaps more meaningful in these ancient cloisters.

Two white tents were to be placed either side of the central stage, representing the opposing English and French camps. In addition, two towers had been constructed behind them, for the leaders of the Greek chorus, the *coryphées,* to give their opposing views of what was taking place on stage. Other circular platforms were placed around the audience for the two Greek choruses representing the dissenting voice of the people. And to hold it all together, a famous actress from the *Comédie Française* was to play Jeanne d'Arc.

At eleven o'clock, there was a service at the cathedral, the girl scouts inside with their families, the boys out on the cathedral steps, where the service was amplified and broadcast on loudspeakers. Following it, the youths and their families were called upon to watch and participate in the performance.

Daniel had asked Tatiana to come later, with the other wives and children. The next few hours were spent checking security arrangements, for many high-ranking dignitaries from the capital and the Loire region would be present, French and German alike. They would occupy the front rows.

Daniel watched the beautiful gardens slowly fill with families. The high-ranking members of the scout movement were directed towards Riou. He sat in front with his wife, the clergy, several Vichy representatives, a military general, and a clutch of German officers.

A stern-looking German censor turned in his seat to watch Daniel issue instructions. Though conscious of the eyes boring into his back, Daniel knew he didn't risk much with the pageant, as it was on the approved Vichy list of works. However, he and the actress from the *Comédie Française* had discussed the direction and staging, what was to be emphasized by a look or gesture.

His thoughts were interrupted by Tatiana walking towards him in a pale blue summer dress with little orange flowers, her heavy dark hair set and waved, her watery, dark eyes fixed on him. Jeanne was holding her white-gloved hand timidly, wearing a pale-yellow dress with a bow around the back, which Tatiana had made of satin curtain material.

"*Bonjour mes chéries.*" Daniel kissed Tatiana's temple. "*Que tu es belle, ma poulette!*" He twirled the laughing Jeanne around. How happy and grown-up she was today. She proudly sat between them.

Sitting on the end of the second row, Daniel nodded to the orchestra, mostly wind instruments.

The general hubbub died down as Jeanne Todd from the *Comédie Française* finally walked out on centre stage in a simple tunic dress. Hair loose around her shoulders, she perfectly embodied the thirteen-year-old Jeanne, from the village of Domrémy, North-Eastern France. Todd stared out at the audience. The narrator on the other side of the stage reported her visions. It was the Hundred Years War, Northern France was occupied by the English. The saints had prophesied that she would one day lead the French troops into battle against the English, save France from English domination, and put Charles VII on the throne.

Whilst the narrator spoke of the occupation, Daniel watched a German official cross his arms and discreetly look back to scan the audience's reaction.

As Daniel's eyes returned to the stage, he saw Vic slip into the end of his row. A uneasiness passed through Daniel. He'd recently received a worrying letter from Lefèbvre about Fort Girard, where morale was low. Preoccupied with the production, Daniel had put it aside.

A neigh echoed round the cloister. An older Jeanne D'Arc had just appeared on stage on a white horse, bearing a banner with cavalry heralds.

Daniel turned to Jeanne, whose eyes lit up when she saw the horse. His smile left him, however, as his eyes met Vic's. Vic was pale and seemed relieved to finally locate him.

Orleans had been saved by the *maid*. At Charles VII's coronation in Reims, where she was guest of honour, two choirs sang a *Te Deum* in praise of the king. Messaien, the composer of this sumptuous and sonorous piece, had been a prisoner in Germany, and part of the proceeds from today's spectacle would go towards the prisoners' fund.

There was loud applause. Daniel watched a music critic feverishly scribble into a notebook. Daniel got up excitedly, but the euphoria soon evaporated as worries of Fort Girard took over. He needed to talk to Vic.

"*Chéri* – I enjoyed the Messaien. Well done!" said Tatiana, squeezing his hand.

"Good. Very good." Daniel saw Vic approaching. "Look, Tatiana, I need to see Vic about something."

Vic followed Daniel through the heaving crowds and out of the cloisters. They walked fast, heads bent, so as to not engage with anyone else. Eventually, they stopped and sat on the cathedral steps.

"Sorry I was late, Daniel. Some problems. Three eighteen-year-old boys have taken to the road without warning."

"*Eh bien*. Sadly, there's not a lot you can do. They're old enough to make their minds up. Anyone I know?"

"Roupp."

"Pierre Roupp?"

"Yes. He was supposed to start his apprenticeship next week and he's taken to the road. Hardly surprising, knowing him," said Vic, smiling. "You know Lefèbvre left too?"

"No?" Daniel's head started to spin.

"Last weekend. Told me he was sorry to leave me in the lurch and that for the time being, he couldn't leave a forwarding address. I'm surprised he didn't write to you."

"He did." Daniel bunched his lips. "I just hadn't got round to answering him. Ah! That's too bad…"

"Don't blame yourself." Vic look genuinely concerned. "And anyway… I myself want to leave."

"You too?"

"Fort Girard has lost its heart."

"*Eh bien,* I might have something for you," Daniel said, getting up.

Riou had spoken of a new centre near Paris he wanted to get off the ground, on the main Orléans-Paris highway.

"Look, Vic, Riou might have an opening for you. A Château des Bezards to refurbish, same as we did at Fort Girard. Your name tops the list of candidates."

"Thank you, Daniel."

The bell had sounded for the next act.

"Even better. Now we should get back."

As Daniel sat down, he realised he had forgotten to ask about Mlle Laviolle. He hoped Vic would be taking her with him. And Lefèbvre, where was he? He recalled the wireless evenings at Fort Girard. 'No address'. It all pointed to one thing.

He would make discreet enquiries. And Roupp? He had most probably joined up too.

Bonne chance, mon gars. Bonne chance.

CHAPTER FORTY-ONE

At the end of a dreary winter's afternoon, several months after *Portique*, Daniel was poring over a scrapbook pasted with news cuttings and letters of praise and thanks from all corners of the Loire region. The project had undoubtedly lifted all their spirits. How good, everyone had said, to sing and work together on such a scale in these dark times.

With some satisfaction, Daniel turned to the last two pages, where he paused on the photo of Jeanne behind prison bars, her white arms reaching out to the audience. Fragments of the speech filled the room now: 'What have I done to deserve this fate? To be betrayed by a Bishop! A Frenchman!' As Daniel had looked back at the audience, all eyes had been riveted on the stage. The tension had been palpable; most of his audience, he hoped, was thinking of Laval – Laval who had sacrificed France's prisoners, their youths, their homeland.

Daniel had found it hard not to exchange knowing glances with Riou – neither had forgotten Laval declaring his wish for a German victory on Radio Paris, the German-controlled station. But Daniel hadn't wanted the play to be an instrument for hate, rather of reflection and hope for the future. And thus, he thought back to the smiles of joy and relief on the girl and boy scouts' faces when they'd taken their bows with Jeanne Todd, as euphoric applause filled the cathedral cloisters. It had taken a while for some to recover from the final scene, when Jeanne had been tied to a stake. What a forlorn figure she had been at first, just a young woman, a maiden, and what a lonely mission, what an achievement to rally the troops and the King to her cause. If she could do it singlehandedly, why couldn't they, together? A country had to be united to be strong. There had been a deathly hush amongst the audience.

"Why are people crying, Papa?" Jeanne had whispered.

"Why?" His throat constricting, he had wanted to say to her, 'one day you will understand. One day, you will know how terrible it is to be occupied'. Instead, he just said, "They're sad for Jeanne."

"So am I," she had said, looking up at him. "What's going to happen to her?"

"She's going to heaven," he replied.

Tatiana, dry-eyed, had given him a doubtful look, knowing how hard he wrestled with his beliefs. But it was followed by a sympathetic one, for she also knew how deeply he felt about his country. It wasn't quite the same for her. It never could be.

With a sigh, he closed the cuttings book and paced the room. After months of frenzied activity he was experiencing a lull, and with a lull always came the uncomfortable questioning, anxieties about the future.

The occupation was entering its third year. Ever since Operation Torch the year before, when the Americans had invaded North Africa, there had been hope of the tide turning in favour of the Allies. But then in September and November, just months ago, the Americans and British had started bombing France, destroying the western suburbs of Paris, the naval port of Toulon, and Nantes, especially Nantes, where raining bombs had killed over 1,200 French civilians. The Germans had produced newsreels of exhausted-looking French families searching through the rubble of their homes, helped by German soldiers. Although he told himself the newsreel had been orchestrated by the Germans, the destruction was real. There were those who were beginning to fear the American pilots. Where were the French bombers? What was De Gaulle doing? Had he abandoned them? This situation couldn't continue.

"*Au-revoir, les gars*. Good luck with Nantes."

Daniel stopped and listened to René let out some young men who had been enlisted in the restoration project of the bombed city.

In April that year, there had been an important development

for the youths. The Germans were no longer asking for them to be shipped over to Germany. Hitler had decided that PoW's were just as able to work in the German factories. Instead the lads were being offered jobs in their own country, often on German contracts. The situation was far from perfect of course, but for now, Daniel and René had no other option.

Daniel had discussed this with the Vichy Minister of Youth, Lamirand, who'd come down from Paris in September. He, Daniel was relieved to find, was not an ardent Vichyite, preferring to talk of the boys and girls whose centres they had visited around the Loire. As Head of Youth Propaganda (the job title still made him wince), it had fallen to Daniel to oversee the Minister's security during the tour of the region. After contacting all the prefectures and gendarmeries ahead of time, Daniel had travelled with Lamirand in a black official Citroen car, which had glided through the French countryside, sandwiched between a cortege of heavily-armed guards astride motorbikes.

Daniel laughed bitterly at the irony now. A Resistance member overseeing the security of a Vichy minister. Not that all Vichy ministers were extensions of the Nazi regime. Far from it. Look at him, René, Riou, Pelletier, Chocho – in Vichy guises, they had been able to accomplish much more.

At the end of the official visit, the Prefecture had run out of fuel. In a freezing prefectural ballroom, everyone, including the Prefect and the Minister, had stood shivering in their coats, clasping glasses of wine, toasting Vichy in perfunctory fashion, exchanging enigmatic looks. No one dared criticise Vichy openly, for in that room there remained staunch Vichyites, and one feared the waiters (or anyone else for that matter), who might be, for one reason or another, Gestapo informers.

A shrill ringing pulled him from his reverie. He was at the counter, staring at the telephone. René was turning the sign round to '*Fermé*' and coming back towards him.

"Do you want me to take it, Dan?"

"No. I'll take it. It may be Lerude."

"Then I'd better stay."

Daniel took the receiver. There was a silence, then a hesitant voice came on the phone.

"Daniel Frrrey. Sacha Kirrrov *à l'appareil.*"

Sacha! Daniel swallowed. The girls' adopted sugar uncle –

chocolates and ribbons still made their way down from Paris. Béa's wax-faced doll, procured, he was sure, from a luxury department store frequented by German officers and black marketeers, had rendered him speechless. But he had held his tongue, for Béa would not be separated from her.

"Tatiana gave me your number."

"Oh!" he stammered, the news forcing the breath out of him. It took all his control not to slam the receiver down.

"Look, Daniel. Can I call you Daniel?"

He heard Sacha order a Russian tea and thank a waiter in Russian. "*Spasibo*. Leave it there. *Spasibo*!" There was a pause. "Still there?"

"*Oui.*"

"Look, it's difficult to talk here," he said, dropping his voice. "Ah, he's gone. Look, Daniel." Sacha seemed to be leaning into the mouthpiece. "You are on the Gestapo watch list."

"What!" Daniel looked at René with alarm.

"Dan?" René asked, concerned.

Daniel bent down over the receiver. "It's alright, René. There's been a problem in Tatiana's family."

Guichet nodded. "Alright. I'll get my case." He walked into the back office.

"Who is that?" Sacha said, warily.

"René – I work with him."

"Be careful, Daniel."

"I am, always... Look, how do you know this? I don't understand."

"Ah! Hallo Boris, my man, is it that time already?" Sacha said, suddenly upbeat. "Daniel, I need to go now, send my best to Tatiana." Then, lowering his voice once more, he said, "Disappear off the radar for a couple of weeks."

"Disappear?"

"*Au-revoir*, Daniel."

The line went dead. Daniel was conscious of standing there with the receiver in his hand.

"Who was that?" René said, walking in with his case.

"A family friend of Tatiana's got into trouble."

"But it's you who looks ill!"

"It's a bad business which I can't go into. Look, I need to go to Paris. Can you hold the fort here?"

"Of course."

A touch of scarlet fever was doing the rounds – he might use that as an excuse. He trusted René, but not his mouth. Riou – he was a different matter. But first of all, he had to talk his wife, who was behind all this.

He rushed home and found her putting Alexandra down to sleep. The other girls were out in the grounds with Monique.

Drumming his fingers on the kitchen table, he waited for his wife to come through to him. She entered the kitchen and seemed to hesitate.

"What is the meaning of this, Tatiana?" he said, well-aware he was glowering. "Stop hovering and sit down."

She sat next to him, folded her arms. "I was worried, Dan. And keep your voice down." She got up again and closed the door, then turned back to him. "Don't you think I hadn't guessed? All these trips to Paris, the huddling around with Riou and the others. How stupid men are, to think that their wives don't know."

"But what did you say to Sacha?" He grabbed her elbow.

She yanked it away from him. "Nothing. Do you think I am so stupid!?"

"You're lying, Tatiana. Look at me!"

She fixed her dark eyes on him and bit her lip. "Nothing of consequence."

"No, no Tatiana!" moaned Daniel, now dropping his face into his hands. "What have you done?"

"Nothing, Dan," she said, recovering herself. "You have nothing to fear – I can trust Sacha."

"You have no idea…"

"Listen," she said, grabbing his right hand, which had bunched into a fist, "he happened to talk about the Shéhérazade last week. About Volodia."

"Who?"

"Sacha's old business partner. The one who produced his film. He has dealings with some high-ranking officers."

"You mean the Gestapo?" He pulled his fist free and brought it down hard on the table, knocking over Alexandra's bottle. "Fine friends you have, Tatiana! And as for that Sacha!"

Tatiana was staring at his fist. "Volodia is not my friend," she said, in a hoarse whisper.

"Then why?"

"Because he has contacts and..." She looked up at him to gauge his reaction.

Daniel felt a deep anger rising within him. "And how do I know Sacha is not trying to get rid of me?"

Tatiana blushed and touched her cheek. "But that's ridiculous, Dan!"

"Always hanging around."

"Stop this!" Tatiana got up. "He's Vladimir's oldest friend, he's been like a brother to me."

"Yes, yes, of course," Daniel said, shaking his head.

"And, listen to me." She leaned forward and grabbed his shoulders. "Sacha has a mistress who sings at the Shéhérazade. She's Jewish. If she's alive today, it's because of Sacha watching over her. She starred in Sacha's film long ago."

Daniel had never wanted to see the film in question.

"Daniel? Dan?" she uttered softly. She cupped his cheeks. The coolness of her fingers calmed him.

"How do I know I can trust him?" he said, miserably.

"Because you can," she said, reaching for his fist and slipping her little hand into his. "If you trust me and Vladimir, you trust Sacha."

Daniel peered into Tatiana's dark eyes, which glistened with resolve. Yes, she loved him, in her proud way, and he loved her. Especially now – she was always so brave and ready to face unpalatable truths.

"Dan. What are you going to do?"

"I'll lie low at my mother's house in Paris. Give me two weeks and, by that time, I'll know what I have to do."

"Why don't you go and see Sacha?"

"No," he said, getting up. "I need to think this over for myself."

The next morning, he asked Riou to meet him in a café before boarding his train for Paris. Riou approached Daniel's table – Daniel had chosen as quiet a corner as he could, for the café was three-quarters full with passengers bound for Paris.

"Thank you for coming." He told Riou everything.

"So, you'll be at your mother's. Don't worry. We'll keep an eye on Tatiana. And of course, we need to watch ourselves at the moment."

"Look," Daniel said, reluctantly bringing up the subject they all feared. "Should I get called in by the Gestapo…"

"You won't. They have nothing on you. They would have come for you by now if they did."

"But just supposing…" He leaned forward and checked his watch. He had ten minutes, but more importantly a policeman had come into the café. He knew a lot of the *gendarmes*. Some would not interfere in resistance activities, had even released some of Daniel's boys bound for Germany. There were others, however, like this young man snooping around, who had to be watched. "I'd like to think I wouldn't talk," he murmured. "But…" He was relieved to see the *gendarme* march out.

"I would like to think that both of us would hold our tongues, Dan," Riou said, smiling sadly. "But I know one chatterbox who should never be arrested."

"René."

"He'd talk before they had even started questioning him. Well, maybe not quite."

Daniel just managed to force a smile.

Riou grew serious again. "Look Dan, I should tell you the latest. I've just received unsettling news which you need to be aware of."

"Oh!"

"Vic suddenly upped and left his new job at les Bézards."

"What!" Daniel noticed people getting up for the Paris train. He picked up his case. "After everything we've done for him. I don't understand."

"It gets worse."

Daniel stiffened. "Let's start walking. I can't afford to miss it."

Riou was looking uncomfortable. He levered himself out of his chair with his good arm.

"Look, there's no easy way to say this. It seems his former Commander-in-chief's car broke down in front of the centre the other night. It was midnight, raining hard. The Commander came dripping wet into the centre and, recognizing Vic, his former valiant footsoldier, fell into his arms. He's set up a new para-military organisation and has taken Vic with him."

Daniel shook his head. "He'll be working for that mad idiot Darnand! For the *Milice*. He'll have Vic goose-stepping through the streets before he knows it. Vic is so naïve."

"Shush – keep your voice down, Dan."

No one, however, was paying any attention. Everyone was too keen to get the Paris train – for who knew whether there would be a next one, now that the Allies had renewed their bombing.

"I can't believe it," Daniel said, almost to himself. "And no doubt some of the boys have followed him to the Paris HQ."

"It's not your fault."

Daniel felt his heart give way. Vic working for the *Milice* – the organisation that spread more fear throughout the resistance network than any other, since its members were French and had local knowledge.

The Paris train was announced. He was aware of Riou's comforting voice, telling him not to worry and to take care of himself as he set out onto the platform.

CHAPTER FORTY-TWO

Through the darkness, Daniel heard the sound of clinking keys and the apartment door shutting. He sat up, gripped the metal sides of his camp bed, and called out, "Maman," in a hoarse whisper.

The footsteps halted momentarily, then continued, lighter this time. A cupboard whined open and he heard the metallic clunk of a pan placed on the stove before silence returned.

Daniel threw his blanket aside and made his way to the kitchen. In the chilled moonlight slanting through the little window, his mother stood at the stove, reheating some coffee.

She started as he entered and then turned her anxious eyes upon him. "Did I wake you?"

"I wasn't asleep," he said, tempering the irritation in his voice. A burnt, sickly-sweet smell rose into his nostrils. "*Attention, Maman.*"

"*Oh non!*" she said woefully, grabbing the small saucepan, which had begun to boil. She removed it from the heat, turned as Daniel's father called out from the bedroom and, without a word, tiptoed down the corridor.

Daniel sat at the kitchen table and grabbed a spoon, drumming it on the checked oilcloth. This closeted existence was slowly driving him insane. Hadn't he had enough of that during his childhood, drifting from room to room, conscious of every sound he made.

The past ten days had revived those sad memories of the Great War. Every day he had watched his father's stooping figure take up work at his desk, his mother don two winter coats for the queue at the *boulangerie*. Meanwhile he had paced the apartment, asking himself how he would beat the Gestapo at their own game. He'd have to know his enemy. To know how they worked, how they thought. To date, no one in his circle had fallen victim to them – it was both a blessing and a curse.

He let go of the spoon and shuffled in his uncomfortable chair. His thoughts turned to Tatiana. He liked to picture her at the stove surrounded by his daughters reading or playing with their dolls. Several nights ago, he had had a terrible dream. He had been lying, beaten and bruised on a stone floor with only a filthy latrine for company, calling out her name.

'Daniel – May I call you Daniel?' Sacha's rolling Russian intonation rang out in his head now. How Tatiana must have pleaded with him. He must have paid dearly for the Gestapo list – a caseload of Krug champagne, an eighty-year-old Armagnac? Thousands of francs.

But he could afford it, bah!

Could he confront Sacha at the Shéhérazade club, as Tatiana had suggested? He squeezed the neck of the spoon. Located in the 9th district, it was an hour's walk from Pré Saint Gervais, where he was hiding. He could go there under cover of darkness. Ignore the curfew and keep to the shadows. Wouldn't it be worth it – bursting in on that smarmy Sacha, just as he was raising a glass to a drunken SS officer.

'Gunter – may I call you Gunter?' It was sickening!

He threw the spoon down. He would never undertake such a plan. Yesterday had put paid to that idea. *What an idiot I was! A moment of terrible weakness!* His parents had been at Sunday worship when he had slipped out onto the tree-lined avenue in front of their apartment building and inhaled a lungful of autumnal air. Feeling human again, he had pulled up the collar of his coat and ventured on through the neighbourhood backstreets. Passing a square, he had seen some pretty little girls of his daughters' age playing on the swings. How their high, happy voices had bounced around the walls of the old apartment buildings. With a heavy heart, he had ended up at a café, which was when that young *gendarme* had got him.

"*Vos papiers, s'il vous plait*, Monsieur."

Daniel's body froze as he recalled reaching into his empty

pocket. He had left his wallet and papers at his parents' home.

"Well come on!" the *gendarme* had snarled. "You know it's an offence to…" And suddenly a police van had pulled up.

"Pierrot," someone had cried from the van. "Quick. We've been ordered to the tenth district. They've captured one of 'em.'"

With a thudding heart, Daniel had watched the *gendarme* turn.

He had been mad to venture out like that. His narrow escape had taught him something. No longer to believe in his nine lives.

"Café?" His mother had slipped back into the kitchen. "I had to give Papa some medication to sleep." She poured the coffee into the bowls.

Daniel looked up at her, suddenly recalling the reason he had joined her in this freezing kitchen at this late hour.

"Where have you been in your robe, Maman? Look, you're shivering – it's past midnight!"

She handed him a steaming bowl, put on one of her winter coats, and sat down. "Daniel, you have enough on your plate."

"Go on…"

She sighed. "A cousin of mine from Alsace, Marie-Claude – you don't know her, but she knew you as a baby – rents a room in this building for a Jewish organisation."

"Oh. Father didn't mention it."

"Your father knows nothing," she said, looking down with embarrassment.

"What?" Daniel had always regarded his parents as inseparable and of common mind.

"I know, I know," she said, lifting her hand. "Papa panicked during those terrible Jewish raids in July last year when we were hiding Friedman's daughters. 'I am already running Friedman's company under my name,' he said. 'I've told Friedman they won't be safe here'." She wrung her hands. "By then, Friedman had made it over the demarcation line to the Free Zone, but his daughters had to wait in Paris. I told Papa that I'd found another room elsewhere in the district for them, but in fact, they moved to Marie-Claude's room in the roof above us, in a *chambre de bonne*; tiny, but sufficient. Every day I took them food and fresh linen or clothes."

"But surely Papa would have understood. Will understand – as judging by tonight…"

"Maybe." She interlinked her thin fingers, as if in prayer.

"Those girls read through the entire collection of *Les Malheurs de Sophie* you know," she said, smiling sadly. "Left the books behind. Thought it would be a comfort for other Jewish children. Your father told me tonight that they have been captured by the police."

"No! How?"

"Their older brother got arrested in a bar. He talked under interrogation."

"Oh, Maman!" Daniel walked over to her. Her angular shoulders, broader than Tatiana's, were shaking. He took hold of them. "It's not your fault."

"They were French policemen!"

"I know, Maman." He hated these discussions. Hated to see his mother so overwrought. "But Maman, remember it's what we're fighting for in the Resistance. For these terrible things to cease."

"Daniel," she said. "What are you going to do? I prayed for you yesterday in church." She reached out for him.

Daniel withdrew to his seat. He had no time for religion, tonight of all nights. He had lain awake before she had arrived and had started to formulate his own plan of action.

But a look of disappointment passed over his mother's face. He hadn't wished to push her away.

"Maman," he said, steering her from thoughts of the Protestant faith. "Who are you hiding now?"

"A woman and her daughter," she said, brightening a little. "The daughter has just turned ten. You should have seen her face light up tonight when I showed her the pink volumes on the little bookshelf. Friedman's daughters would be so happy to think…" Her eyes welled with tears again. "Friedman is beside himself with grief."

"Don't torment yourself." *How much can any family take?* he thought. *There is so much sorrow in the world. But that is why Riou, René, Lerude and I have to act.*

"I am thinking of you too, Daniel. Tonight, I even thought of hiding you in the room. But it would mean…"

Daniel frowned. "No. I couldn't live with that on my conscience. And besides, tomorrow I'm returning to Orléans." There, he had said it. The inevitability made him concentrate.

"But that's walking straight back to the Gestapo!"

"I was told to go off the radar for a few weeks and that is what

I have done. But now I need to do more. It's no use burying my head in the sand."

"But couldn't you all come to live here?"

"No. I have a job to go to. It's time to take control. Go and see the *fritz*. Make him believe that I am innocent of 'terrorist acts', as they like to call them.'

His mother bit into her thin lips.

"Maman. You know this is my only option. I can't remain here and just hope the Gestapo will forget about me. And besides, I am risking your life by staying. And Papa's. Especially in light of what you are doing."

"Daniel, I've told you that I have no fear of death, or the Germans. I have my faith."

"Maman, If I don't go back, the Nazis will smell a rat." The thought of the Gestapo calling in on Tatiana and his children made his chest tighten.

"So how are you going to keep them away?"

"I will go and see the *Propagandastaffel* in Orleans."

"Propaganda what? No, no, Daniel," she said, shaking her head. "You scare me when you are like this!"

"Other people do it. I've pulled the wool over the *fritz's* eyes before. I look like a *fritz* even. Besides," he said, getting up, "I have no other choice."

The following morning, he called Pelletier. "Tell Tatiana I'll be back this evening." As he said this, he felt his heart lurch with longing.

He packed swiftly and took leave of his anxious parents, slipping out of their apartment building with his cap pulled low over his eyes.

It was a beautiful autumn day, cold but sunny. It augured well. With a spring in his step, he entered the *Propagandastaffel* and announced himself: Regional Delegate of Propaganda for Vichy Youth. A young woman in green uniform accompanied him to a waiting room. She handed him a form to complete.

"I cannot guarantee that you will be seen today," she said, crisply.

"I don't plan to take much of his time, Mademoiselle." He gave his most ingratiating smile.

"Well," she said, spinning on her heels, "I will see."

A young male secretary marched in carrying a file. "You're most fortunate," he said, taking Daniel's form without a trace of a smile. He glanced at it and slipped it into a folder. "His next visitor is running late."

Daniel followed the young man into an office, where a sullen, middle-aged man in an open raincoat sat in shadow, at a large desk.

Daniel clicked his heels. "*Mein Herr*. Daniel Frey."

"Yes. Yes. What do you want?" the official said, in a thick German accent.

Daniel swallowed quickly as the form was handed to the official. He seemed to read half of it then dropped it onto his desk in front of him.

"You are no doubt aware that I am responsible for youth propaganda for the National Revolution in this region."

"I am now," said the official. "It is strange, however, that I have never seen you before." The man fixed him with a cold stare.

"It's a recent appointment," Daniel said, quickly, resisting the urge to clear his throat.

Laid out in the chair, his tormentor smirked. Had he believed him? *Chocho can falsify the dates on my work file later.*

"I think you'd better sit." A faint glimmer had appeared in the man's eyes.

Daniel thanked him and sat down stiffly. "I have come here today to seek your help, *Mein Herr*."

"Oh?"

"Yes. You know how disorganised the French are."

The corners of the man's mouth rose for an instant.

"You see, I have so little information available to do my work well, what with the paper shortages, etc. I was hoping I might call on your high office to furnish me with some brochures, for example."

A movement of the man's lips seemed to indicate indecision.

"You know we run a job centre for the youths in this region. And they are still so vulnerable to Jewish-Marxist propaganda." Daniel felt his heart thump against his breastbone. Had he gone too far?

The man got out of his chair, his face flushed with gouty anger. "Yes. Now more than ever." The official dug his knuckles into the corner of his desk, "We need to keep these youths free of lies, propagated by *Juden* and *Communisten* traitors."

The sour-faced secretary had just stepped back in. "Your next appointment is here."

This idiot is about to spoil my performance. "Sir, I thank you for your time – which is precious, I see."

The man fell back into his chair. "*Ja. Ja.* Herr Frey – we have your details. I'll see what I can do." He glowered, then waved him out.

"Of course, *Mein Herr.* I thank you." Daniel bowed his head humbly, clicked his heels, and left the room.

A few days later, a rasping motorbike pulled up in front of the job centre, causing quite a ripple of interest with the youths. Daniel stepped forward to break them up, signed the receipt and took the large box to the back office, where René was standing, open-mouthed.

"What's that, Dan?"

"You'll see." He tore it open and pulled out a leaflet. A soldier's masked head floated in a sea of red ink. Below it, a procession of young workers walked purposely towards a horizon of smoking factories. *'Ils donnent leur sang. Donnez votre travail pour sauver l'Europe du bolchevisme'.* ('They have given their blood. Your work will save Europe from bolshevism').

"Hmm." René laughed. "What do you plan to do with all of this?"

Daniel frowned and handed it over to him. "Is there some way of having this on display?"

"Hmm." René stuffed the brochure into his pocket and removed his round spectacles to clean them. "I could place several on a corner table, out of the way. We'll need to put one up in the window of course. It's not large. In case the *fritz* come round."

"That's good, yes."

"But what about our boys and girls? What do we tell them?"

Daniel sighed deeply. "I'm thinking we don't mention them at all. You know how young people are. Don't notice anything unless it's pointed out to them. You'll just have to keep them busy flicking through index cards and job applications."

René nodded and fished out the leaflet from his pocket. Crumpling it in his hand, he brightened.

"Make good briquettes for the fire."

"Especially now the weather is turning." Daniel grinned.

"And I can think of another use." René turned his head towards the water closet.

"René, really!" Daniel said, his heart lightening.

The telephone rang.

"I'll take it." Daniel walked over to the front desk but reeled back suddenly as he remembered Sacha. The phone rang and rang. Daniel picked up the receiver begrudgingly. "*Allo?*"

"What luck!"

Daniel recognized the voice immediately. He pressed the receiver against his ear.

"Albert," he whispered. He looked up at René. "It's alright. An old friend."

René retreated into the back office.

Daniel uncovered the mouthpiece he was grasping. "Sorry."

"Can I speak now?"

"Yes."

"Good. Rebecca and I need a place to stay near you. A hotel would suit us."

"Of course." He had been taken aback by the panic in Klug's voice. There was a hotel Combleux. Along the canal. Quiet, as the canal was no longer in use. "I have one in mind. He owes me a favour."

"Good, Daniel. Good. Book it in the name of Crosne, will you?"

"Yes."

"We have new identity papers."

"Good."

"Thank you, Daniel." There was a pause. "There is something else…"

"It's Philippe, isn't it?"

"Yes, Philippe and his wife. They've had two children."

Daniel swallowed quickly. He hadn't anticipated this.

"Simon and Clara."

"I'm afraid that a hotel is more difficult."

"I realise this is asking more of you…"

"Let me think."

"Please, I beg of you…"

Daniel could not bear to hear him plead. "Just tell him to

come."

There was a long sigh of relief. "I knew I could rely on you, Daniel. We will be with you in forty-eight hours. Bless you!"

CHAPTER FORTY-THREE

Daniel raced home that evening with Albert in his thoughts. How different things had been in the spring of 1939 when they had last met. Dressed in an elegant camel coat and black trilby hat, Albert had been on his way to make a down-payment for his new office in the ninth district. He had teased Daniel, reading the headlines of the *Figaro*.

'You shouldn't believe what you read in the papers!'

Albert had always possessed an unhealthy amount of optimism. In 1936, when the French workers had occupied the factories countrywide, Albert's immediate response was to instruct them to work further afield, Belgium and the Netherlands, where the dairy factories awaited.

He had been right in 1936. Daniel wondered how he and Philippe had survived the anti-Jewish ordinances. How had they earned money? Daniel couldn't see Albert going to the Jewish charities with a begging bowl. Too proud, and too clever to make himself known to the French authorities. Though how could these soup kitchens and refuges survive otherwise? Or did the charities have a clandestine arm, as in Daniel's mother's case? That was probably how he and Philippe had escaped each successive raid for the past year.

He imagined Philippe, with his wife and children, confined to a tiny room in the ninth or tenth district. A room in which they washed, slept, ate. A room in which they talked in whispers. A room visited every other day by someone with a conscience, someone brave, who didn't suffer from social amnesia. Someone like his mother, with food, clothes, fresh sheets, handed over in an instant before the door was hurriedly closed. For there were the others, the busy-bodies, those with grievances, those who knew there was money to be made through denunciations.

Feeling low, he walked in through the door and found Tatiana alone in the kitchen. Once again, Monique had spirited his daughters away before his return. It was Tatiania's new regime, which had been instituted after the Gestapo scare. Overnight, a household full of screams, giggling and squabbling had given way to regimented calm. Tatiana no longer brought France to him the minute he crossed the threshold. Nor did she disappear to bottle-feed Alexandra in another room. Play with Papa was now for weekends.

Whilst accepting this, Daniel had puzzled over the sudden change in discipline. Until Monique's account of life during his enforced absence in Paris had come to light, that is.

'Madame just stopped eating, Monsieur. It was alarming to see her face so thin. In the second week, I sat with her at mealtimes. Kept a close watch on Jeanne, who picked at her food like her mother. If I hadn't insisted that Jeanne set a good example to her little sisters…' Monique had lifted her plump arm and let it drop, sighing. 'And as for Béatrice, I caught her with Madame's sewing scissors. Cutting that pretty doll's hair! A fortune, that doll cost. I saw the label!' Daniel shuddered with the memory. 'And if that wasn't enough, France and Alexandra went down with a fever.'

Plain-speaking Monique had told him everything, all the while scrutinising him, not cruelly but wishing to make a point. She had been fiercely protective of Tatiana since Alexandra's birth. As if he needed reminding that he had abandoned her in his flight. He now thought back to Tatiana's paleness as he'd rushed through the door after going to the Propaganda office. As he had drawn her to him, he remembered how rigid she had become.

"Just tell me it's over, Dan!"

At that moment, he had thought of ceasing his resistance activities.

"Yes, *chérie*," he had replied, burying his face in her hair to shield her from his uncertainty, for what did he know?

Since then, Béa's cutting frenzy had ceased, but Tatiana had had to ban the doll's matted scalp and large staring eyes from the table.

"Dan!" He noticed that she had oiled her hair this evening, applied red lipstick and a little eye make-up. Around the kitchen she whirled, in high wooden heels, displaying a red skirt she had fashioned with some material Mme Pelletier had given her. It was nipped in at the waistband, accentuating her tiny form. As he sat down at the table, she poured him a glass of wine.

"Look, Daniel." She produced a colander of cèpes mushrooms. "Monique picked them in the woods on her way here."

Daniel leaned over and kissed her temple. Despite his anxiety, his stomach was grumbling with hunger. For weeks at his mother's they had survived on watery soups. Tatiana had already sent off food parcels that week to their parents. In Orleans, at least they could get a little rabbit meat. But mushrooms were a good substitute for the steak he had craved throughout this war. He sniffed their earthy, pungent aroma.

"And we have some eggs from her farm. What would we do without Monique?" she said, throwing two large handfuls of mushrooms into a pan with a sliver of lard. In another pan, she quickly prepared an *omelette aux fines herbes*.

Minutes later, they prepared to eat with eager anticipation; their meal was finished in an instant. Daniel watched his wife dab the corners of her mouth with a gingham napkin and sigh. She turned to him, eyes creasing with profound pleasure.

"I can't find the words to describe how good that was."

Daniel smiled, seizing his opportunity, whilst his wife was in an acquiescent mood.

"Monique has been an angel, true. And we have been good to her, after all, we've provided her with work during these difficult times."

"Yes," Tatiana replied, thoughtfully, "I suppose what you give, you get back." She looked at Daniel quizzically. "What is it?" she snapped.

It was frightening how her moods could change so suddenly. But there was no hiding things from her. It had always been so. Had his keeping his first marriage from her early in their relationship made her forever wary?

"Go on," she said, eyeing him with growing irritability.

"Alright, *chérie*." He patted the table. "I need to talk to you about a phone call I received tonight."

"Oh." The gravity of his voice had made her anxious and, as

usual, she expressed it as fury. "You're not in more danger?"

"No!" He squeezed her hand, but she drew it away.

"Then what?"

"It's Albert. Albert Klug. He called me."

"Oh." She gripped her napkin. "Where is he?"

Daniel poured himself the rest of his weekly wine ration.

"In Paris. But he has left by now with Rebecca. I've arranged for them to stay at that little hotel along the canal."

"Good. Vladimir will be pleased we've been able to help him and Rebecca. Poor Rebecca!"

"Yes." Daniel was relieved the way the conversation was going and now ventured, "There's someone else to consider."

"Philippe, you mean?"

"Yes, *chérie*."

"But that shouldn't be a problem," she said, brightening. "He can join his parents, can't he?"

"If only it were that simple."

Tatiana furrowed her fine dark brows.

"He's got married and has two young children. Simon, five, and a baby, Clara. We cannot put them up in a hotel. They'll be too conspicuous."

Tatiana bit her lip. "Oh, Dan! I've heard such awful things from Sacha. About the children. Separated from their parents, mostly. So that they can go into hiding. For months, some for almost a year."

Sacha again! But this time he let it pass like a foul medicine he needed to take if they were to remain on good terms.

"You're thinking that we could put them up in the other empty cottage, aren't you, Daniel?"

"Well – yes," he said, firming up the idea. "It's right on the edge of the property. Away from the main house."

"And what about Chocho's family and the Pelletiers? We'll need their consent."

This was one of the many reasons he loved her. Tatiana was brave and caring. He took her hand and pressed it to his cheek.

"You are magnificent!"

She smiled, before her expression changed suddenly. "I hope the wives will agree."

"You just have."

"But they'll be worried about their own children, Dan."

"Don't worry, they won't play together. They are older, at school most of the time."

Tatiana nodded. "Chocho is a second-generation Polish immigrant. He will understand, as will his wife, Marianne. As for Sandrine Pelletier, she is always doing good works for the prisoners and the church. I cannot believe that she will refuse me. Besides, if ever... if ever Philippe runs into difficulties with the authorities, we would have to say that we had no knowledge of his origins." Tatiana looked crestfallen. "But it won't happen. I won't let it."

Daniel looked at her uneasily. "You realise that if Philippe were discovered living here by the Gestapo, I might be taken in for questioning. And that could lead to further complications, owing to our other activities."

She raised her arms in protest. "I couldn't live with my conscience if we were to abandon Philippe and his wife. Imagine what they are going through. We had a taste of that with the Gestapo scare. But we will all be careful. It's private here, we're on an estate many kilometres from Orléans. Besides, how often do I ever go into town these days? We get our food from the hamlet or Monique's farm. And winter is coming. Will his wife be able to get a ration book?"

"Yes. Once their new papers are ready. But Riou and René have a contact at the *Mairie*. Albert has already forked out for his in Paris."

"Philippe will need to earn a living."

"Yes. Philippe will have to find work. The rations are barely enough to keep a man or woman alive, as you know. Philippe can't be seen as a drain on our community. Nor will he want to be. Still, René is in a good position to find him something."

Albert Klug arrived a day later, his camel coat thinned and browned with wear, but he still the striking figure Daniel remembered. Rebecca too, her face hardened with fatigue, her tight corkscrew curls (now tinged with grey) pulled up under a large felt hat.

Tatiana stepped forward and enfolded her friend into her thin arms.

"*Dieu merci*, you are here!"

Seeing Tatiana and Rebecca together recalled happier times,

when Rebecca, the gregarious hostess, had served up hearty meals for all of them. Her evenings were always anticipated events after the weeks Daniel, Philippe, Vladimir and Albert spent on the road, selling their machine tools. Tatiana was always welcome and so happy around such a convivial table, where the aroma of warming meatballs, mint, dill and steaming bowls of fluffy rice reminded her and Vladimir of their lost home in the Caucasus Mountains.

Albert let go of his cases and spread his arms. "Daniel, Tatiana!" His defeated voice shocked Daniel as he patted his back in a fatherly way.

Tatiana broke away from Rebecca, sensing the effort it took her to remain standing.

"Daniel will walk you down to the hotel after you've had some mushroom soup." She directed Rebecca towards the table and sat her down. Rebecca's eyes glistened with tears as Tatiana set a steaming bowl of soup before her.

"Ay-Ay-Ay, Rebecca, *kom*," Albert appealed.

"Eat too, Albert," Tatiana said, pushing him down into a chair. He was gripping his suitcases again.

"Let me have those." Daniel took their cases out to a wheelbarrow he had brought to the door. "The light is going. But eat! And I forgot to say, Philippe will be staying in a little house on this estate. We've spoken to our friends." Daniel and Tatiana had been surprised how easily they'd accepted it.

"Bless you, Daniel," Albert blurted out, visibly moved.

Rebecca started to cry. *"Meyn libe,* eat as Daniel says."

CHAPTER FORTY-FOUR

Up ahead, through the chilled twilight slowly enveloping the lawn, Daniel heard a vehicle bumping along the drive. He pushed the wheelbarrow onto the forecourt of Chocho's house, where a van had pulled over and extinguished its blue headlights.

Daniel ran his torch along its darkened windscreen. Two men with berets pulled low over their foreheads were seated in front; one of them, taller with a slighter build, peered out nervously.

"Philippe!"

Philippe threw open the door. There he was at last, in a pair of workman's overalls. They hugged.

Philippe turned and extended a lean arm towards the driver. "Stepan."

A man with a filterless cigarette clamped between his thick lips gave a casual salute.

Ripping off his beret, Philippe threw his disguise onto the front seat. He shivered as he leaned into the car for a rolled-up coat and woollen scarf. He walked Daniel to the back of the van.

"Poor things, we've been unable to stop anywhere. Stepan didn't want to take any chances. He's got an *ausweis* for his niece's first communion."

He wrenched open the van doors. "Isa?"

Philippe and Daniel peered down into the cluttered interior of suitcases and piled-up clothes. Daniel switched on his torch, for the light was fading rapidly, and ran it over Philippe's wife, sitting hunched in a corner in an unbuttoned winter coat.

Philippe leaned in towards her and brought out a bundle from under her thick cardigan.

"Our daughter, Rosa," Philippe said, whilst his wife quickly buttoned up.

Daniel saw Isa blush momentarily and helped her out of the van.

Bleating sounds emanated from the profusion of baby shawls that Philippe now smuggled into his coat.

"Just a minute. Could I have some light please, Daniel?"

Daniel swung his beam back, now sweeping over a curly-headed boy dressed in breeches. He was stretched out in the opposite corner against a pile of coats, a *casquette* dipped over his sleepy head.

"Simon," she murmured. "Wake up. We're here."

The boy struggled to lift his head. "*Ma-ma,*" he said, his eyes still closed. He yawned like a kitten as his mother pulled him up.

"Come on, Simon. We're at Daniel and Tatiana's."

"I'll get the luggage," Daniel said, drawing the boy out of the back with a smile. "*Viens, mon petit.*"

"Put your coat on, Simon," Isa snapped, pushing her son's little arms through the sleeves. Then she marched him round to Stepan. "Give Nina our love." Her voice quavered.

Stepan's hand reached out of the window to ruffle Simon's hair.

"*Merci, mon vieux!*" Philippe peered into the van as the engine started up. In a few moments, it was gone.

Isa wiped her eyes on her sleeve and took a lungful of air.

Daniel pointed his torch down the garden. "We'll be crossing an orchard, then it's down to our cottage, then yours."

"And this is the house where your friends live?" interjected Philippe.

Daniel detected a wariness in Philippe's voice. He shone the torch back over to Chocho's silent porch.

"Yes. I told Chocho and Pelletier not to come out tonight. But you will meet them."

"Thank you, Daniel." Philippe's eyes came alive with gratitude. He turned to Isa and nodded imperceptibly.

What discussions they must have had before leaving Paris.

"*J'ai froid,* Maman!" Simon whined.

"Take your father's hand, Simon! Where's your cap? Don't tell me you left it in the back of the van!"

"Isa! Please. It doesn't matter!"

"But he has so few warm clothes. Let me take Rosa. Take Simon."

"We will find something for him," Daniel said, eager to get them inside.

They made their descent across the frosted lawn. The baby started to cry. It was the high, strangulated cry of a hungry newborn. How many times had Daniel heard it when Tatiana had been nursing his daughters.

"Not far," Daniel tried to say, but his voice was drowned out by the baby. An autumnal mist had descended upon them. An owl hooting and the full moon seemed to disturb Simon. He started to drag his feet.

"Pick him up, Philippe," Isa said, clutching her daughter to her bosom.

"He's old enough to walk." Philippe turned to Daniel. "Excuse us. We haven't ventured out for months. It's just an owl, Simon."

Isa walked on.

"Mind the molehills, Isa!"

Daniel caught up with her. She seemed to be in some sort of trance. Her eyes fixed on the way ahead. They were now in open ground, out of the tree cover. Daniel extinguished his torch, for a little rectangular light had appeared ahead. Tatiana's womanly silhouette was looking out at them from the front porch.

"Daniel? Philippe?"

"Isa, Simon, it's Tatiana," said Philippe, pointing to her. He gave Simon a playful yank. "And you'll see Bubba and Zeude tomorrow."

Wiping her apron, Tatiana held Philippe's hands, and then turned to Isa's pale, tear-stained face. Taking her gently by the shoulders, she murmured,

"You'll be safe here."

Isa's limbs seemed to relax a fraction as she let them drop.

My wife has survived a revolution, Daniel said to himself, proudly. Several times Tatiana had recounted her escape across the Black Sea in a cargo boat. She had been Simon's age when, standing between Elisabeta and Vladimir, she had watched her aunts raise their thin arms from the quay, in what had become an eternal goodbye. Through the squeeze of her mother's hand, she had told Daniel miserably one night, she had felt all the anguish of separation and flight. What Isa was feeling now.

"Tatiana, you'd best shut the door – the light from the house. You don't want the *fritz* coming round."

Daniel saw Isa recoil and hold her baby to her breast. "Where is the house?"

"Straight ahead, Isa," Tatiana murmured, giving Daniel a look which said, 'now what's got into you?' "Daniel will take you. I'll bring over something to eat. Here, take these apples for the time being." She knelt down and offered one to Simon. "They're from our tree. I hope you like them."

Simon nodded vigorously and sank his small teeth into the apple.

Philippe placed his hand on Simon's shoulder. "You say '*merci*'."

"Oh, never mind that," said Tatiana, smiling. "Such lovely black curls," she added, running her slim fingers through Simon's hair.

Tatiana had taken less notice of the little girl swaddled in blankets. A featureless bundle to her. Or was it because the baby girl held no secrets for a mother of four daughters?

As they entered their cottage, Simon watched Daniel light a pyre of kindling he had prepared earlier. It leapt into lengthy flames. Simon's brown eyes sparkled as he threw his apple core into the fire.

"Another apple, please."

"No, Simon. You'll get tummy ache," Philippe said, looking around at his new home.

That day, Daniel had repaired a small table he'd found in the cottage. *Perfect for our chess games. Philippe is so hard to beat.* Philippe loved to read, too –he and Daniel shared the same love of history and poetry. To this end, Daniel had put up several bookshelves in the little sitting room. Philippe was so unlike his father Albert, who was incapable of sitting still, unless he was checking columns of figures.

Philippe was staring at them now with a sad smile. "Thank you. We had to leave our books behind."

Daniel nodded. "Of course. But first things first. You'll be needing new papers. Your father has already been in touch with my friend René. He knows it's urgent. And then you'll be able to work."

Philippe frowned. "You really think that'll be possible?"

"We're banking on it," Daniel said, laughing. But his friend didn't seem to see the joke. Daniel realised he needed to go gently.

"And I've been told food is easier to come by here, Daniel."

Daniel noticed how hollow Philippe's cheeks had become, how feverish his eyes as he stared into the fire. Had he foregone food to feed Simon?

"Yes," Daniel said, happy to be able to relieve his friend of some worries.

"My two sisters are still in Paris. But we couldn't have held out much longer in our tiny apartment. They were good people, those who kept us alive. The people from the Amelot Committee. Jews and non-Jews, like Stepan. Without them, risking their lives every day…"

Tatiana appeared at the door with a stockpot. "Where is Isa?"

"In the bedroom with Rosa."

Tatiana placed the pot on the table. "Cabbage and mushrooms. A little rabbit. Eat whilst it's hot." She pulled the kitchen table drawer and handed one of the spoons to Simon, before stepping into Isa's bedroom.

Simon sat down and clutched the spoon in his little fist. Philippe went over to him straight away and tipped the soup into his bowl without using the ladle. Simon started to slurp hurriedly.

"Gently, son," Philippe said, placing his palm on top of Simon's head.

Daniel saw the holes and snagging at Philippe's lapel, where his friend had unstitched his Jewish Star.

"We'd best go, Daniel." Tatiana had emerged from the bedroom. She turned to Philippe. "Isa is asking for you. Take her some soup."

Daniel placed one more log on the fire.

"*A demain*," Philippe said, taking Tatiana's hand in his. He let go and poured some soup for his wife. Daniel saw Philippe's hand tremble with the weight of the pot.

"Did you see?" he said, walking back with his wife. "Philippe looks terrible."

"And Isa can barely nurse."

"What they must have gone through…"

"They are here at least." Tatiana never liked to dwell on the dark things of this world. At least not out loud. But she recognised those who had experienced them. And somehow, she felt closer to those people, Daniel surmised. It was inevitable.

Daniel and Philippe were playing chess at the kitchen table several weeks later. Albert, sat next to them, was skimming the newspaper while poking his nose into their game.

"Philippe, you've left your queen exposed to his *bischof*." He turned back to Daniel. "Such a *luftmensch*. *Ay-yay-yay*, he's about to lose."

"Papa, please!"

"Daniel, have you heard the latest?" Albert said, grinning. "Two Parisians talking in the *métro*…"

Philippe frowned over his next move.

"First man says to his friend: 'A Jew shot a German in the Luxembourg gardens yesterday evening. When the man was quite dead, he ate part of his entrails, including his heart.'

"His friend replies: 'You'll believe anything you hear, Pierre.'

"'But it's true,' insists Pierre.

"'Impossible,' says his friend.

"'Why?' enquires Pierre.

"'Well,' his friend replies, laughing, 'firstly, Jews don't eat pigs, secondly, Germans have no heart, and thirdly, at nine twenty p.m. everyone is at home listening to the BBC'."

Philippe sighed. Daniel smiled politely. Albert had forgotten he'd already told the joke the day before. But Albert was nervously waiting for René.

"*Salut, les gars*!" And there was Rene's cheerful moon face at the door.

"René!" they all said, getting up and fixing their eyes on the brown envelope he was holding.

"All there," René said, handing it to Philippe. "Here, Monsieur Chalvin."

"Chalvin?"

"Your new identity. Not bad, eh?" René beamed.

Philippe removed the identity cards, handled them delicately, as if inspecting priceless Egyptian papyri. He seemed genuinely moved.

"Papa," he said, tenderly, looking up at Albert. "*Merci*."

"It's only *geld*, son."

"Monsieur Klug, you'll be pleased to know that I've found Philippe work too."

"René, you have surpassed yourself!" said Daniel, delighted.

"At the Prefecture."

"The Prefecture!" Rebecca had just walked in with Tatiana.

"*Ah!*" chimed in Albert, also shocked by the announcement. "What is this?"

"It's not safe for Philippe to work there," Rebecca said, exchanging worried looks with her husband. "We've come so far – if I thought we were handing him to the authorities…"

"Safe as houses," said René, looking very pleased with himself. "Besides, it's enormous. So many departments. Some of them, the *fritz* have little to do with. You'll blend in, Philippe, don't worry. You'll be in Transport. Car permits."

"Oh," Philippe said, laughing for the first time. "When do I start?"

"I told a friend you were available to start immediately. He owes me a favour. I stopped his son being carted off to Germany for the STO…" There was a terrible silence as René realised his blunder.

"Thank you, René," Daniel said, quickly. "You have been most efficient."

René removed his round glasses, a clear sign that he was handing over the matter to Daniel.

"Rebecca," Daniel continued in a conciliatory tone, "Jobs, as you know, are hard to find. And whatever one does these days, one ends up working for the *fritz*. Whether you are sent to Germany, work for Operation Todt on our coastline, or are employed by a French company, the chances are the organisation survives only because it supplies the *boches*. Philippe is discreet and, to be honest, car permits…"

Philippe nodded. "Thank you, Daniel. Maman. Papa. I will be alright. And besides, Daniel and René have taken risks themselves by helping me."

Daniel waved the statement away but felt grateful for the acknowledgement all the same.

Albert nodded. "Of course. Thank you, René. Daniel. And now all of you, I must tell you, it is time for Rebecca and I to leave. Our papers say that we live in the Creuse region and hotel life is not what it used to be."

Albert's funds must be low. But he is happy now. His job is done. And Dieu merci, all will be well.

CHAPTER FORTY-FIVE

Christmas Eve, the snow came, slowly blanketing the patch of lawn in front of the cottage where the children now played.

Daniel had been engrossed in a game of patience and Tatiana darning stockings when they heard a high-pitched cry come through the window.

"Simon," Tatiana said, rushing to the window, decorated in snow.

Daniel got up from the games table and joined her.

"*Laissez-moi,*" shouted Simon, shaking out his snow-filled coat.

Jeanne and Béa were laughing maliciously.

Incensed, Simon bent his curly head and tried to ram them, but he missed, as they stepped aside, and caught France, who had been standing by, packing her own little snowball between her mittens. She was sent flying head-first into the deep snow.

Jeanne ran away towards the orchard, whilst Béa stood there, arms folded, frowning.

Daniel and his wife were poised to come France's aid but saw her lever herself up on her stocky limbs and reappear, a snow creature, rubbing her blonde lashes with her mittens.

"*Pas gentil!*" she said, pointing her tiny index finger at Simon.

Béa went over to hug her little sister. "Don't worry, France. At least you're not a cry-baby like Simon."

Simon stomped his foot and set off home, but Jeanne was already marching back, several heads taller than him.

"No you don't!" she shouted, and from her pocket produced a

spare bit of twine she had no doubt found in the garden. With all her force she pushed him up against one of the apple trees.

Béa clapped her hands in delight, as did France, for she always copied her older sisters.

"Right, that's it," Tatiana said, dropping her sewing onto the sill.

"Leave them, Tatiana," Daniel said, sitting back down at the games table.

"No! Look at Jeanne!"

"Simon needs to learn to stand up for himself. He'll be six soon. Philippe is firmly in agreement with me. It's only Isa who... And now you!"

"But can't you see how unfair this is? Three against one. And Jeanne should know better. She's seven."

Daniel sighed. *Always Jeanne.* He watched his wife fling open the door and rush out in her slippers. Like a fury she grabbed her eldest daughter's arm and started shaking it. "How many times have I told you to leave Simon!"

Jeanne pursed her lips with disappointment and upset. *She so seeks Tatiana's approval. Be gentle with her, Tatiana.*

"It's only a game, Maman," Daniel heard her say in a tearful voice.

Simon started to screw up his face and whimper.

"Oh, stop that!" snapped Béa, in her mother's cross voice.

Tatiana swung round to look at Béa in astonishment. Should he go out and intervene? No, he decided, bringing out the Jack of Spades and placing it on his Queen of the same suit. He was on a winning streak. It was his precious Sunday off, one which had passed so peaceably up until now. He would only undermine Tatiana's authority by calmly striding out, as he liked to do, smiling at them like some magnanimous pasha. Raising one's voice never got you anywhere, he had learnt.

"Just a minute, everyone." Tatiana was back in the house, wiping her slippers on the mat. "I have a surprise. Wait there."

What was she doing?

Daniel heard a cupboard being opened and saw Tatiana fly out of the kitchen with a large bar of chocolate wrapped in brown paper. It was no ordinary bar. It had the distinctive gold Mme de Sevigné label embossed on the front.

"I thought you were saving that for the Christmas table,

Tatiana?" he shouted after her.

Through the window he saw Tatiana produce the tablet of fragrant dark chocolate. *Sacha again!* The children's faces lit up as she dangled it above their heads, looking at them all in turn, lecturing them on good behaviour and consideration for others, no doubt. Satisfied, she proceeded to break up the precious bar before their hungry eyes. Simon stood as straight as a little soldier. He was served first, followed by France.

Still surly, but hunger getting the better of her, Jeanne started to devour her chocolate.

Daniel shook his head, despairing. However, there was silence as they all attacked the fragrant chocolate like hungry wolf cubs.

"More, Tatiana. More," said Simon, standing on tip-toes, lifting his arms up to her, his black curls falling into his eyes. Tatiana's expression was at first stern but Simon pleaded, "Please."

"Well just a little." Tatiana's taut, proud features relaxed as she cupped his soft cheeks.

Jeanne stamped her foot and ran into the house. Within seconds she was burying her white, tear-stained face in Daniel's chest, sending his cards flying to the floor.

Christmas day came. René, being René, was able to procure a large turkey from a local breeder. It fed all three families. The fourth, Philippe's, had made themselves scarce to celebrate Hannukah.

Otherwise, life carried on as normal. Philippe joined Daniel and the other men around the wireless to listen to the clandestine BBC broadcasts. The year had ended well, the retaking of Smolensk by the Russian Army in October, Italy leaving the Axis and the bombing of Berlin, all evidence of the occupier's weakening position. But they dared not hope too much. Corsica had been liberated, however, and this news had Philippe and Daniel performing a mad jig around the sitting room.

In the New Year, Daniel's colleague, the *Préfet* Bussière, ushered him into his regal office. Daniel was surprised to see him lock the door. He motioned him to a seat.

"*Bonne Année,* Daniel, and all that. Now tell me," he said, perching on the corner of his large desk and dropping his chin. "How is the resistance going?"

Daniel scrambled for a reply. He had always been so cautious.

Had René been indiscreet over Christmas? To have come so far and then to realise that their secret business was known to a representative of Vichy; Bussière often lunched with the Maréchal.

"What resistance?"

Bussière gave him a worldly smile.

Having had time to recover from his shock, Daniel continued, "I don't hang around with those terrorists."

"Alright. Alright…" The Prefect raised his hand in apology. "I just want to let you know that I'm always here to help."

"But you have always helped me in every endeavour," Daniel said, guardedly.

"Yes. And I'm now telling you to be careful." He shot him a serious glance and then wiped some cigar ash from his knee. "Certain departments and individuals may take a dim view of what you are involved in."

Daniel left his office a little stunned but felt the warmth of Bussière's handshake long after he had left.

That same month, there was a German clampdown on the youth centres. In January, several were closed in the region, resulting in hundreds of boys and girls being let out to fend for themselves.

Daniel tried to guide them as best he could. The information centre René and he ran was full of young hopefuls searching anxiously for work, but not just any work. No one wished to work in a ball bearings or armaments factory in Germany, whatever the pay. Operation Todt, along the Atlantic coast, was by far the lesser of two evils, Daniel told them. As Daniel had first mentioned to Philippe, it was impossible not to work for the *fritz*, and now that more German workers were called to fight, the pressure on Vichy to provide more French workers had increased.

More and more, Daniel felt his work compromised by Vichy's increasing collaboration with the German authorities. There was a shake-up of the administration. Their job centre was brought into the prefectural offices, while the Youth Ministry, for whom they all worked, was amalgamated with the Ministry of Employment. Chocho found himself shunted to another department. Daniel and Pelletier remained, but found their hands increasingly tied. With jobs thin on the ground and forced labour still threatening the youths, Daniel watched some of them leave civilian life altogether and go off and join the local Resistance groups in the Loir et Cher, where Lerude was recruiting. In most cases, Daniel welcomed it, for those suited to the clandestine life. More worrying however, for Daniel, were the paramilitary organisations. Vic's involvement in them robbed him of sleep. He decided that he would go to Paris at the earliest opportunity.

In the months that followed, the news that Hitler had changed strategy and was drawing labour from the POW camps reduced the pressure on Daniel and René.

But the reorganisation of the Youth Ministry had brought fresh problems. Chocho had been replaced by an individual Riou was wary of, for the new boss, he had been told, had a brother, a notorious Parisian journalist and Nazi sympathiser. Daniel and Pelletier met their new chief of department and were pleasantly surprised by his lack of Vichy zeal. He went as far as to wish for a German defeat.

And yet Bussière's warning had not been forgotten. Riou and Daniel kept their anti-Vichy sympathies to themselves.

Meanwhile, Riou had become watchful of the changes within the Resistance movement, which had grown and become more organised. An important meeting had been planned by a group called *Ceux De la Libération,* with whom Daniel had had intermittent contact. Lerude had decided to take part, with a view to joining forces.

Daniel discussed the impending event with Riou.

"Shouldn't we just try?"

"No, I say!" Riou shook his head resolutely. "The bigger we get, the more visible we become."

"René doesn't see it that way."

"René is foolhardy! And think of it. All these people at a meeting, congregated in one room. Revealing their physical identities. And don't forget, young people can be so indiscreet and gullible."

"Yes," Daniel said, thinking not only of Lerude but now of Vic. "Very."

"We should stay as we are."

Daniel had never been a committeeman, always preferring quick, decisive action and the intimacy of a small, trusted group. Riou was meticulous. A family man, too. 'No suicidal missions,' he would always say. And with this approach, they had accomplished much, on two fronts, working both for the *Gaulliste* army, with Lerude providing intelligence on the ground, and for the British

Intelligence services, with Durand up in Paris, building an arsenal of weapons for the Allied landings – for they would surely come soon.

"My fear is that Lerude is naive," continued Riou. "And the same goes for René."

Daniel nodded.

Earlier, Daniel had told René to think of his family, when René had piped up about the meeting.

'Alright, Dan,' he had replied. 'But shouldn't we keep up with what is happening? We don't want to get left out of things.'

'Left out of things! Imagine how left out you will feel behind prison bars.' Daniel had retorted, angrily. 'And you'll drag us all with you. Who will look after our families then?'

Daniel called Lerude.

"Daniel!" Lerude sounded breathless but ecstatic. He was always rushing around the region these days. Daniel worried about the young man's fragile constitution.

"Lerude," he said, feeling cowardly as he spoke. "Don't take it personally but Riou and I won't be coming. You know our position..."

"Of course."

"We fully support you. Be careful, *mon vieux!*" It seemed strange to refer to his young friend as that. He was only twenty-three.

Lerude laughed. "Look, if they get me, they get me. I don't fear death."

His mother had said the same. Lerude had made a pilgrimage to Chartres. He was considering becoming a priest, after the war.

"See you next week, Dan."

The phone clunked down at the other end.

That night, Daniel ran the conversation over and over in his mind as he paced the cottage. Outside the window in his bedroom, great, silent snowflakes fell. *The meeting might be adjourned because of the weather. Please – let it be adjourned.* Slowly, and without waking Tatiana, he got back into bed, curled up against her, and fell asleep.

He woke with a start. Someone outside, rapping the doorknocker. It had to be Pelletier come down from the house. What was he doing there? He was normally up at the main house by now, waiting for Daniel to appear in the courtyard on his bike.

"Daniel!" came an anxious voice through the door.

Daniel shook himself awake. *Why didn't Tatiana wake me?* He heard her next door, attending to the children. Daniel threw a dressing gown on and wrenched open the frozen door.

Wide-eyed and grim-faced, Pelletier stood there looking at him.

"Come in," Daniel felt himself falter. "What happened?"

Pelletier started to speak in an exhausted tone. "A neighbour saw the Gestapo break down the door. Or maybe it was the *Milice*. Or both. You can bet those French Nazi-lovers thought Christmas had come early."

"How many did they take?"

"Only six. Luckily, most hadn't turned up to the meeting. There was some mix-up on dates. And the weather, of course. But I believe you know one of them."

"Who?" Daniel whispered, feeling his head buzz and whirr with names of people that were dear to him. "Not René?"

"No, Daniel. Lefèbvre."

Tatiana came to the door. "Daniel you're still in your pyjamas. What's happening. Are you alright?"

He was conscious of mouthing his friend's name and of Pelletier and Tatiana directing him towards the bathroom, where Jeanne and Béa were brushing their teeth. The girls scattered immediately, and he just managed to retch down the toilet bowl in time.

"You'd best get dressed, Dan," Pelletier said, now looking truly sorry. "I'll call René and tell him what happened. He'll be grateful he took your advice."

Daniel stared at the purple circles under his eyes in the bathroom mirror then looked away. The Resistance had ceased to be a game.

But René has been spared. And perhaps our lives, too. It depressed him that these were his thoughts. Lerude had had all his life to live. But the young man had been too trusting. Leaving his apartment open to people, day and night. Somewhere a Gestapo agent had infiltrated his network. He would be interrogated. He had told Daniel that he had no fear of torture even though his heart was weak. Lerude wouldn't talk. He could bet his life on it.

With Lerude gone, he, Riou and René had lost their *gaulliste* contact.

Wordlessly, Tatiana got the children ready around him. Daniel was out of the door before he realised that she'd bid him goodbye. He wrapped a scarf over his mouth, felt his eyes water in the chill wind as he leaned forward and pushed his bike up to the house. Who had betrayed Lerude and Lefèbvre? Had Lerude been arrested by the Gestapo? The Orléans *Milice*? He clamped his teeth against the cold and raged inwardly against the madness that had caused one of his members of staff to join the fight for freedom and be a hero, while the other, younger, more impressionable one, joined an organisation that inspired hatred from the resistance movement.

"Darnand!" he screamed out to the wind. *Oh, Vic!*

He had reached the top of the lawn. Pelletier was waiting for him at the front of the house. He couldn't discuss Vic with him. Philippe even less. Thank goodness Philippe had already left for work. His friend had talked of going to Paris, to check up on his sisters in the Latin quarter. There was no fuel, the train tracks had been bombed, so Philippe had resolved to go by bike, much to Isa's despair. And suddenly it all became very clear to him. Tatiana would try and stop him, but he would tell her it was a mission. And as he mulled it over, he realised that he would not be telling a lie.

CHAPTER FORTY-SIX

At the Porte d'Orleans on the outskirts of Paris, Daniel slowed and watched Philippe pedal away towards the southern part of the capital and the Latin quarter.

Picking up speed again, Daniel turned west towards the industrial suburb of Billancourt. On the horizon, grey industrial complexes loomed, many of which had been bombed by the Americans the previous September. Hundreds of French workers in the car, food and silk industries had been injured and killed, Daniel recalled. He remembered one particular headline from a pro-German paper at the *préfecture*: 'Paris Savagely Bombed By Her Liberators'.

Daniel shook his head. His heart lightened, however, as he passed the His Master's Voice factory, where he had procured the gramophones for the centres. What an important day that had been. The day he had entered the Resistance proper. What line would Vic take if he knew?

Daniel recalled happier times with Vic at Fort Girard. Would he be meeting the same Vic who'd huddled around the radio with all of them in Lefèbvre's room, the Vic who'd cheered for the Americans when they'd entered North Africa? Lefèbvre had been carted off to the Mauthausen labour camp. What would Vic think of that?

But I wish for the truth, however messy, he said to himself, leaving Billancourt behind.

He was conscious of pedalling faster now, fury powering his rotations. Glancing at his watch, he saw that it was already midday.

Philippe and he couldn't be caught out by the curfew on the journey back to Orléans; anything could happen to lengthen their trip. But already he had spied, with relief and some consternation, the iron bridge of Saint Cloud. He was almost there. The sun had broken through the low-lying cloud. He pedalled past an eight-storey apartment building that had been prised in two. Swerving around a gaping hole in the road, he continued onto the Place de Saint Cloud, where just the roof remained of an ancient chapel.

Daniel turned to the Seine. A lone fisherman was casting his line over its shimmering waters. He and Tatiana had watched a similar scene from the Pont des Arts when they'd first courted. How the whole of Paris had entered into that first, lingering kiss! Soon after, they had watched six hundred French planes fly over the Champs-Elysees as part of a military celebration. That had been in '35. Where were they now? *De Gaulle will redress this calamity.* His heart leapt at the thought of seeing French planes in the sky again. *Only then will Frenchmen feel truly safe.*

He crossed the bridge and entered the rue de Paris. Ten minutes later, he was cycling through a tree-lined neighbourhood of little shops, cafés, a church. Slowing, he passed *Le Mouton d'Or*, a seventeenth century inn, once the haunt of great classical writers Racine, Molière, and Jean de la Fontaine. How privileged they were to have lived through a century of enlightenment. How would historians sum up the times he was living in now? A time of greed, madness, fear, and chaos. A time where France hung her head in shame.

He braked suddenly. He had spied a squat brick building through some iron railings. Dismounting, he pushed his bike's rattling carcass up onto the pavement. Two young men in navy-blue jackets, ski pants and black berets eyed him warily. It was not unlike what the boys had worn at Fort Girard, except these young men were also wearing black ties.

"What is your business, Monsieur?" said the taller guard. Daniel noticed the pockmarks on his cheek. Shrapnel from German or Allied bombings? Or simply a street brawl?

The stockier-looking young man stepped forward and pointed his machine gun.

"Raise your arms. Look ahead!"

Daniel's heart juddered. He followed his instructions. A hand patted his pockets.

"What are these?"

"Corks, for my tyre. I may have a slow puncture."

The guard hesitated then moved on, right down to his shoes. He raised his head again and stared at Daniel's cap.

"Remove it, Monsieur."

He did so, crumpling the cap in his hand.

"Name?"

"Daniel Frey. I have a meeting with Vic d'O…"

Both sentries perused his tired-looking tweed jacket, his oversized rolled-up trousers. Tatiana had had to punch two more holes in his belt since the beginning of the occupation.

The taller guard brightened. "*Papiers, s'il vous plaît.*"

Daniel produced his identity papers.

"Wait there." The guard marched off.

Daniel unrolled his trousers. Barely a few metres away, some women were glumly queuing outside a bakery. A baby had started to cry. Someone shrieked,

"We'd still have bread if you hadn't given it all away to that *gendarme's* wife!"

The *boulangère* came out onto the pavement, shrugging her shoulders. There was a roar of disapproval as she brought down the metal shutter with a rattle.

The *milicien* looked back at Daniel. His eyes were expressionless. Was this a common occurrence? Probably. This young recruit looked sturdy and strong. Had he joined to fill his stomach? He would argue, no doubt, that he helped the poor in Paris, for the *Milice* were now confiscating black market food and redistributing it to the poor.

What a mess it all is. The people are starving. This cannot last.

"Monsieur Frey?" The returning *milicien's* tone had become more respectful. "Please come through. He's just finishing a class."

The iron gate inched opened, just enough for Daniel to push his bike through. *Just pray that no Resistance member has seen me enter.* He wheeled in his bike and propped it against a wall.

Stuffing his cap into his back pocket, he walked round to the entrance and stepped inside the building.

Vic had emerged from a class. "Daniel!"

A head taller than Vic, Daniel peered over his former protégé's shoulder. *Coat hooks running along the classroom walls.* Had this been a church? Albert and Philippe shot into his mind, hanging their coats and turning towards him with their fringed scarfs and keppas.

"Good to see you!" Vic turned to his charges. "Class dismissed."

Daniel watched the aspiring young officers file out in uniform, all with close-cropped hair, some tall and fresh-faced, resembling the usual offering of Army cadets, others at the back, hardened *banlieusards*, broader and stockier, clutching textbooks in their ink-stained hands.

Vic shook his hand hurriedly. A metal gamma insignia with the sign of the ram had been pinned to his lapel.

"Would you come this way?"

Daniel entered a room that smelt of dust, chalk and age-old wood. Along the wall, behind Vic's desk, ran several long shelves. Proudhon and Maurras's writings, boxes of files and training material filled them. There was a poster on the wall. A French soldier bent double under the weight of a huge cross. '*Grace aux Anglais*' ('Thanks to the English'), ran the sarcastic headline. Above him, Joan of Arc burnt at the stake. Below the soldier, in bold red letters, was written: '*Notre Chemin de Croix*' ('It's the cross we bear').

"Pleased you've been able to make it despite the rail disruption." Vic shut the door. Two brown bottles and sandwiches had been laid out on a tray on Vic's desk.

"A little refreshment after your long ride?" Vic smiled, nervously, as Daniel stared at the beers. "They're chilled."

"Yes. It's been a while since I've had one of these," Daniel said, in a measured voice. He took the bottle and poured himself a glass.

Vic seemed to take pleasure in treating him. "I can imagine. Now tell me, how are Tatiana and the girls?

"Well, thank you." Daniel felt himself wince. "And you?" He brought the dark beer to his lips. How good it would have tasted if he hadn't been sitting in the *Milice* officer training school and facing Vic, now hunched forward awkwardly and talking with such false bonhomie. He put his glass aside.

"I seem to remember it was your favourite."

"Yes," Daniel said, resting his folded hands on Vic's desk. "Thank you – it was."

Vic started to play with his *chevalière*.

"Look. I know what you must think. I owe you an apology…"

"Not only me, Vic. Why did you leave Les Bézards?"

Vic flinched.

"Yes. It was quite a coincidence bumping into your old military commander Darnand like that, in the dead of night." Daniel hated sarcasm – he wasn't used to speaking to people this way. But the anger he had harboured for weeks now fuelled him.

Vic looked away, out of the window, where a youth was being bellowed at in the yard for being out of step.

"I know. But, at the time, it didn't seem so surprising. After all, the war throws up all sorts of situations, doesn't it?" Vic leaned forward. "It was raining, you understand. Heavily." He paused. "My former commander had broken down in his car and was searching for a place to stay."

Daniel listened distractedly.

"When he was brought to me, he was drenched to the bone and furious because he was needed in Paris the following morning. Of course, his features lit up the moment he recognised me. 'Vic. My boy! Such providence!' And I have to admit, I too was surprised and excited by his sudden appearance. You understand, don't you?" He leaned forward. "You're a soldier, Daniel. Darnand had led me into battle against the Germans. I had no reason to doubt his love for France." His face fell.

It was true, Daniel said to himself, Darnand had been decorated twice over, both in the Great War and this one.

"But you left Les Bézards. Just followed him…"

Vic bit his lip. "Yes."

"Leaving all your team leaders to cope as best they could."

"I had trained them well. I had a good deputy, willing to take the reins…"

"You should have discussed it with Riou and I."

"I know, I know. But I was told to say nothing! At least until everything had been made official."

Daniel let out a long sigh.

"Imagine how I felt," Vic continued more insistently. "He had asked me to head up a new officer training school. I assumed he wanted to replicate the elite French one in Uriage, in the Free Zone."

"Yes, Uriage." Daniel had to concede that he'd heard good reports of the French officer training school. He had also heard that it had recently closed. Some rumour of the head being at loggerheads with Laval. It was rumoured that the Uriage head had joined the Resistance. Meanwhile, Darnand, seizing his opportunity, with Laval's consent, moved into the old chateau with the *Milice*, created out of the Legionary Order Service (SOL) he had been running. Unceasingly ambitious, Darnand had now set up a new officer school in Paris.

"My former commander spoke passionately of the new force he was forming to help France get back on its feet," Vic continued. "Of Pétain and Laval allowing him to do it. To balance up the inequality between the *fritz* and us. We have no army, after all."

"I see." Daniel visualised Darnand praising his former officer to the skies as they warmed themselves by the fire, exchanging war memories. Daniel gripped the chair, still nursing his anger. "So, you followed him…"

"Yes. And, at first, I was so proud to be part of this new force. I had plans for training the best, the noblest, the bravest officers in the land. I was able to start sifting through the ex-soldiers, but most had been imprisoned in Germany. I went to Les Bézards…"

Daniel shuddered at the thought of his boys joining such an organisation.

"But I was surprised how few young men of quality presented themselves. The ones that did… well you can see for yourself who Darnand is making me take on." Vic's face twisted with disgust. "Petty crooks, some of them. He has complained, of course. I'm being told I'm too choosy." He wrung his hands, then reached into his desk drawer. "And recently I came across this." He pulled out a newssheet entitled '*Combats*'.

A headline ran along the first page: 'Alert to all *Miliciens!*' Daniel skimmed the lines, stopping on 'Waffen-SS', 'triumphant Jew', and 'destroy bolshevism'. He pushed it back towards Vic.

"So, you'll be joining the SS, I see. The price of being armed now, for it's the only way the Germans are going to trust Darnand. Goosestepping through the streets and *siegheiling*. Oh Vic! What are you doing in this synagogue, too?"

"I promise you I didn't know anything of this." He looked genuinely upset, wringing his hands over and over again. "And now it's all getting out of hand," he continued, almost hysterically.

"Yes, now that Darnand is head of the French police."

Vic shuffled in his chair.

"You had visions of creating an army to reclaim our country.

But it seems…"

Vic shook his head and looked miserably out of the window.

"Rounding up Jews and Resistance groups. Turning on your own kind. Hardly noble!"

A deep silence followed. Vic turned back to him, his expression one of shock and disbelief. Daniel decided to stop his attack. He had to be careful. He had been so used to guiding Vic that he had forgotten the risk he was running talking to him like this. He hoped they hadn't been overheard.

Daniel got up and walked over to the large window. The cadets were saluting their sergeant.

"I haven't got long. They'll be back in soon."

"What are you going to do now?"

"I don't know."

Daniel turned. "You must leave and join us down in Orleans. Before you're made to do something you regret."

"If only it were that simple," wailed Vic. "How I wish Darnand would tell me to go. But he won't, I know."

Daniel, sensing a crisis approaching, sat down.

Vic's voice had dropped to a whisper. "I'm turning the question over and over in my head. But how do I explain myself? Someone walked out recently, and he was found dead in the gutter – supposedly shot by the *FTP-Moi* resistance.'

"What do you mean, supposedly?" Daniel looked puzzled. These young communist partisans were regularly taking down German officers, and now the *Milice,* in broad daylight. Quite fearless. He had to admire their pluck. "If it's not the *Moi,* you're not suggesting that the *Milice* are…"

Vic had grown white and silent.

"In which case, you simply resign, claiming that you don't feel yourself up to the job. That you have failed Darnand."

Vic let out a bitter laugh.

"Alright – just disappear. Go underground. If the Allies continue to… there will be plenty switching sides, going to join the Resistance."

"I've already thought of that. But they'll torture my younger student brother at the Sorbonne, terrorize my parents. No. They know everything about me."

Daniel was suddenly on his guard.

"I'm trapped here."

"I will do whatever I can, Vic," Daniel said, getting ready to leave. In reality, his head swum with confusion. "At least we've had this conversation and I have you on record as wanting to leave and regretting your actions."

Vic got up and shook his hand vigorously. "Thank you. I'm relieved that we have talked."

Daniel left the synagogue in a hurry. Pulling up the collar of his jacket and dipping his cap, he pushed his bike rapidly out of the forecourt. Anger, shame and finally pity filled his heart. *Who hasn't made mistakes?* How reckless, rebellious and foolhardy he had been in his youth. Wasting his school years, marrying in haste, only to regret it bitterly when he met Tatiana, whom he loved with his whole heart. The Army at least had taught him some self-discipline, trained him physically and mentally to deal with complex war situations. But what they were facing in France was something else.

Look how we have all been deceived by those we trusted. Pétain – a war hero, too. Petain's fight to get back millions of French prisoners had dominated his regime. The old Maréchal had failed miserably in his endeavour, compromising France, compromising his people, letting Laval, Darnand take over.

A little light came to dispel his despair. *Perhaps, just perhaps, Vic can be useful to us.*

On the return journey, Philippe, relieved that he had been able to see his sisters, was as anxious to get home as Daniel. They pedalled furiously, eager to gain Orleans before nightfall, but as they were cycling along the Artenay rails, an American Lockheed appeared above their heads.

Fearing the worst, they raced off at speed, down a bumpy path bordered by elm trees. Throwing themselves under one of them and flattening themselves like rats, they felt a torrent of bullets rain down on them, shattering and splintering the wood within centimetres of their rigid bodies.

The plane motor faded. A smell of moist earth and burning wood filled the air.

"Alright, *mon vieux*?" Daniel said, peering down at Philippe, who was spitting out earth and spume. "Idiot!" Daniel dusted off his jacket, his trousers. "Target practice."

"Why us?" Philippe said, bitterly.

"I don't understand anything anymore," Daniel said, exhausted. "Let's take the backcountry for a while. It'll take longer, but we'll have more cover."

They reached St Jean de Braye much later than anticipated. Too tired to speak or celebrate their luck, they clapped each other on the back and pushed their bikes across the moonlit lawn, down to their respective homes.

CHAPTER FORTY-SEVEN

"The Lockheed was a warning."

Daniel frowned and ran his eyes down *Le Républicain*. Blasted apartment buildings, piled-up tombstones in Orléan's main cemetery and fractured cathedral towers occupied the front page. Funerals, the article read, would have to be held in the church of Saint Marceau, on the opposite shore of the Loire. However, the bombing of Les Aubrais railway station, in the north of the city, was the lead story. In a night raid, the RAF had targeted the main rail junction, taking with it the surrounding factories and workmen's houses. With no electricity, no water, no gas, the city had temporarily ground to a halt.

Daniel thought back to when it had all started, the day after their return from Paris, when sirens had rung out all over Orleans in broad daylight. He had spilled out of the Préfecture with Pelletier and Chocho. Two streets running west from the Place du Matroi had been struck by a stray American bomber shot down by a German fighter plane. 47 dead and apartment buildings burnt to the ground. And now, ten days later, they had been woken during the night by the sound of distant bombing.

"The RAF released fifteen hundred bombs in twenty minutes." Daniel looked up from his paper and watched Philippe retrieve a box of chess pieces from the sitting room shelf. "One hundred dead. One thousand homes destroyed around Aubrais. They're calling the Allies 'massacring liberators', as usual." He folded the paper angrily and handed it to Philippe. "Want it?"

Philippe tossed it aside after a cursory glance.

"Come on, Daniel. Instead of getting all worked up." Philippe picked two chess pawns out of the box and thrust two bony fists forward.

"Right hand," Daniel said, distractedly.

Philippe opened his fist. "Black."

Without comment on Philippe's advantage, they started to set up the pieces on the board.

"It's a tragedy when Allied planes claim innocent lives. And what about that brave pilot! It's about time these Allied landings became a reality!"

Philippe sighed and moved his pawn.

Daniel automatically brought out his knight. "That first bomb came down near our old house. Riou should move out of central Orléans." He looked up. Philippe was deliberating his next move. "Hopefully the air raids will cease for a while."

Philippe wearily brought out his bishop. None of them had been getting much rest, but Philippe, with a teething baby, seemed to be sleepwalking through the day. Although his complexion had improved since coming to the Loire, today he was looking particularly drawn.

"Philippe. Why don't you go and get some rest?"

"I'm fine, Dan," he said. "It's your move. And this was supposed to be a rest!" He frowned, concentrating on the board.

The following week, news came that the Germans were simply repairing the damaged track at Les Aubrais.

Daniel and Riou met in a café after work.

"I just don't understand it, Dan. We need to talk to Davaine, he works for that engineering company, Campenon-Bernard. Lerude always said he was to be trusted."

Davaine received Daniel and Riou in his office the next day. He was a solid man with a big, open face.

"No one can understand it," he said, shaking his head. "The German goods trains have started running again, even though the track up to Paris is still not in use."

"Can we take a look?" Riou said, tentatively.

"Best I'm not seen up there with you," Davaine said, suddenly wary. "However, I can put you in touch with some of the old boys supervising the repair of the track. You'll have to watch your back. Perhaps Daniel… You could always say you've come down to see how your boys are getting on. Heard some of them have work down there."

"Seems sensible," Riou said, eyeing Daniel.

Daniel nodded and watched Davaine go over to the coat rack where a black button-up jacket, trousers and cap hung.

"Put these on for good measure," he said, sizing Daniel up. "They may be a bit loose but you're about my height. Ask for a Monsieur Bazin."

Dressed as a *cheminot*, Daniel cycled up, with some apprehension, to Les Aubrais. A team of young men were rebuilding the track, as part of their obligatory STO service (Service du Travail Obligatoire). They were supervised by an old man leaning on his shovel.

"I'm Daniel. Davaine the engineer sent me."

The old man looked up. "Oh ay!"

"Everything's ground to a halt around here but I hear some trains are getting out…"

The wily-looking fellow called over his shoulder. "Carry on with your work, *les gars.*" His weather-beaten face returned to Daniel. "There's an old line running out of here, through the Orleans forest." He jerked his head in that direction. "There are trains running out of there at night. But you didn't hear it from me, right?"

"*Merci*, Monsieur!" Daniel hopped back onto his bike and sped back into town.

"Why hadn't anyone spotted it?" Daniel asked Riou later.

"I'm not sure," Riou said, poring over a map. "But it would make sense, the line would be invisible from the air. Daniel, can I ask you to look into the possibility of sabotaging the line?"

A jolt passed through him, fear and excitement seizing hold. He had been itching for something to do. Since the railways had gone down and there was little or no fuel, he had been stuck in his pen-pushing job, not even able to visit the remaining centres.

"Yes," he said. "Of course."

'No suicide missions', Riou would always say. He had clearly thought this one through. The night watchmen guarding the track were their boys. Should they sabotage the track they had only to stage an ambush of the security staff, tie them up, reward them later.

"You'll need to go with someone who knows about laying explosives," Riou said, softly.

"Of course. Davaine can put forward someone. We have some dynamite, Bickford tape, detonators."

"You're sure you want to do this, Daniel?" Riou said. "We have *maquis* hiding in the woods if we run into any difficulty. The Germans don't know that we know about the trains. And as for those minding the track, they're our boys…"

"Yes, yes…"

"I'm also organising a team to sabotage the electrical transformer post in Cercotte. It's not guarded, I hear."

Over the next few days, Daniel and a man named Jules hid out in the forest for a few hours every evening. At around 21h00, a train left a concealed siding in Les Aubrais, trundling past them fifteen minutes later. They timed its journey from the station to the point in the woods precisely, for the French driver was always uppermost in their minds.

Lying on their fronts the third evening, satisfied with their findings, they discussed the materials they would need.

"Several sets of explosives, each five kilos in weight, which we bury under the ballast."

"Alright," Daniel said.

"But the train is shunting along slowly at this point. Perhaps a bigger charge. Something like twenty-five kilos."

"That sounds a lot! How do we hide it?"

"Yes, it's bulky. We have to bury it one metre under the track."

"If we don't get caught digging, what is that going to do?"

"Blow the locomotive three metres into the air."

"Sounds dramatic, but wouldn't we be better off having several charges divided down the track. Just in case one of the charges doesn't work?"

The rail started to tremble, sending them rushing back into the bushes. As the locomotive shunted past, the ground shook under them. Daniel quickly peered up at the driver checking the moonlit track and at his colleague shovelling coal. A passenger window opened in the second carriage. Daniel and his colleague pulled their caps down over their heads.

"Gaston! *Ferme la fenêtre!* Idiot!"

"Oh, come on. Just a quick smoke."

"Are you mad? Do you want the *fritz* coming in here!? We've got a way to go before Cologne!"

Daniel and Jules jerked up their heads in surprise.

"I can't believe it!" whispered Daniel.

"Yes – good thing we came back to check tonight. French youths going out to Germany! *Fritz* are filling the trains with French youths for their own protection."

Daniel shook his head. "We could have blown the lot of them away!"

Several weeks later, Daniel was at his desk, in his airless office at the Prefecture he had grown to hate, thinking back gloomily on the aborted sabotage.

There was a knock at the door.

"*Entrez.*"

In stepped a slight, bespectacled young man in a black beret and *Milicien* uniform.

Daniel leapt from his chair, then locked the door. Tempering his rising panic, he stared at the boy, who stood erect and ready to speak.

"Alright. So, what is it?" Daniel felt his stomach tighten. *Surely they haven't come for me!*

"You have a René Guichet working for you. Vic has overhead talk that he may be arrested."

"What!"

"Vic has advised you to tell Monsieur Guichet to make himself scarce."

Daniel unlocked the door. "Thank Vic for me."

The boy nodded and, before marching out, added, "I was at Fort Girard, Monsieur."

"Alright, *mon gars*," was all Daniel could reply. He hadn't recognised the boy and felt suddenly very low. Had he been there after he'd left?

His heart pounding, he made his way over to the new job centre, a brisk 15-minute walk across town. What had René got himself into? Always wanting to meet new people, never heeding Riou's advice to limit his activities to their immediate circle. And Vic?

What he'd just done could have cost him. Or was he looking for a way out of the *Milice?*

Daniel swore silently. When he reached the bureau, the sight of René merrily locking up for the day, looking so pleased with himself, infuriated him all the more.

He slammed the door behind both of them.

"*Qu'est-ce qui se passe*, Daniel?"

"Lock up and let's go to your office."

The telephone rang; René turned to answer it.

"Leave it!"

Eyeing him suspiciously, René locked up, and Daniel followed him into his office.

"The Gestapo are on to you."

"What? Who says?"

"A *milicien!*"

"Fine company you keep," said René, mockingly.

"René, this isn't a joke! Leave! Make yourself scarce – understand?"

"But there is so much to clear. Paperwork, passports, false ID, intelligence maps. You don't want to be left with all that."

"Just gather all that up. Put it in a case. And give it all to me. Understand?"

René looked startled. He stared at the wall-to-wall files running along the bookshelves.

Daniel's heart dipped. "I need to get back to work in the Prefecture. Paris office snooping. You promise to be out in twenty minutes?"

"I promise. Well, maybe not twenty minutes... But don't worry."

Daniel got up at dawn and pedalled furiously back into town.

"Daniel!" René's white, bespectacled face peeped around the door. "Oh, thank goodness it's you." He was clutching a briefcase. "All ready to go."

Daniel threw him a disgusted look.

"I know, Dan. I'd misplaced some files belonging to Lerude."

A bell rang out by the main door in the hall. Daniel and René froze.

"Give me the case," Daniel snapped.

Two men were shouting in German and pounding the door.

"Stay there, René. I'll get it. Before the concierge..." Daniel ran down the staircase with his briefcase. "I'm coming, Messieurs!" He pulled open the heavy oak door. "*Désolé*, Messieurs – can I help you?"

One of the two Gestapo officers flashed his SIPO card. "We have come for a Mess-sieu Guch-ey."

'Guch-ey'? The fritz can't speak French! "There is no Monsieur Guchet here as far as I know," Daniel said, shaking his head apologetically.

The Gestapo officer eyed him severely. "*Vous-zete* Monsieur Guchet?"

"Oh no, I assure you."

"Show me your papers!"

Daniel put his case at his feet and started patting his pocket. "I think you're mistaken. You may want to ask the *concierge* but she is not yet up and about it seems…"

"What is the problem, Messieurs?"

Daniel's body went rigid. The two SIPO officers were no longer focused on him. He turned and forced himself to smile at his friend, grinning inanely down at them.

"These gentlemen want to know whether there's a Guchet here. I've told them…"

"It's not Guchet, it's Guichet," René said, lifting his arms like a pantomime clown stoking up an audience.

Daniel stood there, horrified.

"That's me!" he heard his dearest friend say. "A simple mistake to make. Why don't you come through. Good day, Monsieur," he said, addressing Daniel. "You weren't to know. Good day to you."

"What?"

Daniel had no other option but to shrug his shoulders.

The Gestapo looked at him, but then stormed up the stairs with his colleague. The sound of their boots echoed in the vast hallway.

His heart breaking, Daniel watched them shove René back into his office. There was a muffled cry. Then silence.

Daniel stepped out into the street, tears pricking the corners of his eyes. Willing his legs forward and clutching his case of documents, he ran down the cobbled street to Riou's office.

CHAPTER FORTY-EIGHT

Daniel opened his desk drawer, full of pencils, paperclips, newspaper clippings, letters of thanks from the boys they had trained and placed. He pulled out several photographs of René standing in front of the first job centre they had established in that old scout hut across the other side of town. Moon-faced René grinning, his little round spectacles glinting in the sun. He was pointing at the camera, at him taking the photograph. 'He's the boss,' René was saying, laughingly. Loyal, conscientious, fun-loving, infuriating René.

Daniel replaced the photograph and shut the drawer. *It has to stay. As long as it stays, René is alive.* He started to remove his raincoat, but the chill in the air made him change his mind. *It's May – why am I so cold?* He hadn't slept for two days.

Riou had insisted that they carry on as normal.

'If anyone should be arrested, let it not be that chatterbox René.' Riou's damning words rang out in the silence. How bitterly Riou regretted them now; they'd sealed René's fate. And behind them lay the terrible truth of the matter. Neither he nor Riou had trusted him.

There was a knock at the door; a young man carrying brochures.

"I've come on behalf of Riou," he said, putting the brochures on René's desk. "He has news."

Daniel followed the boy over to Riou's office.

Riou was standing, staring out of the window. "Shut the door, Daniel."

"Well?" he said, weakly, feeling his throat constrict.

"A colleague of Lerude's has just been to see me. The young man had been held for questioning by the Gestapo but was released yesterday."

"I didn't know anyone ever came out of there."

"Lucky for us he did," Riou sighed. "Before being shoved out into the street, he saw René making his way across the Gestapo yard... on his hands and knees."

Riou's voice had become hoarse.

The image of their friend crawling triggered a series of violent scenes. He wished he didn't possess such imagination.

"René recognised Lerude's colleague, although by then he could barely see, his eyes were so swollen. 'Tell the guys I didn't talk', he said." Riou's face had turned a ghastly grey. "The guard screamed at him. René cowered like some sickly dog."

There was a terrible silence. René had withstood the greatest urge within him. Had clamped his jaw, bitten his tongue until it had bled.

Daniel felt his throat swell. "We should go and see his family."

"Yes. We'll do it together."

That night, Daniel had barely fallen asleep when he was shaken awake by the sirens.

Tatiana raised herself with effort and slipped into the children's bedrooms, adopting that false singsong voice she had begun to use with them. Jeanne, Béa and France had fallen asleep, bulked up with sweaters and coats. It was still cold at night and Béa and France had developed persistent dry coughs. Tatiana feared that Philippe and his family had infected them with scarlet fever, even though they'd been quarantined in their cottage for the past week.

Daniel dressed hurriedly and ran out into the garden. He stared up at the night sky, filling with 'Bengal fires', hundreds and hundreds of them spilling out into the rumbling darkness. A wind was sweeping them north, illuminating the fields in red and orange lights. And then, inexplicably, a great gust, a counter-wind brought some back, towards St Jean de Braye. It was no use going to Chocho and Pelletier's overcrowded shelter. They already feared contagion up there.

He raced back into the cottage and to Philippe's.

"*Sortez!*" He was conscious of his thin, reedy voice competing with the thunderous thrumming which had now started up above them. A fleet of flying fortresses were starting to scream past at high altitude, like golden crosses shooting in the direction of the Aubrais train station.

Tatiana came running out, Alexandra in her arms. Daniel swept up pale and sickly Béa and France.

"Jeanne, run with us!"

"Daniel!" A feeble cry – Philippe, with Rosa in his arms, was making his way painfully across the lawn behind them. Isa dragged Simon by the hand.

"Can you make it?" Daniel shouted back.

Philippe nodded.

They ran in an easterly direction, out into the open countryside.

"Quick, that clump of trees over there," Daniel shouted. They headed towards them, flung themselves into a damp, cold ditch.

As Daniel and Tatiana lay there, catching their breath and clinging to one another, the bombs started to rain down on Aubrais, and then across Orleans and closer to their village. The German ground defence let rip and started to scatter the planes, which had released their cargo, and the sound of booming and splintering explosions filled the air, each boom piercing their very cores.

"Papa!" Jeanne cupped her ears and pressed her face into Daniel's chest.

France copied her sister, letting out a hacking cough. Tatiana crouched on the other side of him with Béa, who was so quiet, numbly watching the skies. Alexandra, Daniel noticed, had started to suck her thumb.

For what seemed a whole lifetime, the thunderous bombs filled the air around them.

There was silence. Daniel looked up.

"*Regarde,* Papa. *Le feu,*" shouted France, excitedly.

The whole horizon was ablaze.

The next morning, a car passed by with a megaphone, asking for all available men from the region to come to Aubrais station to help clear the track after the bombing.

Whilst Philippe stayed in bed with a temperature and rashes, hundreds of men, Daniel, Pelletier and Chocho amongst them, were taken by truck towards the northern outskirts of Orleans. A train packed with German troops and two cargo trains had been waiting at the station when the vast junction had been struck. In a world of intense heat, the soldiers had leapt out of the carriages and packed themselves into an underground shelter, but it too had received a direct hit. The first volunteers had had to remove the charred carcases and severed limbs. Daniel held a handkerchief to his nose, the stench of human skin and blood catching in his throat.

An SS guard with contorted features screamed, "*Schnell! Schnell!*"

They had to clear the track of disembodied carriages and tangled rails further ahead.

Walking down in the intense heat, Daniel came across a burst wagon, filled with barrels. One had rolled out and was issuing a dark red liquid. Daniel dipped his index finger and tasted it. Sweet, like burnt peaches. And the label: '*Banyuls*'. Wine! The coveted dessert wine from the PyRenés! It had been bound for Germany.

"Banyuls," he told his neighbour, and the word spread down the line of workers.

Almost at the same time, someone shouted from another wagon, "We've found some tin cups here."

A young German guard told Daniel and his men to fill the cups and pass them round to the troops. The cups of strong dessert wine started to circulate, the German guards even helping dispense the full tin mugs to their entourage, and then to Daniel and his colleagues.

By late afternoon, a euphoria had taken hold of everyone, for the wine was strong and sweet, and how much sweetness had they had in this war? They went about their work, together, as one, their stomachs burning with the warming liquor. The German officers gave out garbled orders.

Daniel, in the warm alcoholic haze, saw the zealous SS guard striding towards them with a pistol. He waved it at Daniel, who grinned incredulously before stepping back into his other colleagues in a panic.

"Ay! *Calmez-vous!*" He struggled for the German words as the guard pointed the weapon at him.

"*Du bist verrückt, Werner!*" Two German officers wrestled their colleague to the ground.

Seemingly oblivious to what had happened, a German and his

newly-acquired French friend loaded one of the remaining barrels onto a wheelbarrow. They pushed it for several metres, only just managing to stay upright by pulling at one another's sleeves. One tripped over a twisted rail, taking the other with him, leaving the barrow to roll down a small embankment. Nonplussed, both men got up and went careering after it, like joyful children.

"*Eh. Viens ici!*"

"*Komm hier!*"

Heaving the barrel back up into the barrow and rocking backwards and forwards on unsteady legs, they proceeded back up the little hillock with their precious booty. "*Attention, mon vieux. Un peu plus, et voilà, cette fois-ci!*"

"*Ho Ho. Regardez-les…*" said Daniel's neighbour, laughing.

A German officer joined in the banter. "*Dumbkopf, Willi!*" His broad shoulders shook with laughter.

Wiping his dripping forehead with his handkerchief, Daniel looked on, grinning and numb. *How stupid this is. How stupid. Killing each other one minute. The next, united in laughter. And not so long ago I was sabotaging the track.* Laughter burst out of him and the sound of it rang out in his head that night before going to sleep.

CHAPTER FORTY-NINE

And all it took was several barrels of Banyuls! Daniel stared listlessly at the piles of paper littering his desk. He hadn't drunk like that in quite a while. *Stupid! I was a sitting duck for that madman, Willi – or was it Werner!? If it hadn't been for his colleagues…*

How many of the Germans with whom he'd shared a cup of sweet wine truly believed the Nazi ideology? A handful? Certainly, the guard who had brandished his gun!

How many lives have I remaining? I must be more careful. I have mouths to feed.

Daniel carried on with a job he barely tolerated. Since the Germans had ordered the closure of many youth centres, his days consisted largely of stamping and signing off training, and writing and signing references. He made continual appeals to the Prefect to prevent young men from being sent to Germany, claiming one was too sick or had specialist skills needed on a farm in the region. He did what he could, but it was never enough.

By the time he came home, his one wish was to sit on a chair in the garden and watch his daughters play with Simon. With a sketchbook in his lap, and when the light permitted, Daniel traced the children's games of hide and seek; wild, spiralling pencil lines for Simon, who, following his fever and growth spurt, was proving to be the fiercest of wolves.

One balmy evening, Alexandra, crawling around his feet, levered herself up to her feet with his chair. No doubt she had been watching her sisters shriek with delight and wanted to join them.

Abandoning his sketching, Daniel let her grip his outstretched fingers and led her haltingly across the lawn to her siblings.

Though a welcome event, Alexandra's first steps were a reminder of time passing. Daniel started to wonder whether the war would ever end. The thought of Jeanne, Béa, France and Alexandra growing up under Nazism filled him with dread. He thought of the Allied landings, the ones they had been expecting for the past two years, and his anxiety grew.

If we are not killed by the Allied bombs, there could be a civil war. It seemed sacrilegious. He sincerely wished for an Allied victory, for De Gaulle to reclaim their country, but an uprising in his country was being talked about, and not only by the *Milice*.

Vic still plagued his thoughts. He couldn't eradicate from his mind the day Vic had received him in that synagogue in Auteuil. The shame he felt spilled out in Philippe's company, where they had grown irritable with each other. Their chess games had become uncomfortable, as Philippe would inexplicably sacrifice a queen, or two precious knights, and let Daniel finish him off suddenly, without warning. Those sorts of hollow victories brought no pleasure to Daniel. Daniel wanted a proper battle. A proper fight, which Philippe seemed unwilling to give him.

One May evening, Tatiana, perhaps sensing his growing restlessness, summoned him to the stepladder she had positioned under the loft.

"Dan, remember I need a little table for the kitchen, for my sewing. Will you take a look up there?" She was already on the middle rung, standing on tiptoes.

"Very well," he said, eyeing her smooth white calves. He could think of better things to do. He reached for her dress but was thwarted by her rapid descent.

"Such a clutter, *chéri*." And then she was out in the garden with a basket of laundry. "Girls, keep an eye on Alexandra."

Sighing and levering himself up into the attic, he switched on his flashlight. The beam illuminated several large trunks. Their owner, Daniel had been told, had made it to England. Had he joined up with De Gaulle? Was he involved in the planned Allied landings? How he envied him.

He moved the beam along to a pair of table legs then to the table-top, where a piece of furniture had been covered in calico. He pulled away the cloth. A grill, two knobs. It couldn't be.

"Tatiana!"

The door went. He extinguished his torch and, relieved to see his chess opponent, scaled down the ladder, bringing the table with him.

"Philippe. Help me, will you."

They brought down the wireless and plugged it in. It took a while to warm up but, as the lamp lit the stations, Daniel started to turn the bakelite knob feverishly. Nothing at first except the German-controlled Radio Paris. An orchestra played some saccharine music. Philippe crossed his arms. Daniel frowned and continued turning until, through the crackle and burble, a faint voice came through.

"*Ici Londres. La France parle aux Français.*"

Daniel and Philippe stared at one another.

"*Voici quelques communiqués…Il n'y a plus de tabac dans la tabatière.*" ('There's no more tobacco left in the tobacco tin.') "*Le cheval bleu se promène à l'horizon.*" ('The blue horse is walking along the horizon').

Philippe threw his head back and laughed. "Sounds like something your Paul Fort cooked up!"

Daniel joined him in his mirth. It was good to see his friend laugh. "Yes – the poets are having a field day over the Channel!"

Tatiana walked in with an empty laundry basket. "Ah good, you've brought down the table. But what's that? Are you mad? You don't want to get caught with that wireless."

"We'll take it up when we're not using it. Don't worry."

Tatiana sighed and laid out her patterns on the table.

"That's our listening over for tonight, Philippe, but come over tomorrow night."

Every night after dinner they listened to the messages and laughed at the more outlandish ones.

"*Avez-vous vu les oiseaux dans la barbe de Charlemagne?*" ('Have you seen the birds in Charlemagne's beard?') in particular. In amongst the gaiety, Daniel yearned to know of the military preparations taking place.

Even with this beacon of hope, they dared not dream – too much. They had been oppressed for so long and had learned to be mistrustful of good news.

For comparison, they listened to Radio Paris, where they were assured of the impenetrability of the Atlantic Wall defences along the west coast.

"The Allies, when they strike, are unlikely to attack from there," Daniel shouted at the radio. "It'll be from the south, or the north."

From the BBC they learnt, however, of Germany's increasing difficulties in Russia, prompting Daniel, Pelletier and Chocho, who came over one evening, to talk of Napoleon and the loss of supply lines. The same thing was hopefully happening to the *fritz*, they said, but they were still in awe of the mighty Wehrmacht, who seemed so invincible, like the Grecian Hydra, whose head you chopped and who grew back two.

At least in the air, the Americans seemed to be winning. Night after night, Daniel and Tatiana woke to hear the thrumming of high-flying American aircraft, which the German artillery was unable to reach. Night after night, the planes passed and left them alone.

Just as Les Aubrais was put back into operation, albeit with a reduced service, the bombers returned. They came under the cover of darkness again, this time unleashing their bombs on the town of Orleans.

Morning came and, unable to reach Riou by phone, Daniel and Pelletier rushed over to their friend's neighbourhood in the eastern part of town. A fire engine parked outside Riou's house made them stop dead in their tracks.

A bomb had demolished Riou's house.

Feeling his legs grow leaden, Daniel let Pelletier go on ahead and converse with the *Chief Pompier*. He watched his friend's face iron out with relief and, unable to believe such providence, rushed towards him.

"What is it, Pelletier?"

"Riou's children have been taken away to their grandparents. Amazingly, aside from vision problems, they escaped unscathed."

"*Dieu merci!*" Daniel stared at his friend, whose eyes were focusing on a medic in galoshes and gloves carrying a bundle of sheets out of an ambulance.

Pelletier swallowed hard. "He didn't make it, Dan."

Daniel felt the blood slowly drain from his face. "But we need to go down there…" He staggered to the smoking cellar and nearly ran into a medic blocking the entrance.

"Monsieur! It's out of bounds."

"Let us in."

"Step aside, Monsieur." Two gloved men entered the cellar.

"We're family. Let us through!"

"I'm warning you, Monsieur. The parents, by covering their children with their bodies…"

Daniel's mind raced with panic and confusion. He could only think of Riou as solid, as whole, as part of him, part of all their lives.

"I know," he said, in a quavering voice.

"In which case…" The paramedic turned to him wearily. "Follow me."

Daniel and Pelletier descended the stone steps, still glistening where the fireman's hose had been. Towards the bottom, they entered a wall of acrid smoke and darkness. Daniel felt something lodge in his throat. A piece of burnt wood or grit? The thought that it might be human ash brought about a fit of coughing. He spat it out and, removing his handkerchief from his jacket pocket, clamped it over his nose and mouth. He turned to Pelletier, who had done the same.

In the main chamber, sunlight slanted through the enormous gash left by the bomb. Ducking under a fallen beam, Daniel followed the medic's galoshes through the puddles, water seeping through his leather shoes.

Daniel felt himself go cold as he peered into the shadier corners of the cellar. Blackened, uneven shapes rose and fell. A crumpled blanket caught Daniel's eye. The medic was moving towards it.

"Wait!" Bracing himself, he peeled away the material. "Oh." His plaintive cry echoed around the chamber. On its side lay a charred head.

"Leave it, Daniel," said Pelletier, coming up beside him and grabbing his elbow. "The stretcher-bearers will take it."

"Perhaps it would be better to concentrate on your friends' possessions," said the paramedic, coming over with a cloth bag.

Daniel nodded weakly. He crouched down in the rubble and ran his flashlight over the piles of slippery stones, splintered wood, shattered glass.

Pelletier came over, holding out a curled-up wedding photograph of Jean Riou and his young bride. He wiped it on his sleeve, before slipping it into his pocket.

"I fear for the children," Pelletier said, shaking his head. "But the temporary blindness – it was an act of God."

Daniel was half-listening, queasily picking through viscous objects around him. He fell upon a tin box and wiped off the sodden ashes with his sleeve. Inside it was a little notebook. He flicked through several scout songs, work notes, and turned to the last page. In the inside cover Riou had inscribed something. Daniel drew his torch nearer: 'Life is a dream. A charming dream that we must all know how to leave in song.'

Daniel handed it to Pelletier and, amongst the broken bricks, smoke and ashes, he dropped to his knees and wept for his friend.

On the day of the funeral, the church of Saint Marceau was not only packed with mourners. Riou's coffin was one of the one hundred and fifty filling the church nave.

Rudderless, Daniel tried to resume normal life.

He cycled into Orleans every morning, flanked by Pelletier and Philippe. No one spoke of Riou, of René, of Lerude. It seemed too soon to speak of them, to bring them back into the present, for as far as Daniel was concerned, they hadn't left it. Daniel trudged into his office, head bent and heart closed off. Cut off from his Resistance friends, a weariness overwhelmed him. He had grown tired of the war. It was time it ended, he told himself, so that he could disappear, with Tatiana and his daughters – just live quietly, that was it.

Even the games of whist he now embarked on with Chocho and Pelletier gave him no relief. As for chess, he and Philippe had lost their appetite.

One evening, as he sat with an unopened edition of *Les Miserables* in his lap, he watched his wife applying the finishing touches to a pale blue summer dress for Jeanne. She caught him staring.

"Put on some music, Dan," she said to him, gently. "You haven't had the radio on in weeks."

It was true. *A resistance message is a dagger through the heart without Riou.*

"But softly – we don't want to wake the children."

A little music, why not? *If it gives her pleasure.*

He brought the radio down from the attic and turned on Radio

Paris. They heard Maurice Chevalier's voice rise over the airwaves. Another preposterously cheerful song about Paris. He reached for the tuning button.

"Do you mind, *chérie?*"

"No. Go on," she said, now looking happier with the bow she was adjusting.

The signal was very hard to reach, but he persisted. The sound of a kettledrum broke through. His heart leapt as he heard a voice, a jovial but insistent voice: *'Il est temps de cuellir des tomates. Je repète, il est temps de cueillir les tomates.'*

Tatiana dropped her sewing. "Something is happening, Dan." Her eyes now gleamed at the wireless. "Something momentous."

The following evening, Daniel, Philippe, Pelletier, Chocho and Tatiana crowded around the set.

"At nine-thirty this morning, under the command of General Eisenhower, allied naval forces, supported by strong air support, began landing allied armies on the northern coast of France."

They hugged one another.

"It will raise Lerude's, Lefèbvre's and René's spirits," Daniel said, quietly, once their elation had worn off and they'd all regained their seats.

"If they get the news," Philippe said, frowning.

"Of course," Daniel said, tuning into Radio Paris. Hopes of victory were dampened by the news that allied troops were being held back by the fortifications along France's northern coast. They were suffering heavy losses and the German reinforcements were making their way over there in haste.

In the ensuing days, Daniel and his circle returned to the BBC, which spoke of victories. In truth, they didn't really know who and what to follow, but he wanted to believe the British and disregard the German propaganda that had left them in the dark for so long.

In Orleans, the excitement was palpable. A buzzing optimism electrified the air. People had even started to hum the *Marseillaise* quietly, though it was soon drowned out by the sound of heavily armed German soldiers pounding the cobbled streets. The troops' expressions had hardened, to such an extent that Daniel wondered whether the Banyuls incident had been an alcohol-induced fantasy.

One morning, at the beginning of July, Daniel was passing a rail bridge in the centre of town when he heard a locomotive grind to a halt. He stared down the track and was amazed to see a line of German tanks and artillery guns, submerged in camouflage netting, fill his view.

"Get lost!" shouted a soldier guarding the track.

Daniel rushed back to his office and called Davaine.

"I know. I'm coming round, Daniel!"

Perched on Daniel's desk soon after, the engineer explained the situation. "The train has been forced to terminate its journey as the line towards Pithiviers has been damaged. The cargo is no less than the precious élite division *Das Reich!*"

"No!"

"Probably want the panzers to prevent the English from crossing the Seine at Rouen. At least, that is our information."

Daniel stared at Davaine, barely able to believe what he was hearing.

"Our company, Campeon-Bernard, is getting a convoy together to transport wood parts needed to repair a damaged bridge over the Seine. The Germans have told us that the construction work needs to be completed in three days, after which the tanks and other military equipment will, I presume, power on towards Rouen."

"So, I was wondering, Daniel…"

Daniel sat up in his chair, realising that this wasn't a social call.

"…whether you have what you need to sabotage the line. We need incendiary equipment and slow release charges."

"Not enough. This requires an almighty charge."

"Several. The mission mustn't fail."

Daniel's heart thumped loudly against his breastbone. "Leave it with me," he heard himself say. Without thinking, he had plunged right back into action, without Riou. And it felt good.

Not wasting any time, Daniel made his way to a youth centre still in operation outside Orleans. The centre leader had known Riou; he was a man to be trusted. They marched over to his office, locking the door behind them.

"I need one of your young group leaders," Daniel said, hurriedly. "Someone who can think on his feet."

The centre leader looked at him gravely.

"His mission will be to go up to Paris, retrieve some vital equipment from a colleague of mine, and to cycle back. All in one day."

The Chief sighed. "That's a tall order. However, I do know an audacious fellow. Plucked from the streets of Belleville. Father a communist and locked up in Fresnes. He's grown up having to defend himself."

A red-haired, freckled youth of about seventeen glanced at Daniel warily when he stepped into his office twenty minutes later. He was wearing the same *Narvik* uniform they had worn at Fort Girard. He reminded Daniel of Roupp.

"*Mon gars,* what is your name?"

"Alfred."

"Alfred. I'll come straight to the point. I have a vital mission for you."

The youth cocked his head.

"I'd like you to go to a music shop near *l'Opéra Comique* and meet a man called Durand. Tell him Daniel, Riou's colleague, sent you. I'd like thirty lighters with detonators. Some Bickford cable and five kilos of explosive."

Alfred's eyes widened and shone. "Right, sir."

"Here's a large rucksack and a case. Can you get that on the back of your bike?"

"Think so."

"Here's a torn bank note."

"What happened to the rest?"

"It's your pass, Alfred. Durand will have the other half. I'll expect you back by tomorrow at the very latest."

If Alfred was nervous, he didn't show it.

That evening, Daniel raced home to Tatiana in a state of agitation. As he stepped through the door, he ran into Monique on her way out.

"Madame has just come in. Madame Chalvin is still not well."

"We'll have to be careful." Tatiana rushed into the kitchen. "I had to leave some soup for them on their doorstep. Jeanne is already looking so pale. And as for Béa and France, they've not shaken off their coughs."

"Don't worry, *chérie.*" Daniel drew her to him. "Please – we must remain calm."

But all that night, Daniel tossed in his bed, thinking of that young man who had gone up to Paris on a bone-shaker, armed with just his wits. He imagined Paris's streets filled with trigger-happy troops, *Milice* gangs and Gestapo gangsters. The Resistance was suffering terribly. Big names, it was rumoured, had been captured, probably murdered. He remembered the boy's freckled face and toothy grin and felt bolstered by the image. But what sort of life was this for a boy? For any boy. Tatiana could count herself lucky she hadn't given birth to one.

He went in to see Jeanne, who was calling for him from her bedroom.

"Why are they dropping bombs on us, Papa?"

"They're not dropping the bombs on us, *ma poulette*."

"The newspaper is full of pictures, Papa."

"Yes. But these people are trying to help us."

"Simon cries at night and still wets the bed. I heard Maman and Isa talking."

"Some boys do. He'll grow out of it. You mustn't worry about him."

The following afternoon, the phone rang in his office.

"Alfred is here," said the centre leader, sounding much relieved. "Amazingly, he's brought what you asked for."

"Not a moment too soon!" Daniel said, barely able to contain his elation. "Davaine will come immediately to collect it. Everything is set for tonight. The track has been repaired, the trains are due to leave tomorrow morning."

Davaine called round at his office two days later.

"Just in time. Our team set the detonators so that they went off a good distance from Orleans. I'm not sure where exactly, but you can be sure that the bridge repair won't take place now."

Waves of unadulterated joy passed through Daniel as he sprang from his chair.

At the centre, Alfred was in the Chief's office, waiting for him.

"Congratulations, Alfred. Our mission is complete!"

Alfred smiled crookedly.

"How did it go in Paris?"

"That Durand's a trooper. Invited me to dinner, let me have a bath whilst he got everything ready. I slept well, and set off with a good breakfast inside me."

"Yes. How was Paris?"

"Everyone panicking. Troops everywhere. I got talking with these German soldiers on the back of a truck along the Orleans road."

"German soldiers?"

"Yeh – It was risky. But my legs were tired. That case! I was worried I wouldn't make it back in time."

"I see."

"Anyway, a couple of *fritz* saw my uniform and thought I belonged to the *Milice*. I didn't put them right on that one, of course." He laughed boyishly. "They allowed me to hook up to the truck for a while with my bicycle."

Daniel buried his head in his hands, incredulous.

"Then they stopped to relieve themselves – they'd all been drinking, see."

"Ah, that was why you felt able to…"

"Yep, and then I got talking to the driver. He asked me where I was heading. I told them Orleans. He asked the guys I had been speaking to whether they minded. And they said, 'No, anything for one of our boys'."

"I can't believe it, *mon gars*. You got into a truck full of *fritz* with your bomb-making equipment?"

Alfred beamed. "Yes, sir."

"And they didn't ask what was inside your case?"

"I had it on the floor in the front seat before they could even notice it."

"Didn't they ask you what you were doing in Paris?"

"No – too busy singing. They gave me a beer."

It was Daniel's turn to laugh.

It was now easier to follow the Allied movements on the wireless, for they were receiving information from everywhere. Patton's army was progressing towards Paris from the south. General Montgomery and Leclerc, meanwhile, had succeeded in breaking through the German divisions in the north. The *Das Reich* division had arrived in Rouen, but not in time to stop the British and French troops from crossing the Seine.

Listening to this, Daniel's heart filled with pride; with Davaine and the boy, he had played some small part in making it happen.

CHAPTER FIFTY

The satisfaction was short-lived. He woke up one morning barely able to lift or turn his head. Weakly, he watched a bluebottle ram a windowpane continuously.

Through the open door, he heard the faint clinking of bowls. Tatiana was up preparing breakfast. He heard Pelletier's jubilant voice at the door, shouting his name. His friend burst into his bedroom.

"Daniel, Le Mans has been liberated! The Americans will be in Paris soon. We'll have to watch the *fritz* around here…"

Pelletier's thick brush hair and owl-like brows hovered over him menacingly. The features blurred and the room began to swirl. Through the painful ringing of his ears, he tried to speak.

"Tatiana!"

The doctor was droning on. His tongue still throbbed from the spoon that man had used on it. So hard. He could taste that foul metallic thing.

"Err…" He pulled his head up. He wanted to be sick.

"Monsieur, please. You must sleep."

And back he turned to Tatiana, who nodded and nodded, her shiny, dark eyes fixed on the man who was packing up his things. He scribbled a note, gave it to her. A briefcase left his bedside, as did Tatiana.

Tatiana, come back! His head had started to pulse with pain. Through his hazy vision, he felt relief when she returned. He felt his bed sheets tighten. He moved his head to follow her around the room but then gave up trying. She brought a glass to his face.

"Drink," she said, softly.

He wanted to please her. He opened his mouth with effort. How thirsty he was. He felt the glass rest on his lips and water bathe his teeth. He gulped, half-choked and coughed it out. As soon as Tatiana pulled the glass away, the thirst returned, but it was too late, she had already slid a glass stick into his mouth.

"No!" It slid out again and Tatiana was peering over him and frowning.

She removed a pillow from below him, he felt himself drop onto a cooler one, but the room had started to swim.

He awoke, his head pounding. He rolled onto his side miserably and felt his lids close.

This is not the time to fall sick. What time is it, Tatiana? He opened his eyes. She was removing a dry compress. He felt something cool bathe his forehead.

Aroused from a deep sleep, Daniel awoke in the darkened room. The shutters were closed. Tatiana was whispering to someone. He heard the words "milk" and "farm".

Tatiana! Tatiana! Be careful. He remembered the war. The *fritz.* Pelletier.

There was a shuffle of slippers at the foot of his bed.

"Tatiana?" No, it wasn't her. The figure had shrunk and was standing in her night clothes in silvery darkness. "Tatiana?"

The figure went over to the front door and opened it. The stars were out and the heavens cold.

"Lock it," Daniel said, feebly. He turned over on his side.

He was woken by banging.

Jeanne's tear-stained face rushed past him. "Maman!"

The woman ran through the bedroom to the other rooms, then returned, hovered, said something in a high, agitated voice. He heard "soldiers", "bike", "milk", "hid", "die".

Oh Tatiana! He opened his mouth, but he was so thirsty. The girls came out of their bedroom.

"Go to the kitchen. Jeanne will give you some milk."

The following morning, he was able to say her name properly.

"Tatiana!" She had presented him with a bowl.

"Gazpacho. Tomatoes are in season. It will do you good."

He opened his shrunken lips. She dropped a spoonful onto his tongue.

"More."

"Not too fast, Daniel," she said, tremulously.

He took several spoonfuls and tried to focus on her. Her eyes were red. He tried to mouth something again.

"Ta…"

But she had already left the room, for there was the sound of Alexandra crying. He rolled himself into the sheet, sweating profusely. He rolled over in the other direction and felt cooler. He stared at the ceiling and thought, *What day is it? Where is that fly?* His lids closed once more.

He dreamt of Riou. They were walking in the garden at Fort Girard, he was telling him something. But Daniel couldn't hear him over the sound of the planes, and his feet were wading through a field of squashed tomatoes. As he turned to face the planes, one of them turned into a gigantic fly.

He woke with a jolt – the girls were running into the bedroom. "Maman! Maman!"

"Can't we go to the shelter, Maman?"

Jeanne.

"No. Not with Papa ill," Tatiana said, jumping out of bed. "We'll be fine here. Girls, bunch yourself into a ball on the floor by the window. Jeanne, you show them. Make yourself as tiny as possible."

He heard France giggle. Béa too. Jeanne told them to be quiet. The planes got louder and she too broke out into nervous laughter.

Tatiana touched Daniel's shoulder. "Dan," she said, gently. "Can you slide off the bed?"

He stared at her, uncomprehendingly. A booming sound and sub-machine guns. Ta-ra-ta-ta-ta.

"Dan, move your legs, quick! There, that's right."

The noise. The noise. Ta-ra-ta-ta-ta.

"Daniel, lie down on the girls," she said, with urgency.

Must lie down. I'm lying down over France and Jeanne. Will I make them ill?

"*On se couche les filles. On se couche.*"

*That's Tatiana, telling the girls to lie down. Ta-ta-ta. Funny,
the guns. Ta-ta-ta-ta. Ta-ta-ta. France, don't wriggle, ma poulette.
And Jeanne, why is your little heart beating so? And Alexandra,
you're gurgling, Béa too. And now, why so quiet? So quiet. It's so
noisy here. Deafening! It's a good game. Ha-ha. Boom! Why is the
floor shaking?*

They awoke entangled in blankets and sheets. How long they had
been lying like that as one, Daniel didn't know. He lifted his head;
the headache had gone. The relief of it. He tried to recall the
night before. Had it been the night before? Or the night before
that?

Tatiana stirred next to him.

"Dan," Tatiana murmured. "We're all here." She started
laughing, but then tears rolled down her thin cheeks.

"Don't cry, Maman," Jeanne said.

Alexandra had started to suck her thumb again.

"It's alright, Jeanne," she said, stroking her hair. "It's alright.
Now, Dan," she said, wiping her eyes on her apron. "Can you get
up and back into bed? Can you do that?"

He nodded. The effort was enormous.

He lay back down on the mattress and felt his lids droop again.
He heard Tatiana's long sigh.

"Come on, *les filles*. We'll make some breakfast with the milk."

And then he heard Pelletier and Chocho outside in the garden,
through the open window.

"Tatiana. Thank goodness you're alright. What a night! The
garden is full of roof tiles, cartridges."

"Béa, Jeanne, you're not to let France put any of that in her
mouth – do you hear!?"

And then it was late morning. He was out of bed. Light-headed,
but with his temperature gone.

"Daniel, what are you doing up?" Tatiana cried.

Pelletier and Chocho had come to the door. The whirring of
wheels and rumbling of machinery could be heard across the
fields. It seemed to get closer.

"Can you walk?"

He nodded.

"Take your time. We'll go ahead. We'll leave a place for you."

Pelletier and Chocho started to run in the direction of the road. Forgetting the weakness in his legs, Daniel took several rapid strides, then broke into a run. Feeling his body buckle under him, he sat down in some long grasses and watched his friends join a long row of people by the roadside ahead. He heaved himself up again and stumbled towards them on trembling limbs.

"*Bravo more vieux*!" Pelletier said, tearing his eyes from the spectacle they were all mesmerised by.

A procession of dazzling machinery: armoured vehicles, tanks, artillery guns, heavy military trucks grinding towards them. Standing or sitting on the sides of these trucks, in their metal helmets and clutching their sub-machine guns, grinning and waving, all resembling mechanics (it was impossible to tell the grades), were the first Americans he had ever set eyes on. How different they were from the proud, stiff, blond storm-troopers in dark uniform who had filled them with ghastly awe.

Twenty minutes later they were gone, and the three friends walked excitedly back to their houses, this time keeping in step.

Lunchtime that day, Daniel heard the troops had stopped off at the youth centre outside of Orleans, where Alfred was stationed. Monique told Daniel that she'd dropped off a tray of tomatoes from their farm but had found herself queuing for the privilege. People were coming from miles around to reward the troops and to stop and stare.

"A barrier finally had to be put up," she said, gesticulating excitedly. "To let them rest."

Late afternoon, the American troops toured St Jean de Braye and distributed their 'K' rations. Daniel returned to the cottage, laden with sugar, coffee, tea, and all number of luxuries. Jeanne and Béa had their first chewing gum. The others had a spoonful of sugar.

"I've invited a Sergeant Riley to tea, Tatiana, and several others at five p.m."

"But Daniel," Tatiana said, before realising that she had a basketful of plums she had gathered from the tree with Jeanne. She had just enough flour, several powdered eggs and milk to make a *clafoutis*.

"Perfect, they'll love that!"

"By the way, Daniel," she said, laughing. "You're better!"

Daniel stepped back. He hadn't thought about it. "Yes, I suppose I am."

The morning after, Daniel was alarmed to see Vic's tormented face at the door.

He walked in guardedly, checking to see he hadn't been followed. Tatiana threw her arms up in the air as she came across them.

"*Quelle joie,* Vic!"

Vic walked over timidly. Daniel waited for the pleasantries to be over. "Tatiana, *chérie,* would you mind? We have some business to discuss."

Surprised, Tatiana went out to the garden to mind the children with Isa.

"Sit, Vic. Tell me."

Vic plunged his face into his hands. "The last forty-eight hours have been terrible! I escaped a mock trial at the *Milice* headquarters in Paris by holding the jurors at gunpoint. I ran out a back door. Luckily, I was able to slip into the crowds around the building. I changed into some civilian clothes a friend lent me and cycled here. I don't know what to do, Daniel! It's the communists I have to watch now."

"You'd best go to the Americans. Ask for a Sergeant Riley, say I sent you. But quick. They're leaving Orleans soon."

"Thank you, Daniel."

"Good luck."

From then, everything accelerated. On August 15th, the French army and navy came through Provence with General Lattre de Tassigny, and then finally, on the 24th, General Leclerc with his armoured division entered Paris. The church bells rang out in Orleans as everyone started to celebrate.

A boy came to the house, sent by Vic.

"He's safely in the hands of the Americans. He's going to stand trial, but he's ready for that."

By going to the Americans, Vic had at least escaped the wrath of the communist FTP (*Francs-Tireurs et Partisans)* who had taken the law into their own hands, shooting notorious collaborators up against a wall. It was understandable – the *Milice* paramilitaries had focused their manhunts on them.

The *gaulliste,* Lerude, René and Lefèbvre had received better treatment, if being interned, beaten and tortured rather than shot could be regarded as such.

Monique came running in after Vic had left, a look of horror on her face.

"Two women have just had their heads shaved. They're staggering through the village with their hands bound, everyone jeering at them."

What should have been a time of national unity was turning into a civil war. There were attempts to bring order. Loudspeakers announced a meeting for all those who had fought in the Resistance at the gymnasium in Orleans.

Expecting two or three hundred men and women at the most, Daniel raced along there and was shocked to find one thousand strong filling the hall. The auditorium was heaving with angry, over-excited people wishing to see their representative on stage. Where had all these people come from?

On the podium, a fight broke out between two men, each wishing to say his piece at the microphone. Each political faction, resistance group, probably bogus in some cases, fought to be heard. Each felt mandated to oversee the running of the *comités d'épuration* set up to eradicate traitors.

Thank goodness De Gaulle has already elected a Commissaire de la République to run the Prefecture in Orleans. Sickened by the spectacle, he marched out, feeling light-headed. He ran straight into Duvillard from the Arnouville Centre, with whom he had run the arms operation.

"Where are you going, Daniel? You should stay. We need people like you."

"Have you been in there?"

Duvillard laughed. "Now everyone's been in the resistance, eh? Oh well, suit yourself." He dived into the crowds.

That evening, Tatiana invited Philippe and Isa to dine with them. Philippe had decided to move to Marseilles. He and Albert were keen to settle as far from the capital as possible.

"Down on the coast. If we ever need to leave in a hurry!" Philippe said, looking at Isa, who appeared decidedly uncomfortable.

"Leave?" Daniel shook his head. "No, No, Philippe! This will never happen again."

Isa shuffled in her chair. "Certainly – we never want to return to Paris. Not after I was turned away from our local park with Simon. He was too young to wear the star, but not me." She jabbed her chest. "Véronique, my friend, offered to take him, so that he could play with her son. I left the sandpit. Such disapproving looks I received. Simon started to cry. It was awful! He thought I was leaving him. And then the July raid came soon after…"

Tatiana took Isa's hand. "Oh, Isa!"

Isa lifted her hand away. "Paris was supposed to be civilised. We should have learnt from Dreyfus. And to think that Philippe had to work at the Prefecture – for Vichy!"

Daniel and Philippe exchanged uneasy looks.

"And the stories we hear from our friends…" She rushed out of the room.

"I understand, Isa," Tatiana said, calling after her. "Really I do…" But Isa had gone.

Daniel stared at his wife. *Tatiana, normally so hot-headed and proud, is taking it all. But look at what happened with Stalin's purges and her aunt. I feel nothing but sadness for both of them.*

Philippe hovered miserably.

Isa walked back in. "Philippe – don't say that you're not feeling the same," she said, choking with sobs.

He gave his wife a helpless look. "But Tatiana and Daniel are not to blame!"

Feeling criticised, Isa retraced her steps towards the door. "Tatiana, I'm sorry to have spoilt your evening. Of course, I don't blame you or Daniel. But you and others like you could be counted on one hand."

Philippe and Isa left the next day. Simon rushed to plant a kiss on Tatiana's cheek, which had grown so thin. Daniel watched her wipe away a single tear. Isa followed a second behind.

"I'm so sorry," she said.

"Isa. You, Philippe and the children are forever in our hearts. And Albert and Rebecca. We owe so much to them, too."

Daniel watched Philippe leave with a heavy heart. Separation. How many more would he have to endure?

"We will exchange Christmas cards," Tatiana said to Daniel,

kissing him tenderly on the cheek.

"Hannukah cards, you mean. They will want to start afresh. Create a new life for themselves with their children. Even if Philippe and Isa don't want to travel up to Paris, maybe Simon will visit Jeanne one day, when they are university students. Why not? And we need to do the same, *chérie*. Start to plan, that is."

As he said this, he felt his heart hark back to Philippe, in the days when he, Vladimir and Philippe had taken to the open road for months on end, with just a passport, three shirts and a raincoat, peddling their new machine tools. They had just cornered the dairy market in Belgium and the Netherlands when war broke out. All their dreams of villas on the Côte d'Azur – maybe Philippe had taken his first steps towards them.

CHAPTER FIFTY-ONE

The future was on everyone's lips, but for any progress to take place, for people to move forward, they had to forgive and to forget, they were told, and for many it would take many long years, Daniel thought, if it happened at all.

Every time Philippe looks at me, he'll be reminded of the war and his vulnerability. And Philippe is proud. Perhaps he was wrong – he hoped so.

Vic, meanwhile, faced a difficult trial, one in which he would be held up as an example. He had been young, impressionable, had had the misfortune to be inadvertently linked to the most hated man in France. To be branded a traitor was a terrible thing. Daniel hoped his family would support him. At least he would feel he had paid his dues. And in time, hopefully France would forget. Meanwhile, there were those with money and power who had fled the country. Would they be allowed to spend the rest of their days in some distant land in some amnesiac dream?

He swept the enraging thought aside and turned to things closer to his heart. Pelletier, Chocho and he were all that remained of their close circle of friends. Philippe and Isa had slipped off to Marseilles, and there was no news from René, Lefèbvre and Lerude. The war seemed to be reaching its apogee in Germany.

A little candle of hope illuminated his mind – he pictured them all returning and sitting at his table, painfully thin and frail but alive. He felt suddenly proud to be their friends and was aware of his spirits lifting.

And in a few minutes' time he would, with the rest of Orleans, be listening to De Gaulle deliver his speech from the magnificent balcony of the city hall. The *Général* had come to take charge, to take over the reins of their struggling nation now reeling from internecine political battles. It was no surprise. De Gaulle disliked political parties and, for Daniel, the Resistance meeting in Orleans had been enough to deter him from politics for life.

With growing anticipation, Daniel made his way down to the Place du Martroi in central Orleans with his family. Daniel looked about him at the crenelated walls and collapsed buildings, the work of both German and Allied bombs. The square had been reduced to an archaeological site of dust and rubble, which the authorities had cleaned up as best they could for the occasion.

Daniel shook his head and returned to his sombre reflections. A way of life had been obliterated in Orléans and all over France. Things would never be the same. Not for him. Not for anyone. How many ghosts floated above his head today: Riou's, maybe René's, Lefèbvre's, Lerude's? His heart tripped as he thought of them.

"Riou," he mumbled. His dismembered body lying in that smoke-filled basement. Daniel shivered involuntarily and felt the misery of that day rise up in his chest.

"Papa!" Jeanne tugged at his arm. "Are we really going to see the *Général?*"

"Yes, *ma poulette,*" he croaked.

"And the Germans, where have they gone, Papa?"

"Back to Germany, *ma poulette.*"

"Back to their homes." Jeanne took his hand thoughtfully. "And what about us, Papa?"

He stared at her, blankly. Strange, he hadn't thought that far ahead yet.

"We will see, *ma poulette.* We will see." Tatiana give him an anxious look. No doubt she wanted to return to Paris. But they would have to wait. Food was more plentiful down here and he still had a job working for the Prefecture. Dull, repetitive and administrative. Everything he hated. He would start looking around for alternative employment the minute he could. The fresh green vineyards carpeting the Jurançon hills still beckoned, but it was too soon, he told himself. Perhaps when he saw Vladimir. Ah, Vladimir.

His spirits rose. He looked across at his family, walking alongside him, Tatiana leading the way proudly in her pale-yellow dress, her hair flying in the September breeze.

"And in the meantime, we have the *Général* to meet," he said, letting a sudden laugh escape. He stopped at a street-seller to buy little paper Tricolores on sticks for his daughters.

Béa sat on a wall with Jeanne, having mock battles with their flags. Daniel intervened, eager to point out to them and France the statue of Jeanne d'Arc astride her horse, rising above the crowd in the middle of the square.

"Look at her, girls! Look how proud she looks up there!" Only part of her plinth had been blown off. It was a miracle she had survived the bombings.

Daniel looked back over his shoulder, at the haggard but relieved *orléanais* awaiting De Gaulle. How long this war had been! Was it really over? He turned back towards the *Mairie,* to the infantry unit, brass band and cavalry soldiers standing there, not only for show. There had already been several assassination attempts on the *Général* at the Liberation of Paris.

"Papa!" France's clear blue eyes peered up at him, expectantly.

"*Oui, ma petite?*" He swept up his daughter and carefully lowered her soft legs onto his shoulders.

"*Regarde.*" Her toddler finger pointed towards the city hall, where two doors had opened. A tall, stiff, military figure with a prominent nose and small keen eyes walked out onto a majestic balcony. There was a swelling roar from the crowd as he raised his arm and gave the victory sign. For years, Daniel had seen the 'v', the word 'victory' painted or scratched clandestinely on walls, benches, trees, and now here it was, manifested as flesh and blood. The *Général* was no longer an indistinct, distant voice reaching out over the airwaves, but someone like them. Well, not quite like them, perhaps.

The people in the square went wild. France shook her Tricolor wildly with her sisters.

"*Vivre France,*" she sang out with them, in her baby voice. Jeanne and Béa giggled.

Daniel felt Tatiana's slender arm about his waist. Rarely had she shown any enthusiasm for a politician, but De Gaulle was different, she said. What would they have done without him and the Allies?

De Gaulle lowered his arms to calm his audience. It took a while for the waves of "De Gaulle" to die. He smiled indulgently then grew serious.

He started to speak in a strange, reverberating voice, of a France that had been mutilated and ruined. In Orleans, he said, pointing to the statue of Jeanne d'Arc, the spirit of liberation had, however, been kept alive. And now it was up to them, the citizens of Orleans, to join with the rest of France, to work hard to rebuild her. To walk along this new road, one which rejected the corrupting influence of political parties. He lifted his arms.

"And now I would like us to all come together to sing our national anthem, the *Marseillaise. Vive la France!*"

France jigged up and down on Daniel's shoulders, thrilled by the impact and power of her name. Rows and rows of raised arms sprung up to give the victory sign, to repeat, "*Vive la France!*" The band sprung into life.

With the *Marseillaise* still ringing in his ears, Daniel followed Chocho into the reception inside the *Mairie*. Chocho, as former Regional Delegate for National Education, had been summoned, as had Daniel as his delegate. His predecessor, having compromised himself by zealously enforcing the German laws that obliged France's youth to work in Germany, had gone on the run.

They formed a line to shake the *Général's* hand. Chocho and Daniel stood shoulder-to-shoulder, halfway down the row of functionaries. Nervously, Daniel watched the *Général* progress down the row, exchanging a word or two with each of them.

Daniel felt his knees grow weak as he anticipated his impending encounter with the great man. Barely a metre away now. Oh, how he wished to take his hand! Was this idolatry? He had always scorned hero worship. Of course, he had had mentors – his employers, Paul Fort, Albert Klug, around whom he had felt safe and valued. But no, what he was experiencing was quite new. Aged thirty-five, he was experiencing what it was like to admire someone to the point of madness!

De Gaulle. Charles. Oui mon Général, he repeated inwardly. *We did have a few narrow escapes, but I was proud to play my small part in our victory.*

The General was within breathing distance, shaking Chocho's

hand, who seemed to be blushing and blustering.

"Yes, *mon Général,* we both worked in the regional department for Education. And I'd like you to meet my right-hand man, Daniel Frey."

Daniel bent his head and smiled.

De Gaulle peered down at him from a height and offered his slim, white palm. How thin and elegant his wrist was.

"He was in charge of propaganda. But you see..." Chocho chuckled, manically.

Daniel froze.

De Gaulle's hand didn't retract. He frowned. "Who nominated you?"

Daniel looked up, trying to mask his horror. He wanted to cry out 'Chocho!' Chocho, who had waved away the Vichy job description as a mere detail. Of course, the title had borne no relation to the work he had undertaken. But De Gaulle was already giving him a withering look.

Chocho's face went grey. He dived in again. "But Daniel's services have been exemplary, *mon Général!* The *Commissaire de la République,* who you selected to run the Prefecture, would not have allowed him to stay in his position otherwise. The title was created by Vichy and formed no part of..."

"*Mon Général.*" One of De Gaulle's staff leaned in and pointed to his watch.

De Gaulle nodded, and Daniel felt De Gaulle's dry palm slip out of his feverish grip.

The *Général* turned on his heels and directed his prominent nose towards the side door, his escape route. Daniel's last image of him was of his tall, lean figure, in full uniform, forging its way through the waiters carrying buckets of champagne, the wide-eyed guests clutching their flutes to their chests as he passed.

FIN/END

Author's Note

The main events in the book truly happened and my resistance heroes are real.

François Lefèbvre really was arrested January 1944 by the Gestapo and local Milice and taken to the Mauthausen labour camp in Austria where he died from exhaustion working in the mines. His gentle character and 'natural elegance', as remembered by René Guichet, who was also incarcerated there, made Lefèbvre a target for sadistic SS officers.

Young Claude Lerude really did head up the "Vengeance" resistance movement in the Loiret and helped hundreds of boys avoid enforced labour by letting them camp out in the woods and join the maquis. Already of fragile health, Lerude sadly died at the Neuengamme labour camp in Northern Germany in 1945, aged 25.

René Guichet survived the Mauthausen labour camp. It was notorious for its 186 steps which the detainees had to climb at the end of the day with a boulder on their back. At a celebration tea given in honour of his release, his friends recall 'a small boy descending from a taxi.' It was Guichet, their friend, who broke down before a table laden with cakes. After the war, he worked in the family textile business before entering Henri Duvillard's ministry for war veterans in 1968.

In May 1943, Henri Duvillard joined Lerude's network, "Vengeance". He also entered SOE's network "Etienne Leblanc". As an agent in the "Buckmaster Jean Marie" network, he also facilitated several parachute drops, between June 1943 and

June 1944 around his Centre, Arnouville. Today the centre is synonymous with resistance. In 1948 he received the 'Médaille de la Résistance' personally from General De Gaulle. From the 1950s onwards he worked in the political arena as a Gaulliste member of the Cabinet and député in the Loiret. He died in 2001.

Préfet Bussière – After serving in Vendôme and Orleans, the Préfet Bussière moved to Marseilles. In May 1944 he was arrested by the Gestapo for resistance activities (part of the network Super NAP made up of public servants). He died in the Baltic Sea, May 1945, when the prison ship, on which he was a passenger, was bombed by the RAF.

Finally, my grandfather Daniel, did indeed receive a cold reception from De Gaulle due to a misunderstanding about his role in the resistance. However years later his services to the Resistance were recognised. Henri Duvillard had proposed him for the L'Ordre National de la Legion d'Honneur when Daniel died suddenly in August 1986.

Acknowledgements

My huge thanks goes to the Mayor of la Ville-aux-Clercs, Isabelle Maincion, who spent time helping my research.

Also to Maryse Redon, owner of *Le Manoir de la Fôret* hotel (formally the Fort Girard youth centre), who provided such a warm welcome.

Finally to my grandfather and his friends, whose bravery I can only fully appreciate now having written this book.

Printed in Great Britain
by Amazon

85663036R00192